03/01

PENGUIN BOOKS

THE LEPER'S BELL

Paul Micou is an American who, after living in London for many years, recently moved to Provence with his family. He is the author of six previous novels.

D1236942

PAUL MICOU

The Leper's Bell

PENGUIN BOOKS

PENGUIN BOOKS

Published by the Penguin Group
Penguin Books Ltd, 27 Wrights Lane, London w8 5tz, England
Penguin Putnam Inc., 375 Hudson Street, New York, New York 10014, USA
Penguin Books Australia Ltd, Ringwood, Victoria, Australia
Penguin Books Canada Ltd, 10 Alcorn Avenue, Toronto, Ontario, Canada m4v 3b2
Penguin Books (NZ) Ltd, Private Bag 102902, NSMC, Auckland, New Zealand

Penguin Books Ltd, Registered Offices: Harmondsworth, Middlesex, England

First published by Viking 1999
Published in Penguin Books 2000
1 3 5 7 9 10 8 6 4 2

Set in Monotype Sabon
Printed in England by Clays Ltd, St Ives plc

For Anna U.

Innocence always calls mutely for protection when we would be so much wiser to guard ourselves against it: innocence is like a dumb leper who has lost his bell, wandering the world, meaning no harm.

GRAHAM GREENE, *The Quiet American*

I

From the moment he stepped out of the aeroplane into the sunshine at the top of the ramp, Ben knew he wanted the job. This is it, he thought, this is the place. I can take this step, it's as easy as anything – easier than what I would be leaving behind. How many people do this? How many people promise themselves they will one day, but they put it off and for ever wonder what they have missed? I can bring my family here. The children won't even know it's out of the ordinary. And so what if it doesn't work out, for whatever reason? There is always retreat.

Already the crush of people thrilled him. The dilapidated pieces of luggage – string bags, canvas sacks, tattered leather – did not revolve antiseptically on a conveyor belt but were brought by hand and deposited on a sooty floor. Ben's polished-leather suitcase stood out from the rest of the baggage just as he stood out from the dark skin, the moustaches, the heavy wool clothes, the black eyes and the babble pointless to foreign ears. Soldiers smoking cigarettes collected their kit, weapons and all. Women, headscarves knotted beneath their chins, retrieved not only sacks of conventional belongings but bags of produce. It was inexplicable, really, the sense of belonging that arose from feeling so out of place.

Out in the hot dry air, into a fuming taxi, sliding on a plastic-covered seat, Ben leaned well to one side so the driver couldn't see him grinning like a fool. Ben couldn't stop smiling. His heart beat audibly in his ears, and he wanted to sing. He *would* sing, the moment he was alone. He would throw open the curtains of his hotel room, open the window wide, stretch out his arms to his new city, and *sing*. He rolled down the car window and breathed the hot smell of his new country – a smell of roads built yesterday on top of roads built ten thousand years ago. What had seemed daunting challenges – the move, the language, the schools, the job itself – fell away and became a natural transition. Ben was made for this. It was going to be easy. Ellen would adore it, she would throw herself into the new life with her customary energy, she would know instinctively how to deal with servants and time on her hands. The children, being children, would adapt like chameleons. Their horizons would effortlessly be broadened before they knew what had happened to them. They would be handed a new language on a plate, maybe two languages. It seemed clearer to Ben than ever that this leap was unarguably the right thing to do. Nothing would ever be the same, but it would always be impossible, *impossible* to say that it had not been the right thing to do. No matter what. He felt like someone repaying a favour tenfold, and he revelled in the joy of his own generosity. He had promised himself this break, this escape. He had promised Ellen variety and adventure. It was all too perfect and luxurious, and he felt he hadn't earned the privilege.

Everything Ben saw as the taxi fumed its way into the city was novel and exactly as it should have been. There were, just as he had imagined, dwellings made of dung, overloaded trucks, men riding donkeys, people walking slowly by the side of the road with no destination in sight. The rough, dry terrain was a mixture of rocky desert and abandoned building sites. Soldiers gathered here and there wearing such heavy wool uniforms that Ben could imagine steam rising from their shoulders. The city began without much preamble: petrol stations, army barracks, crowded buses, parks, whitewashed houses, uniformed children walking home from school. Ben perspired in his stiff khaki suit; it was the first time he had worn the garment. He found that he was still smiling, excited. He knew nothing about this country, none of its language or culture. He felt absolutely at home here.

Ben had been vaccinated against cholera, yellow fever, polio, diphtheria, tetanus. His right hip still ached from a gamma-globulin booster. He carried traveller's cheques handed over by the organization that was in the process of recruiting him – the people to whom it seemed he needed only say an enthusiastic 'Yes' for the job and the life to be his. In his briefcase he carried a pristine, once-stamped passport. The briefcase was light, but heavy with potential. His stay was supposed to last four days, but he wanted simply to *summon* his family, not to break the spell by returning home and overseeing a tedious move. He couldn't wait to see his new house, his office, his car, his chauffeur, his cook and his maid. All of these awaited him.

Wild dogs patrolled the street-side open sewers. The traffic grew dense and noisy. Apartment buildings, many still under construction, replaced the broken little houses of the suburbs. The road widened to a boulevard and suddenly there was the city itself, choked in smog in a basin ringed by dried brown hills. Ben realized that he'd had a premonition of this panorama, he had seen exactly this view in his mind or in his dreams. It was the filthiest place, gloriously so. In its centre the dome-like old town stuck up like a beehive.

The taxi driver turned on the radio and the cab was filled with a ululating song that sounded to Ben like someone struggling in the wrong register to find the proper tune. He drove through the traffic in lunges, so that his passenger had to hold on to the door handle. Impatient, the driver shot down a side-street and on to a different avenue. Still not satisfied, he nosed down another side-street and gunned the engine. Ben never saw a thing, but there was a sudden lurch to one side and a thud.

3

The driver shouted a single word, straightened out the car and accelerated again. Ben sat up and turned around. In the middle of the street lay a dead or dying dog.

2

The American who was to be Ben's boss had been unable to meet him at the hotel, but had sent his wife along in his place. Also American, Candy Mancini warmly greeted Ben as he came into the lobby. She was an attractive, athletic-looking woman of about forty, nearly as tall as Ben.

'To the bar,' said Candy, smiling and taking Ben's arm. A uniformed porter had already taken his suitcase to reception. The bar was at the back of the modern hotel, and it gave on to a terrace and garden. The couple sat outside at an iron table beneath a tall eucalyptus tree that must have been preserved and sheltered there during the construction of the building. Carp nosed about in a small pool nearby. Ben had taken off his jacket and not bothered to straighten his tie. He told Candy about the dog.

'You're off to a good start, then,' she said. 'Anyway, don't worry. Most of the dogs are wild. No one will miss it.'

'That's nice to know,' said Ben. 'I just thought the driver ought to have stopped.'

'That's never a good idea. Someone would have claimed the dog and there would have been trouble.'

A waiter appeared. Candy ordered a vodka and tonic. Ben noticed that she didn't say 'please'.

'The same for me, please,' said Ben, stressing the word and making eye contact with the teenage waiter. He had spent the last few years trying to teach his own children to behave this way, and it would have been a betrayal not to do so himself.

'I'm starved for gossip,' said Candy. 'Tell me everything.'

Ben wondered why Paul Mancini had sent along his wife rather than an underling from the office. He supposed it was meant to be a gesture of hospitality, but it made him tense. Candy's directness seemed to assume a formal agreement that had not yet been established.

'In what . . . sphere?' asked Ben.

'Oh, anything. Tell me about your family. Would they be happy to move here? Not everyone is.'

'Perfectly happy.' Ben didn't want to say too much. 'Absolutely game. Ellen – my wife – is the more adventurous of the two of us, if anything. The kids aren't quite sure what it all means but . . . they're kids, they'll love it. Do you have children?' Ben, who was a lawyer, wouldn't have asked this question if he didn't already know the answer.

'Paul Junior and Caroline,' said Candy, as the drinks arrived. 'Eight and five.'

'*Thank* you,' said Ben, making eye contact with the waiter again.

'My advice,' said Candy, not having looked at the waiter, 'is fire them, fire them, fire them until you find someone perfect.'

'Pardon me?'

'Sorry, the help. I went through – it must have been *six* hopeless girls before I found Tamina. She's an angel and she doesn't know she works about three times as hard as she has to. Right now she's taking the children skiing.'

'Skiing?' Ben looked up at the hot blue sky.

'A dry *piste*, of course. Brand new. I haven't seen it myself but judging from the bruises it does the job.'

Ben sipped his drink and tried to relax. He thought it odd that Candy hadn't thought to toast his arrival before downing half of her drink. He tried to relax. Killing the dog had upset him and taken away the elation he had felt on arrival. The last thing he wanted to do was get into some sort of drinking and gossiping session with the wife of his potential boss.

'Paul's very sorry not to have met you himself,' said Candy, as if remembering a line she had rehearsed in front of a mirror. 'He's been in the hinterland for three days and won't be back until late tonight. He always comes back grumbling about something. He's an impatient man. It's as if he wants to turn this country into – I don't know – upstate New York, in one generation. He thinks this is his last job, his swan song. He wants everything done yesterday. He says the local engineers are tops but the workers are slipshod. He never relaxes, never enjoys the things you can enjoy here. Doesn't slow down, adapt to the pace. The children think he lives somewhere else and visits on birthdays or to throw a grown-up party they're not invited to. It drives me *crazy* when Paul says I spend too much time at the club, when of course he's working so hard he's never around and doesn't have to deal with the day-to-day.'

Ben made a mental note to tell his wife never to talk to anyone about anything.

Candy finished her drink and said, 'Paul's seeing you tomorrow morning, is that right?'

'That's right.'

'You should come up to the house. It's marvellous. You'll be in the same neighbourhood, no doubt. I mean, there's only the one.' Candy leaned forward conspiratorially. '*Insist* on a pool,' she said. 'You'll get a pool.'

Ben felt the stubble on his chin. 'Sorry, I must look like a tramp. It's a hell of a long trip.'

'You look great,' said Candy. 'Let's get another drink.'

Ben was relieved to hear and see that there wasn't the slightest innuendo in what Candy said. She was fulfilling one of an overseas wife's many duties, and getting a couple of drinks out of it if she could. She knew better than Ben did that they would be seeing a lot of each other, their children would probably become lifelong friends, they would take turns hosting parties and presiding over barbecues. Candy was going to be Ellen's best friend for at least two or three years whether either of them liked it or not. Ben's relationship with Paul Mancini would start off on a formal footing, then gradually evolve into mutual respect and friendship. They would drink too much one night and vent their frustrations and a bond would be formed.

'It's very strange for Paul,' said Candy. 'He thinks he's nearing retirement but he has these two *babies* at home. He'll be seventy when Caroline's in college. What are your children's names?'

'Sean and Nicole. My wife's grandparents' names. Five and three. A little younger than yours.' The twelve hours or so it would have taken to explain even a portion of one of his children's lives to Candy Mancini loomed up for a moment in Ben's mind. He couldn't tell if she knew there had been problems.

'The American Hospital is super,' she said, indicating that she did. 'Did you know Little Paul blew two of his fingers off with a firecracker and had them sewed back on?'

'Jesus.'

'I fell in love with the surgeon. He'd been in Vietnam and said he'd sewed on smaller fingers.'

'Jesus.'

'It worked out fine. It's his right hand, so he can still play the violin.'

'He plays the violin?'

'No, but I mean he *can*.'

Ben noticed that Candy didn't wear jewellery of any kind, not even a watch. There were subtle pink indentations on the sides of her nose that suggested she usually wore dark glasses. She wore a beige linen suit and a tall woman's flat-soled shoes. She spoke precisely, with a neutral American accent, as if she were used to trying to make herself understood to foreigners. She and her husband had lived in Brazil, Sri Lanka and Zaire,

8

each tour separated by a single year in Washington, DC. Ben had never met Paul Mancini, nor spoken to him on the telephone. They had communicated by letter. Mancini's reputation, so far as Ben had been able to decode it, was one of plodding careerism tinged with frustration at never having been made an ambassador. He had fought during the early years of the war in Vietnam and been awarded two Purple Hearts, one of which may have been the result of hitting his head against the ceiling of a destroyer's cabin: Mancini was said to be inordinately tall, like his wife. The other Purple Heart had been earned for being shot in the sternum by enemy fire. Like any man whose generation had been spared even conscription, Ben was intimidated by men who had experienced combat.

'So you do think you want the job, don't you?' Candy asked. Her directness really did make Ben tense. Whatever he said now would reach Mancini's ear the moment he came home tonight.

'All I can say is that the moment I came out of the plane I felt the strangest . . . comfort.'

'I know exactly what you mean. I only felt that way in Africa. I *made* Paul take that posting, he was against it. He thought Little Paul was too young – Caroline wasn't born yet, but African women with babies, as you probably know . . . Anyway we had a wonderful time.'

'I've never been to Africa.'

'Well, Ben, there's always the next tour. Do you want another drink? I have to go home in a few minutes to feed the kids dinner. I try never to miss that.'

'I won't, thanks. You go ahead.'

'There's so much for you to be filled in on. You'll find it's a pretty small circle here.'

'If I take the job.'

'If you take the job. I believe there's only the one other candidate.'

This was news to Ben. He hadn't been told. He felt his lips tighten and his eyes squint as he took in what Candy had said.

'You didn't know?' she asked, seeming to enjoy having sprung the news.

'I . . . did, actually. I did know,' Ben said. He lied because he thought it would be a sign of weakness to admit that something so important hadn't been related to him. He had flown all this way thinking the job was his for the taking. 'I just never found out who the other person is.'

'I met him yesterday, right here,' said Candy, as her third vodka and tonic arrived. 'His name is Ross Howard.'

'Thanks,' Ben said to the waiter, on Candy's behalf. Then, to Candy, 'He's here? He's here now?'

'Sure. I suppose Paul wants you to get the guided tour together. It will save time. May the best man win, right?'

Now Ben felt his hands turning to fists beneath the iron table. He was being auditioned, right now. Paul Mancini would not be able to make up his mind, so he would ask his wife at the last minute. 'Oh, just *you* make the decision,' Mancini would say. Candy would base her choice on which of the two men looked like more fun, more likely to be an entertaining conversationalist at her dinner parties – the one whose *wife* sounded like good value. Ben now wished he had joined her in the third drink, to appear sociable and at ease. It had been such a psychological leap for him to have come this far down the road to a new life, and it galled him that all was still uncertain. It also frightened him, for complicated reasons.

3

Ellen had at first not been made fully aware of the terms on which Ben had left his law firm. In fact she had been deceived. It was a pure lie, and something Ben had known at the time he would find difficult to live with. He still didn't know exactly what had driven him to an uncharacteristic economy with the truth – no, it had been worse than that, it had been a dangerous, treacherous lie. At the beginning he had said to himself that he would tell Ellen the truth one day, when the dust settled, when their new life had been deemed a success. There had seemed little sense in troubling her at such a tricky juncture in their lives, when she had been under so much pressure herself. Ben still winced inwardly when he looked at the cold facts of what had happened to him.

Ben had been an associate at a large corporate law firm with, in his own mind at least, partnership very much on the cards in the relatively near future. He had risen sufficiently high in the ranks that, after six horrendous months when four major clients walked away, he found himself senior enough to be spending a great deal of his time firing those lower down on the tree. He hated this duty as much as anyone would – he lost sleep, he awoke each morning groaning at the prospect of what the day held in store, he resented the senior partners for not taking on this unpleasant chore themselves. Still, he tried his best to be *good* at giving people the bad news. He honed his speech, which always began, 'I'm sure you know why I needed to see you today.' He promised to keep in touch. If he knew the victim well he would invite him or her out for a drink. He had a short list of other firms he thought might be hiring even in the present climate, and he vowed to make his references absolute jewels of the genre.

Ben fired a dozen people in this way over a period of three wretched weeks. Only one former employee took the news so badly that Ben worried the poor young man might harm himself: he was engaged to be married and actually *begged* Ben to change his mind. On the whole Ben agreed that these people – *some* people, anyway – had to go if the firm were to survive. Now that the purge seemed over, he looked forward to returning to his primary focus, which was the defence of a water utility accused in a class-action suit (absolutely rightly, it had emerged) of gross negligence and the near-fatal poisoning of eleven hundred people in rural Massachusetts. He cleared his desk of heartfelt references and recommendations, and prepared for his future. Then, on a Friday afternoon after lunch, he was summoned to a senior partner's office – Victor Wiesman, the same senior partner who had hired Ben straight out of law school. Ben and Wiesman had become friends – insofar as Ben could have any social life at all any more with two young children at home. They went to lunch together every other month or so and talked about 'anything not to do with the office', as Wiesman put it. His three children were grown up, and he had been a source of guidance and comfort to Ben and his wife when Sean and Nicole were unwell.

Ben put on his suit jacket and walked the short distance to Wiesman's office. He assumed this meeting was to do with the water utility, whose managers insisted against all the odds and Ben's advice that their stonewalling denials were the way forward. Some of the evidence Ben had seen was so fraudulent it wouldn't fool a child. Wiesman stood up behind his desk when Ben knocked and entered. Wiesman had gained weight in the past two or three years. His white hair sprouted only over his ears. He had a big, pugilist's face, blue eyes and short limbs. Most people took him to be Irish until they learned his name. He gestured at a chair and Ben sat down.

'I'm sure you know why I wanted to see you today,' Wiesman said. In a blur of hurried talk that caused Ben some initial confusion, Wiesman continued a prepared speech. He promised to keep in touch, he asked if Ben wanted to go out for a drink later, he named three or four firms he was under the impression might be hiring even in this climate, he guaranteed referrals of such tribute and veneration they would read like eulogies.

'I got canned once too, you know,' said Wiesman, whom Ben had never seen so uncomfortable.

'Really?'

'Sure. My first job. I was just a paralegal, but it felt like the end of the world. You'll look back on this and it'll seem like a blip. Nine out of ten times it's for the best. You're a young man. You'll see, trust me.'

Paralegal, thought Ben. What, when Wiesman was twenty-two? I've got two broken children and a wife and a mortgage on a house that belongs to my *father-in-law* and I promised, I *promised* Ellen this was going to work out, there wasn't any doubt, no doubt at all, our plans were based on that promise – I was going to be sitting in *your* chair in five years or sooner if anyone had the good grace to *die*. Besides, I'm not made for this, I'm not the sort of person you *fire*.

'I'm sure you're right,' said Ben, boiling inside his suit.

'You're probably relieved,' said Wiesman, trying to make himself feel human. Ben had used exactly these words with the people he'd fired. 'You were heading for about two years, maybe three, being jerked around by Freeman and the water people. Take a holiday. Look around and don't jump at the first offer. You're too good, Ben. This is *entirely* a structural thing, as you know better than anyone. At this rate we're going to have to sack our*selves*. It's a sinking ship and I think you've known that all along.'

'Who else is going? I mean, at my . . . level.'

Wiesman actually flinched. He looked down between his hands at his desk, as if searching for a long list of sackings he was only beginning to work his way through. He didn't reply right away.

'Johnson? Fluornoy? That fucking Innis?'

'Not just . . . yet,' said Wiesman. He looked up from his hands. 'I don't want you losing your temper, Ben.'

Ben had already so thoroughly lost his temper, if only inwardly, he found it difficult to breathe. 'I am willing,' he said, slowly, sucking air between the words, 'to pretend we never had this conversation. I am willing to walk back to my office and to continue as if nothing happened. Just take it back, Victor. This is *not* a good time.' Ben felt himself falling into a pit. He didn't want to, but he knew he was about to sound like the young fiancé he had sacked only a week ago. He was going to beg. Ben's life, until only moments ago – though strewn with predictable unhappiness, disappointment, struggle and frustration – had been a tolerable pattern of compromise that he had learned to take pride in and even enjoy. 'Fire Innis,' he said. 'Innis is useless.'

'I won't get into that. You will not draw me into that line. I'm not going to say any more, Ben, except that, with the greatest regret, my decision is final. You know how hard this is. Don't make it any worse. It'll work out fine, you'll see. Just take a break and –'

Ben was on his feet. His mouth was clamped shut and he was breathing heavily through his nostrils. He was dizzy with anger and felt for a moment that he might lash out at Wiesman.

'You must have seen this coming,' said Wiesman. 'You must have.'

Ben had seen *nothing* coming.

4

When Candy Mancini went home, somewhat flushed after her three drinks, Ben left the hotel to take a walk and get his bearings. It was after six o'clock, but the July sun still hung high in the notorious smog. Expatriates lived and sent their children to school up in the hills. The city, where they still burned coal and the cars and buses fumed so much they seemed to be on fire, was considered a health hazard to children. Ben put on dark glasses and walked in a random direction down one of the city's broadest avenues. In the first five minutes of his walk he heard more car horns blaring than he thought he had in the rest of his life until then. Amazingly, he could hear human voices over the traffic and the beeping horns and the grinding of buses' gears. Everyone who was not entirely alone seemed to be shouting. Occasionally Ben spotted a Westerner wearing a suit, and he wondered if the man might be his competition. Candy had said nothing more about him, but already Ben had built up an image in his mind: younger, clean-cut, no children to complicate his new life, experience abroad – probably Peace Corps before that. He needn't be a lawyer, this wasn't a legal job. He could be CIA, he could be State, he could be AID, he could be closely related to someone important in Washington. He could be a trained engineer. He could be a little proto-ambassador cutting his teeth on practical work. It said something about Ben's fragile state of mind that the man he imagined was in every way superior to him and more likely to get the job. He even saw the other man as a wit, a daring lover, someone Candy Mancini had found so alluring that she had already made up her mind. Whoever he was, he had almost certainly joined Candy in that third drink, if not a fourth. Only a rock-climbing injury had kept him out of professional tennis. He spoke the local language fluently. His foreign-service exam was framed on some bureaucrat's wall.

Ben had started actively to search the crowds for this man. The air was filled with babble and the smells of roasting corn on the cob and pretzels and coffee. Giant eucalyptus trees lined the boulevard, their leaves hanging black and heavy with soot. Workmen, their rough hands stained with plaster-dust and paint, headed home from countless construction sites – the whole city was a construction site. Ben had walked only a few hundred yards before he felt uncomfortable and needed to retreat to his hotel.

Back in the cool lobby, he avoided eye contact with the other male guests: any one of them could be his competition. He took the stairs to his floor, found his room, and only when his key was in the lock did he remember with a spasm of fright that he had left his briefcase in the bar. While rushing back down the stairs, he had time to think that this mistake was going to cost him the job. Someone would have stolen his briefcase and his passport and his traveller's cheques and all the papers that related to the posting. He would have to tell Paul Mancini that he had been stripped of his crucial documents and money before the sun had set on his first day in the country. He would appear foolish and disorganized and unprepared for travel. He came to the foot of the stairs into the lobby and walked with panicked gait to the bar and out into the garden. He could see right away that the briefcase was gone. There was another briefcase in its place and another man sitting at the wrought-iron table, reading a newspaper. Ben looked around for the young waiter, but couldn't see him. The man looked up from his newspaper and saw Ben standing there looking worried and indecisive.

'Excuse me,' said the man. He had an American accent. 'I'll bet I know what you're looking for.'

Ben let out the breath he'd been holding and slumped his shoulders in relief. The man folded his newspaper and put it down. He stood up and extended his hand. 'You're Ben Pelton?'

'That's right,' said Ben, shaking hands.

'Sorry, I figured I'd look in the briefcase to see who it belonged to. I left it at the reception desk. I hope you won't mind, but just to be on the safe side I kept these for you.' He reached into his jacket and pulled out Ben's passport and his traveller's cheques. 'I'm Ross Howard,' he said, handing over Ben's possessions. 'Looks like we're here for the same reason, my friend. Care to join me?'

5

Ellen Delaney Pelton had fed the children their supper, bathed one of them and put both to bed by eight-thirty. She had been on her feet since six in the morning, but – except for a period of half an hour during the early afternoon when she had wanted to lie down on the kitchen floor and go to sleep – the day had been a pleasant one full of chores accomplished, errands run, games played, appointments kept. Ellen had a great deal of physical and mental energy and she kept moving, like a feeding shark, dispensing her duties and ticking them off a mental list of Things to Do that had become second nature. This was a Friday. The family's Dutch au pair had been in bed with a chest cold since Tuesday, emerging only late at night to eat toast with tuna fish and mayonnaise. Ellen found herself unable to sit down even now in the quiet house, her body humming with the leftover pulses of energy that kept her moving, moving through every long day.

It was a rare evening that Ellen's husband came home from work in time to see the children before bed, and there had been no chance of that tonight. He'd phoned to say he had to attend a reception in honour of a despised former colleague's retirement. This was not an unusual thing for her husband to be doing instead of coming home to his family; it had become quite as routine as her own chores, doctors' visits, outings, errands. When this regular procedure had at first begun to impose itself, Ellen had enjoyed her evenings winding down, staring with disbelief at the news on television, thinking uninterrupted, escapist thoughts. Only recently had she found herself restless when the children were mercifully asleep, in need of conversation or something less repetitive than the news on television and less potentially dangerous than uninterrupted thinking. She hated to go to bed before Ben came home, because she couldn't lie down with a book for more than ten minutes without falling asleep. Her principles forbade a television in the bedroom. By the time Ben came home he was usually good for no more than a quick précis of his journey, a considerate question or two about Ellen's and the children's day and a one-minute shower (Ben always showered before bed). Ellen had set self-improving tasks to fill the evenings – studying the history of her ancestral Ireland, writing letters to friends and family, listening to music in an organized way – but none had lasted more than three days and the television news eventually won out.

Ellen had a crush on a British foreign correspondent who frequently popped up on satellite television to tell her how ghastly it was somewhere else, how lucky she was to be safe in her annually appreciating house, how grateful she ought to be. She especially liked the foreign correspondent because in all his subjective humanity he seemed to her naïve and childlike. Evan Court – as the foreign correspondent was known, and perhaps was really named – took the view that the world was naturally a peaceful and bounteous place, and daily he conveyed his outrage that it did not live up to its promise. Artillery shells burst on hillsides over Evan Court's shoulder; naked, starving children grasped his sleeves and stared at him with pleading eyes; selfless missionaries recounted the morning's atrocities; men were hanged before the lens of his cameraman. Two or three Evan-less evenings would pass, and he would appear again in another place with the same grim story to tell. Tanned, handsomely balding, sometimes allowing the sweat to show on his slender brown chest, Evan Court and his humanitarian eyes pleaded with the viewer to share the agony of his surroundings just as the naked, starving children pleaded with him for deliverance.

Evan Court reported tonight on the riotous aftermath of a sub-continent suicide-bombing. The political implications of the attack were hard to predict, its historical context vague, even the likely perpetrators impossible to pinpoint at this stage. The rioting crowds had killed more people than the terrorist. Evan Court stood steady in a rushing river of shrieking humanity as dust rose up from the street to swirl about the strands of the reporter's wind-blown, thinning hair. His staccato mid-Atlantic voice listed the figures of dead and wounded, remarked on the unexpectedness of the event, predicted worse to come. He signed off and stiffened his jaw. The American anchorman at home solemnly wished him Godspeed. Ellen sighed, still standing in her kitchen (where her principles did not forbid a television), and turned down the volume. She listened in the direction of the staircase, because her five-year-old son could still come down at any time. She listened in the direction of the drive, because Ben had promised to be home by nine-thirty. All she could hear was the dishwasher, a new dishwasher that was supposed to be 'whisper quiet' but that at this time of Ellen's day sounded like a waterfall.

Ellen cleaned and dried the kitchen-counter surfaces, set aside milk in a bottle for Nicole at dawn (Ellen liked to give her daughter her first drink of the day in bed). She went into the playroom and with a blank mind put away loose toys and deposited stray clothing in the hamper. She felt the clothes in the drier and decided to give them another twenty minutes. She went back into the kitchen, prepared the automatic coffee machine and set its timer for five-thirty. She went into the living room and rearranged the sofa cushions that had been thrown about after Sean came home from kindergarten. She performed these chores with her mind deliberately empty. She no longer needed to know or think about the things she had known and thought about so sharply only a few short years ago. She was like the whisper-quiet dishwasher, toiling efficiently through her cycle of chores. Tomorrow would be the same.

It was nearly ten o'clock. Ellen went back into the kitchen and stared at the silent television. There was something exciting happening – somewhere else, to someone else – something of such importance that it was broadcast as it happened. The people involved looked American. Most likely it was a natural disaster or an assassination or an awards ceremony. A perfectly beautiful young policeman was asked for an opinion. Ellen turned up the volume and discovered that the beautiful police-man's partner had been wounded in a 'foiled robbery hostage situation' in San Diego, since happily resolved by the per-petrator's suicide. Ellen looked at the clock above the stove: ten o'clock sharp, time for the headlines and perhaps a glimpse of Evan Court.

Sean came downstairs, as he had done often in the past few weeks. Ellen could hear his tread on the stairs, but didn't turn around. She turned down the volume of the television again. The boy would announce a pretext for his appearance – thirst, hunger, a question – and then he would go back to bed.

'Mama,' he said.

Ellen turned around. 'Yes, my darling?'

'I just wanted to say something.' He stood with a hand on the door frame, left bare foot casually placed *en pointe* on right bare foot.

'Yes?'

'I forgot to say it before. I wanted to say it to you now.'

'Go ahead then, my angel.'

'Happy birthday, Mama.'

And so Ellen floated across the kitchen to take Sean in her arms. Closing her eyes, she picked him up with one arm around his shoulders and the other beneath his thighs. Ellen's were complicated tears. The boy in her arms – a thin child with thin blond hair and a serious gaze – had, like his sister, been through a medical nightmare and was not yet out of the woods. And it was, indeed, Ellen's birthday – her twenty-eighth.

Ellen put Sean back to bed after drying her tears from his cheek. As she came downstairs she saw the lights of Ben's car flash across the living-room wall as he turned into the drive. She hurried into the kitchen, splashed cold water on her face and dried it with a paper towel. Moments later Ben entered, suit jacket over one arm, tie loosened. He looked like someone who was about to say, 'I could use a drink.'

'I could use a drink,' said Ben. He smiled at his own rudeness and added, 'After I've given you a kiss and said happy birthday.' Ellen felt the tears rise in her eyes again as the couple met halfway across the kitchen and kissed each other.

'Have a beer,' she said, letting go of him and moving to the refrigerator. Ben draped his jacket on the counter. 'It's all we have, I think. I'll join you.'

Ellen had to fight off the more and more frequent realization that she was a living cliché, that she lived a whole *raft* of clichés that she would have scoffed at only a few years ago. In medical school, before she had dropped out to have Sean, she had written in her diary a list of ways she didn't want to turn out, and here – under this roof, her hand reaching into the refrigerator, the exhausted husband home late from work with his tie loosened, the children upstairs asleep, the whisper-quiet dishwasher roaring in the corner, the silent television on the counter glowing with other people's lives, the certainty that tomorrow would be no different – here was half the list. She lived the other half of the list as well, but none of that was tangible, it was hidden in a secret chamber of her imagination.

Ben accepted a can of cold beer and drank nearly all of it before speaking. 'In the car I promised myself I wouldn't bore you with what happened today, that I'd sleep on it.'

'Something happened?'

Ben licked his lips. 'It's your birthday. We should talk about you.' Ben smiled again and Ellen had the feeling that whatever had happened was important. 'Or the kids. How are the kids?'

'Oh, go on,' said Ellen.

Ben untied his tie and drew it slowly out of his unbuttoned collar. He reached inside his jacket pocket for the box containing the antique emerald ring he had bought only a week ago, a purchase that would be unthinkable today. 'What would you say, my most beautiful birthday girl, if I said your husband, your middle-aged husband' – Ben had recently turned thirty-three – 'was in *every likelihood* going to throw it all in for something different, something exciting, something . . . something *not like this*?'

Ellen ignored the unopened present for the moment and responded in the way Ben would have hoped: a little snort of sarcasm, a swig of beer. She thought he was kidding, or dreaming. She thought he'd had too much to drink at the farewell reception. She didn't suspect a thing.

6

Ben hadn't lashed out at Wiesman. He had taken a deep breath and clenched and unclenched his fists and then turned on his heel and walked out of Wiesman's office with the senior partner's voice trailing off behind him. 'You'll see, Ben. Trust me. Don't walk out of here like that, Ben. Everything will work out fine.' And then the horrible words, 'Take it like a man, for Christ's sake, Ben. Take it like a man . . .'

Ben walked to his own office, packed his briefcase with the few personal effects he had ever brought to work, put on his overcoat and left the building without saying a word to anyone. Breathless with a sort of puzzled rage, he tramped uphill to the deli where he sometimes bought sandwiches for lunch back at his desk. He paused outside and gathered himself. His face was burning hot. He looked inside the deli and saw that there was only one customer at the counter and she was already paying for her food. Ben hated queues. He opened the door for the woman as she left, smiling at her as if he'd just been promoted rather than sacked. It hurt the muscles in his face to smile. He entered the deli and ordered a tongue sandwich on rye bread with mustard and mayonnaise and salt and pepper. He took a can of beer out of the refrigerator and put it on the counter. He stood there with forced casualness as his sandwich was quickly prepared. He paid the man and left. He walked farther up the hill to the little cemetery that he'd walked by hundreds of times on the way to work but never entered. The headstones were pitted with age. He sat down on one of them without looking at the name of the grave's eighteenth-century occupant. He unwrapped his sandwich and opened his beer and thought, What did I do wrong?

Ben didn't think he had done anything wrong. This made things worse. It couldn't have been that meeting a month ago when he was just *slightly* sarcastic in front of a client? No, he hadn't done anything wrong. He was not prepared to be a casualty of fate. People like Ben didn't go to Harvard, then to Harvard Law School, then get married to pretty women they loved, then have children who were sick but fixable, then turn thirty-three, then get . . . *fired*, have everything stop, become damaged goods, become failures, negotiate the rest of their short working lives regretfully and from a stance of pitiful weakness. Ben couldn't imagine this had ever happened to anyone else in his position, with his background. He thought very hard about this. He tried to think of relatives, classmates, friends, acquaintances who had been similarly treated. There was no one. It was a nightmare. Ben remembered conversations with friends and associates where they all laughed at their good fortune, but behind the laughter there was the certainty that success was deserved. A corollary of this line of thinking was that *failure* was equally deserved. 'Show us the corpses,' they used to say, meaning that if one persevered, if one were really *good*, success and security would trundle along as surely as the next commuter train. Ben had persevered. Ben had been good.

Ben sat on a pile of corpses in the shady little cemetery and felt that he was a corpse himself. It was unimaginable to him that he would make his way home early, explain laughingly to Ellen that he'd been fired but that it was OK, it's nine out of ten times for the best, he'd *taken it like a man*, everything would turn out fine, he wouldn't be damaged goods, a corpse, others were hiring even in this climate and he'd climb straight back on to the ladder on just the rung from which he'd been pushed off. Ben never made a conscious decision to lie to Ellen,

25

he simply didn't tell her the truth right away because the truth still wasn't real to him.

He had four hours to kill before his usual train. He walked to the station and stowed his briefcase in a locker. He didn't know what he was going to do next, but he knew it was going to be out of the ordinary. After half an hour's stroll he found himself in the city's quaintly tolerated red-light district. He smiled for the first time since the phoney smile at the woman in the deli – he smiled because he had been pretending he hadn't deliberately been walking straight here, straight to a stinking cubicle where he could put quarters in a slot and watch young women making love on film. Ben always called it 'making love', no matter how sickeningly degraded the women were. He had even watched a film like this at home with Ellen, and made her laugh when he said, 'Look, how romantic,' as some poor thing was debased for all time on celluloid. 'They're making love. They're *in* love, just like us.'

The fact was these films inflamed Ben. He believed them, he believed *in* them. He believed the plots, even. Now, in the stinking cubicle, a sacked man and a failure, Ben became engrossed in the five-minute story of a teenager who, washing her car in the driveway, spied her fat old neighbour leering over a hedge and simply had to *have* him, right there, on the hood. Aroused to the point of fever, Ben left the cubicle and looked at his watch. He had three hours. Bewildered and shocked by what he was doing, he went around the corner to a staircase that led to a girl he'd heard about from his debauched friend Donald Murphy. He rang the bell and was admitted. He gave the girl, who was beautiful if Ben didn't look too closely at her, fifty dollars. In exchange for the money the girl undressed and swiftly relieved Ben using only her mouth and hands, then sweetly closed the door on him as he went back down the stairs. Shaking his head in disbelief, Ben went straight across the street to an Irish bar and ordered a whisky, which he had never done on his own in the afternoon in his life. Two hours of being a failure, he thought, *two hours*, and I'm a drunken, whoring monster. Twenty-five years of childhood, school, college and graduate school, eight years of important and well-paid legal work to keep the fabric of society in one piece, and in *two hours*, after my first real, personal setback, I am a drunken, whoring monster. If he could sink so low in two hours, Ben thought, where would he be next year?

7

'So have you met Candy Mancini?' asked Ross Howard, as the sky darkened over the hotel garden.

'I did meet her, yes,' said Ben.

'What did you make of her?'

Ben shrugged. He was still trying to decide what he made of Ross Howard. He looked about twenty-five years old, if not younger. He had a long, dark face and curly black hair that would thin to baldness in about five years. He had very white but crooked teeth, he hadn't shaved that day, his cheap blue suit was too tight in the legs and shoulders. He was overconfident and too familiar for someone his age. He didn't wear a wedding ring. Ben thought the house and the pool and the car and the chauffeur and the maid would be wasted on an unmarried, childless man in a cheap suit.

'Mancini's back tonight, correct?' asked Ross.

'That's what his wife said, yes.'

'I hear he's taking us on the grand tour tomorrow.'

'That's right.'

'You know anything about dams?'

'Not a lot. Do you?'

'Great big blockages in rivers, is my guess.'

Ross Howard was too relaxed, in Ben's opinion. He didn't look as if he wanted this job, *needed* this job, the way Ben did.

'You're a lawyer, right?' Ross asked.

'That's right. How could you tell?'

'Candy Mancini told me.'

'What else did Candy Mancini tell you?'

'Oh, nothing, really.'

'I take it you're *not* a lawyer?'

'Oh, God no.'

'Then what . . . *are* you?' It was rare in Ben's experience for a man not to be a lawyer.

'I'm a banker, I guess,' said Ross.

'SD Bank?'

'How could you tell?'

Ben shrugged again. He found this conversation exhausting. He would excuse himself as soon as he'd finished his drink. 'It just makes sense,' he said.

'Wouldn't you be nervous bringing your family here?' asked Ross.

'No. Why would I?'

'Well, I mean the filth and the disease and the probability of war or revolution, the schools, the *hospitals*,' Ross stressed the word, so Ben knew Candy had told him whatever she knew about the children, 'the language, the disease –'

'You already said disease.'

'Anyway, you know what I mean.'

'I really ought to go to bed,' said Ben.

'What, no dinner?'

'I've had a long day, a long trip. I haven't even been to my room yet. Thanks again, by the way, for the briefcase.'

'No problem.'

'Put the drinks on my bill. It's room twenty-seven.'

'Hey, thanks, Ben.'

'See you tomorrow.'

'I guess so.'

The men shook hands and Ben left the darkened garden. He retrieved his briefcase from the reception desk and went back upstairs to his room. He went inside, checked that his suitcase was there, took off his jacket and hung it in the closet. The room smelled of fresh paint. He opened the window, which gave on to the garden downstairs. He could see Ross Howard still sitting there next to the carp pool, back at his newspaper and reading by candlelight. Ben was certain that Ross was a spook. He had to be. Ben also thought Ross had to be a Princeton man – there was a misplaced sense of superiority about him, a second-rate figure who had no idea he was second rate. It offended Ben that this . . . this *youth* was in contention for the same job as he was. His being a trainee spy would explain that. And if he were a trainee spy, did that mean there would be pressure on Paul Mancini to hire the boy? Mancini had done his diplomatic tours, but this posting was private development. Ben wondered if the United States intelligence community pressured private organizations to hire their people overseas, and then he snorted aloud at having had to think this through. Of *course* they did.

8

For Ellen it was a normal Saturday. For Ben it was an excruciating test of his nerve. He couldn't believe yesterday had happened to him – to *him*, to Benjamin Pelton: Wiesman like a fat old boxer behind his desk, firing Ben, taking away Ben's career; in the cemetery sitting on a man's grave, swallowing a cow's tongue; the wretched cubicle and the pretty teenager on the screen being so in love with her neighbour that she needed him on the hood of her car, immediately; the stairs leading up to that girl's room and the way her long blonde hair touched his legs as she went about her work; ordering first one then two more whiskies in an Irish bar and just drinking, doing nothing else but drinking; coming home and cheerfully telling his pretty young wife that there was going to be a change.

'I have a terrible feeling you're serious,' said Ellen, who really had no idea.

'I think I am. We've talked about it enough. Time for action. You love me when I take *action*.'

'I always love you. Oh, thank you Sean.' Sean had come into the kitchen with a painting. Nicole sat on the kitchen floor eating a croissant.

'I've got half a mind to give Wiesman my notice on Monday,' said Ben, who was unemployed.

'Don't use just half your mind on something so important,' Ellen said. 'Not that I'm against a change. You know I'm usually in favour, depending on my mood.'

'Anyway, we won't be able to talk about it now. The children.'

Indeed, the couple spent the next day and a half with the children without having a moment to discuss their collective future, not even at night because Ellen was so tired. Ben was tired too, but slept in fits separated by spasms of disbelieving panic. His body felt weak and trembly and sore. On Monday morning Ben got out of bed at five-thirty, shaved, put on a suit, ate a piece of toast and drove away. Ellen went about her duties, relieved to have Else, the au pair, awake to help out (Else had a long history of unpredictable illness). Ben drove to the train station, parked his car, bought a newspaper and a cup of coffee, boarded the train, found a seat. He read the paper and filled in the crossword as casually as he might sign his name. Half an hour later the train pulled in at its terminus. Ben disembarked, tossed the newspaper into a bin, strode manfully out of the station and stopped dead. The moment he stopped he felt people were staring at him. No one else had simply stopped, they were moving, moving, getting somewhere. Ben had stopped. People really were staring at him, now. They were annoyed by this man with a suit and a briefcase who wasn't moving. There were mutters of impatience as they broke stride to get past him.

Ben slowly walked to a coffee shop, went in, looked around, sat down. He ordered coffee and toast. The word 'hobo' sprang to his mind. He felt unshaven and unkempt, though he was neither. He had a lunch date at one o'clock with a lawyer friend named Alan Yates whom he had known since sophomore year at Harvard. He had more than four hours to kill. He would spend them trying to decide if he should tell Alan Yates – recently poached and made partner by a firm so exquisitely glamorous they didn't have a sign on the door of their office building – that he had been fired. Ben knew he could trust Alan to keep the news to himself. On the other hand, it would be the first time in Ben's life that he admitted defeat to a contemporary. It would be impossible not to sound as if he were asking Alan for a job. Unlikely as it was that Alan *would* offer Ben a job, if that happened Ben would be in Alan's debt for ever and consider himself to be Alan's employee. He could prostrate himself before Alan, beg for a job, pretend to Ellen that he had been poached; or he could say nothing to Alan and hope to find a job so radically different from the law that his departure from Wiesman's firm would look deliberate and in many ways enviable.

Alan Yates was a lazy, inconsiderate man whose career had ballooned out of all proportion to his abilities because he was well-born. Until now Ben had considered this phenomenon a fact of life that he could do nothing about; now he wanted to hang the well-born by their Achilles' tendons. Alan had breezed through Harvard as if he'd been there before: he seemed to know all the faculty and coaches and bartenders and the other people who made university life possible. Alan had never seemed to 'apply' to law school, he just came back from summer break and moved his things a few hundred yards away to his new digs. He never 'applied' for his first job, he just packed up his car and drove to his apartment and put his things away again and went to work wearing perfect clothes he had always owned. Alan had no personal problems. After law school he had spent five years having a grand time dating unsuitable women until he married the girl everyone knew he was supposed to marry in the first place. He had a healthy boy and a healthy girl. He was a partner. He earned an unnecessary amount of money to pile on top of the unnecessary amount of money his great-grandfather had killed himself amassing.

Ben drank two further cups of coffee and let his fury rise to such a pitch that he thought he might attack the waitress. Options, all of them desperate, swam before his eyes: rush straight back to Wiesman and resume begging; call Ellen, tell her the truth, get her advice; type up a CV and apply for jobs all over the country and live with being a soiled lawyer, rather than a pristine one like Alan Yates; find out when that lovely whore opened for business, and that Irish bar; confide in no one but his parents, who would pretend not to be horrified and would offer whatever support they could while Ben got his life back on the rails; shoot, poison, cut or hang himself.

9

'The thing is,' said Ross Howard, who looked refreshed and relaxed, 'the General needs us more than we need him.'

'I understand that,' said Ben. The two men were eating breakfast together before their collective audition with Paul Mancini.

'I've met the General, you know.'

'No, I didn't know that,' said Ben, sarcasm heaving inside him but invisible on the surface. The General had been running this country for fifteen years, off and on. He and an inept, divisive parliament took it in turns.

'At the United Nations,' said Ross.

'Of all places,' said Ben.

'He's the good guy, Ben, believe me.' It was true that this country was practically unique in the world for having a sophisticated intelligentsia who, just every now and then, preferred the General to democracy.

'I'm sure that's right.'

'He's a strictly military ruler. Corruption isn't in his nature. He's ruthless, sure, but not in a kind of *criminal* way. He gets things done. He has a country to develop, and he's developing it. He doesn't have that crazy African thing, that ego, that syphilitic power-mad thing. He's really a bit of a visionary, and the people recognize that he's . . . what's the word?'

Ben searched Ross Howard's face for a clue. 'Benevolent?'

'Exactly. Thank you. The General is benevolent.'

'As are his junta?'

'I don't think that's the appropriate word, Ben, and I wouldn't use it around here if I were you.'

Being lectured by someone younger made Ben dizzy with rage. It was the first time in his life that he had resented someone for calling him 'Ben', even though Ross Howard had little choice in the matter. 'I wouldn't dream of using the word in any other context, *Ross*, but let's be honest. Anyway I don't care who runs this country at the moment. They're at peace. They're on our side. They're just taking care of business and that's why I'm here. To help.'

'Well I suppose you're to be commended for wanting to leave the good life behind. Didn't you like being an attorney?'

'Hated it,' said Ben. This was to be his stance. 'There was absolutely nothing I liked about it. Except the Law, of course.' Yes, this was Ben's new stance: hold up the loftiness of the Law, which he had memorized; disdain the practice. He had a higher calling, now, but could hold his knowledge of the Law in reserve. 'Why did you leave the bank?' Ben had a feeling young Ross Howard hadn't been fired.

'Oh, well, I haven't left. This would be a secondment, if all goes well.'

'I see.' Ben didn't see. 'You're not married?'

'No, no. I live with someone.'

Ben prayed that Ross Howard would reveal himself to be homosexual, and that this would count against him in Mancini's eyes.

'A great gal,' he said.

'Is she eager to join you in this disease-plagued pit of revolutionary violence?'

'I don't think so. She's got her own thing going at the UN.'

You're *both* spies, Ben thought. 'So you'd come alone?'

'That's the idea. I mean, I don't really care, either way. I thought it would be a laugh to check it out. This is a great country and I like the language.'

'How the hell,' said Ben, who had been eating quite a lot of black olives and salty white cheese, 'did you learn the language?'

'Oh, you know, one of those courses.' Ross said this as if he had learned to be a sous-chef. 'Can you get by, at least?'

'I don't know how to say anything but "Beer, please."'

'How do you say that, then?' asked Ross.

'Oh, all right. I say it in English. Or I will given half a chance this afternoon.'

I could go out west somewhere and teach law, Ben thought. I could live in a sunny place and have girl students who respect me to the point of wanting me to commit adultery, which I would never do, God bless my beautiful Ellen. I could put on a pair of rubber gloves so that I wouldn't leave fingerprints when I packed the rattlesnake in the box that I mailed to Victor Wiesman and marked 'Confidential'. I could phone Alan Yates from my sunny patio and ask him how many billable hours he'd logged that week.

A man wearing funeral-director's black came into the restaurant and asked Ben and Ross if they were ready. This was the chauffeur. He had a tidy black moustache and his black shoes were highly polished. He introduced himself in English, and to Ben's ear his name sounded like 'Chauffeur'. Chauffeur led the way outside to his long black car, an antique American car with tail fins that gleamed with recent polishing. In this town a car had to be washed every day. Ben and Ross installed themselves in the back seat, which had been covered with tiger skin to protect the original plastic. Chauffeur obviously took pride in his vehicle and in the art of driving in this noisy, congested city. He used the horn judiciously and once or twice he deigned to give another driver right of way.

The offices of Planning and Resources, Ltd took up two floors of a large house that had once belonged to the General's brother-in-law (who was now the country's temporary Treasurer). There was still a residential feel to the place – antique carpets, chandeliers, a great spiral staircase, carpets and tapestries on the walls. An American receptionist, who had painted her long fingernails pink, led Ben and Ross upstairs and along a corridor to Paul Mancini's office. Mancini was elsewhere, and the receptionist went away to fetch him. The office was beautiful, parquet-floored, and once would have been a ballroom. Two crystal chandeliers hung from the tall ceiling. Mancini's desk looked tiny at the far end of the room.

'A Maliki,' said Ross Howard, gesturing at a painting of mountains on the wall opposite the windows. 'Local man, still alive. Probably the country's greatest artist this century.'

You son of a *bitch*, thought Ben. 'I like it,' he said.

'It's of the Berevan Mountains, about two hundred miles away. They have ski lifts, these days. The General skis, you know.'

'No, I *didn't* know that, Ross. Funnily enough.'

The receptionist returned with Paul Mancini at her side. 'Ah, my men,' he said, loping across the ballroom office with his hand outstretched. Ben had the conscious thought that the first of them to shake Mancini's hand was the more likely to get the job, but that the one who showed the most initial eagerness to get the first handshake might compromise the advantage. The geography of the room and Ross Howard's slightly closer proximity to the door meant that Ross got the first handshake. Ben congratulated himself on not having lunged to the fore.

Mancini was more than six-and-a-half feet tall. He had kept his white hair close-cropped, as if to remind people that he had been a Lieutenant Colonel in the Green Berets. He had a thin, smooth face and high cheekbones. Ben thought that if it weren't for his exaggerated height Mancini would look like an astronaut, steely and self-confident, immune to fear. It also occurred to Ben that one of the reasons Mancini was frustrated not to have been made an ambassador was that he already looked exactly like one.

'Good, good,' said Mancini, now shaking Ben's hand. 'Right. Sit down, both of you. We'll have tea, Celia. On the double, all right? We're off in just a few minutes.'

Ben felt a twitch in his cheek – his right cheek had actually started to *twitch*, and this would be visible in his right eye. As he sat down he smiled harder to drive the twitch away. He was a twitching, sacked lawyer sitting in an office on the other side of the world with a combat veteran and a man who had known the painting on the wall was a Maliki. A thought dawned on Ben.

'I notice you've got a Maliki,' Ben said, smiling through his twitch.

'Yes, yes, I like him very much. It was a gift from the General.'

Ben crossed his legs. 'The Berevan Mountains. I understand there's skiing out there these days.'

'Yes, that's right,' said Mancini. 'We've skied there, just once.'

'The General's known to be a skier . . .'

Throughout this exchange, Ben didn't look at Ross. He felt the twitch subsiding. He held Mancini's gaze. He composed his features and relaxed his body in the chair, hoping this would convey his relative maturity. Having stolen Ross's intelligence about the painting and the geography of this country, he was reminded of the courtroom. Every so often Ben had walked into court knowing he had a lock on a case, something that would get the whole thing thrown out before lunch. It was a terrific feeling of power. He could sit in his chair with his legs crossed listening to his doomed opponent unravelling his argument without knowing it. It was only on these occasions when Ben had been happy in court. The rest of the time he was so nervous and so in awe of the judge and the whole

39

procedure that he had sometimes relied on medication not to lose his composure.

Celia brought in tea – tea from the street, served in little steaming glasses on a brass tray held by a tripartite chain.

'We try to go in for the local customs,' said Mancini. 'Thanks, Celia.'

The tea tasted strong and sweet. As he sipped, Ben caught Ross's eye. Ross was angry. Ross thought Ben had been unfair. Now it looked to Ben as if Ross really did want this job as much as he did. Ben also noticed that Ross hadn't shaved perfectly, he had missed a spot just to the right of the centre of his chin; no doubt this would become more apparent as the day wore on.

'Here's the drill,' said Mancini, tightly wound inside his long suit. 'We'll take a drive out to the Meheti Dam, such as it is. Take a look around. We'll have lunch out there at a restaurant on the bank of what will be the reservoir. We'll meet a few people and then hurry back, all right? We'll have a drink at my house with some friends. You've already met my wife. This is all just sort of to break the ice and then for the next couple of days we'll have further chats, not together. I want you to know I'm decisive in these things and we'll know what's what by the time you leave on Thursday.'

'Good,' said Ben, firmly.

'I've changed my ticket,' said Ross. 'I'm not leaving Thursday. I thought I'd travel around the country for a week while I'm here. I'm particularly interested in seeing the Baram Caves.'

Ben had never heard of the Baram Caves.

'Oh, well, marvellous,' said Mancini. 'Absolutely marvellous place, the Baram Caves. Every time someone visits from stateside we take them or send them to Baram. The children love it too. It's only about a two-hour drive.'

Ben tried to think of something to say. He didn't say anything.

Mancini had finished his tea and risen from his chair. He had a very erect bearing for so tall a man. Ben imagined himself sitting behind Mancini's desk in a few years' time, after Mancini's retirement, a seasoned overseas gent telling prospective employees about the Baram Caves, whatever the hell they were.

IO

After several cups of coffee, Ben had made the firm decision not to tell Alan Yates that Wiesman had fired him. He might hint that he was looking in other directions, looking for a radical change to enrich his life – but he would not confess that he had been sacked. He would ask plenty of questions and let Alan do the talking, which Alan usually did anyway. They would talk about their wives and children and schools and property values. If necessary, Ben would hint that his likely partnership was the main reason he hadn't already struck out for a different job; and that at the same time the thought of a partnership – so long-term, so soul-destroying – was something he dreaded in a way, something that made him want to take life by the horns before it was too late.

Ben spent the next two hours wandering around being unemployed. He went to a book shop and bought a novel for the first time since Christmas. He liked novels, but rarely had time to read. It occurred to him that he really only read two books a year. If he lived another fifty years, just one hundred more books would enter his imagination. He looked up at the shelves of books surrounding him – mountains of books – and he felt absurd. He went outside and sat on a low wall in the sunshine. He opened the book he had bought but found he couldn't concentrate. He relived over and over again the feeling he'd had on Friday in Wiesman's office, of falling into a pit where no one could hear his screams for help. He was short of breath and slightly nauseated. He closed the book, put it in his briefcase, walked away again trying to fill his lungs with air. He felt weak and tired. Minutes passed unnaturally slowly. For years, Ben had watched the hands on the clock in his office sweeping by too quickly for him to get everything done. Now he found himself looking at his watch at intervals of seconds. He charted a walk in his mind that would use up the remaining hour before his lunch with Alan Yates, one that wouldn't take him anywhere near his former office building.

An hour later Ben was in sight of the restaurant. He slapped his cheeks to make himself look healthy. He practised smiling. He was more convinced than ever that to tell Alan the truth would be a humiliating error. They would have a normal lunch, perhaps even a glass or two of wine, they might reminisce about a particular girl at Harvard. Alan would continue to think of Ben as his old pal who'd gone down the same road, who'd made it in life, who as well as being a good provider for his beautiful wife and fixable children, was a damned good lawyer. Ben set his jaw and accelerated into the stride of a busy attorney. He entered the restaurant and immediately saw Alan Yates, who was handing his coat over to the hat-check girl. Alan had gone the tiniest bit grey, which suited his stature at his exquisite law firm. He kept trim by being wealthy. He turned around and saw Ben standing in the doorway. Ben puffed out his chest, smiled and waved as if acknowledging an ovation. Alan came over.

'Jesus, Ben,' he said. 'I'm so sorry.'

II

The drive to the Meheti Dam Project was an uncomfortable one for Ben, because he had to sit in the front seat of Chauffeur's car. He could only converse with Mancini and Ross if he turned sideways and spoke over his shoulder. The result of this arrangement was that Mancini and Ross relaxed on the tiger-skin back seat and chatted like old friends – or like father and son – while Ben was left craning his neck and unable to hear everything that was said. It was hot and Chauffeur's car was not air-conditioned. Ben felt his hair going limp with sweat. He opened the car window, but this only made it more difficult for him to hear what Mancini and Ross were saying. For all he knew they were talking about the Baram Caves.

Chauffeur drove at a stately pace. The city gave way to scrubby, rocky desert and a canyon containing the river that would power the Meheti Dam hydroelectric plant, creating a reservoir not only for drinking-water, sanitation and irrigation but also for what was called 'leisure activity'. Leisure activity meant a yacht club and a hotel. The dam was the biggest project Mancini's company had yet been involved in, and it was financed both privately and by the governments of the United States, Canada and Great Britain. Ben was not unaware that there were geopolitical stakes involved in this country's solicitation of Western funds for such an enormous engineering endeavour.

Overhearing what he could of the back-seat conversation, Ben admitted to himself that Ross Howard sounded likeable despite his youthful arrogance. He had done his homework, as perhaps only a spy could. He was well-spoken and intelligent, and he struck a sensible balance between flattering Mancini and asserting his own qualities. He seemed to know the names of everyone in every department of every organization Mancini asked about. Worse still, Mancini knew Ross's father, who had recently retired from State. Ben slumped in his seat and stopped making the effort to listen to their chat, which had become so relaxed and incestuous that Ben's cause already appeared to be lost.

After an hour's journey, the modern road gave way to dirt, and climbed into craggy hills. Chauffeur then turned on to a track used by the hundreds of vehicles involved in the dam's construction. Ben saw how Chauffeur winced with every bump and every cloud of dust – these were insults to his treasured car. At a high turn in the track Mancini asked Chauffeur to pause. The three men got out of the car and surveyed the project site from above. The dam was almost finished. The river, which had its source in the Berevan Mountains to the north, had been diverted through a fork in the gorge half a mile away. It was going to be a high and slender dam. Mancini said a few words about delays and cost overruns, then the men returned to the car and Chauffeur drove on. Soon they came to another construction site, this one for the hotel and yacht club. At the moment it was situated on top of a gently sloping hill, but in only a few months it would be at the edge of a reservoir almost seven miles long and two miles wide at its broadest. Ben looked down at the desiccated landscape and tried to imagine the space above it filled with water, and wondered if he ought to ask if fish would be introduced or if they would simply appear on their own.

Ben had forgotten his dark glasses, and had to squint into the glare of the hot sun as he followed the other men to an unfinished terrace where tea awaited. Ross asked questions about the dimensions of the dam, source of materials, rate of work. Ben said nothing and sat stiffly next to Ross, one place removed from Mancini. A team of workmen on the hillside seized his attention. They were sifting gravel, using rectangular sieves propped up at forty-five-degree angles. The first man threw shovel-loads of gravel at them, creating a cone of sifted gravel on the other side. The next man would use this pile against a finer sieve, creating finer gravel. A third man in turn used the new pile against an even finer sieve, turning it to sand. Ben was transfixed by this process and by the intensity of the men's labour in such heat. In the dazzling sunshine Ben's vision was blurred and for a moment the middle sieve, with white gravel pouring down its face with each shovelful, seemed to take on the features of Victor Wiesman. Ben had been sifted. The pain seized him again and for a moment he didn't hear that Mancini was speaking to him.

'I beg your pardon?' Ben asked, turning and looking at his own double reflection in Mancini's dark glasses.

'I said tell me about yourself, Ben.'

12

When Ben looked back on his life he saw it as divided into four sections, or phases. His childhood, in a New England town, could not have been more peaceful nor happier nor more secure. His father was a local lawyer with a proper shingle hanging from the eaves of the little house in the centre of town where he and a property firm had established their offices. Ben's mother serenely raised him and his two younger sisters. Ben liked to think of the second phase as one of academic excellence. In a high-school class of thirty-five pupils, Ben had little difficulty in emerging as valedictorian. The third phase – Harvard and Harvard Law School – put him in his place academically, but still he had succeeded. These were years of such intensity, both socially and intellectually, that it made him breathless to revisit his diary. The fourth phase began on the day he met Ellen Delaney outside a Boston theatre. She was not yet twenty years old, just starting out on the years Ben had recently put behind him. By successfully courting this fresh young woman, Ben effectively took away the greater part of the exhilaration and despair, passion and insecurity she might otherwise have experienced. She moved in with Ben in her junior year and was cut off from the traditional whirl of campus life. This would become a paradox- ical source of guilt for Ben, especially at the traumatic close of the fourth phase, as if he should have left Ellen alone to enjoy her youth and only then have returned to claim her. At least she didn't get pregnant until graduate school. The next few years of work and children were a blur of anxiety and exhaustion that, looking back, ceased abruptly in the jowls of Victor Wiesman.

Ben mulled over what had become of his life as he took the train home after lunch with Alan Yates, where Ben had presented himself in a miserable combination of phoney bravado and false optimism. It was all for the best, Ben had said repeatedly, smiling and ordering a whole bottle of wine: under normal working conditions it was not done to drink at lunch. Alan promised to help, which only made Ben more convinced that he had to break away from the law entirely. He didn't want to be indebted to anyone, but especially not to Alan. When Alan had to leave, he did so with a pitying frown and a pat on the back that said, 'So you turned out to be a loser. What a crying shame.' Alan insisted on leaving cash on the table so that Ben could pay the bill when he had finished his wine. This gesture was so predictable and so profoundly irritating that Ben ordered brandy and a cigar and then another brandy and stayed in his chair, fuming, for a further hour. He left the restaurant, bought a magazine, walked to the train station and sat there until after six o'clock. He caught a slightly earlier train than usual and was home in time to help put the children to bed. He went through this charade for the rest of the week and the following Monday, spending his days walking, drinking coffee, visiting museums, reading. It took this long for his situation really to sink in. Ellen seemed pleased that he was able to come home earlier than usual. On that Monday, then, ten days after being fired, he was again home in time to help put the children to bed. When this was done he and Ellen sat on high stools at the kitchen counter, watching the television news.

Evan Court was in Africa. Ellen thought he looked frightened, which she found endearing. The men and boys causing this current difficulty looked drunk or drugged or both. Evan Court's pictures tonight showed them roaming around a village where they had just killed every resident foolish enough to have stayed behind after the general evacuation of their nook of Africa. Sensitive to the network's viewers, Evan's cameraman filmed dead bodies from a distance, so that they looked like bundles of rags. This was a big story primarily because a Finnish aid worker had been among the dozens killed. Evan was blunt and self-deprecating enough to admit that he and his crew would be getting out of the area as soon as possible in the interest of their own safety.

'I'm in love with him,' Ellen said.

'I know you are,' said Ben. 'Don't keep reminding me.'

'Sorry.'

'Would you love me more if I were a far-flung war correspondent?'

'Only *slightly* more, Ben.'

'Well, how about if I worked in the glamorous field of international development, or diplomacy, or if I were a spy?'

'Only *slightly* more, as I said.'

'I'm not kidding this time, Ellen.'

'You didn't really quit today, did you? Say you didn't quit.'

'I didn't quit.'

Ben wondered how long he could keep up the deception. If Alan Yates already knew, lots of other people did too. Ellen didn't socialize with anyone who was likely to find out, and she never dealt with the bank accounts, but Ben was going to have a hard time going through the motions of still working. He couldn't just drive around in the car, because Ellen might notice a sudden leap on the odometer. He hated himself for having deceived her, but already he thought he had done so much damage that there was no turning back. He wasn't thinking clearly. Here was Ellen, the one person he could count on for support, the closest person to him in the world, and yet he was keeping her in the dark even when someone like Alan Yates knew the whole story.

'I'll tell you the truth, Ellen. I hope you won't be angry. Today I asked Wiesman for two weeks off so I can look around for something else. I didn't tell him that, of course. I told him you weren't feeling well and I had to help with the children.'

Ellen looked shocked. 'Two weeks? But what about this summer? And how could you lie like that to Wiesman?'

'Just a routine white lie. In this climate I can't have him thinking I want to leave. And I'll still have enough time off left for the summer, don't worry. Anyway, what if I find something else by then? I'm going to turn our little world upside down.'

'Please be careful,' said Ellen.

'This is no time for caution,' Ben said, finding that he was swallowing hard. 'No time for caution.' Ellen's face was only inches away. Her pure, familiar features were beautiful to him as always – but now, with a cowardly lie hanging between the couple, he wilted under the trust and concern in her eyes. 'I don't . . .' Ben began, swallowing again. 'I don't think you should worry. I'll . . .' He tried to laugh as he swept a hand before him and said, 'I want to take you away from all this.'

The television was still on. Evan Court had reappeared to be interviewed from Africa, where a horrible new morning had just begun to dawn. Ellen turned away from Ben to watch her beloved reporter. Ben couldn't look away from his wife. The light of distant atrocities played off her pale and lovely face. Ben felt himself breaking down. This hadn't happened to him for years. The contrast between that apocalypse and this run-of-the-mill setback – a 'blip', Wiesman had called it – made Ben all the more sorrowful in his self-pity. Despite being conscious of the great gulf between what was important and what was not, he could not prevent himself from gazing on Ellen's trusting, pretty face and falling, falling: he felt that something permanent had happened. It was not all in his mind; his body felt weak again and his flesh crawled. He was breaking down. He didn't have the strength to make an excuse and leave the room. His shoulders began to heave and his nostrils flared and his mouth opened silently as if he were trying to catch his breath after being punched in the stomach. Ellen hadn't seen yet. She was still watching Evan Court as he helped his crew and four wounded Africans into a military helicopter. It had always been her face – the set of her mouth, her long eyelashes, her delicate hair – that affected Ben this way, rather than her voice or the things she said. Ben and Ellen had a deal – and it was not unspoken, it was quite explicit because Ben had insisted on making grand promises. He had taken her youth, but he would make it up to her by living only for her happiness and comfort. Ellen had left a boyfriend for him, a man who these days showed up on the op-ed pages of the *New York Times* being brilliant and funny and mixing in interesting circles and dropping hints that it wasn't as easy as it seemed juggling homes on both coasts. The ex-boyfriend was still single and had once written a piece about lost love in which, with what appeared to be sincere sentimentality, he wrote the words, 'You know who you are, my love.' Ellen had tried to hide the magazine in which the piece appeared, but a mutual friend kindly pointed it out so that Ben wouldn't miss it. Ben was breaking down, now, the tears had begun and would not stop until he had sobbed them all away.

'Oh, Ben,' said Ellen. 'Jesus, Ben. What is it? What's the matter?' She put her arms around his shoulders and squeezed. She pressed her face against his and he felt her hair on his cheek, which only reminded him of the girl at the top of the stairs. Now he moaned and the tears poured between his clenched eyelids. He tried to say 'I promised,' but couldn't find his voice.

'Oh, Ben.'

Trying to hold back his sobs only contributed to the ugliness of the sounds Ben made. Ellen held him and looked on in horror as he convulsed in her arms. She could feel the spasms of the muscles in his back. She could smell cigars and alcohol on his breath. He covered his face with his hands. Ellen couldn't imagine what the problem could be. Ben was unable to speak, and she knew enough not to press him until he regained control.

'There, there, Ben,' she said, as if she were comforting one of her children. 'There, there. I'll get you a paper towel.'

Ben cried into the paper towel for a while, then into another. 'I promised,' he managed to say, his face a grotesque mask of pain. 'I promised you.'

'Don't worry,' said Ellen. The thought came crashing down on Ellen that Ben was having an affair. 'Whatever it is, it's all right,' she said, having trained herself to say these words at precisely this moment, a moment she had always considered inevitable. 'It's all right.' She stroked his hair as his head bobbed up and down with the spasms of weeping.

'I promised you,' Ben said, opening his mouth in an ape-like grimace, so that strands of saliva stretched unattractively between his upper and lower lips.

Ellen closed her eyes. 'I know,' she said. She hoped Sean wouldn't come downstairs now, as he so often did at this time. Ben was so far gone he wouldn't be able to pull himself together even in front of their little boy.

Ben could just about speak now, in a kind of torture-victim moan. 'I don't want . . .' he said.

'What?'

'I don't want the children to know.'

Now Ellen had her suspicions confirmed. She was going to have to add the Adulterous Husband to the list of clichés she lived every day. 'It's all right,' she said.

'It's not,' said Ben, still sobbing but with a bit of hysterical laughter finally bleeding through the tears. 'It's not.'

'Look, whatever it is it's all right. Why don't you go ahead and tell me.' Ellen imagined a woman's name. It had to be someone in the city, not out here. She would have found out instantly if it were someone out here.

'I don't want my parents to know. In part—' here Ben hiccuped. 'In particular I don't want your *father* to know.'

'It's all right,' said Ellen. In her mind, Ben was about to say 'She's called Francine' or 'Her name is Abigail' or 'It's Cheryl'.

'Wiesman fired me,' Ben said.

Ellen experienced the odd physical sensation of simultaneously breathing out with relief and breathing in with alarm. 'Oh, *baby*,' she said. 'He didn't.'

Ben nodded helplessly. His red face was wet from forehead to jaw. 'He *did*.'

'Oh, *baby*.'

'I'm so sorry, Ellen.'

'Don't be silly.'

'I'm so sorry, Ellen. I love you so much.'

'I love you too. Don't be silly.'

'I'm so sorry.'

'OK.'

'Don't tell your father.'

'Oh, Ben. I won't tell my stupid old father.'

'He's not stupid. He hates me.'

'Of *course* he hates you.'

Ben's laughter was getting through, now. He laughed through his nose and thought, While I'm at it, why don't I just tell her I visited a prostitute? 'You know what?' he asked his wife, really laughing now. 'You know what?'

'What,' said Ellen, still stroking his hair and now kissing his cheek, her arms around him like the protective mother she was.

'Last Friday, after it happened . . .'

'It was last Friday?'

'Well . . . Actually it was the Friday before that, now that

53

you mention it. I didn't want to tell you. I didn't want it to have *happened*. I didn't want the kids to know.'

'Oh, baby.'

Ben was so enthusiastic about Ellen's response that he really did want to get to the drunken, whoring monster part of his recent past. 'Anyway on the afternoon it happened I just didn't know what to do with myself. I should have come home but everything was just sinking in. I walked around. Do you know, I ended up at . . .' Ben caught himself. His eyes went wide with horror at what he had almost done.

'Where, Ben?'

Ben shook his head. 'Sorry, sorry about this. I was just saying . . .' Ben could not believe what he had almost said, on top of what he had already admitted. 'I was just saying I did the stupidest thing, it's a cliché. I ended up at an Irish bar drinking whisky all by myself and just sitting there, not even reading, not even watching the golf on television, just sitting there.'

'I can't believe you didn't tell me,' said Ellen, now at arm's length.

'It's a nightmare,' said Ben. 'I couldn't believe it was happening. My life is over.'

'Sure,' said Ellen, firmly. 'Now wipe your eyes and blow your nose and listen to me. Look, look there.' She pointed at the television. Evan Court had flown his evacuees to a large African city, but two of them had died *en route*. 'What does the word "perspective" mean to you, my darling?'

Ben buried his face in his hands again, but this would be the last wave of self-pity to sweep over him. He had confessed. He felt cleansed. In a few days he would take action and start again.

13

The lunch and meetings at the Meheti Dam were inconsequential, as far as Ben was concerned. He and Ross Howard were introduced to engineers and foremen and three token workmen. They ate braised lamb and drank local wine. Paul Mancini exuded confidence and initiative. Chauffeur lurked in the background, washing and polishing his car even though he would have to cover rough terrain again as soon as they left. When they did leave it was Ben's turn to sit in the back seat with Mancini. The wine and the sun and his long journey had made him so tired he found it difficult to make conversation, especially as he could see how bored Mancini was with small-talk. Ross sat unassumingly in the front, speaking the local language with Chauffeur.

Mancini's house, up in the hills to the north of the city, was surrounded by high stone walls. Chauffeur parked in the street, and the men climbed a steep staircase that led to a carport underneath the house, which was built on stilts. On the next level was the swimming pool, a California-style pool house, a tennis court and a long formal garden that was out of place against the adjacent rocky hillside. The house itself was brand new and not quite complete. Already a drinks party had developed outside the house, and Candy Mancini waved her glass in greeting. Ben was introduced to British, Canadian and American members of the Planning and Resources staff. He was handed a longed-for glass of wine by a thin and dignified servant who wore a starched white jacket over black trousers and plastic sandals.

In the bright sunlight, which was amplified by the swimming pool, Ross Howard's blue suit looked tatty, ill-fitting and hot. The spot of stubble he had missed shaving was now as visible as a birthmark. Ben felt cool and appropriate in his khaki suit. He avoided Ross for the moment and went over to reacquaint himself with Candy Mancini.

'We had a good day,' Ben said. 'The dam is spectacular.'

'I'm so glad,' said Candy, who looked as if she hadn't had a chance to shower after playing tennis. There were spots of dried salt in the corners of her eyes.

'I love your house.'

'Thank you. They've built it all around us. The garden was here before.'

'Where are your children?' There were at least ten children running around.

'There's Little Paul, over there by the ping-pong table. I don't know why we have that outside, it's almost always too windy. There's Caroline saying hello to her daddy.'

'Beautiful. I miss my kids and I've only been away – what, thirty-six hours?'

'The children are in heaven here. It's an easy life. Look, here comes Little Paul now.'

Candy's son came over to ask if he could have a piece of the chocolate cake that had not yet been cut.

'Not yet, darling. Here, meet Ben Pelton.'

Little Paul – at home his father was known as Big Paul – was an astonishingly poised boy. He made direct eye contact and shook hands firmly. He had dark brown hair and large blue eyes. He wore a white T-shirt and blue bathing trunks, and was barefoot. He spoke clearly but there was something about him – Ben couldn't quite say what – out of the ordinary. He stood comfortably among the adults with one hand on his hip and a weary, grown-up expression on his face. He was going to be tall, like his parents. It occurred to Ben that he was really going to enjoy his own son at that age, just a year or two from now. Someone to have a conversation with, someone who would contradict him and turn out to be right.

'Have you seen the Meheti Dam?' Ben asked the boy.

'Only about sixty times,' said Little Paul.

'Well, I saw it for the first time today. I was very impressed. Your father is doing good work. He said he's going to take you out to the reservoir and teach you to water-ski.'

'Did he? That'll be terrific.' Paul Junior really did have a charming air about him. Ben was so taken by his looks and his poise that he thought this must be an overreaction because he missed his own children so much. He thought how nice it would be if this boy could be Sean's best friend, an early mentor.

'Your Dad said you once went skiing in the Berevan Mountains.'

'That's right,' said Paul. 'I'm afraid I wasn't very good at it.'

'Oh, of course you were,' said Candy, who still lingered at Ben's side despite the arrival of new guests. 'For your first time you were fabulous.'

'I wasn't,' said Paul. 'I was scared and the instructor said so. I didn't like falling down and I didn't like the sound the skis made on the ice.'

Just then Ross Howard insinuated himself into their midst to say hello to Candy Mancini. He did not even acknowledge the child until he was introduced. It was Little Paul who first extended his hand in greeting. Ben was so moved by the boy's good manners that he had to turn away for a moment to collect himself. When he turned back, Ross was speaking to the boy in the local language.

'I'm terrible,' said Candy. 'I really can't bring myself to say a word. My husband is *very* good about it, though. How amazing you are, Ross.'

Ben picked a piece of fried squid from a passing tray, and ate it. Ross and Little Paul reverted to English. More guests arrived and Candy excused herself to perform her duties as hostess.

'Do you know most of the people here?' Ben asked the boy.

Little Paul looked around. 'Not all of them,' he said. 'I don't go to the same school as their kids. Mostly everyone goes to the American School. Caroline and I are at the French School just down the street.'

Ben waited for Ross to break into French, but Ross hadn't been listening – he was searching the growing crowd for a waiter to refill his glass of wine. The boy's manners and speech were remarkable, but Ben didn't know many eight-year-olds and therefore could draw few comparisons. 'Do you enjoy school?'

'A *lot*,' said Paul, with adult sarcasm. 'Actually, it's pretty strict but I like my teacher this year.'

The waiter returned and poured wine into Ben and Ross's glasses, and patted Paul on the head.

'That's Yelam,' said Paul, when the waiter went away. 'He's our houseboy.' Ben had never heard anyone say the word 'houseboy' before. 'If I do well in school he bakes me a special kind of cake. He can carve toys out of watermelons. He made me a machine gun out of pieces of wood the workmen left around – a machine gun that really goes "tak-tak-tak-tak-tak". He was in the army for three years. He won't talk about that.'

'Does he speak English?'

'He's getting better.'

Candy Mancini returned with a group of new arrivals. 'Come meet the *jeunesse dorée*,' she said, referring to Ben and Ross, but – to Ben's paranoid ear – mostly to Ross. Ben was introduced to an Englishman named Jenkins and a Canadian named Wright. Jenkins was a tiny, bald man with a paunch who let it be known that both of his sons were at boarding school back in England, and that this was a good thing. Ben looked at Little Paul and wondered how anyone could voluntarily be separated from their children for more than a few days at a time. Jenkins was an ex-Foreign-Office man – no doubt a spy, thought Ben – who, like Mancini, considered himself to be nearing retirement even though he was only in his mid-fifties. He had the air of private wealth. Ross chatted to him about London, a city Ross knew well, while Ben tried to think of something to say to the Canadian. Wright was a fair-haired, amiable man of about forty who knew a lot about mining. His job was to seek out the mineral wealth of this country and to put into place the machinery of its exploitation. His three children were at the American School – he'd fought bitterly with his Québécois wife on this score. 'The French School frightens me,' he said. 'Looks like a prison camp.' Little Paul didn't rise to this. Ben thought he wanted his kids in school with Little Paul, whether it looked like a prison camp or not.

Ben was aware that there would be a meeting at Planning and Resources and both Wright and Jenkins would be asked their opinion of the two candidates for the new job. He fought through his exhaustion to try to think of something he could say that would make him shine, even as Ross turned to Wright and began a conversation not about children, not about schools, not about the weather, but about *bauxite*.

Ben still couldn't think of anything important to say. The truth – that he was quite obviously not so qualified as Ross Howard; that he was encumbered by family and therefore more expensive to hire; that he was *desperate* for this job – was not what he thought Jenkins and Wright ought to hear. Ben had paused long enough now for Jenkins to ask the inevitable, tricky question:

'So you're a lawyer?'

Ben searched his mind for inspiration, and was rewarded. 'Once a lawyer, always a lawyer, I guess,' he said, casually.

'I've wanted a change for quite some time, though. My wife is all for it.'

'It certainly would be a change,' said Jenkins.

'It's what we want. Long ago I suggested politics, but my wife, Ellen, was never in favour. I sometimes say, "I could be Lieutenant Governor by now," and she says, "See what I *mean*?"'

Jenkins smiled. Ben felt that this was his first victory. 'Chap has a sense of humour,' Jenkins would report at the meeting with Mancini. 'Threw away a political career, as well. Decent man.'

'It was all the social posing and hypocrisy and outright lying my wife objected to,' said Ben, socially posing, being a hypocrite, lying outright – he'd never said a word to Ellen about politics.

'How do you vote, then?' asked Jenkins.

Ben almost answered this question truthfully, then he almost answered it untruthfully. Finally he said, 'I don't think it would be appropriate to say. Anyhow, I'm open-minded.'

'Quite right,' said Jenkins.

'I've never voted,' said Ross, rather rashly in Ben's opinion. Was this a second victory?

'I don't blame you,' said Wright, the Canadian mining expert. 'Not voting is a form of voting, if you see what I mean.'

So Ross had escaped that particular trap.

'Ah, more wives,' said Candy, who for the last couple of minutes had been leaning down, whispering about something with her son.

Jenkins's wife was small and round and cheerful; Wright's wife was tall, dark and elegantly dressed. Ross immediately complimented Mrs Jenkins on her earrings, which he correctly identified as local; and Mrs Wright on her light cotton dress, which he correctly identified as Parisian.

'We always go to Paris on leave,' said Mrs Wright.

God, do I want this job, Ben thought. The idea of 'leave in

Paris', of Little Paul coming over to play with Sean after French School, having an equivalent of Yelam to be his *houseboy*, for Heaven's sake . . . His face began to twitch again. He allowed Yelam to refill his glass for the third time. He wanted to dive into the pool.

The view from the hillside pool house was of an enormous compound surrounded by a high brick wall. Through the trees Ben glimpsed the top of a squat white building. Its roof bristled with antennae, the largest of which looked like an outsize washing line.

'The Soviet Embassy,' Candy said, noticing Ben's interest.

'I once shot a crow out of one of their trees with my air gun,' said Little Paul.

This description of an act of violence reminded Ben of Little Paul's injury. He looked down at the boy's right hand, which showed only a faint V-shaped scar between his index and middle fingers, pale against his tan.

'I don't know if I killed it,' he added, looking ashamed and remorseful. 'I hope not. It fell out of the tree behind the wall. I won't do *that* again.'

'That's my angel,' said Candy.

Ross piped up again. 'The Ambassador's residence is inside those walls as well, or so I'm told.'

'Yes, it's the whole thing. It's rare for anyone to come in or go out – sort of like their country, as my husband says.'

Ross brayed with forced laughter. Ben kept staring at Little Paul's hand, while trying not to. He thought of his own children and their past and future wounds. He remembered the first time Sean had been hurt, when he was only two years old and stepped on a dead bee on the porch. Sean had fallen first to his knees and then on his back, his little baby face split by a grimace and a cry so horrible Ben almost couldn't move. The boy had cried out, 'Papa, Papa!' and Ben had taken this as an accusation. He lifted the boy up and comforted him and

61

wondered for a moment if he ought to call an ambulance in case Sean were allergic. In a minute he realized that everything was going to be all right. Still sobbing, Sean managed to say, 'I was stung by a bee,' and Ben experienced a perverse flush of pride in the child's inexplicably perfect use of the past tense, which almost seemed to make the bee sting worthwhile. When Ellen had come home Ben first reported Sean's clear and correct grammar, then the injury.

Jenkins and Ross were now trading pontifications on the Soviet Union, a country of which neither man approved. Wright was less dogmatic, when he could get a word in. The wives expressed no opinion.

'But I think you'll find,' said Jenkins, as the subject somehow drifted back to domestic servants, 'that the *character* of the people here is indomitable. And do you know why? It is simply because they were never colonized. They had an empire of their own, you see. They are proud. They are nothing like your African or your Indian or your – I was going to say American but I suppose not. Those people are naturally servile. That is also why they are dishonest, murderous, really *mad*, is what they are. You won't find that sort of thing here. You will find stoicism, pride – national as well as personal pride. And I insist they are honest – not like your mad African.'

Obviously Jenkins was the weak link in the organization – the drunk whom either Ben or Ross was going to replace. Ben wondered if Jenkins knew, and guessed that he didn't.

'You were in Kinshasa, weren't you, Candy?' Jenkins asked rhetorically.

'I –'

'Well, the people are simply *mad*. Hack you to bits as soon as look at you, as the expression goes. Oh I'm not saying the colonial years and the Empire were a great treat for everyone everywhere, but for God's sake, to look at these people today – pullulating, violent, ravaged by disease . . .'

On Jenkins went, and Ben was reminded of Ross's remark about 'power-mad, syphilitic' African strongmen. Perhaps Ross would take Jenkins aside and agree with him on every fatuous point he made.

'Now that's enough of that,' said Candy, expertly. 'Let's let these boys mingle. They might like to see the garden.'

The group broke up. Ross made a beeline for Paul Mancini. Ben wandered around to the other side of the pool and introduced himself to a husband and wife who pretended they weren't having a terrible argument about something. The man was called Joseph DiMarko, and had been working as an accountant for Mancini since the inception of Planning and Resources. His wife, Megan, taught English at the local university. Their children attended the American School, so Ben asked them about that.

'It's a little slice of America,' said DiMarko. 'Little-league baseball, the works. All the servicemen's children go there.' There was a substantial American military presence in this country, as it was still a powerful buffer against the menace of Communism. 'And you get the PX for groceries, of course. I don't know what we'd do without the PX.'

'They have peanut butter,' said Megan.

'And of course there's the big swimming pool – the children love it. Very clean,' said DiMarko, who wore loud yellow trousers and a shiny green jacket. 'Tennis too, but we don't play.'

Ben looked past DiMarko at Ross and Mancini, who were engaged in animated conversation. It pained Ben to think that he would have to go through the motions of auditioning for the job for a further three days, when the outcome already seemed so certain. He knew there were thousands of jobs out there, but he wanted *this* one. He had promised Ellen, he had said it was a *fait accompli*. To return with the news that the job had been usurped by a gangling youngster like Ross Howard would be like telling Ellen he had been fired all over again, that he just wasn't *good* enough.

DiMarko had been talking politely for some time about the amenities available to expatriates, but Ben wasn't really listening. He was looking at Ross and Mancini and wondering what he could possibly do to turn things around. It didn't look as if Ross would get drunk and make a fool of himself, even though Yelam was doing a good job of keeping everyone's glass full.

'Excuse me,' Ben said to DiMarko. 'I thought I would explore the garden.'

Ben walked alone down a stone path that led to a broad lawn surrounded by midget pine trees. A stooped gardener laboured in the undergrowth. The hiss of sprinklers explained the garden's viability in the hot, dry climate. A hill rose behind the trees; nothing at all grew there. A house was under construction at the top of the hill. On the other side, the grounds of the Soviet Embassy compound stretched all the way to the end of the street. From this vantage point Ben had a better view of the office building itself, and in an upstairs window he saw the silhouette of a lone Communist sitting at his desk, plotting world domination. In the distance the city centre was just visible, an ancient cone of humanity choked in modern smog.

Ben turned around and started back towards the pool. People had begun to say their goodbyes – but not Ross, who still had Mancini's ear. Ben approached and remarked that the garden was lovely.

'It's very special. We're lucky to have it,' said Mancini, who looked pleased with himself. He was so tall Ben found himself wondering what it must have been like to be such a big target in the jungles and paddies of Vietnam. 'Excuse me just a moment, men,' he said. 'I have to have a word with my wife.'

Ben and Ross were left alone. Little Paul had taken off his T-shirt and dived into the pool.

'Quite a place,' said Ross. 'One of the better houses around, I would have thought. Look at it, it's huge.'

'Yes.'

Ross looked puffed up, self-confident. He knew the job was his. He had a broad, crooked-toothed smile on his face. The spot on his chin that he had missed shaving had grown darker. Ben thought his only chance was if Mancini had some visceral horror of facial hair or if he could not abide men who didn't shave thoroughly. This was a slender hope.

Then something happened that changed both of their lives for ever. When Ben looked back on the incident he was struck by how absurdly arbitrary life was: just a series of accidents and random bifurcations.

Ross had his back to the house and the sun in his eyes. He was watching Little Paul swimming in the pool.

'Strange kid,' he said, in a normal voice.

Over Ross's shoulder Ben could see Mancini and his wife coming back to say goodbye.

'Yes,' said Ben, encouragingly. He established eye contact with Ross and didn't make the slightest suggestion that Ross might be overheard. 'Very strange.' It was almost as if Ben knew what was going to happen, as he fixed his gaze on Ross and didn't let his eyes travel to Mancini, who was now just feet away from Ross and closing fast.

'If you ask me,' said Ross, so ebullient in his supposed success that he was in a pronouncing mood, and now gesturing at Little Paul, 'that kid is going to turn out queer.'

'We can cancel,' said Ellen, referring to Sunday's visit to her parents' house.

'No, that would only make your father suspicious. We'll go. We'll tell him our plans in the vaguest way. We will *not* tell him the truth.'

And so they went – Ben tense behind the wheel, Ellen turned sideways to placate the children. She had been so good, so supportive – even conspiratorial. Ben was still numb and ill with disbelief and frustration, but relieved to have his wife in the know. They had talked for hours on the night of Ben's confession and managed to turn his humiliation into a positive act of rebellion against the conventional life. Ellen had made it seem as if they had needed this jolt in order to fulfil their destiny.

Ben dreaded seeing Ellen's father, who was a pretentious, bullying, repressed and hateful old man. He was a bigot. Ben had never lasted two hours in his company without getting into an unpleasant argument. He set out on these Sunday trips telling himself that he could manage, that he could be accommodating, that he could match Judd Delaney's racism and anti-Semitism slur for slur if necessary to avoid confrontation. Every time he was driven over the edge.

Ellen's parents lived an hour and a half away in a sturdy old farmhouse on seven acres of land. Before retiring, Dr Delaney had made a good living as an ear-nose-and-throat man. 'In this town it's seventeen Jews and me,' he had said, several times. 'I'm the only Irish doctor within a hundred miles.'

Ben had converted to Catholicism in order to marry Ellen and to curb Dr Delaney's rage when the couple moved in together beforehand. 'Conversion' had been an odd word to use, since Ben had no religion whatsoever to begin with. Still, Ben could honestly say that he was as good a Catholic as his wife, who despised the Roman Catholic Church and in front of her parents had once called the whole Christian phenomenon 'infantile'.

'Well, here we are,' said Ellen, with a sigh. She always said 'Well, here we are,' and sighed, when they pulled in to the long drive to her father's pretty house.

Dr and Mrs Delaney had just returned from Mass, and stood next to their car outside the front door.

'Smile, everybody,' Ellen said.

Ben smiled like a made-up clown as he brought the car to a halt. He got out and said, 'Beth, Judd, how *are* you?'

Ellen's mother was mysterious to Ben. She gave the impression of being an absolute cipher, but he suspected that she lived a reasonably full life in her mind, behind the outward appearance of total deference to her boorish husband. They had been married for thirty-two years, and Ellen was their only child. Dr Delaney had once said to Ben, in his wife's and daughter's earshot, 'She busted her tubes. It's her fault. I wanted six children. Three boys, three girls.'

Ben helped Sean and Nicole out of the car and everyone kissed and hugged and said how happy they were.

'Sorry you couldn't make it in time for Mass,' Mrs Delaney said. 'I know how difficult it is to pack up a family and get a move on.'

'Indeed,' said Ellen.

Ben continued to smile. He had to get through the next four hours or so without spitefully telling his father-in-law that he'd been fired. The old man would be devastated: his little girl, married to a *loser*.

'There's a lot to talk about,' Ben said, as they all entered the house. 'We have some news.'

'News, is it?' asked Judd Delaney, who had never been to Ireland but was fiercely proud of his distant roots and affected the accent on weekends. He was going deaf, so his every objectionable remark carried a long way.

Ellen helped her mother in the kitchen. The children played on a swing in the back yard. Ben and Delaney drank gin and tonics on the patio.

'So what's the news, then?'

'We're thinking of a change,' Ben said, wanting to play out the suspense. Delaney would be furious at the thought of his daughter leaving the country.

'What would you want to change?' Delaney was a handsome man but his features were cruel. He had severe white eyebrows over squinting, paranoid blue eyes. He had fought in Korea and wouldn't let anyone forget it.

'My job, for a start,' said Ben.

'What, now? At this point?'

'Yes.'

'Craziest thing I've ever heard. Unless of course you're going to be a judge. Are you going to be a judge?'

'No sir.'

'What, then.'

'We want to go abroad. See the world. We're bored, to tell you the truth. Everything's become so routine. We thought it was time to shake things up a bit. I'm going to look into other things.'

'Other things?'

'Other than the law.'

Delaney laughed. He was the sort of man who had unshakeable beliefs. Christ was the son of God; lawyers practised law. 'You don't honestly . . . You don't mean that.'

Ben was enjoying this. 'Yes,' he said. 'The farther away the better.'

'You can't do that to Ellen and the children. Look at them.'

'Ellen is in favour. The children will be fine.'

'I don't understand you, Ben. Think what you're throwing away. Anyway I don't think you're serious.'

'Dead serious. And I'm only throwing away a pretty standard life, Dad.' Ben sometimes called Delaney 'Dad', just to annoy him.

'Ellen!' Delaney shouted. 'Ellen, come out here!'

Ellen came out to the patio, wiping her hands on a kitchen towel. 'What could it possibly be?' she asked, smiling sweetly.

'What's this nonsense about a so-called "change"?'

'Have you two got to that already?'

'Are you out of your minds? What about the children?'

'Daddy, the children will be happy anywhere. Let me get both of you another drink.'

'Just like that?' asked Delaney. 'Just like that? You're not even going to *discuss* it?'

'Of course we can discuss it,' said Ellen, taking the men's empty glasses. 'But you make it sound as if we have to ask permission.'

'Well . . .' said Delaney. 'Maybe you *ought* to ask permission. What about your mother and me?'

'Let me just get those drinks.'

Ellen took the men's glasses and went back into the house.

'This is a lot of foolishness,' said Delaney. 'What, aren't things going well at work?'

'Things are fine at work,' Ben lied. 'It isn't that. I already explained. We've been thinking about this for a couple of years at least. It's a departure.'

'A departure. I see. A departure. A big leap into oblivion, more like.'

'I disagree.'

'Where in hell are you thinking of going?'

'I don't much care. South America? Asia? Africa?' Ben said 'Africa' mischievously, knowing the word would get a rise out of Delaney.

'Oh, fine, *terrific*,' said Delaney, as Ellen came back out with the fresh drinks. 'I hear you're going to *Africa*, Ellen. It isn't bad enough having them in your own street, you've got to go to the *source*?'

'Daddy . . .'

'Perhaps you'll live in a leper colony?'

'I don't think Africa, necessarily, is where we're going.'

'Ben just said so.'

'No I didn't,' said Ben. 'I just mentioned it as a remote possibility. Anyway "Africa" covers a lot of ground.'

'Well what are you going to *do*, Ben – become a missionary?'

'That hadn't occurred to me, funnily enough. I'll find something. I'm interested in development. What I'm doing now is so dry, and when it isn't boring it's dishonest.'

'Oh, *dishonest*, is it? For goodness' sake, Ben, you're a *lawyer*.'

'Not for long,' said Ben, glancing at Ellen.

'And what is "development"? Just shovelling money into a black hole. Pun intended.'

'Not always, I don't think.'

'Ellen, tell me this isn't serious.'

'It's serious, Daddy. It'll be fun, think of it that way.'

'Not for us,' Delaney said, with customary bluntness.

'You could visit.'

Ben tried not to wince.

'When is this all supposed to happen?'

Ben let Ellen answer. 'As soon as possible,' she said.

'What about school for the children? You can't just take Sean out of school.'

70

'People do it all the time, Daddy. We'll make sure to go someplace where they have schools.'

Ben couldn't believe he had set all of this in motion. The pressure was really on him now. It had been the oddest feeling to turn to the employment classifieds in his daily newspaper and to look down the columns of inappropriate openings. He sensed that personal connections were going to have to come into play.

Ellen's mother came out on to the patio. She wore a red-and-white-striped chef's apron over her church clothes.

'Beth,' said Delaney. 'Did you hear what these kids are planning to do? They're going to go to Africa to develop the savages.'

Ellen's mother laughed sharply. 'All of my dreams have come true,' she said.

It was one of the peculiarities of Beth Delaney's personality and demeanour that even her own daughter couldn't tell when she was joking.

'Not Africa, Mom,' said Ellen.

'Oh no, maybe not,' said Delaney. 'But certainly somewhere in need of *development*. I take it this would not be Paris? Why so sudden about everything? Can't you sit back and think about this for . . . for a few years? Until the children are grown up? Until we're dead?'

'Daddy, please.'

'I thought you wanted to be a judge, Ben.'

'I never said anything like that, ever. Anyway lawyers in my line don't normally become judges. You can forget about my being a judge in any case. What is it about judges?'

'I thought that's what top-notch lawyers did when they took early retirement.'

'It doesn't work that way, I assure you.'

'I don't want to be indelicate here,' said Delaney, working his jaw around an ice cube in preparation for indelicacy, 'but wouldn't a drastic switch like this mean a pretty hefty pay-cut?'

'Not necessarily,' said Ben. 'It's a different way of living, when you're overseas. Lots of things are taken care of, I gather. Low cost of living. And it could lead to very interesting opportunities.'

'But can you be sure the firm would have you back if things went sour wherever you ended up?'

'To tell the truth they probably wouldn't. They wouldn't, no.'

'Good God, Ben. You've really got to be careful. Don't do anything stupid. Think of your future. Think of Ellen. Think of the children.' Sean and Nicole had tired of the swing and were making their way back up the lawn, holding hands. 'Have you told the children anything yet?'

'Not directly,' said Ellen. 'But they've overheard enough. Yesterday Sean asked if he ought to start packing his little suitcase. We'll tell them when we know something firm, maybe before, because I'm worried Sean will get the impression we're leaving and not taking him and Nicole with us. You know how children are.'

'I suppose I do,' said Delaney, stroking his chin, 'except that I've only had *just* the one.'

Beth went back into the kitchen. Ben marvelled at her restraint. Delaney had mentioned his regret at not having more children and implied Beth's responsibility every single time Ben had seen him – what must he be like when there were no guests in the house? Ben could now hear Beth in the kitchen vigorously chopping vegetables.

'I have to ask you a favour,' Ben said to Delaney. 'Please don't tell anyone about this until we're set, all right? I wouldn't want my bosses to know I was thinking of leaving, in this climate. Jobs like mine are scarce.'

'Oh, sure,' said Delaney. 'Like they'd *fire* Benjamin Pelton. What a laugh.'

15

'If you ask me,' Ross Howard had just said, 'that kid is going to turn out queer.'

Ben's eyes darted to Paul and Candy Mancini. They had stopped abruptly as if they'd forgotten something. Had they heard? Ben couldn't be completely sure. Ross noticed them now and turned quickly. His face went instantly red, as if he had been slapped. Candy walked away again and Mancini came over looking stern and military.

'Right, men. See you tomorrow afternoon. Celia's left an itinerary at your hotel. Go ahead and see the sights in the morning while you have the chance. I've hardly had a moment for tourism so everything I know about comes from Candy. Off you go then,' he said, shaking hands with both men. 'Chauffeur's waiting downstairs. I don't need him tonight.'

Ben and Ross shook hands with Mancini and departed, thanking Candy on their way out. Ben searched her features for evidence that she had overheard Ross's gaffe, but she was as poised as ever.

In the back seat of the car Ross swore repeatedly under his breath, loosened his tie, leaned low against the door frame. Ben rolled down his window and let the freshening evening air cool his face. Ross stopped muttering and sat up. He looked ill. He rolled down the window on his side and ran his fingers through his damp, curly hair.

'Mancini couldn't have heard, could he?' Ross asked, keeping his voice down in case Chauffeur had exceptionally good hearing and comprehension of English.

'I don't know what you mean, Ross.'

'What I said about his kid.'

'Oh, that. No, I don't think so. I wouldn't worry about it.'

'This means a lot to me.'

'What does?'

'This job.'

'But you said you didn't care either way.'

Ross groaned. 'I was only *saying* that. I got *axed*, man. I made a stupid mistake.'

'Jesus, you poor bastard,' said Ben, pursing his lips so he wouldn't smile. 'What kind of mistake?'

Ross groaned again at the recollection. 'The kind of mistake where you take a lot of someone else's money and turn it into not very much of someone else's money when you had no real business playing around with someone else's money in the first place.'

'Did you, by any chance . . . break the law?'

'It's a grey area,' said Ross, dismally. 'Let's just say I wanted to get out of town. I mean, I made the mistake on a Monday morning – I wasn't feeling well, I don't know what came over me. I was on the street by lunchtime.'

'How awful for you.'

'I don't know what came over me. My girlfriend dumped me during dinner when I tried to explain.'

'Some girlfriend.'

'Mancini doesn't know anything. You wouldn't . . . Jesus, you wouldn't *tell* him, would you?'

Ben thought about the question. 'It depends. And let me guess: the bank gave you glowing recommendations to cover their own *derrière*?'

'That's correct. I shouldn't have told you anything.'

'Don't worry, Ross. Consider me your lawyer, if you want.'

'You're a pal,' said Ross. 'I mean, at least you have nothing to lose. You have something to fall back on.'

'Sure.'

'Mancini probably didn't hear me. I'm sure he didn't hear me. He couldn't have. He would have blown a gasket on the spot, then and there.'

'You're right.'

'I feel better. I feel good. Say, you want to hit the town tonight? We've got tomorrow morning off. I got a hint at the hotel that there are . . . services available.'

Ben raised his chin. 'I don't do that,' he said. 'I'm going straight to my room to try to get through to my wife, then hit the hay.'

'Suit yourself.'

'And don't worry.'

'Me and my big mouth.'

'Don't worry.'

The sky had darkened over the hills and a single, distinct thunderstorm broke over the exclusive neighbourhood where Mancini lived. Chauffeur guided his gleaming car downhill to the city. He took the same two shortcuts as Ben's taxi driver had when coming in from the airport. In the narrow side-street near the hotel Ben saw the dead dog still lying in the gutter, its legs stiff in the air with rigor mortis, its jaws frozen open.

They thanked Chauffeur and entered the hotel together. At reception they were given their itineraries for the following day. There was also a message for Ross, which he unfolded and read at the desk. He crushed the piece of paper in his hands and looked up at the ceiling.

'Let me guess,' said Ben, calmly. 'Mancini overheard?'

16

'This isn't fair,' said Ellen, as the Pelton family drove off to visit Ben's parents. It was the Sunday following their visit to the Delaneys. 'We didn't tell my father, why should we tell yours?'

Ben tried to be diplomatic. 'There is only one reason. It isn't that my parents are in any way "closer" to us than yours or necessarily more sympathetic. But they may be able to help.'

'And my parents couldn't?'

'That's what I'm saying. My father has contacts in that world, just by accident. If I were in medicine we would have confided in your father and not mine.'

'What kind of contacts? I'm not buying this, Ben. You could get their help without telling them you were you-know-what.' They never used the word "fired" in front of the children. 'I know what you want. You want absolution.' As usual, Ellen had put her finger on Ben's real motivation. Ben wanted to tell his parents because he wanted them to share not only in his disappointment but in his struggle.

In Ben's view his parents were in a different category of humanity from Ellen's – genteel, tolerant, fatalistic and culturally refined; in Ellen's view, Ben's parents were posing, pseudo-intellectual, threatening and repressed. She loved them but she dreaded seeing them because they put pressure on her to conform to their family's ways. She resented the idea that Ben was allowed to *say* he dreaded seeing her parents, but she had to pretend that every audience with the wonderful Peltons was a privilege. Today was going to be particularly stressful. Much as she had tried to be light-hearted about and supportive of Ben's radical departure in life, it had been all she could do to conceal her trepidation. She would have to pretend to Ben's parents that she was firmly behind the change – that in fact the revolution in their lives had been her idea.

Ellen hated to admit to herself that she felt as disappointed *in* Ben as she did *for* him – but there it was. Even though none of this was likely to have been his fault, she still felt let down. She'd had her own plans, after all, vague as they were. She had been willing to break her back for a fixed number of years – about seven, she had estimated – raising her two children and blanking out her mind and keeping the household together. But one thought kept her going: that the regime would end. She had been plucked so young from independent life that she had never even had a proper job. When Sean was born she couldn't imagine working or continuing medical school, and eighteen months later – just as she had been able to start focusing on what she might do – along came Nicole. Soon Ellen was able to add to her list of clichés the most dreaded thought of many modern women: she was turning into her mother. It caused Ellen some distress that she often found herself consciously fantasizing about the things she could already have done between the ages of nineteen and twenty-eight: this was an excruciating subject for reflection. The solution was to ask herself how she might turn the situation to her advantage. She would never – contraceptives willing – have to interrupt a career for children, a hiatus that these days was the norm. She would still be young when her children were grown; in fact Sean would be in college when some of Ellen's contemporaries would still desperately be trying for a first or second child. This thought gave her some comfort, but Ben's reversal had changed everything.

Ben's parents had lived in the same house since they were married thirty-six years ago. It was worth a fair amount of money now but they would go to their graves without selling.

Ben's father had still not retired, though he had recently hired two more associates. The town had grown substantially over the years, and Ben's father now worked out of a modern, glass office building with, as Ben's father put it, 'telephones and everything'. At sixty-four he was in excellent health and possessed an endearing love for his work.

'You're nervous, I can tell,' said Ellen, minutes away from their destination.

'Well. Let's think why that should be. I'm about to tell my lawyer father that his lawyer son has been *you-know-what*.'

'Yes, but it's a completely different sort of job. You earned more than your father the first day you walked out of Law School.'

'True enough,' said Ben, recalling his father's expression when he'd learned the news of Ben's starting salary: a look that said, 'The world is upside down.' 'But I still couldn't afford a proper house, could I? The world *is* upside down.' Judd Delaney had bought the house and Ben paid off the mortgage. In effect he was renting the house from his father-in-law. This was a source of irritation that contributed to Ben's eagerness to flee the country now that he had a chance.

'Here we are,' said Ben, guiding the car up the switch-back asphalt drive. His parents' house was concealed within a hilltop wood. Ben had been taken to this house one week after he was born. He had lived in this house for seventeen years. His memories were mainly of sneaking around in the woods and spying on his sisters doing the same. 'Everybody smile.'

Mr Pelton was the first to emerge. He squatted down and extended his arms to hug both of his grandchildren at once. He wore clean woodsman's clothing and boots – as men in his neighbourhood invariably did at weekends – as if the practice of law were merely an annoying weekly interruption of one's truer calling in forestry. Mr Pelton had always been a cheerful, even jovial sort of man to the outside world, but sometimes moody and unpredictable at home. His hair had thinned and whitened, but his substantial eyebrows were still rust-coloured and wiry. The corners of his blue eyes creased attractively as he winced and laughed under the burden of his grandchildren. He greeted Ben with a handshake and Ellen with a kiss on the cheek.

'You both look exhausted,' he said. 'Terrible. You're overdoing it, I can tell. Come inside and get some fuel.'

Mrs Pelton emerged from the kitchen looking, Ben thought, somewhat overwrought.

'You look overwrought, Mom,' Ben said, kissing her.

'So would you if . . . Oh, I won't go into it. Trivial household stuff. Come sit down and have a drink. I want to show these children their presents and get that over with.'

The children ran into the kitchen with their grandmother. Ellen almost followed them, but she didn't want to miss the men's conversation. If necessary she would initiate it herself. She found that she was angry.

Mr Pelton poured three glasses of beer and took them out to the glassed-in patio. Pleasantries took no more than five minutes. After a long enough pause, Ben said, 'Actually Dad, we have rather momentous news.'

Ben should have known how this remark would be interpreted. 'I'll get Mary,' said Mr Pelton, rising from his wicker chair. 'She'll be delighted.'

'Oh, no, sorry. Sit down. It's not that.'

Mr Pelton sat down again and said, 'Well, what a relief. I'm sure she would have been horrified.' He chuckled. 'Go ahead and tell me what it is, then.'

Ben cleared his throat and swallowed. The wicker chair creaked beneath his legs. Sitting across from him was the man who had raised him to be a lawyer and footed the monstrous bill; who had failed to control his emotions when Ben phoned in with the news that he had been admitted to Harvard Law

79

School; who had swooned with a combination of pride and disbelief when Ben had explained the terms of his first job. For a relatively provincial lawyer, Mr Pelton was a great student of the Law and had shaped Ben's outlook on its nobility and importance more than any Harvard professor had ever done. Mr Pelton's days may have been filled with divorce and easement and the drawing-up of wills, but his mind was in the clouds of the Constitution. He knew the literature and lore of the United States Supreme Court as thoroughly as an evangelical minister would know the New Testament. He prided himself on the precision and clarity a legal education had lent to his and Ben's thoughts and speech. He saw in the mechanics of the Law the greatest genius of his country's government. He enjoyed the local prestige attached to having built up a law firm on his own. He had lived such a perfect American life – so perfect he had been able to disdain most of its spoils. He had seen his daughters marry lawyers, and seen his son enter one of the loftiest modern realms of practice.

Ben cleared his throat and swallowed again. 'Maybe we could have another beer?' he asked. 'I'll get them.'

'Let me,' said Ellen. She got up and left, and returned with three cans of beer before Ben had managed to say a word.

Ben's father was supremely good at waiting people out. He had asked his question; he awaited his answer. Ben opened his can of beer and smiled meekly at Ellen as he refilled his glass. He shouldn't have brought up the subject. He thought he should take the same line as he had with Delaney, even though Mr Pelton would probably be just as furious. He imagined his father reddening, possibly standing up, shouting, ordering his son out of the house. Quitting the Law! It was unthinkable. Even worse, he visualized his father saying, 'This is not a problem. You will work with me. Pelton and Pelton. It's perfect, and not a moment too soon.'

'Why don't you tell him?' said Ellen, pleasantly.

Ben smiled at her again, as if to say, 'Thanks a lot.' He took a sip of beer and wished he'd never confessed to Ellen. He wished he'd just found another law job, anywhere, and done his best to make it look like a positive move.

'All right, here it is,' said Ben. 'The point is, Dad, we've been thinking about a big change for some time. The idea being to shake things up, you know? To make a move. Perhaps to leave the country for a couple of years, branch out.' Out of the corner of his eye, Ben could see Ellen glaring at him. 'It needn't be permanent,' Ben continued, delivering a version of events that was, if anything, softer than the one he had used with Ellen's father. 'For no particular reason the area of Third-World development comes to mind, if we're really going to make this break. I thought you might have some words of advice, or contacts, is all.'

Coward, thought Ellen. Initially she had thought it unfair to tell Ben's father the whole truth; now she was livid for the opposite reason. She wanted to see Ben's confession and his father's reaction. Ben deserved to face this. Before Mr Pelton could reply, Ellen broke in. 'That's not the story, Ben. Tell your father the truth.'

'Oh, my,' said Mr Pelton, sitting back in his chair and crossing his legs.

Ben's throat had gone dry. He gave Ellen a disbelieving look. He felt betrayed on all sides, forced into a corner by his own wife.

'All right, look,' Ben said, his voice low. 'Dad, I got fired. Wiesman fired me. I could have stuck around for a while but I just walked out. I haven't been back to the office since. I should have told you right away, but . . .'

Ben hoped his father would say something, but the man just sat there nodding, his rusty eyebrows raised.

'It was entirely a structural thing. Everyone's getting the axe. Just bad luck. I didn't do anything wrong.'

Ben's father took a sip of his beer.

'The idea is,' Ben continued, 'to go for a big change. It actually *is* true,' he added, glancing significantly at Ellen for an instant, 'that we have been thinking about this for a long time anyway. I want to get out of the rut, now that I have this unexpected chance. Does this make any sense?'

Ben was almost curled up in his chair, now, waiting for the onslaught. When Ben's father lost his temper it was wise to be elsewhere. But still Mr Pelton sat there, nodding his head, as if waiting for some critical mass of anger to be achieved within him.

'Look, Dad, I know what you're thinking. And if you think a little more you'll say "What about the children?" The children will be fine. We're sure of it. Our plans are vague at the moment. There's no rush . . .'

Mr Pelton stood up. He turned his back on Ben and Ellen and moved to the glass wall of the conservatory to look out at the old trees in the back garden. He folded his arms and sighed. The children could be heard laughing delightedly in the kitchen with their grandmother. Outside it was a cool, sunny day and the perfume of spring blossoms permeated the room. Ben's father held his contemplative pose for two minutes or more. Ben and Ellen exchanged a look that combined anxiety with mutual antagonism.

When Ben's father turned around he was working his mouth as if to dislodge a piece of food from between back molars.

'Stand up, Ben,' he said.

Ben reluctantly stood.

'Ben, Ben, Ben,' said Mr Pelton, approaching.

Ben tried not to flinch as his father extended an arm. He put his arm around Ben's shoulder and squeezed. Then he smiled and, with a laugh of such warmth and solidarity it made Ben swoon, he said, 'Ben my boy, this is the *best* news I have *ever* heard in my *life*.'

17

Paul Mancini, seated behind his desk, smoked a cigarette. Ben couldn't remember having seen him smoke the previous day. Mancini did not appear to be in a good mood. It was mid-afternoon, and although all six windows of the ballroom were open, the office was as hot and dry as a sauna. The noise of traffic outside reflected off the walls and the parquet, and that – combined with the heat and the cigarette smoke and Mancini's evident ill-humour – made the office quite an unpleasant place to be.

'The job's yours,' said Mancini, so bluntly Ben blinked as he registered the news.

'I'm so glad,' Ben said.

'You must know why,' said Mancini, nervously tapping his cigarette on the edge of a glass ashtray.

'I'm tempted to say it is because I am so superbly qualified, Mr Mancini,' Ben said, smiling sincerely for the first time in months.

'Call me Paul. You're perfectly well qualified, Ben. But I'm asking if you know why this . . . *procedure* has been cut short.'

'Yes, I think I do,' said Ben, who hoped he would never have to lie again in his life. 'It's because you overheard what Ross said about your boy. I can assure you that I was in no –'

'Prick,' said Mancini. 'That *prick*.'

'Well, he –'

'That sorry little prick. I hated him the moment I saw him. I had to say "I don't think you're going to fit in here," all that crap.'

'I didn't think much of him either,' said Ben, smiling, trying to be good-humoured.

Mancini took a long drag on his cigarette and leaned back in his big leather chair as he exhaled a cone of smoke. 'I want to ask you something, Ben. I want to know the truth. You have children, right?'

'Yes. A boy and a girl.'

'Now you don't think – rather, *do* you think, just between you and me – and nothing whatsoever rides on this, I just want your candid opinion – do you think there might be any . . . *validity* to what Ross said?'

Ben considered this question momentarily, and found that now the pressure was off his answer came easily. 'Of course not. As you say, there's nothing riding on this so let me just tell you. I was inspired by your boy. I really was. He's the best-mannered little kid I've ever met, I'm not just saying that. I want my son to be just like him. Ross is an idiot.'

'He's a prick,' said Mancini, leaning forward again to stub out his cigarette in the ashtray.

'That too,' said Ben. 'I'm not excusing what he said, but he doesn't know a thing about children and he may have been thrown by how grown-up Little Paul is for an eight-year-old.'

'Do you think?'

'Yes.'

'You don't think Ross . . . *saw* something? I mean, Jesus.'

'Oh, come on.'

'It just suddenly made me worried.'

'Don't.'

'Maybe you *can* tell,' said Mancini. 'You hear stories. "I knew I was queer from the age of five," that sort of thing. I mean, it's not as if he dresses in his sister's clothing, or anything.'

'Of course not. I'm certain you have nothing to worry about.'

'Let's hope so. Candy was so upset she couldn't sleep last night. She's the one who made me send the message right away.

She said she couldn't face that . . . that *prick* for one more second.'

'I don't blame her.'

Mancini pushed back his chair and stood up. 'Anyway, look. I shouldn't have bothered you with this unpleasantness. Welcome aboard, Ben, we're delighted to have you.' Mancini, from his great height, extended a hand.

'I can't tell you how pleased I am,' said Ben.

'Chauffeur's downstairs if you need him to get back to your hotel.'

'No, thanks anyway. I thought I'd walk.'

'Ignore the beggars,' said Mancini. 'One coin each and you'll be broke by the time you're downtown.'

'I'll keep that in mind. Thanks, Paul,' said Ben, as he turned to leave. 'I'm very enthusiastic about everything. I can't wait.'

Ben left Mancini's office and walked down the corridor to the broad spiral staircase. He took off his suit jacket and slung it over his shoulder as he slowly descended, bouncing on the balls of his feet. He loosened his tie. He waved to Celia, the receptionist, as she crossed the marble foyer. 'See you in about six weeks,' he said, so cheerfully he might have been announcing the birth of his child. He pushed a button to unlock the massive cedar doors, and left the building for the heat and chaos of the boulevard outside.

His walk was downhill all the way. He bought a large, soft pretzel from a man who cooked them on a street corner along with corn on the cob and some sort of purplish nut. He passed building site after building site. Men sifted and sieved, sifted and sieved. Buses rumbled by, so packed with travellers that people – even small children – rode on the roofs or on the luggage racks. Old men played board games at tables on the pavement outside tea shops. Ben noticed a number of shop windows displaying nothing but flick knives and cigarette lighters.

85

A cooling breeze swept up the boulevard. Ben paused at a school yard to watch young boys playing soccer on an asphalt court. When he turned away from this spectacle he noticed two soldiers walking uphill towards him. Unarmed, off duty, they walked slowly in the sunshine with their caps hooked in their belts. They were about the toughest-looking young men Ben could recall seeing – full moustaches, hair close-cropped, paratrooper boots, heavy olive-green uniforms, cigarettes loosely dangling from their lips. A moment later Ben noticed they were holding hands. Trying not to stare, Ben passed them, then turned around. They were not exactly holding hands. Their little fingers were interlocked.

Ben continued down the boulevard, breathing in, breathing out, his heart pumping strongly in his chest. He had done it. This was his city now. He was elated, just as he had been when he first arrived and had his first glimpse and scent of this country. He couldn't wait to see his house, his pool, his chauffeur, his *houseboy*. He had never felt so optimistic in his life, nor more in control. Ben had done this all by himself. He had deviated from the beaten track. He had taken the reins of his family's future in his own two hands. He had taken a mighty blow on the chin and hauled himself back to his feet to exact his revenge. In Ben's mind, Victor Wiesman was a small, petty man, his features now dissolving in memory to a grey past he couldn't be happier to leave behind. Ellen needn't know that he had been saved by a ludicrous accident. Judd Delaney would slaver over photographs of the children swimming in the pool, clambering over amphitheatres, exploring the Baram Caves – whatever the hell they were. Alan Yates would pause over his interminable briefs and wonder, wonder, if life could have been different. Ben's father, whose categorical support for departure was the most pleasant surprise of Ben's life, would visit at the earliest opportunity to bask in his son's interesting new world. The children would be fine.

18

Ben and Ellen Pelton held hands as the aircraft began its final descent. Sean and Nicole had only recently fallen asleep again, for the second time during the journey. It was past four o'clock in the morning local time – the connecting flight in London had been delayed by several hours. The couple travelled with four large suitcases neatly packed with clothes and necessities. The rest of their possessions would follow within three weeks. Ben carried a piece of paper with his new address written on it – a house they had rented sight-unseen, thanks to Candy Mancini. If Ben understood correctly, it was the house still under construction on the barren hillside above the Mancinis' house.

Ben leaned over the children so he could look out of the window and try to make out landmarks below. There was nothing at all to see – not a light, not a car – until suddenly the wheels touched down and the airport's runway lights illuminated the cabin. He squeezed Ellen's hand as the engines howled in reverse and the jet slowed to a crawl. We're here, Ben thought. I have done this. I have made this happen. He looked down at his children, who slept identically curled up with a red blanket tucked under their chins. I've brought my family here, Ben thought, to this alien place. We will never be the same. He turned to Ellen and they exchanged an excited, nervous look.

When the aircraft came to a stop, Ben picked up Nicole and passed her to Ellen. He lifted Sean on to his shoulder and carried him to the front of the plane. When Ben stepped out into the cool night air and the bright airport lights, Sean lifted his head and dozily looked around.

'Are we home?' he asked.

'Yes, indeed,' said Ben.

The boy looked up. 'Look at all the stars.'

'It's a beautiful sight.'

The plane had been almost empty, so it took only minutes to collect their luggage and pass through customs. In the arrivals hall a weary young man introduced himself as their driver. He wore a shiny black suit and a skinny black tie, just like Chauffeur, and said his name was Sammy. He apologized for his poor English. Ben apologized for being so late.

'Hotel?' Sammy asked.

Ben thought for a moment, and looked at his watch. 'If it's all right,' he said, 'we'll go to our house first.' He took the address out of his pocket and handed it to Sammy, who nodded in comprehension. 'I believe it's on the way,' said Ben.

Ellen and the children slept on the back seat of the car. Ben sat silently in the front next to Sammy. The journey to the northern hills on the outskirts of the city took only forty minutes at this time of morning. The stars gradually disappeared as the eastern horizon paled to rosy blue. Ben recognized the Soviet Embassy compound from some distance away, then Mancini's house. The road curved around the desiccated hill and narrowed to a dirt track. Up and up they climbed, until Sammy stopped the car outside a half-completed wall and said he would wait. Ellen awoke looking disorientated.

'Come on,' said Ben. 'We can leave the children here. Is that OK, Sammy?'

The driver nodded.

Ben helped Ellen out of the car and over a low section of the unfinished stone wall. He smelled wet concrete and fresh paint.

'Where are we?' asked Ellen, still waking up.

'Far, far away,' said Ben, who was exhilarated. Holding Ellen's hand, he led the way up a concrete staircase and there, low and white against the brightening sky, was their new house.

'What is this? Why are we here?'

'Come along,' said Ben, leading Ellen around the house to a terrace and an empty swimming pool. 'You're going to like this,' he said, pulling her by the hand. They walked around the pool to an iron railing where the hillside fell steeply away. Below them, to the left, was Mancini's house and garden. Beyond was the vast Soviet Embassy compound, dark and mysterious. And beyond that, still in the shadows as the sun's rays first illuminated the surrounding hills, was the city centre.

'This is where we live,' said Ben. 'This is our house.'

Ellen turned around and looked at the house, then back to the panorama at her feet. At that moment the sun edged over the horizon and coloured the hillside. Ellen didn't know what she had expected, but it was nothing like this. The waking city looked magnificent to her – pricked with slender minarets, the old town tumbling down the sides of an almost perfectly dome-shaped hill, broad modern boulevards dotted with early traffic.

'Can you believe it?'

'I can't. It's beautiful. We really live right here? This is our house?'

'In three weeks it will be.'

'Wonderful.'

Ben put his arm around his wife's shoulders and they watched the sun complete its rise. The past few months of anxiety and doubt melted away as the heat struck their faces and gleamed on the fresh-white walls of the house.

'We should go,' said Ben. 'I feel sorry for the driver. He's been up all night.'

'Just another minute,' said Ellen. She looked around and said, 'We'll have to be vigilant around here, with the kids. The pool makes me nervous. And this hill, it's like a cliff. Look, rusty nails everywhere. We're really going to have to be careful.'

'Don't worry. They'll be fine.'

'And hiring people.'

'Candy Mancini will help. She's an old hand at these things. Her advice is "fire them, fire them, fire them" until you find the perfect one.'

'I feel more like a wife than ever,' said Ellen.

'A beautiful wife.'

'Can you see me striding around ordering servants to do things? It's ridiculous.'

'Don't stride around. Lounge in a deck-chair with a drink in your hand and order them to do things from there. It's important to get off on the right foot with staff – let them know who's boss. You mustn't get too friendly with them.'

'Now what the hell do you know about servants, Ben?'

'Nothing. Thank God I can leave all of that to you. They will fear and respect you.'

'Unlikely.'

'It's going to be a lot of work, you know. Seriously. You'll have to bear the brunt of all these adjustments. I'll be working like a slave.'

'Oh yes,' said Ellen. 'I've been meaning to ask you. Could you just tell me, please, what services you are going to provide to Mr Mancini and the rest of them? What precisely you will *do*, starting on Monday morning?'

Ben sniffed the warming air. Calls to prayer, quaveringly sung, wailed from the city's minarets, causing crows to rise from the trees in the Soviet Embassy compound. The smog was so heavy it seemed to fizz in reaction with the sunlight.

'I don't have the *faintest* idea,' said Ben, kissing Ellen's hair above her ear. 'Isn't that marvellous?'

19

'Mind if I pop in and say hello?'

Ben looked up from his empty desk. He had been in the office for fifteen minutes, wondering what to do. An egg-shaped head wearing thick spectacles had poked around Ben's open office door.

'Come in,' said Ben, standing up.

The figure who entered was wire-slim and wore a brown corduroy suit with unnecessary buttons and pockets and even, Ben noticed, epaulettes. Shod in desert boots, he looked like a Victorian Egyptologist. He was about Ben's age, perhaps a little older. He was sickly pale but his balding head had been sunburned.

'I'm Dominic Thrune,' said the man, giggling at his own name.

'Ben Pelton.'

'*Marvellous*,' said Dominic, as the men shook hands over Ben's broad wooden desk. 'Welcome, welcome, welcome.'

'Thank you.'

'Do you mind if I shut the door?'

'Go ahead.'

Dominic Thrune shut the door and returned to sit down opposite Ben. 'Do you mind if I smoke?'

'Not at all.'

'There's an ashtray in your left-hand drawer, I think you'll find. This used to be my office.'

'Did it?' Ben located the ashtray and set it on the far side of his desk.

'Yes, in the glory years before they started hiring so many people. I like to smoke these local things. Care for one?'

'No, thank you.'

'Settling in all right, are you?' Dominic's English accent was musical and exaggerated. When he asked a question he raised his eyebrows high on his forehead and opened his eyes wide, as if he were trying to take alarming news on board.

'I've only been here a few minutes.'

'I meant the *family*,' said Dominic, pronouncing the word gravely. 'The wife and kids?' Up went his eyebrows.

'We're staying at a hotel for a few weeks while the house is finished.'

'Oh, which *one*?' asked Dominic, the eyebrows going sternly down this time.

'The Chevalier.'

'*Marvellous*. Are they all right with the kiddies?'

'They seem to be.'

'I'm not a *family* man, myself,' said Dominic. This news was not surprising to Ben. 'No, it's just me in my little hut in the hills. I've been here nine years – ten years in March, it'll be. I was hired *in situ* when they set up shop.'

'What did you do before?'

'I was an itinerant teacher. That's not to say I taught only itinerants.' Dominic giggled again at what must have been the hundredth time he had attempted this joke. 'I was always nomadic. After university I went to India – I was born in India, you know – and I simply *walked* here. Took years. It was a circuitous route, you might say. Or it must have been because I was in China for months.'

'You actually walked?'

'Well, no, that would be going too far.' Dominic giggled again. 'I took the occasional bus or truck. I always wanted to write a *book* about my experiences.'

'You must have had a lot of adventures.'

'Yes, of course. I will bore you at length about them, given time and a glass or two of *karat*.'

'I don't know what that is.'

'You soon will. It's the local firewater. It tastes like paraffin mixed with liquorice and if you drink more than about four fluid ounces you start to have hallucinations of purgatory.'

'I'm not a big drinker.'

'We'll fix that. Have you met Diane?'

'Who's Diane?'

'Diane, dear boy, is your secretary. The girls don't usually come in until nine-thirty.' Ben had never had his own secretary before. At the law firm the girls worked in a pool. 'My poor darling Colleen fell pregnant and had to go home to Belfast. Her replacement,' said Dominic, whispering now, 'is a local girl. Not very bright. Not that the two things are related, of course. You'll love Diane. Frightfully organized.'

'What is it you do?' asked Ben.

'My *very* grand title is "Director of Communications". Anything that needs publishing, that's me. And I have a crack at The Great Mancini's speeches every now and again. He's a rather important figure, right now. It's people like Mancini who have their finger in the dike against the Communist Scourge. Interesting man, Mancini. Know him well?'

'Not at all. I met him when I came over to be interviewed.'

'Have you a very grand title yet?'

'I'm told it's "Associate Director".'

'Good *lord*, Ben, you're my *boss*. Quick, tell me to do something.' Dominic giggled.

'I'm going to be doing a lot of "liaising", to use the jargon.'

'Good man.'

Someone knocked on the door. It was a feminine knock.

'Come in,' said Ben.

'Ah, Diane, here you are,' said Dominic. 'Let me introduce you.'

Diane was a petite woman of about forty-five. Her elaborate blonde coiffure had preceded her into the room. She wore oversized, pink-rimmed glasses. She failed to conceal her disapproval of Dominic Thrune as introductions were made.

'Diane used to work for Jenkins,' Dominic said.

'I've met him,' said Ben.

'Jenkins is no longer with the firm,' said Dominic. He worked his eyebrows significantly and mimed the act of drinking. 'Home to the Shires and a retirement full of drizzle. Strangely enough he took the news rather badly, didn't he, Diane?'

'I wouldn't want to say,' said Diane loyally.

'Oh, such a lot of anguished gnashing of teeth. My word. I don't think he took too kindly to accusations of *loose lips*, if you follow me. He was friendly with a Bulgarian. Played chess with the man and after a few vodkas he –'

'Really, Dominic,' said Diane. 'I don't think Mr Pelton –'

'Call me Ben.'

'– is interested in any of this.'

'I'm just saying that with the mood the world's in it doesn't do to drink vodka with Bulgarians.'

'Hush now,' said Diane, who had an authoritative Texan accent.

'I'll be off then,' said Dominic. 'Do come and visit me in my little cell downstairs. I think of it as the engine room.'

'I'll do that,' said Ben.

Dominic blew a kiss at Diane and walked knock-kneed to the door. When he had left, Diane shut the door behind him, then came back to Ben's desk and sat down.

'He's not so bad as he seems,' she said. 'He speaks the language like a native. He writes well. He's a frustrated novelist, I think.'

'I thought he was very entertaining,' said Ben.

'Anyway I just wanted to say welcome.'

'Thanks.'

'Anything you need settling-in-wise, just ask. I know my way around.'

'That's very kind of you. Everything has happened so fast. My son is starting school today, already.'

'Where are you sending him?'

'The French School. It's just down the street from where we'll be living.'

'You're very brave.'

'How so?'

'Oh, sorry. I didn't mean to worry you. It's just that they're supposed to be very strict up there.'

'Mr Mancini's children go to the French School,' said Ben.

'Well, that's really more to do with . . .' Diane stopped herself.

'More to do with what?'

Diane looked flustered. 'I only meant that perhaps Mr Mancini wants to mix widely, you see. Not just with other Americans. The children from the French School are from all over. Also a lot of locals with French wives.'

'I understand.'

'Remember, anything I can do. Anything at all. Your first meeting is at eleven o'clock in Mr Mancini's office. He'll want you to tag along for a few days until you know who everyone is. It's always go-go-go with Mr Mancini.'

'I look forward to it.'

'And don't worry about Dominic's nonsense about poor Mr Jenkins. It's not really like that around here. We're really very relaxed.'

'Glad to hear it, Diane.'

'Would you like me to get you some tea? I can send out to the street. A boy brings it up.'

'That would be wonderful.'

Diane waved cheerfully with her fingers and left Ben's office, closing the door behind her. Ben looked down at his empty desk. The noise of traffic on the boulevard was a dull roar in the background. He felt as if he were in hiding, in exile. No one could see him here. Even his father, who had indirectly got him this job with one telephone call, wouldn't understand how Ben felt. None of his friends, his relatives, his former colleagues had any idea what he would be doing from day to day. They would not be able to visualize his office, his house, his city. Ben had dropped out. He was an invisible man. From the day he was fired until the day Mancini had said 'The job's yours,' Ben had slept fitfully, eaten poorly, drunk more than usual, been short of breath. Now he felt safe. No one could see him here.

Diane's knock came on the door again. She opened the door and ushered in a small boy, no older than Sean, who carried a small brass tea-tray by its chain. The boy confidently approached, plucked a fluted glass of tea from the tray and placed it on Ben's desk. The boy smiled up at Ben – he was missing his two front teeth. Ben looked up at Diane and shrugged his shoulders, meaning to ask if he ought to pay.

'It's taken care of,' said Diane. She said something in the local language to the boy, who bowed to Ben and turned on his heel to leave.

When the door closed again, Ben sipped the hot, sweet tea. He had an hour to go before the meeting in Mancini's office. He reclined in his leather armchair and put his feet up on his empty desk, glass of tea close to hand. No one could see him here.

20

'Do you remember the most important thing I told you about your new school?' Ellen asked her son, holding his hand and Nicole's as they walked downhill from the building site that would soon be their house. She had asked Sammy to drop them off there so she could time the walk to school. The street was dusty from construction work on several new houses. There were workmen all over the neighbourhood, who seemed to do nothing but sift gravel through sieves.

'What?'

'Well, I told you what the name of the school is, didn't I?'

'Yes,' Sean said. 'It's called the French School.'

'Correct,' said Ellen. 'And what is going to be particularly different about the French School?'

'The classes are taught in French,' said Sean.

'Yes,' said Ellen, holding Sean's hand much too tightly and almost dragging him and Nicole along the dusty pavement. 'The French language.'

'That's all right,' Sean said.

'I hope so,' said Ellen. It was a warm day and she wore only a light cardigan over her print dress. She also wore large dark glasses. The tendons stood out on her wrist as she squeezed her children's hands. She was an anxious woman.

The French School First Grade occupied a yellow house set back and down from the street in a leafy gulch. Other children were being led into the school wearing a uniform of navy-blue shorts or skirts, navy-blue jackets, white socks and blue shoes; shirts were white and ties were red, so that the pupils bore the colours of the French flag. Ellen was so nervous she half hoped Sean would rebel at the thought of being taught in French, and demand to go home.

'All right, let's practise one last time,' she said, hanging back from the other children and their parents. 'What will you say to your teacher?'

'I'll say, "*Bonjour, Madame Soubrier*."'

'Perfect. It's going to be a breeze.'

'You're hurting my hand,' said Sean, who looked perfectly relaxed. Candy Mancini had arranged for his uniform to be delivered to the hotel.

'Sorry, angel. Look, Nicky and I are going to come in with you just to see your classroom and meet Madame Soubrier, all right?'

'Sure.'

'Here we go,' said Ellen, who had a knot in her stomach as if she were approaching a final exam. 'You'll see, everything will be fine.'

Ellen followed the other parents and children down a brick staircase to the front door of the house. Just inside, Madame Soubrier greeted each pupil in turn as they were handed over by chic mothers or local nannies.

'Now,' whispered Ellen, still gripping Sean's hand so hard she could have held him off the ground.

'*Bonjour, Madame Soubrier*,' said Sean.

Madame Soubrier, not much older than Ellen, was a thin-lipped but pretty woman who wore her long brown hair tied back so tightly it seemed to stretch the skin over her cheekbones. She smiled and shook hands with Sean and spoke several sentences so rapidly even Ellen couldn't understand her.

'Do you speak English?' Ellen asked her.

'*Non*,' said Madame Soubrier, guiding Sean into the house.

In broken, embarrassed French – and using some sign language – Ellen asked if she and Nicole could come in for a minute.

'*Une minute,*' said Madame Soubrier. '*Pas plus.*'

Upstairs, in a cool, airy room overlooking a small playground surrounded by tall trees, was Sean's classroom. Twenty wooden desks were neatly arranged in pairs. The desks had inkwells in the corners and grooves to hold pens and pencils. Madame Soubrier stood behind a large table at the front of the room. Sean was assigned a desk in the middle of the classroom. Ellen and Nicole stood at the back corner, so that Sean's profile was just visible as he sat with his hands on his desk, next to a little blonde girl. Madame Soubrier picked up a clutch of coloured chalks and addressed the blackboard. In seconds she had drawn an empty bird's nest, and written '*Le nid*' beneath it in clear, sharp handwriting. She turned around and pointed at her drawing.

'*Le nid,*' said the class, except for Sean.

'*Sean?*' asked Madame Soubrier. '*Le nid.*'

Sean's little voice piped up. '*Le nid,*' he said.

'*Bravo, mon garçon,*' said Madame Soubrier.

Ellen swallowed and felt her face flush. She pulled Nicole along with her as she made for the door.

21

After a two-hour meeting devoted to scheduling a banquet for the American Ambassador and a road-opening with the General, Paul Mancini took Ben out for lunch. Ben had to walk at a trot to keep up with Mancini's long, impatient strides.

'We can sit out in the garden, it's still warm enough,' Mancini said. 'That way we can talk more openly than is advisable at the office.'

'Do you mean –?'

'Yes.'

The restaurant was located in a pretty square next to an open market. Mancini led the way straight to the kitchen, where patrons chose their meals directly from a glassed-in counter. Ben let Mancini order for him.

'How's the stomach?' Mancini asked.

'No problems.'

'There will be. You'll become immune after a while. I drink the tap water now with no ill effects.'

The two men sat at a table in a sunny courtyard. Mancini had ordered local red wine 'to keep up appearances'.

Ben and Mancini were the only foreigners in the restaurant. Well-fed businessmen wearing Western suits cheerfully harangued one another over tables piled with plates and cutlery.

'It may seem paranoid,' said Mancini, 'but I try never to go into any details in the office. It's like this all over the world, you know. That's just a little something I wanted to say: assume they're listening. Even now, really, but we can't clam up all the time. Still, you'll be surprised how often something you've said privately comes back to you from a different quarter. I've said things at my own dinner table that got into the newspapers. Happens all the time.'

'You'll have to tell me what's secret and what's not, then,' said Ben.

'Everything's secret,' said Mancini, smiling.

'That's easy. I'll never open my mouth.'

'It's not all that bad. But just to give you an example. The road we were discussing this morning?'

'The one the General's opening?'

'Correct. Well, it's a sort of ring road – you drove on a short stretch of it coming in from the airport. What you didn't drive on was a straight section of four-lane highway that appears to lead to nowhere. It's over twenty miles long.'

'And we're funding it?'

'In part.'

'Where does it lead?'

'It leads to a model city and a technical university. Among other things.'

'I see,' said Ben. 'Am I allowed to ask?'

'Sure. There is a military component to just about everything we do. It is part of the service we provide. It's only natural. This won't be a surprise to you.'

'No.'

'There's no need to get into the details, but you will have to know broadly what's what. Parts of that highway will be used as an airstrip in an emergency. The university is attached to weapons research of various kinds – the General is keen to be hands-on in that area, keep things under his own control. His technical boys are very good and we set them up with what they need.'

Mancini paused as two waiters arrived with platters of food: cold cucumber-and-yoghurt soup; baby artichoke hearts with their long stems still attached, drenched in olive oil; cigarette-shaped *mille-feuilles* filled with melted cheese; sliced tomatoes.

'Dig in,' Mancini said, when the waiters went away. 'The point I'm making is that in this business there are areas of . . . *politics* involved and sometimes it's best not to try to second-guess the General or anyone else. The man is his own master, but he knows where his dollars come from.'

'Do you know him personally?'

'I wouldn't say that. I mean, you don't have heart-to-hearts with the General, but our relationship is getting stronger all the time. We have met privately half a dozen times.'

'How long does he intend to stay in power this time – any idea?'

'Anyone's guess is as good as mine. I suppose ideally they'd bring back the parliament, have an election, show that side of the process, but keep the reins in the General's hands. In the background, of course. If there isn't a war I don't see why that shouldn't happen next year or even sooner.'

Ben didn't take the threat of war too seriously – he'd read up on the problem and it seemed to him to amount to nothing more than eternal posturing over three or four minor territorial disputes and two major ones. Even if war did break out, it would happen at a distance and would almost certainly be decided quickly in the General's favour. There were Cold War implications to the ongoing dispute, but it was hard to imagine the Soviet Union coming down too strongly against the General even in the worst case. They had their hands full elsewhere.

'I'm looking forward to meeting your wife,' said Mancini, as main courses arrived: braised lamb, cut up in kebab-like chunks, with pilaf and pine nuts; spicy meat balls with stuffed peppers on the side; chicken in pureed walnut sauce. 'I understand she's interested in ballet?' he asked, politely.

'Yes she is. Or was,' said Ben. He swallowed a piece of lamb and washed it down with red wine. Ellen's interest in ballet was not something he had mentioned in his CV, not something he had mentioned to Candy Mancini, not something Ellen had spoken of in years. Ben knew he had been vetted, but not so deeply. Before his first trip to meet Mancini – and to compete with Ross Howard – he had been flown to Washington head-quarters for what was candidly called a 'background check'. Ben hadn't known what to expect, but tried to be cheerful as he underwent three separate polygraph examinations, two blood tests and an interview on a park bench with a man who introduced himself as 'Hank Campion, FBI'. At the time it had occurred to Ben that these procedures were harder on someone who had nothing to hide – as if a concession of malfeasance here, of disloyalty there, might be thrown like sops to the inquisition and convince them of the subject's inherent decency. To reply in the negative to every single query pertaining to drug or alcohol abuse, homosexuality, adultery, membership of subversive organizations, atheism, admiration for social reformers, theft grand or petty, veniality, dark moods, Satanism – this painted Ben as almost inhuman. Hank Campion, FBI, had chatted pleasantly about such matters as where Ben bought his suits, if he cut his hair in the city or closer to home, if he liked playing catch with his son – as if Ben might inexplicably blurt out that he had once helped pick spinach with illegal immigrants, that he smoked Cuban cigars, that his father read European novels, that *Das Kapital* had made a huge and positive impression on him at an early age (all of which were true). Hank took Ben to lunch, and when Ben ordered mineral water Hank said, 'Do you have a problem with drinking?' Ben searched his mind for a misdemeanour to which he might confess, and could only think of the girl at the top of the stairs. The polygraph examiners had asked, 'Are you faithful to your wife?' and when Ben answered 'Yes' he felt it was as truthful an answer as he could give – and he felt his heart lurch beneath the straps. Perhaps that is what swayed them to believe Ben was honest: that he had lied only about faithfulness to his wife

– the guilty memory of a blonde girl cheerfully servicing Ben as if she were opening a valve in an overheated boiler.

Ben continued to converse automatically with Mancini. A breeze had come up that toyed with the leaves overhead and sprinkled the courtyard with light. Ben consciously wondered if Mancini or some Washington functionary knew something about Ellen that he didn't – an affair, a fling, an hour's play on a suburban afternoon, even an inchoate yearning she had never revealed. Two or three times Mancini seemed deliberately to let slip a nugget of information that suggested he knew things so close to Ben's private core that with one word or phrase he could bring the whole structure down.

'We'll have a *karat*,' Mancini said. Soon a waiter arrived with a jug of cold water, two glasses full of ice and a blue bottle. 'It's better when the weather is really hot, but what the hell.'

'Dominic Thrune told me about *karat*,' Ben said. 'Warned me, rather.'

The liquid Mancini poured was white and sticky – Ben was somewhat repulsed until the water was added and the mixture turned almost clear.

'A local would spend half a day drinking just two glasses,' said Mancini. 'Here's to you.'

'Cheers.'

Ben followed Mancini's lead and took a great gulp of the drink, which tasted vile at first but had a pleasant numbing effect on the lips and tongue.

'There's a story about this stuff,' said Mancini, contemplating his glass. 'All about a boy who fell into a vat of *karat*, and became invincible. The problem was that he . . . I can never remember stories. Something about how he led his people to victory after victory against their oppressors, he knew no fear, but when the crunch came he was asked a riddle by someone – it was a crucial moment and he confidently answered the riddle but was a million miles off and his own people cut off his head for being so stupid. There's a moral there I think.'

As Mancini poured them each a second drink, Ben became aware that his constitution was being put to the test. There was no other point in getting drunk in the afternoon. The *karat* had a powerful effect – it speeded the heart and relaxed the nervous system and generally made Ben want to conquer foreign lands and rape every woman he could lay hands on. All of this he managed to keep under wraps, as little sweating bowls of lime sorbet arrived and a third glass of *karat* was poured. Ben watched carefully to make sure Mancini was really drinking his share; he seemed to be.

Mancini's icy, astronaut's gaze was not affected by the *karat*; his speech was, but only slightly, and this was noticeable in content rather than in tone. He reminisced about the days as a very young man when he had considered the priesthood – a path in life his pacifist brother had taken back home in Chicago. He spoke of what a good sport Candy had been over the years, and how she thrived overseas. He smoked another cigarette and said he had quit smoking for three years after Caroline was born, but couldn't resist any longer. He asked if Ben agreed that daughters were different, that one became more emotional about daughters. Ben pretended to agree, when almost all of his emotion had already been expended on Sean, when the boy was ill.

As someone with practically nothing to hide, Ben felt secure as the drink wormed its way into his brain. His speech sounded clear to his own ears as he replied to Mancini's questions. It occurred to him that he loved this restaurant, this food, this life. He resisted one of the devious effects of the *karat*, which was that of truth serum. He did not ask Mancini – as he now had the strongest compulsion to do – to raise his shirt and show him his battle scars.

Mancini smoked another cigarette. The restaurant's courtyard gradually emptied. Mancini relaxed his normally military posture and began to philosophize. Ben concentrated on keeping a strictly businesslike demeanour, even as Mancini set off on a rhapsody concerning his daughter. 'Caroline,' he said. 'I don't know why we called that sweet little girl Caroline. You've seen her. You've seen her. She just *is* Caroline.'

'Indeed.'

'I want her to love me as much as I love her.'

'I'm sure she will.'

'What's your girl's name again?'

'Nicole.'

'Nicole. She had her jaw busted up?'

'My son is Sean.'

'Sean and Nicole. Sean had a problem too, am I right? He had a problem?'

Ben nodded and drank.

22

Ben had just come back to the office from court. It had been a wasted morning because Judge Ladatt had flu and called a recess until the following week. It was a stinking loser of a case anyway – the sort of case Ben seemed to get more and more often in those days, a client who thought he knew better than his attorneys and was on a self-destructive ride towards extraordinary damages. In chambers a very ill Judge Ladatt had snuffled about how the case was a 'ludicrous farrago' and joked that he was going to kill himself and make it look like an accident so his children could afford Law School.

There was a message on Ben's desk to ring Ellen urgently. With blank mind, Ben dialled his home number. Karin the Swedish au pair answered, coughing and sneezing at the same time. Ben held the receiver away from his face, as if he might be infected through it, then put it to his ear again and asked what the matter was.

Karin sniffled and said Sean was unwell, he was at the hospital with Ellen.

'An accident?'

'No.'

'He fell down or something?'

'No.'

Ben heard himself breathe through the receiver. 'Tell me what, then, Karin.'

'He had a pain. He had blood.'

'Blood? Where was he bleeding? His nose?'

'No. Blood in his urine.'

'Blood in his urine,' Ben repeated. 'How much blood? What kind of . . . *proportion* of blood to urine?'

'I didn't see. Ellen saw.'

Sean was then three years old. Ben looked down at his desk. There were four hours of work lying there that had to be gone through today, no later, despite Judge Ladatt's flu.

'Would you please call Ellen at the hospital and have her call me at work? I can't come home now. I'm sure she's in control.'

'She's upset. White as a sheet.'

'Are you with Nicole?'

'Yes.'

'Good. Just tell Ellen to call me, Karin.'

Ben hung up the phone and addressed his work. His was not the sort of job where mere attendance counted for anything: progress had to be made. He started on a list of matters he could delegate, writing points on a memo and dabbing subordinates' initials in the margin next to each one, his mind pulsing with the words 'renal failure'. One of Ben's priorities was to pull this case out of the fire so that next time Wiesman assigned him to something it would be a clear winner – some dicey lawsuit where the judge or jury could be driven mad with expert boredom regardless of the preponderance of evidence. Ben *had* to clear his desk. 'Renal failure,' he thought. Last night Sean had seemed fine – he had assembled three plastic tubes from the frame of his toy house and rushed about pointing them and saying 'Be careful, everybody – it's a hydraulic gun.' His health problems to date had been: six weeks premature; anal stenosis; a suspected irregular heartbeat (since resolved and blamed on chocolate); the aspiration of a pebble (solved on the spot by Ellen, who had required sedation after the experience); legion colds and bronchial attacks; the loss of a toenail when Ben had dropped the kettle on his foot . . .

Ben's phone rang. Ellen sounded calm. 'You've got to get over here.'

'All right,' said Ben. 'Right away?'

'Of *course*, right away.'

'Tell me what it is.'

'They don't know. I think kidneys.'

'You're not a doctor.' Ben always had to make an effort not to bring his courtroom voice home. 'But of course –'

'Just get here.'

'I'll be there as soon as I can.' Ben wanted to ask what possible help he could be, and to add that he had a ludicrous farrago of a case on his hands, that a few hours wouldn't make any difference. Then he caught himself thinking this way, loathed himself momentarily, and said, 'I'll be right there.'

Ben attacked his work in a most irresponsible way, aiming at compromise. He left the office ninety minutes later, making an effort not to be seen doing so. If he were caught by Wiesman or another partner he could announce that his son probably needed a kidney transplant; he could tell Ellen he had missed the early train and been stalled in the car park at the station.

Ben arrived at the hospital in a clinical frame of mind. It reminded him of the day Sean was born, when Ben had felt so coldly detached he might have been watching an educational film for the tenth time, its happy outcome certain. He did not take off his overcoat, did not put down his briefcase, did not loosen his tie – did not even break into a sweat before the moment he found himself looking down at Sean, skinny as a two-by-four, unconscious. Ben reached over and pulled the cotton blanket down to cover the exposed toes of Sean's right foot, as he might have done in the middle of a normal night.

'He's just asleep,' Ellen said, her voice low. 'The doctor's looking at some scan results, or will be shortly.'

'Do we know the doctor?'

'Not this one. He's about fifteen years old. Doctor Friend.'

'Terrific name. Is he a paediatrician?'

'Of course he is.'

'Specialist?'

'I haven't asked, Ben. I saw him for ten minutes and he was poking and prodding Sean the whole time.'

'Let's get someone we know. Let's get Vanetti in here or someone, get a referral once they have an idea what's going on.'

'I've called Vanetti's office and he's not available. He's going to his kids' Easter Pageant, or something.'

'How much blood was there?'

Ellen closed her eyes for a moment and breathed out to try to calm herself. 'Ben,' she said, 'it was like red wine.'

Ben winced. He led Ellen out of the room into the bright hospital corridor. There wasn't much to say before they had more information, except to imagine optimistic diagnoses.

'Probably a stone,' said Ben. 'Poor little fellow. But they can explode kidney stones these days with hydro-shock or whatever it's called.'

'Lithotripter,' said Ellen, who had been raised in a medical family.

'Sure. They put the little guy in a bath and zap the stone and he pisses it out with no pain.'

Ellen shook her head. 'They eliminated that with the first scan. They saw something that made Doctor Friend grunt in that way doctors have, you know, as if it's all so inconvenient. Or that it's silly and irresponsible for a little boy to have a screwed up . . .' Ellen controlled herself.

'I want this solved *immediately*,' Ben said.

'Tell me about it.'

'Poor old Karin sounded terrible on the phone. Are you sure Nicole's all right with her?'

'Well *I'm* not going home. You can if you want.'

'I don't think so. We can check in every now and then. Where the hell is your Doctor Friend?'

'You don't want to know. He said, "I think we've got a priority here," when they rolled in this little black kid who'd been burned. I mean so badly you could *smell* him –'

'Please, Ellen, no.'

Ben and Ellen sat down next to each other in upholstered armchairs. Ellen waited in a state of extreme tension and of unwelcome, vestigial Catholic prayer. Ben waited coldly, tapping his fingers on his knee, willing the problem out of his mind. He didn't want Sean to suffer and he didn't want Sean to die – probably in that order – but the damning, selfish thought intruded that as a man and as a citizen he was going to change categories: he was going to be the father of a broken child. He narrowed his eyebrows at this cruel line of thinking, at its utter self-centredness. He shook his head to drive it out and pinched the bridge of his nose. He reached out to hold Ellen's hand.

'It'll be all right,' he said. 'He'll be fine.'

'I have to go back and look at him,' Ellen said, but as she and Ben stood up a thin and rosy-faced young doctor rounded the corner and approached. He wore perfectly round, gold-rimmed spectacles.

Doctor Friend smiled at Ellen through the distress caused by the burn victim, and shook hands with Ben. 'You're Sean's dad?'

'Father, yes,' said Ben.

'Good,' said Doctor Friend. 'Well, we know a great deal about your Sean, now.'

'And?'

'And we're going to need to know a little bit more.'

Ben heard himself ask, 'Can you give us a range of possibilities?'

'I *could* do that, but then you might be needlessly worried.'

'Which means it could be serious.'

'Oh, it's serious, all right,' said Doctor Friend, rubbing

his clean pale hands together. 'But whatever it is it's almost certainly fixable.'

'Fixable,' Ben repeated.

'All right, look. He's got either a tumour or what's called a duplex kidney or else a very serious infection. I've put a call through to Doctor Fang – you may have heard of him?'

'No.'

'Max Fang. Extremely good. It's like he's psychic, you know what I mean?'

'No,' said Ellen.

'Vaguely,' said Ben.

'Fang will have a look and then we'll proceed, depending.'

Ellen said, 'Chances are he loses the kidney.' All the colour had drained from her face. 'Right?'

'That's correct,' said Doctor Friend.

'Is this Stubbs' Tumour?' asked Ellen. Ben looked at her sideways. He had never heard of Stubbs' Tumour.

'Mrs Pelton, please. One step at a time, now. And I'm sorry but I've got to get back there . . .' He gestured down the corridor.

'Is that little boy going to be all right? The burned boy?'

Doctor Friend shrugged his slender shoulders and smiled. 'I don't think so, no,' he said. 'OK? You two relax and I'm sure everything will turn out fine – Fang's the best. I'll try to get him in here by tomorrow morning at the latest.' Doctor Friend shoved his hands into his coat pockets, turned and walked away with his head bowed.

Chastened by the tragedy of the other little boy on the ward, Ben and Ellen didn't say anything for some time.

'Wouldn't want his job,' said Ben, eventually.

'I would,' said Ellen, so angrily Ben flinched. 'I was going to *be* a doctor, remember?' she added, sounding very much like her father when he implied that it was somehow his wife's fault that they had only one child.

Ben managed to hold his tongue – even the mildest admonishment at this moment would have caused a terrible argument.

'Go home,' said Ellen. 'I'll sleep here with Sean.'

'I can –'

'Go home.'

Ellen walked back into Sean's room without looking at her husband, and closed the door behind her.

23

'Do you play tennis?' asked Candy Mancini.

'Not very well,' said Ellen.

The two women had just met for the first time. They sat in cool sunlight by the Mancinis' swimming pool. Little Paul and Sean were at school – it was Sean's second day. Caroline and Nicole were being looked after by Tamina inside the house.

'You'll be better than most of the old bags,' said Candy, who had masculine muscles in her arms. 'But I warn you I'm *really* good.'

Ellen didn't want to talk about tennis. She wanted to talk about the bomb that had gone off about a quarter of a mile from their hotel. It had exploded at eleven o'clock at night. The children were asleep. Ben was not just asleep but insensate after his first day at work. He had returned to the hotel early with his eyes spinning in his head, unable to form clear speech. He had struggled to take off his clothes, given up on trying to take a shower and, after pronouncing the single word '*karat*', fallen face-down on the bed. Ellen had been sitting on a chair close to the television – watching Evan Court reporting from somewhere that used to be on the other side of the world but was now roughly in Ellen's neck of the woods – when the blast occurred. She half expected Evan Court to duck when she heard the noise, which sounded like a gigantic oil drum dropped on marble from a great height. It said something about the age Ellen lived in that she knew right away it was a bomb blast.

'No one told me there were going to be bombs,' Ellen said.

Four people had been injured, according to official reports. That didn't mean only four people had been injured.

'Oh, that,' said Candy.

'I mean, I *heard* it, it was that close.'

'Let's hurry those workmen along, then,' said Candy, gesturing up the hill towards Ellen's unfinished house. 'The bombs only go off downtown, and not very often. It's nothing to worry about up here.'

'Who's responsible?'

'There's a long list,' said Candy. 'Last night was outside a night-club, so probably religious right. The political left goes for government buildings or – I love this word – "infrastructure". Paul's afraid someone will blow up his precious dam.'

'I don't like the sound of this.'

'Oh, honey,' said Candy, 'don't you worry. Just think. A few people cut up by a little bomb. Do you know how many people will be killed in car crashes in this country today? That's what you ought to worry about. Their filthy cars and buses – the brakes don't work. Pedestrians just trust in God and throw themselves into the traffic. The roads out of town can be a nightmare. If you go up into the Berevan Mountains the place is just littered with wrecks up one side and down the other.'

'Yes, but bombs?'

'Read the papers much? There was a bomb in London yesterday as well – a much, much bigger bomb. A couple of days ago they blew up an airport bus terminal in Paris, for about the tenth time. You know how it is. Bombs everywhere. You can't get away. When we were in Sri Lanka one little man got about eighty people. Dead. How many people do you think were murdered in the US last night? Two hundred? Three hundred? Let's be wild and have a drink. Yelam!'

24

'The *karat* hangover,' said Dominic Thrune, 'is untreatable.'

Ben had dropped by Dominic's office for advice on this subject, carefully lowering himself into a chair opposite Dominic's desk.

Dominic sighed and said, 'That was awfully naughty of the Great Mancini. He has a cast-iron gut for some reason — perhaps he drank an antidote in Vietnam. There's only one thing to do and that's to have another glass of the stuff, but I can't recommend going down that *particular* road to ruin. I did warn you.'

'It's poison,' said Ben. 'I'll never drink another drop. How do the locals do it?'

'Well, you aren't supposed to gulp it down like a gin and tonic, you know. I think they swirl a small amount around in their mouths and let it osmose through the gums and palate.'

'When I woke up this morning I thought I'd been hit by a truck. My wife says I slept through a bomb blast.'

'Indeed. I drove past the wreckage on the way to the office this morning. I think it hurt more than four people, which is what today's radio reports claim.' Dominic pointed at an antique radio on his desk. 'They had a mechanical street-scrubber out on the pavement, and I've never seen one of those in this city before, only in Paris.'

'My wife is worried.'

Dominic scoffingly waved a thin hand in the air. 'I'll tell you the worst thing about the bombs,' he said. 'The worst thing is that they force the General's hand. They make him round up people who are obviously guilty and put them in rather ghastly gaols without charge. They can portray themselves as political prisoners and the victims of human-rights abuses, when of course they are bombers and murderers who manage never to be caught in the act. I can tell you there are acquaintances of mine at home who I would adore the freedom to detain indefinitely without charge.'

'You agree with the General's stance, then?'

'Absolutely. As should we all. We are not here to tear down this country, but to build it up.' Dominic spoke theatrically, trying on a speech-writer's phoney words. 'There is no real opposition to him here – least of all from politicians at the moment – just eight or ten political, religious or ethnic groups with fancy initials and whose only PR is murder. If they're not all kept in abeyance there will be war.'

'How does that follow?'

'The General, once weakened, will start a war himself if he has to. How many of us, nationally speaking, can say we haven't done the same?'

It gave Ben a lift to think that he might be involved, however peripherally, in the fate of millions. Only months ago he was concerned principally with keeping the billable hours at a maximum, balancing that number against the harmony of his family. It had never occurred to him that a single case he had ever been associated with might be important.

'Anyway, to business,' said Dominic. 'What's on your plate today?'

'Meetings. I never used to have "meetings" before, *per se*.'

'You'll be meeting some of the natives. *Liaising*.'

'Right.'

'My only advice about the natives is that they are deceptively honest. You think you're being taken for a ride but in fact they are simply saying exactly what they mean. Funny, that.'

'I'll keep it in mind.'

'Otherwise everything fine? Settling in?' Dominic was a fidgety man. Throughout the conversation he had been adjusting papers on his desk, opening and shutting drawers, smoking local cigarettes. He wore the same unusual, brown-corduroy Victorian-Egyptologist suit.

'It's all happening very quickly. My son is in school. I'm picking out our car this afternoon.'

'Oh, what *kind*?' asked Dominic, his dark eyebrows raised towards the ceiling.

'Well, with two children . . . Diane advised me to go with the four-wheel-drive Euphoria. I haven't even seen one, just a photograph. It looks like it means business.'

'Splendid choice. What colour?'

'Colour? I didn't specify a colour.'

'Well you must. Everyone's driving the Euphoria and you have to be distinctive. Do not allow them to give you forest green. Mancini has forest green. And of course white is out of the question – too dirty here. If I were you I would insist on black, to give you that diplomatic look.'

'I'll make a note of that. Black Euphoria.'

'Yes, with air conditioning and tinted windows. I'm sure Diane has thought of all this.'

'I'll check with her.'

'Lovely woman, Diane. Tragic story, though.' Ben wasn't sure he wanted to know Diane's tragic story, but there was no stopping Dominic Thrune. 'She was from quite a well-off family in Texas, went to university, decided to see the world. She met and married an *Italian*, of all people, which caused a terrible rift between her and her parents. She lived in Rome with the young man, who worked in his father's property business. Then the cad began to mistreat her. She bravely left the Italian – can you imagine? A Texas girl all alone in Europe, estranged from her parents, divorcing some lunatic of an Italian man? She spoke the language, and there began her secretarial career.' Dominic picked another cigarette out of the pack, thoughtfully applied flame with a brass lighter. 'I suppose it was lucky she didn't have children. She found temp work with various international organizations, met and fell in love with an American, a *married man*, who left his wife for her. Hard to believe, isn't it, the passion underneath the surface of that woman? They moved here, when the new man got a job on the coast with a tourism outfit. Then he died suddenly, in his early fifties. Just dropped dead. Poor Diane. This time they did have children: a boy and twin girls. Seems to me a normal woman would have called it a day and gone home, but she came here to the capital and raised the children alone. Frightfully brave of her, don't you think? I suppose she had some money from the Italian and from the dead American, but it must have been a struggle. She started working here at the same time I did, seven years ago. It was during her second or third year, on holiday on the southern coast, that one of her twin girls drowned.'

Ben rubbed his eyes. He supposed he was glad to have this information – he would have learned it eventually – but he didn't like Dominic's clear relish in relating the terrible facts of Diane's life.

'She was ten years old, I think. Imagine. Of course I've never asked Diane directly, but the story is that the little girl was swimming in a harbour – the local kids like to swim around in the harbour and the people on yachts throw coins into the water for them to dive down and retrieve. The little girl joined the locals, as did her twin sister. Apparently she hit her head on the keel of a boat as she came up from a dive, and no one saw her float up unconscious on the other side of the boat. No one missed her for some minutes, by which time it was too late. Imagine the guilt.'

Ben had started to sweat. He didn't know if he would be able to look Diane in the eye when he went upstairs to his office. His head still ached from the *karat* poisoning, a sharp pain straight across the eyebrows. 'Awful,' he said. 'Just awful. And you're making my headache worse.'

'*So* sorry.' Dominic craned his head to one side and looked searchingly at Ben. It was a look Ben vaguely recognized. 'Care to let me show you some sights when you have a chance? No sense being cut off from it all up on the hill.'

'I'd enjoy that,' said Ben, politely.

'I promise not to take you near any public hangings.' Dominic waved his cigarette in the air and said something with a proverbial ring in the local language.

'What does that mean?'

'It means, "Never close your ears to the leper's bell."'

'How many languages do you speak?'

Dominic had to think. 'Seven, if you want to include the two dead ones.'

'That's amazing.'

'Not really. I knew four of them by the age of eight.'

'What was that about lepers? Are there lepers in this country?'

'My dear,' said Dominic, stubbing out his cigarette as his telephone rang, 'there are lepers *everywhere*.'

25

Ben made the decision to go along and lease the black Euphoria on his own. He might have asked Sammy, the driver, who knew all about cars; he might have asked Dominic Thrune, who spoke the language so well and knew the ways of the locals; he might even have asked Diane, even though he had been doing his best to avoid her since hearing about the tragedy in her life. Instead he slipped away from the office alone after the last meeting of the afternoon, eager to taste the hurly-burly of native commercial life.

The city growled around him as he picked his way through the crowds. The boulevard he walked down led like the spoke of a wheel to the mysterious old city at its centre. Refracted through smog, the low sun glowed purple-orange and so large it wouldn't be obscured by the palm of one's hand at arm's length. On either side of the boulevard ran swiftly moving streams of water over concrete beds: these were the sewers, which were gradually being replaced with subterranean plumbing. On the previous day, staggering back to the hotel from his lunch with Mancini, Ben had seen an old woman crouched down next to one of these streams, washing a pair of men's trousers. There was no stench that Ben could detect – but, downtown, one had to allow for a fierce competition of odours.

Ben found the Euphoria dealership with little difficulty. The Euphoria dealer himself stood on the pavement outside, smoking a cigarette, wearing a sharp black suit, white shirt and salesman's loud yellow tie. He was a thin man of indeterminate youth – probably not yet thirty. Like almost every one of his male compatriots over the age of sixteen, he wore a moustache. Behind him, a modern showroom displayed three different models of Euphoria, none black. Ben approached and introduced himself in English; Diane had called ahead. The young man said his name was Tito, and guided Ben to a little round table on the pavement just next door to the Euphoria dealership. With elaborate charm, in good English, Tito welcomed Ben to his country and expressed the wish that he would have a wonderful stay. Tito added that he had enjoyed a friendly and mutually satisfactory business relationship with Planning and Resources – who would be contributing to the lease or purchase of the Euphoria as part of Ben's employment package.

'Lease, I think,' said Ben.

Tito wagged his head from side to side, considering this proposal. A boy arrived with two glasses of tea. 'That's OK,' said Tito, patting the boy on the head. 'Leasing is OK. It's standard deal.'

Negotiating was not beyond Ben – that had been part of his old job. Bargaining was a different matter, and he was well aware that he now lived in a country where bargaining was not just an art-form but a source of cultural pride: to try to bargain with Tito, Ben imagined, would be like a tourist trying to cook for an Italian peasant family. Still, he had to try. The Euphoria was not an inexpensive car.

'First of all,' Ben said, 'I need it in black. Black?'

'Sure.'

'Air conditioning?'

'Standard.'

'Tinted windows?'

'Optional.'

This exchange happened at almost shouting volume: the two decayed old buildings on either side of Tito's dealership were being torn down. A film of dust had settled on the surface of Ben's tea.

'Delivery?'

'Ten days.'

'Price?'

Tito frowned. 'Standard deal.'

'I was told about the standard deal. I was told that's too high.'

Tito put a palm to his chest and smiled wistfully, as if he had been complimented on his beautiful singing voice. He changed the subject to the weather, which he claimed was unseasonably warm. It was during this digression that Ben noticed the loping figure of Dominic Thrune on the other side of the avenue, about a hundred yards away.

'A colleague,' said Ben, nodding in Dominic's direction. Ben wasn't pleased about this interference. He wanted to pull off this deal all by himself. Then he realized that Dominic hadn't seen him, wasn't coming to the Euphoria dealership. He stopped at a news stand and bought a magazine. He moved on from there to the next street corner, stopped again, opened the magazine and began to read. If it hadn't been for the trunk of a eucalyptus tree on his side of the avenue, Dominic might have had a clear view of Ben. A moment later he leaned his back against the wall, crossed his ankles. He looked at his watch, as if he were waiting for someone.

Ben and Tito discussed the standard deal, the convenience of getting a black Euphoria in only ten days when a six-month wait was the norm, the impossibility of Tito accepting a dollar-currency cash bribe (not impossible at all), the rarity of tinted windows (optional). Still keeping one eye on Dominic Thrune, Ben found himself agreeing to the standard deal, extra for the tinted windows, *and* the dollar-currency cash bribe, plus delivering the promise that he would take his family to Tito's older brother's restaurant the following Friday evening: one *karat* on the house.

A young man approached Dominic Thrune. He wore a white

T-shirt and blue jeans. He looked like a teenager. He was clean-shaven. Dominic put the magazine under his arm and lit a cigarette. The young man leaned his shoulder against the wall. Ben tried not to stare. He tried to concentrate on what Tito was saying – child seats extra, four-wheel-drive extra, spare tyre extra, extra for a set of snow tyres (extremely important; it would snow suddenly, and very soon), insurance extra, registration extra, tax extra, import duty extra, express delivery extra. The young man across the avenue was smiling – a smile so white it was visible even at such a distance. Dominic looked one way, up the street, then the other way, down the street. He pushed at the young man's bare forearm and the pair rounded the corner into a side-street. Ben soon lost sight of them, but not before he saw Dominic Thrune use the folded magazine to pat the young man's buttocks as if he were prodding a mule.

This little drama reminded Ben of his unreal encounter with the girl at the top of the stairs. For a few weeks he hadn't been able to think about the event without physical symptoms of shame and guilt. After a while he told himself not to be so silly – the world was populated with selfish men who got up to things that amounted to the most astonishing betrayal of their families. Ben's own desperate little detour was nothing – and, when he thought about it after a sufficient interval, strangely satisfactory and cleansing for so clinical, brief and silent an act. He knew he would do it again, and more – though definitely not here, not in this country, not if he could help it.

Ben declined Tito's offer of a test-drive, and shook hands on the deal. The paperwork would be delivered to Ben's office.

Tito said, 'The Euphoria is very good for the children. Very safe.'

'That's the idea,' said Ben, getting up to leave. 'To take care of the children.'

26

Life at the Chevalier Hotel soon lost its charm and novelty. It was too cold in the mornings to sit on the balcony, and the restaurant always smelled of cigar smoke, so the family ate breakfast in their suite. Sammy picked them up at eight-thirty. He dropped Ben at the Planning and Resources offices, then headed into the hills to take Sean to the French School. He then drove Ellen and Nicole to the new house, where Ellen did her best to oversee the sifting labourers while keeping Nicole entertained. Just before noon Ellen escorted Nicole to Candy Mancini's house, and left the little girl there in Tamina's tested hands.

Each day Ellen had a long list of errands to accomplish, and a window of three hours in which to do so. She was grateful for Sammy's services. His English wasn't quite good enough for her to enlist him as a translator on the site of her nearly finished house, but he was patient and accommodating and knew every street and shop in the city. Ellen hated decorating, but the house was in need of very little. It was laid out for summer but insulated for winter. The floors were tile or white-washed cement. Anticipating the arrival of their belongings from home, Ellen had a fairly short list of things she had to buy: curtains, pool furniture, furniture for the servants' quarters out behind the pool house, local carpets, a couple of broad brooms to fend off the city's particulate atmosphere that rained plaster and soot all day and night.

Candy Mancini had set up an interview with relatives of Yelam's, who lived in a small village in the hills fifty miles away. 'You want a couple,' Candy had said. 'I never found a couple, but if you ask me Yelam and Tamina will be one soon if they aren't already. Watch yours like a *hawk*, though.' Ellen's requirements would not be so grand as Candy's: the Mancinis had – in addition to Yelam and Tamina – two gardeners, a laundress, a pool man, a chauffeur who spoke three foreign languages, and a man whose only job was to sweep the steps and carport. The house on top of the hill – Ellen and Ben's house – stood on no more than an acre of plateau cut out of the hillside and flattened by a bulldozer. Like the Mancinis' house, only in miniature, it had been built on stilts over a carport – taking advantage of the hillside's steep incline.

The excitement and novelty of a new city were enough to keep Ellen's mind off the meaning of her new role in life – the overseas wife, the memsahib. She liked Candy Mancini – admired her, in some ways – but Ellen didn't want to emulate a life of tennis, socializing, drinking too much by the pool, talking in a condescending way about the locals. To say, 'They really are *marvellous* people' sounded patronizing to Ellen's ears. In many ways Ellen's life would be easier than it had been at home – on the level of domestic drudgery, at least – but there were new ways in which demands would be made on her time. She had resolved to tutor Sean in English for at least one hour every afternoon before supper; to take French lessons so that she might keep up with her son in that language; to learn to speak, if not to write, the local language; to organize weekend family trips to study the ancient culture of this fascinating land; to be at Ben's side at parties and banquets like an ambassador's wife, head cocked in admiration of her dashing husband; to keep a hawk's eye on her staff, as Candy had advised. She would keep Nicole out of school until the following autumn, when the little girl would be four years old. The French School had a small nursery programme.

Ellen would write to her parents weekly – not so much to

keep them informed, but to expiate her own guilt at having moved so far away. Her father had been furious, so resentful of Ben's decision that he made threats about disowning his only child as well as his grandchildren, just to spite his irresponsible and ungrateful son-in-law. Ellen's mother had feigned support, but was obviously as unhappy as her husband to be losing one of the only consistent threads in her mostly empty life.

Ben had assured Ellen that money wasn't going to be a problem, despite his dramatic cut in pay. One goal in their married life had been to set aside enough for the children's education – assumed, to be on the safe side, to last in each case until the age of approximately thirty – and this was no longer a possibility. Inroads had already been made during Ben's career as a lawyer, but now even college was not completely guaranteed. It had been a theme of Ellen's class and generation that to maintain the standards they had known as children and students, one had to be a millionaire. Ben and Ellen, apart from the children's education fund, had only a few tens of thousands of dollars in the bank. Ellen's father and mother could not be counted on for support later on, thanks to her father's obstinate investment in a power company whose first nuclear plant had mistakenly been built on a minor but still significant geological shift. Dr Delaney had still not found a buyer for Ben and Ellen's house – now denuded and in a slowly sinking neighbourhood: Ellen's father had personally counted *three* black families in their street. Ben's parents might conceivably be of some use but they were acutely aware – Mr Pelton having drawn up so many wills, only to see parents outlive children – that costly retirement lasting thirty years was not out of the ordinary.

Where had Ben's income and severance pay gone? The Peltons did not live at all ostentatiously. Taxes were not outrageously high. The mortgage had been dear but not crippling.

Sean's medical bills had been a drain, though, and Nicole's operations on her jaw and knee. A robbery had cost them fairly dearly when both cars, both televisions, the stereo, the silver, the jewellery and much of the furniture had to be replaced and the insurance fell short by a mile. Ellen's married friends back home, most of whose husbands had jobs as highly paid as Ben's, worked outside the home. The money had gone on the children, and on optimism. It was true that expenses here were relatively low, but Ellen's guilty material expectations were now unlikely to be realized.

This afternoon Ellen paid a visit to the country club, not too far from her house – just on the other side of the enormous Soviet Embassy compound. Candy had said it would be unthinkable for Ben and Ellen not to join, that the children would love the pool, that it could be fatiguing to eat in local restaurants all the time. Sammy drove Ellen and Nicole to the club, through gilded gates with the national crest on the ironwork, up a drive to the main building that contained the restaurant, locker rooms, two bars and a gym. As always, Sammy leapt athletically out of the driver's seat to open the back door on Ellen's side. Nicole crawled along the seat and got out with her mother. They walked around the side of the main building to the clay tennis courts, where Candy Mancini, wearing a white visor and sunglasses, was playing singles against a man. Ellen had only played tennis in high school, and didn't much like the game. She had never seen a woman hit the ball as hard as Candy. When she served she tossed the ball so high she could rock back on her heels, knees bent, racket way behind her back, and *wait* there with her body a store of kinetic energy, then leap into the air and bring the racket crashing through the ball from a great height. She had long legs and a figure that middle age had only slightly thickened. She perspired unashamedly, so that the binding back of a sports bra was visible through her soaked tennis dress.

Ellen wondered if, for political reasons, Ben would ask her to take tennis lessons. She would have to tell him that lessons or no lessons, she would never take a game off Candy Mancini.

Candy made short work of her opponent – a local by the looks of him – a paunchy, brown-pated man who wore wrist bands, a headband, white socks and shoes stained with clay from running and sliding back and forth chasing Candy's teasing ground-strokes. Towelling herself off, Candy came over to Ellen beaming with satisfaction. She introduced her opponent, who soon departed for the showers.

'That,' said Candy, as she led Ellen and Nicole to the terrace bar, 'is the man they call the Beast. He's going to be a billionaire sometime pretty soon.'

'The Billionaire Beast.'

'Exactly. An arms dealer, naturally. It all makes you wonder. Hello, little Nicole.'

Nicole was a three-year-old of very few words. Unlike her brother, who took after Ellen, Nicole was a solemn and mysterious child. Her appearance unnerved strangers: she had dark, almost purple circles under her eyes and a faintly sour expression on her face, as if she were a defeated politician after a long campaign. She hadn't had an easy life. It had been difficult to pay much attention to her during Sean's illness. Fixing her skewed knee, only eighteen months ago, had been painful and confining – she wore a brace for six months and still limped slightly even though there was probably no need for her to do so. Ellen was worried that her favouring one leg would be bad for her back and pelvis. The doctors said not to worry. The jaw operation had been even more serious.

'I said "Hello, little Nicole,"' Candy repeated, somewhat sternly. Ellen could see where Little Paul got his striking articulateness: Candy was an imposing and uncompromising mother when it came to her children's manners and speech.

'Say hello, Nicky,' said Ellen softly.

'Hi,' said Nicole.

'You sure don't say much, Nicole,' said Candy. 'Your mom and I are going to the bar. Would you like to come with us? Do you want something to *drink* at the *bar*, Nicole? *Juice?*'

Nicole did not reply.

'She might have milk,' said Ellen, who resented Candy's tone with Nicole, as if Candy were patronizing the child the way she did this whole country. Who was to say she hadn't created a monster in her own son? Little Paul, only eight years old, had shaken Ellen's hand firmly, sat down in a chair, crossed his legs, and conversed with the solicitousness of a cultured Southern judge.

Nicole wore almond drain-pipe trousers; she always wore almond drain-pipe trousers these days; she was inconsolable without almond drain-pipe trousers. 'Look, a trampoline,' she said.

'Not now,' said Ellen. 'Mrs Mancini wants to go to the terrace bar.' Ellen knew Candy needed a drink more than usual: she'd hit one of the supports of her carport with the Euphoria – it was her second accident in two months, she said – and dreaded having to tell her husband.

'Oh, it's all right,' said Candy. 'They'll bring us a drink. I'll help you spot Nicole.' Then, leaning down, '"Spot", in this context, Nicole, means to stand by the trampoline to catch you if you bounce off.'

Nicole bounced reticently on the trampoline while Ellen and Candy spotted her. Gin and tonics were produced.

'Has my husband spoken to your husband,' Candy asked, 'about getting a gun?'

'I beg your pardon?'

'A gun. You'll need a gun.'

'Why do we need a gun? We don't need a gun.'

'Yes you do. We always say, you need a gun for the wild rabid dogs in the city and, in the mountains, for the wolves.

That's not what you really need a gun for. You need it to protect yourself against robbers. Robbery is one of the consequences,' Candy said, in her precise voice, 'of having a few hundred rich people living upstairs, if you will, from a few million poor people downstairs.'

'How often have you been robbed?'

'Never, here. But it will happen. Paul will shoot at them and that will be the end of that. In Kinshasa we were robbed three times in two years.'

'Did you have a gun?'

'Yes, but we were always away when the robbers came. "What an *unbelievable* coincidence," as Little Paul might say. We were never robbed in Sri Lanka – except for little things the servants took. In Rio Paul accidentally wounded a boy, so we had to leave.'

'We were robbed, back home.'

'See what I mean, honey? It's like the bombs. There are robbers and murderers everywhere.'

Nicole stopped bouncing on the trampoline. 'Robbers and murderers?' she asked.

'That's right, darling,' said Candy.

'Everywhere?' asked Nicole.

'*Everywhere*. Let's get another drink, honey. Then we'll talk about that gun.'

27

'This doesn't feel like much of a gun,' said Ben, standing next to Paul Mancini on the rough hillside between their houses. In fact in its own way it was rather a lot of gun for Ben, who had only fired rifles and shotguns in his life: its manoeuvrability was shocking to him; it was just an extension of his arm. Mancini had placed four empty American beer cans on the side of the hill in a safe-enough place: an errant shot might kill a Communist across the way, nothing more.

Mancini, who in Ben's mind had killed hundreds of human beings, took the gun in his hand. It was a beautiful object, black and compact, oily to the touch, heavy. It held a clip of nine rounds plus the one in the chamber. Mancini bent his knees, stretched out his arms, aimed the weapon at the beer-can targets. He squeezed off four rounds, dead-sounding thuds absorbed by the leafy trees of the Soviet Embassy compound. The beer cans were untroubled.

Ben didn't want to embarrass his warrior boss, so he said, 'Probably the breeze – and it's a long way to those cans for a handgun. Must be forty feet.'

Mancini fired four more times, even more quickly, then twice more. The beer cans remained where they had been placed, though Ben had seen soil rise in their vicinity. Mancini removed the clip, checked the empty chamber, put on the safety.

'Probably the breeze,' Ben said, knowing it was his turn next.

'Take a look,' said Mancini. 'I'll reload.'

Ben walked unsteadily over the rocky terrain to inspect the

beer cans. Each had two clean bullet holes side by side in their centre; the two central cans each had a further hole in the brewery's label closer to the top. Gripped by his natural competitive instinct, Ben returned to Mancini determined to make his mark on the cans. 'Good shooting,' he said, as if he had expected to find the beer cans surgically holed under Mancini fire. 'I just thought they'd be knocked down,' he added, taking the gun in his hands.

Mancini muttered something about muzzle velocity as Ben took his stance and aimed convincingly at the can on the far left.

'I'm pretending I'm shooting at a rabid dog,' Ben said.

'OK,' said Mancini. 'Take the safety off, then.'

Ben did so, aimed again, fired. The beer can on the far right was tossed into the air. 'I should quit while I'm ahead,' Ben said, not admitting that he had missed his intended target by four feet.

'Go on,' said Mancini. He was so tall, he was such a *soldier*, Ben felt minuscule and incompetent by comparison. He fired through the rest of the clip, managing in the end to topple two of the remaining cans – probably by bouncing stray rocks against them.

'You're fine,' said Mancini. 'Keep it in the bedroom. They'll come at night. And don't shoot at people. Shoot at the ceiling. That's why the clip – you can shoot up the whole place. If you hear someone in your house it's because they want something they know is there and they'll know where to find it. Your servants will have told them. They won't be armed. Shout and shoot, shout and shoot. They'll skedaddle and they won't come back. Remember, don't shoot *at* anyone, you'll just kill one of your kids.'

'Jesus, Paul.'

'It's been known to happen.'

28

Ellen had never been comfortable when there was nothing for her to do; it gave her time to think. Now, lying alone in the sunshine by the club swimming pool, wearing shorts and a polo shirt, her children being entertained by Tamina, a glass of iced tea inches from her hand, her eyes shut behind dark glasses, she felt idle and useless. She wished she had a short-wave radio or a book. She thought it unhealthy that she had to force herself to relax, as if relaxation itself were a chore. She wondered if idleness would prove to be habit-forming, if she would waste away her stay in this country with servant-freed afternoons doing this: lounging, inert, trying not to think.

Instead of thinking – which really amounted to worrying: worrying about Sean, worrying about Nicole, worrying about Ben, worrying about her parents – Ellen chose to fantasize. She fantasized now about Evan Court. She wondered about his love-life. She couldn't imagine that a man who travelled so constantly could be married, nor that he had a steady girlfriend. He was a gentle-looking man for someone whose job was to seek out and report on the worst violence he could locate anywhere in the world on any given day. His compassionate eyes suggested someone who did not treat women casually. His affairs were likely to be profound – with intrepid female colleagues, perhaps – if necessarily brief. He and his lover would sponge themselves off in a stagnant river rife with bilharzia, then make love in a canvas tent on a narrow camp bed beneath a canopy of torn mosquito netting.

Ellen laughed silently, through her nostrils. She lay there

in her under-utilized twenty-eight-year-old body, wanting to laugh louder. The only sound she could hear – there was no one in the swimming-pool – was that of Candy Mancini pounding tennis balls past the Billionaire Beast. Ellen wanted to laugh because, as her Evan Court fantasy grew more intense, she had to recall an infuriating secret she had kept from Ben. It was more than a secret; it was a deception.

There was Ellen – just nineteen, a sophomore in college, whose father claimed Irish extraction – coming out of a Boston theatre. And along came Ben, looking dazed because he had not yet finished Law School. He walked up to her and her two friends – fellow dancers – and he said to Ellen, 'Hello. You are *so* pretty.' Ellen had never been approached by a stranger in this way before. By midnight she had kissed him.

She found him somewhat intimidating, distant – she also found him beautiful, and her friends agreed. He was drawn and exhausted from his scholarly exertions, but there was no mistaking his beauty: his ambitious eyes, his taut jaw – 'just the shape of his *head*, really,' as one of Ellen's friends had put it. Self-confident, dry, well-read, focused, very different from the posturing innocents Ellen knew. She didn't like him very much, she told herself. She found him arrogant. But of course she liked arrogant men – or *told* herself she did; or should. Ellen had no idea. The reason she had no idea was that she had no experience. She had not been sheltered, she had gone to a co-ed school, she had been popular with boys, she loved the idea of boys – but she had no experience, no proper experience with boys. After meeting Ben and looking back on her lack of proper experience, she had no explanation. Her current boyfriend, the one who would go on to mention her in print, never forced the issue of taking her to bed. As an outgoing, gossipy girl, she knew for a fact that she was alone among her friends in this regard – she was the *only one*. It was not out of fear, nor out of morality that she had taken this course. It was an accident, not a choice. She had loved her boyfriends – both of them. They seemed happy enough too. There was dance and choir and schoolwork and summer camp and every damned thing to do every week. From the day in her life – she remembered the day – when she had a clear view of what she longed for with a boy, six years slipped by with plenty of opportunity and – accidentally, not by choice – no action taken. Then she met Ben and thought, I am going to have to lie about all of this.

In a perverse reversal of what her mother and grandmother probably went through, Ellen found herself exaggerating her sexual past. She kissed Ben that first night and said, 'I have a boyfriend.' This was true, but not in the way Ben would have understood the remark. Ben said, 'Now you have two,' and she kissed him again. She really fell into his arms, now, and she could tell this was a man who was exhausted and lonely. He said he loved her that first night, and she said, 'Don't be ridiculous.' He said, 'If you think that's ridiculous, I don't want to see you ever again.'

Ellen spent more than an hour that night sitting on a sofa with Ben, cheek to cheek, hypnotizing herself with the single act of drawing her finger from behind his ear, over his jaw to his chin, then back again. She did not consider herself a virgin, although her best friend said, 'A panel of technical experts would say that you are.' Ben took her home intact, that night. Only in retrospect did she see herself in Ben's eyes – a teenager, the girl he never had when *he* was an undergraduate because they were all dating graduate students. It made her happy, in a way, to think of herself from that perspective. Ben must have been salivating. And yet he courted her with efficient care, to the extent that a full week elapsed before they slept together, which was an almost Victorian ritual by comparison with her generation's norm. Immediately before that happened, Ellen and Ben had the following exchange:

136

'Were you in love with your last boyfriend?'

'I thought I was. There was a terrible problem.'

'You don't have to tell me, Ellen.'

'You can probably guess.'

'Probably.'

'Well,' said Ellen, feeling as she lied as if she were riding an out-of-control toboggan, 'we took care of it.' This was a dark refrain from her adolescent years: girls were always taking care of it. She had no idea why she was speaking this way. She was telling Ben she'd had an abortion: that she was experienced.

'Awful,' said Ben. 'I'm sorry.'

'Have you had a lot of girlfriends?'

'No, not many,' said Ben. The truth was: *many*.

29

Ben and Ellen stood at the edge of the terrace, watching their
first sunset as occupants of the hilltop house. Sean and Nicole
were indoors being fed their supper by Ama, whom Ellen had
employed along with her husband, who liked to be called Haz.
Ama and Haz had been married only three months, but did
not plan to have children for several years. They were both
twenty-three years old. They had grown up in the same small
village – Yelam's village. Their marriage had been arranged.
They were probably cousins. They spoke very little English.
Ama was a stout young woman with long, thick black hair
and a prominent mole on her right cheek. Haz was a boyish
young man with a pretty smile and an understated moustache.
They were well paid and looked as if they couldn't believe
their luck to be living here. They lived in a small, self-contained
apartment attached to the back of the house. Between them
they had seventeen younger brothers and sisters, so they knew
something about children.

The Peltons' belongings had arrived only three days late.
Everything had been moved in to the house, which itself had
been finished on time. They had been in the country ten weeks.
Sean spoke French. Nicole could name basic groceries in the
local language. Ben had learned that his job required little more
than attendance and a measure of diplomacy. Ellen had a
fantastic tan. Winter had not yet moved in, but the black
Euphoria and its spare tyres were prepared for snow in the
carport.

Ellen leaned her head against Ben's shoulder. She had been

moving, moving, for weeks. With Sammy's help she had ferried
Sean to school every morning, orchestrated the workmen and
movers as their tasks overlapped, hired Ama and Haz, made
friends at the club, enrolled on a language course, insisted on
a satellite dish so that she wouldn't lose touch with Evan Court,
taken a tennis lesson, test-driven the black Euphoria, tried to
reassure a worried-looking Nicole, debriefed Ben about his
job, cleared the boundary of the property of rusty nails, hinges
and wire, learned to say 'A dozen eggs and a bottle of milk,
please' in the local language, bought the most beautiful carpet
she had ever seen – all greys – for only two-hundred dollars.

'Do you know what Sean said today?' she asked.

'What.'

'He said – I swear to God he said this – he said, "*Je veux
voir les lépreux.*"'

'I want to see the lepers?'

'Right. I don't know what's stranger – his wanting to see
the lepers, or his being able to say so in French after only a
few weeks.'

'Do you ever speak French with him?'

'No. It's just that the new things he learns he has to say in
French, obviously.'

'But lepers? Who told him about lepers?'

'He has a friend named Daniel.'

'And Daniel has seen lepers?'

'Look,' said Ellen, turning Ben around and pointing at the
barren mountains to the north. 'You see that? There's a long
white building in the middle of the mountain. From this far
away it's just a dot, but you can just make it out from down
here when the sun's shining on it. It looks like a ski chalet but
it's supposed to be enormous.'

'I see it.'

'Sean says Daniel told him that's a leper asylum.'

'Good old Daniel.'

'Sean really wants to see the lepers.'

'Oh, come on.'

'Well, why not? Will you take him to see the lepers?'

'Ellen, please.'

'Why not?'

'That's just weird. Morbid. Have you ever seen a leper?'

'No.'

'Why are we even talking about this? Those poor God-damned people. There's a leper outside my office building. His hands and feet are bound with dirty rags. Jesus.'

'Well, Sean said he wanted to see them.'

'Jesus, Ellen. My colleague Dominic says there isn't any leprosy to speak of in this country. Sean will think leprosy is everywhere if that's his first tourist excursion.'

'Do you know what leprosy is?'

'No.'

'It's caused by a bacillus. Hard to catch, though.'

'Well, my beautiful and knowledgeable medical wife, do you honestly think it would be a good idea to take Sean – deliberately – to have a gander at lepers? Come on.'

'Of course not. I just thought you could drive out together somewhere, this weekend. Show him the lepers from a distance.'

'What, like a zoo? Those poor God-damned people, Ellen.'

'Make it into a game – a funny game.'

'Oh, hilarious. The leprosy game.'

'You'll think of something. I just think you and Sean ought to have an excursion, get him out of the house for a day or two while I wrap things up around here.'

'I could take him to the Baram Caves, I suppose,' said Ben. 'Do you have any idea what the hell the Baram Caves are?'

'As a matter of fact I know exactly what they are. A new friend at the club told me. They were hideouts for Christians about a thousand years ago. The Christians fled into the moun-tains, dug out their caves and lived there for a few generations.

When they were allowed out again they spoke a language no one else understood.'

'Who's your new friend at the club?'

'Oh, I forgot to tell you. We have our first dinner invitation. We're going to socialize. Her name is so beautiful, listen to this: Nadejda Tumarevna. You call her Nadia, though. She's a former ballerina. She's the real thing. She's gorgeous. She was an actual Russian ballerina, can you believe it?'

'Russian?'

'Sure.'

'What does her husband do?'

'Something at the Embassy, obviously,' she said, gesturing before her. The Soviet Embassy compound stretched away at their feet. 'I really didn't ask about him. His name is Denis, isn't that funny? I talked to Nadia about ballet. Her English is really good. She's been everywhere, danced everywhere.'

'It might not be a great idea for me to have dinner with Russians,' said Ben.

'What, are you a spy, now? Or afraid they'll spy on you?'

'No, of course not. It's just that my predecessor got fired for playing chess and drinking too much with a Bulgarian.'

'Well, you don't play chess and you don't drink too much. It'll be fine. You'll fall in love with Nadejda Tumarevna.'

'I have a feeling I ought to ask Mancini's permission.'

'That's no way to live. We were cordially invited to a dinner party by a very charming woman – someone who could be my friend. We'll go.'

Ben thought about this for a minute, looking out over the darkening city. 'All right,' he said. 'Just don't tell anyone. And on Saturday I'll take Sean to the Baram Caves.'

30

'I'm afraid the news isn't great,' Dr Friend had said, confirming that Sean's illness had proved to be Stubbs' Tumour. 'The bad news is he's going to lose a kidney. The good news is that he's got two of them. There will also be radiotherapy.' This was reported to Ellen – Ben was at work.

'Get it out,' Ben had said when the information was relayed to him, referring to his son's cancer. 'Solve this.'

For the next six months Ellen lived in a fury. She accepted that it was her job to deal with Sean's treatment, and Ben's job to continue being a lawyer so they would have money; she hated this. Watching Sean nearly dying was beyond sadness or grief. She went so hot with anger she often found she had bruised herself somehow – gripping the steering wheel too tightly, kicking the dishwasher. There was no humour in their lives any longer, nor could they imagine there ever would be again. Nicole looked up at the world and saw a gloomy, stressful place. Back at home, Ellen watched Sean sitting in a chair on the terrace – pretending to read, which he hadn't yet learned to do, his little head cocked to one side and his mouth moving, his sandalled feet tapping on the armrest, wearing a watch cap – and she had to support herself against the wall and cover her face with her hand.

Ben's reaction to the crisis was to withdraw into himself, to work harder than ever, to have difficulty even looking at Sean. He took sleeping pills in the evenings. He complained of a stiff jaw caused by grinding his teeth at night. Inwardly he felt detached and, though he hated himself for this, *annoyed* with Sean. On the rare occasions when he was home while Sean was awake – the boy's treatment exhausted him – Ben held Sean in his arms and thought selfishly that he didn't deserve a sick child. The horrendous stress in his household caused him to lose his temper with Ellen on occasion, something he profoundly regretted the moment his anger subsided. He resented even sincere sympathy from friends and colleagues, though he knew how difficult it was for them to say the right thing. Victor Wiesman, for example, infuriated Ben one day by drawing a parallel between Sean's illness and one of his own children's broken fibula fifteen years ago. In his unsettled state of mind, Ben suspected both of his sisters – neither of whom yet had children – of taking morbid pleasure in the drama of their nephew's unspeakable misfortune. Ben had to tell himself over and over that it was Ellen who needed his support, Ellen who was truly suffering, Ellen who would never get over this if it came to the worst. When Ben blew up at her – always over matters so trivial he sometimes couldn't even remember the cause of his outburst – it made him feel guilty and useless.

Nicole's doctors had said she ought to have the operation on her knee when she was eighteen months old; this coincided with the news that Sean's recovery was complete, or at least the best that could have been hoped for under the circumstances. For six months afterwards it was Sean who was relatively ignored, and Nicole who had to be carried up and down stairs in her cast, then later in her brace. As before, it was Ellen who threw herself into the back-breaking tasks involved in Nicole's recovery, who had to repress her violent emotions and soldier on; while Ben worked hard, took sleeping pills at night, and thought to himself without *quite* saying so that his life's trajectory had been thrown off course by these inconveniently broken children. He told himself he was only being honest. When both children seemed all right again, Ben had figuratively cleared his throat and said, 'Back to normal.' Then Victor Wiesman sacked him.

31

Nadejda Tumarevna and her husband Denis lived in a concrete apartment block halfway down the hill towards the city centre. Because Ben and Ellen were not yet comfortable leaving their children alone with Ama and Haz, Tamina had come over to help look after them; Candy Mancini, unusually for her, was at home for the evening. Ben was more nervous about this arrangement than Ellen, but she had seen Tamina playing with the children for several days and had every confidence in her trustworthiness. On Ben's instructions, Ellen had told Candy only that they were going out for dinner, not that they were socializing with dreaded Communists. Ellen hated lying and would have told the truth had Candy asked where they were going.

Ben parked the black Euphoria in the street outside the drab, sooty apartment building. Laundry had been hung out to dry on some of the balconies. Boys played football in the street, rode bicycles in a vacant lot across the way; girls chatted in groups, played hopscotch. Ellen was surprised by the shabbiness of the neighbourhood, the dilapidation of the apartment building. Nadejda Tumarevna was one of the most glamorous-looking women Ellen had ever met.

'It's on the fifth floor,' said Ellen. 'Are you sure you don't want to take the elevator? We're in a new country now.'

Ben never took elevators. This was one of his few obvious neuroses, and was associated with his mild claustrophobia. It had started at the beginning of Sean's illness, when Ben found that he couldn't bear to push the button to call the elevator because he had the strongest feeling the doors would open and there would be a dead or badly wounded person lying inside. He couldn't explain this petty phobia, and it embarrassed him, but even with colleagues at work he had to insist on walking up or down stairs. When Ellen said she could call the elevator, inspect it, then tell Ben the coast was clear, he said he was just as worried about the doors opening at the other end and revealing the same dead or badly wounded person. It was the doors opening he couldn't abide; not knowing what the opening would reveal.

Ben smiled, shook his head and made for the stairs. He thought it only a minor psychological aversion – it wasn't as if he couldn't fly, or drive, or leave the house – and he was willing to brave the stairs. Ellen always walked with him, but she made a point every time of asking first if Ben hadn't finally shucked off his peculiar and inconvenient dread. Ben held her hand as they climbed the dusty stairs. The stairwell was full of the smells of cooking, of lamb and rice and pastry. The walls were bare – back home in a similar building they would have been daubed with elaborate graffiti. They stopped just before the fifth landing for a few seconds, so they wouldn't be out of breath when they met their hosts. They climbed the rest of the way under the light of a single bare, yellow bulb.

Ellen rang the doorbell. The door opened and Nadejda Tumarevna was revealed. Ben almost gasped at the sight of her, at the contrast of her appearance with her dull surroundings. She extended a long arm to shake Ellen's hand, her face lighting up and her cheekbones rising high beneath her glowing blue eyes – she might have been reaching out to her partner on stage. She shook Ben's hand and nodded her head in a gracious, miniature bow. Her soft brown hair was pulled back in a pony tail behind her long, ivory neck. She wore a black cashmere dress and no jewellery, only a plain watch on her slender left wrist. She was slightly taller than Ellen even in flat-soled black pumps.

Ben and Ellen entered the apartment and were introduced to Nadia's husband. He was not at all what they had expected: Ellen had thought of him as a dashing former aristocrat, with wavy black hair and perhaps the hint of a duelling scar; Ben had pictured a barrel-chested, rheumy-eyed, melancholy, grey-haired bureaucrat in a cheap wool suit. Denis turned out to be a small, quick-looking man in his early thirties. He shook hands brightly and cordially. He had a small, dark head but a broad and unusually white smile. He wore a black silk suit and a thin black tie. He spoke English with a vaguely French accent beside the Russian one, while Nadia's inflections were British.

Ben and Ellen were handed small glasses of chilled vodka even before they were shown through to the sitting room. A toast was made in Russian, then Denis said, 'You are most welcome.' All four drank, then looked significantly at one another before putting down their glasses. They were guided through a small dining room before reaching the sitting room, which looked as out of place in this concrete building as the elegant Russian couple did. It was a long and narrow room, voluptuously decorated: a fine carpet, an oak coffee table, a peach sofa, two crystal vases of roses, a bronze bust of Nadia, a black upright piano, wintry Russian oils on the walls, two antique armchairs, soft-gold box-pleated curtains, column-and-urn lamps with tasselled shades. It was as if a tiny corner of a Russian palace – a waiting room, perhaps – had been moved into this unprepossessing space.

Everyone sat down – Ben and Ellen on the sofa, Nadia and Denis in the armchairs – and champagne was poured. This was not local sparkling wine, which Ben had unhappily drunk during business lunches, but proper French champagne. Nadia did the pouring, into fine crystal flutes. Ben had to make an effort not to stare at her as she did so. He had never had this conscious thought before: 'She is more beautiful than my wife.'

Conversation was stiff for only a few minutes, thanks to the vodka and champagne. Ellen leaned in Nadia's direction and spoke about children: Nadia said she wanted at least three, and envied Ellen for having given birth so young. Ben leaned towards Denis, and made the mistake of mentioning he drove a Euphoria; Denis drove one of the ubiquitous local Fardis.

'We live across from your Embassy,' said Ben.

'On the hill?'

'That's us. The house is brand new. We're very lucky I suppose.'

'I can see it from my office. You have a pool. And a fantastic garden.'

'Oh, no, that's someone else. My boss, Mr Mancini.' Ben had been in this room for five minutes and already he thought he might have said too much. 'We're in the small house on top of the hill.'

'Not so small,' said Denis.

'Well, no. It's comfortable of course.'

'My wife is very taken with your wife – they were both dancers.'

'Yes, but I don't think . . . there can't be any comparison. Your wife was a professional . . . a great dancer, I understand. I don't know the first thing about ballet.'

'She was good,' said Denis – he couldn't be overheard because the women were chatting away. 'She was never great.'

'How did you meet?'

'Through my brother. He knew her first. He worked with the ballet – really he was a travel agent. He met her and introduced us. He doesn't go with women.'

'I see.'

Denis had quite an intense stare. Ben could read a great deal of frustration in the Russian's eyes: he drove a Fardi, he lived

148

in an ugly building in a poor neighbourhood, he worked for a rotten government, he didn't have any children. Ben supposed that even being married to a woman who was as lovely as it was possible for a woman to be could eventually be taken for granted.

'Do you have a cook?' Denis asked.

'Yes, yes we do.'

'And someone to look after your children – Sean and Nicole?'

'Yes. How good of you to know their names.'

'Nadia told me. And all of your projects – the Meheti Dam, the Ring Road, the mines and so on – you are very busy?'

Ben definitely wanted to avoid discussing business with this character. 'How about you?'

Denis heaved a great Russian shrug. 'Diplomat,' he said. 'Visas and so on. Have some more champagne.'

The bottle was soon finished. A glorious colour had risen in Nadia's unearthly cheeks.

'After dinner,' Denis said, 'I want to show you a film.'

'That would be fine,' said Ben, scanning the room for a television. He couldn't see one.

The conversation became more general. Nadia gave advice on fitting in with the locals, which came down to elaborate generosity. The people here, she said, had a high standard of etiquette and foreigners were best advised to learn their ways: gifts, infinite hospitality, respect for the family, piety.

'You will make wonderful friends,' said Nadia, 'in the government, in the arts, in the academy.'

Ben could see now why Ellen had insisted on this dinner. Ellen and Nadia were naturally attracted to each other: two good-looking women, energetic and culturally transplanted. It thrilled Ben to think they would be friends, that Nadia would become pregnant and Ellen could show her the ropes. They would shop together and study the language together and talk about ballet.

Denis said, 'One little drink and we will dine.' He produced a vodka bottle and new glasses from a cabinet next to the piano.

'Who plays the piano?' Ellen asked.

'We both,' said Denis. 'I play, Nadia dances. Nadia plays, I weep.'

Four more glasses of vodka were poured, another formal toast in Russian made, then Denis said, 'We are both so happy to welcome you here.' Everyone drank down the vodka and smiled.

Ben was thoroughly in love with Nadia as she took his elbow and led him into the tiny dining room. Ellen swooned under the influence of drink and Denis's chivalrous charm. He pulled out her chair and eased it beneath her as she sat down; seeing this, Ben did likewise for Nadia. The men seated themselves, and there was a pause as the Americans wondered who would serve. Swinging doors opened from a kitchen the size of Ben and Ellen's cloakroom, and out came a young man in a starched white uniform. He bore two bowls of soup. He placed these at the women's settings and returned to the cramped kitchen. As the doors opened again a female cook was briefly visible. The young man returned with two more bowls of soup and placed them carefully, from the left, before Ben and Denis.

'This smells wonderful,' said Ellen.

'Wonderful,' said Ben.

Denis poured wine. Nadia raised her glass and said, 'To our new friends. Welcome.'

'Welcome,' said Denis.

All drank.

'Now Ben,' said Nadia, when everyone had tasted their lobster bisque. 'Tell me everything about your . . .' Ben thought she would say 'work'. Nadia glowed and grinned as she paused before saying '. . . children.'

Ben replied in platitudes for half a minute, then said, 'They've both had . . . health problems. They're fine now. The children are fine.' He looked to Ellen not just for confirmation of what he had said, but for a change of subject.

'Ben's taking Sean out to the Baram Caves tomorrow. An excursion.'

'He will love it,' said Nadia. 'We have been many times. We always take visitors there.'

'That's what my boss does,' said Ben, wincing as he mentioned Mancini for the second time.

'Actually,' said Denis, lighting an American cigarette as the hired waiter cleared the soup bowls, 'you are going to be moved by what you see. Martyrs to their religion. Artists. You won't believe the wall paintings. Trust me, I have been there twenty times. There are tunnels and caves and chambers no one has seen, not yet. You go deeper and deeper and you don't believe people lived in there. They made fire. They took care of their little babies. They prayed and they painted and they made music. Inside these caves. For a hundred years – more. Tell that to your son. Make him understand. They dug deeper, made more tunnels and chambers – a chapel in every one. This is what I have to tell myself when I visit the caves: there were people, like me, living inside. I imagine someone like me sitting in one of the chambers trying to entertain children. Magic? Stories? Songs? More than one hundred years, Mr Pelton.'

'Call me Ben.'

'Call me Denis.'

The second course arrived: grilled sole.

'It is flown in fresh,' said Denis. 'We are fortunate at the Embassy. There isn't any fish in the restaurants – not fresh fish.'

'It looks delicious,' said Ellen, who had been holding back on the wine.

Nadia raised her chin and said, 'Forgive me, but I have to say how *happy* I am.'

The others laughed supportively and drank. Ben had to remind himself that she was the enemy. She and Denis were the wall Mancini was trying to tear down. Her lips though, her *lips*. When she smiled – 'I have to say how *happy* I am' – it was like a sunrise. Ben glanced at Denis and had the very clear thought that he was envious of someone who awoke with Nadia's legs entwined with his, her pure ivory body and her lips and hair just an inch away or closer. Ben could not tolerate envy. His father had once said, 'The day I envy another man is the day I know I've failed.' That's why I'm here, Ben thought – because I will be envied. I have made this break. I am dining with a Soviet diplomat and his inconceivably beautiful wife. Alan Yates would envy me. Alan Yates would *choke* on his envy if he saw me sitting here with a Soviet diplomat and his inconceivably beautiful ballerina wife. Alan Yates, as I fork this fresh grilled sole into my mouth, wash it down with exotic white wine, will be staring into a shaving mirror in his bathroom in his suburb before embarking on another day of unholy toil – I was there, I knew it, I knew the lazy, condescending stare of Judge Ladatt. Ben thought he should invite Alan Yates and his wife and his two perfect children to visit. Nadia and Denis could be on hand, by the pool overlooking the massive, threatening Soviet Embassy compound.

'Ben?' asked Ellen.

'Sorry?'

'Nadia asked you about your "sports".'

Ben was drunk. He hadn't heard the question.

'My . . . sports?'

'Yes,' insisted Ellen. 'Your sports.'

'Well, you know, my sports . . .' said Ben, now clawing his way through the vodka and the champagne and the wine. 'I have few sports.' He laughed. No one else did. 'I rowed.' He made a rowing motion with his fists. 'They told me, "All you have to do is get up at five o'clock in the morning. Chip the ice off your hands. And pull." I wasn't any good. I ski. I love skiing. Do you ski?'

This last question came as 'Russkie?' Ben didn't know why Ellen had to cover her mouth with her napkin, and couldn't understand why his question wasn't greeted with a reply.

Ellen came to Ben's rescue and changed the subject yet again. This was a delicate matter, she realized: too much on schools or children and she might offend the childless Russians or even open up a wound; anything about politics was off-base and potentially dangerous with her tipsy husband across the table; they had already covered food and sightseeing. Ellen said, 'Do you like to read books in English?' The couple nodded. 'We've brought over our whole library. Feel free, if you want,' she said. 'Right now I'm reading an English novel called *Front and Centre*. It's about the . . .' Ellen had been about to say 'war', but this was also not an area it was best to explore, at least at their first collective meeting. 'About the . . .' she was going to say 'class system,' but thought better of that too. 'About . . .' she was going to say 'politics', she was going to say 'spies', she was going to say 'public school', she was going to say 'the aristocracy', she was going to say 'the Cold War'. 'It's mostly about gardening,' she finally said.

Ben squinted at his wife. He was fully aware that he'd had too much to drink, but he wasn't a bad drinker and knew that he could manage to keep mum for the rest of the evening. He had a sip of wine and finished his sole. Salad and cheese were served.

Denis said, 'Shall we have coffee in the other room? I want to show you the film.'

'Coffee' turned out to mean 'coffee and more vodka'. Denis, who did not look or behave like an alcoholic, smoked and drank even as he went about the task of setting up a screen and eight-millimetre film projector. Ben and Ellen sank into the peach sofa and held their glasses of vodka in their laps.

Nadia sat in one of the armchairs, glowing. Denis turned off the lights. He turned on and focused the projector. Film clattered through this antique machine. Music filled the small, narrow room. There, on a stage, alone, was Nadia – dancing. The film was of good quality: steady, colourful, edited together from two angles. Denis sat down.

'An audition,' he said, over the music. 'Sixteen years old.'

Both Ben and Ellen looked at Nadia in the darkness, then back at the screen. Ben finished his glass of vodka and it was refilled. Nadia danced on the screen, wearing a white silk skirt over a white leotard. A chamber orchestra was briefly shown sawing away in the pit: all men, all in shirtsleeves. The music was unknown to Ben; Ellen recognized it as Girov. Ben, who thought ballet was absurd, marvelled anyway at Nadia's shape and control and prettiness. Ellen, who had danced for years, recognized a talent and poise she had never known herself. Ben's response to the film was overwhelmingly an erotic one. Ellen's response was cultural and artistic. It was a good film, ten minutes long, and the American guests applauded when it was over.

Denis turned the lights back on. Ellen said all the right things to Nadia. Ben drained his glass. He felt that this was a personal assault on him as a man. Ben was depressed now, like a Russian who'd had too much vodka to drink. He was dizzy with nostalgia. He remembered his first kiss, which had haunted him ever afterwards. She had said, 'You've never done this?' 'Of course I have,' he'd lied, a twelve-year-old with half a bottle of cheap wine in his brain. 'And I . . . I really like you.' 'You do?' 'I like you fine,' Ben had said, and this sentence had plagued him ever since: 'I like you fine.' What kind of grammar was that? And yet it was one of the most truthful things he had ever said, until the night he approached Ellen and said, 'You are *so* pretty.'

Ben was still *compos* enough to regret that he had drunk

too much, knowing that he had to get up in the morning to drive Sean to the lepers and the Baram Caves. He thought, drunkenly, that when it came time to say goodnight he would circle Nadia's slender waist with his hands and kiss her just *slightly* too close to her mouth. And he would register her response. She might put a hand to the back of his neck – she might signal something. He might even place his palm on her dancer's hip, and draw her to him as he kissed her just slightly, *slightly* too close to her mouth.

'Ben?'

'Sorry?'

'Denis was asking if you had met the General.'

'Ah, sorry. The General? I have *not* met the General. I will do so in about ten days. We're going to open a road. He'll be there for the ceremony.'

'I have met him,' said Denis, pointing an index finger at his own chest. Then Denis scowled with distaste, which reminded Ben that while Americans thought the General was a reasonable compromise at a tricky time and were showering him with dollars, the Soviets were doing everything they could to undermine his regime. 'He is a brutal and dishonest man,' said Denis. 'He lies to his people.'

'Well I –'

'He lies to them and he does not listen. He will fall.'

Ben, thanks to the coffee somewhat more clear-headed than he had been, wanted to enter into a conversation with Denis on the subject of unhealthy governments. He wanted to say that he felt sorry for Denis for having to work for a failed, miserable government and coming from a country where that sound you heard in the night wasn't a teenager breaking in to steal a carpet, but the boot of a leather-coated policeman who was going to take you away to be murdered. This was Ben's understanding of conditions in the Soviet Union at the time. He wanted to dare Denis to visit the United States and try not to *throw up* when confronted with such bounty and freedom.

'That's your opinion,' said Ben. 'I've no doubt you know a great deal more about the situation than I do. Perhaps we shouldn't get into it just now.' Ben caught Ellen's eye and could see how relieved she was that he hadn't risen to Denis's provocative remarks.

Denis, whose voice was hoarse from smoking, made two further attempts to get Ben to open up about his perspective on current events. Both times Ben politely declined. He was proud of himself. He had been lured into this Russian's cramped apartment, plied with liquor, seduced by his wife and a film of her as a girl when she could slowly, slowly raise a pointed toe from the floor to above her head, and he hadn't said a single compromising word about his views or his work. When he looked at Denis now – wearing his sharp suit, speaking his good English, married to his beautiful wife – he saw a man who could have only one kind of job, and it wasn't the approving of visas. Presumably he armed and supported the Left, a small group of parties that were not tolerated under the General (but whose leaders were released from prison and allowed to run for Parliament when the General sometimes nominally ceded power to the politicians). This was bound to be tricky work, and Ben wished he could ask Denis how he went about it.

'I wish one of you would play the piano,' said Ellen.

'Aha!' said Denis, standing. He drained his glass and bowed to his guests. He went to the piano, pulled out the bench and sat down. 'You will sing along,' he said, and launched into 'Yankee Doodle'. This was not at all what Ben and Ellen had expected; nevertheless they sang along, as Denis enjoyed his little joke. Ben wished he knew how to play the *Internationale*.

Nadia played next. Ben didn't know the piece but Ellen recognized it as something-or-other by Maurice Ravel. Brief and haunting, the music was cause for Denis to pour more vodka.

'My friend,' he said to Ben, sitting on the arm of the sofa and placing his hand on Ben's shoulder, 'what a great deal we have to talk about. No?'

'I'm sure that's true.'

'I will tell you about Russia and you will tell me . . . how to have babies.'

Nadia returned from the piano. 'I think it is past my husband's bedtime,' she said.

'Nonsense! Music!' Denis looked drunk for the first time.

Nadia said something to him in Russian that could only have been a rebuke. Ben was now completely sober in comparison with Denis, whose eyes were wide and who let ash fall on the carpet from the tip of his cigarette. Ellen stood up understandingly. Nadia gracefully led them through the dining room to the front door, with Denis taking up the rear shouting 'Nonsense! You must stay! Music! Songs!' Ellen kissed Nadia on both cheeks, then suffered a bear hug from Denis. Ben shook Denis's hand – Denis trying to pull Ben back into the apartment. Ben kissed Nadia just *slightly* too close to both sides of her mouth, placing a hand on her hip.

'We'll take the elevator,' Ben announced, when the apartment door had closed. Now that he was separated from Denis, he seemed drunk again. He pushed the button and stood facing the doors, arms akimbo, *daring* a dead or wounded person to be inside. The doors opened and Ben leapt back as if he'd been struck: a toothless, one-legged old man stood at the back, leaning on a stick.

32

Ben didn't have the hangover he deserved; he was still drunk
when Sean came into the master bedroom at six o'clock in the
morning. Sean had dressed himself. He had even put on his
'mountaineering boots'. He had been looking forward to this
excursion for days. Ben got out of bed and put on the trousers
he had left on the floor. He remembered it was a weekend,
and took the trousers off. The bedroom smelled of Denis's
cigarette smoke. Ben located more appropriate clothes, washed
his face, brushed his teeth and said, 'Breakfast?' While Ellen
slept, Ben prepared French toast. This was quickly eaten, in
relative silence. Sean ate eagerly: he wanted to get going, to
see the lepers and the Baram Caves. Ben drank two mugs of
instant coffee, but knew he was still drunk. Ellen had driven
them home from the Russians' apartment, or so Ben surmised.

Father and son went downstairs to the carport, but not before
Ben had surreptitiously packed his handgun. The Euphoria
growled into life. Ben guided the vehicle down the unfinished
road, past Mancini's house, around the north-west corner of
the Soviet Embassy compound, higher into the hills. It was a
crisp, blue morning, perfect for seeing lepers.

'Here's the map,' said Ben. 'You navigate, my boy.'

'North,' said Sean.

'I can get us to the Meheti Dam. From then on it's unexplored
territory. Isn't this fun?'

'Yes!' shouted Sean. He was excited, sitting up in the passenger seat, buckled in, snacks in a picnic basket in the back,
lepers and caves in his future.

158

Ben was excited too, despite his dizziness and nausea. Here he was with his boy, on deserted streets, climbing into the mountains in a black Euphoria. On the verges of the road men tended their sheep, women carried loads of firewood, smoke plumed from the chimneys of houses built of mud. Ben began to sing: he imitated the sound that wailed across the city every morning, every evening. He was still drunk. Sean joined in. Father and son ululated together and laughed together as they climbed the hills towards the Berevan Mountains and the Baram Caves beyond.

'Do you know what?' asked Sean.

'What.'

'The lepers wear white robes.'

'Do they?'

'Of *course* they do. White robes. They wear white robes like monks and they wear bells around their necks so people know they're coming.'

'Do they?'

'Yes. Robes and bells.'

'Did your friend Daniel tell you this?'

'Yes he did. *And* pieces of their bodies fall off wherever they go. You can pick up their fingers and toes.'

'I don't think so, Sean.'

Father and son wore corduroy trousers, work shirts and grey sweaters. Sean's hair had gone nearly white from the sun, even though it was almost winter.

'My teacher shouted at me yesterday,' Sean said.

'*Did* she? How terrible. What for?'

'I spoke to the girl next to me. Her name is Anne.'

'All you did was speak to her?'

Sean blushed. 'I asked her to be my best friend.'

'Good for you, Sean. I can't believe your teacher shouted at you just because of that. It's unfair.'

'We're not allowed to talk in class. If I'd done it again I would have got a *claque*.'

'*Claque?*'

'Madame Soubrier comes down the aisle and slaps you across the face as hard as she can. That's a *claque*.'

'Has this happened to you?'

'Not yet,' said Sean, smiling. 'But it will.'

'I do hope not.'

'Anne is called "*La Reine des Claques*". She gets slapped about ten times a day.'

'What for?'

'Bad penmanship. Bad spelling. Talking in class. Telling everyone that Constance wasn't wearing undies.'

'This all rings a bell,' said Ben. 'Do you know, when I was at Harvard I got in trouble with a teacher once.'

'Aardvark?'

'Yes, Aardvark.' Sean always called Harvard 'Aardvark'. 'When I was at Aardvark I sat next to a girl I really liked. One morning I spoke to her in the middle of a lecture by a very famous professor. He looked up from his notes, over his glasses, and said, "Please, *Mister* Pelton." I couldn't believe he knew my name. There were about seventy of us in the class and it was early in the semester. "Please, *Mister* Pelton." I just froze. I was frightened. I was so embarrassed. But do you know what? The girl was really impressed. Either that or she felt sorry for me. We became . . . good *friends* for a while afterwards. So the lesson is, Sean, flirting with girls is more important than school.'

'At least the professor didn't give you a *claque*,' said Sean.

'As far as I'm aware they don't give out *claques* at Aardvark.'

'One of the boys at school, an American boy, made an escape attempt.'

'Really?'

'Yes. He ran for the fence. He was at the top, almost over the fence, when they got to him and pulled him down. He was covered in mud. They made him stand in front of the class with his pants down.'

'They did?'

'Yes. And they rapped him on the butt with a ruler.'

'Does that sort of thing happen a lot?'

'That was the only time. So far. His name is Tom and he's dangerous.'

'How so?'

'He carries switchblades and rope.'

'How old is he?'

'Seven.'

'And he carries knives?'

'And rope.'

'I see.'

'He says he can do what he likes because he's the Ambassador's son.'

'The American Ambassador?'

'Well I said he was American, didn't I?'

'What's his last name?'

'I don't know.'

'I'd be surprised if the American Ambassador sent his son to the French School.'

Sean looked up and parroted something he'd heard his father say: 'Are you calling me a liar?'

'Of course not, Sean.'

The city was out of sight behind them now. There were times when there wasn't a car, a building, a person – not even a shrub to be seen in the bright morning light. Ben was elated, even though he thought at any moment he might have to pull over and vomit at the roadside. He tuned the Euphoria's radio to a station that played religious music. Sean tried to sing along, and laughed at the random-sounding melody. Ben thought that there was nothing more beautiful than Sean's laughing. He thought, I'm a good man, I'm a good father.

Their route took them near the Meheti Dam Project. Sean was eager to see it, especially because he enjoyed saying the word 'dam'. Ben turned right at the place Mancini's chauffeur had done during Ben's audition with Ross Howard. He followed the pitted track to the top of the hill, pulled over, stopped the engine. Sean was impressed with the dam, which had doubled in size since Ben had last seen it. It was almost completed.

'Dam, dam, dam,' said Sean, with some relish.

'Do you want to drive down to where the reservoir will be? It's on the way to the lepers.'

'Sure.'

They got back into the Euphoria and drove down the track on the steep wall of the canyon. As they approached the 'leisure activities' building site, now almost finished, Ben spotted Paul Mancini's forest-green Euphoria parked in a vacant patch of ground, next to three other cars and a military van. A group of people stood nearby on the terrace. Unmistakable among the group was Paul Mancini, towering over everyone and wearing weekend clothes.

'Look, it's Mr Mancini,' Ben said. 'Your friend Paul's father. And there's Little Paul, playing with the cement.' Sean already idolized Mancini's son.

Intending to say good morning to his boss, Ben drove to within one hundred feet of the terrace. Now he could see Dominic Thrune in the group of six men. He rolled down his car window. He smiled and waved to Dominic. Mancini hadn't yet seen Ben or registered the sound of the Euphoria. Just then Dominic made a sudden sideways jerking motion with his head – lips thin, eyes full of warning: 'Get away!' Ben must have looked confused, because Dominic repeated the gesture even more forcefully, and added a motion with his left index finger, pointing decidedly *away*. Ben had no explanation for this behaviour unless it was a sensitive meeting that would have been spoiled by the arrival of a father and son on a weekend outing. Ben didn't recognize any of the other men. They weren't from Planning and Resources. They were locals. One of them wore a military uniform.

'To the lepers,' said Ben, accelerating up the track. 'It's not far now. Do you have the binoculars handy, my boy?'

'Got 'em.'

'Look! Look! There's the long, white building! It's the lepers!'

Sean trained his binoculars on the long, white building, still miles away. 'It's too bumpy,' he said. 'I can't see a thing. Go close, go up the mountain. Go closer and stop.'

'I'll put her in four-wheel drive,' said Ben, though there was no real reason to do so. 'Now we're in business,' he said. 'Now we're really having an adventure.'

Up and up they drove. The diversion in the river was visible a thousand feet below them, and the dry river bed leading to the dam.

'That makes thirteen,' said Sean, referring to the carcass of a small truck rusting at the side of the road.

'How do you say thirteen in French?' Ben asked.

'*Treize*,' said Sean, without having to think.

'Clever, clever boy,' said Ben.

'*Quatorze*,' said Sean: a Fardi, denuded and rusting, lay on its side on the verge. There were also pieces of cars, trucks and buses, but they didn't count: drive shafts, doors, engines.

'We can stop here,' said Ben, having pulled into a lay-by that overlooked the long, white building.

They got out of the car and cautiously approached the edge of the canyon precipice. Sean raised the binoculars to his eyes.

'Can you see anyone?' Ben squinted down at the building and thought he could detect movement in the fenced-in yard.

'Yes,' said Sean. 'A large number of lepers.'

'Really? A large number?'

Sean counted. 'Thirteen,' he said, for the second time that day.

'*Treize?*'

'*Oui.*'

'May I have a look?'

Sean passed the binoculars to his father, his tanned little face severe. 'This is *sensational*,' said Sean, using one of his mother's favourite adjectives.

Ben squinted through the binoculars, adjusting them for his more widely spaced eyes. There was the long, white building, its windows barred, its compound fenced in by razor wire. At one end of the compound thirteen men were assembled. They wore white uniforms. There were no crutches on view, no wheelchairs. The men were guarded by soldiers who carried automatic weapons.

'Do you see the lepers?' Sean asked. 'Do you?'

'I see them,' said Ben, as he watched the men being lined up by the soldiers at one end of what was really a parade ground or exercise yard. Four more soldiers rounded the corner of the building, escorting a white-uniformed man who shuffled along between them. The man's hands were bound behind his back.

'May I see?' asked Sean, reaching up for the binoculars.

'In a second,' said Ben, as the prisoner was led to the centre of the parade ground, fifty feet from the other men. The four soldiers unshouldered their weapons and walked a few feet away. The man in the white uniform fell to his knees.

'May I see?'

'Yes, Sean, just a sec, all right? I'm trying to focus.'

'I want to see right now. It was my idea to come see the lepers.'

'I know it was, Sean. Just a minute, little guy.'

The men in the white uniforms jerked to attention; an order must have been given. The bound prisoner kneeling in the centre of the compound bowed his head. This activity took place hundreds of yards away, but Ben thought he could see the sweat shining on the shaved heads of the prisoners. The four soldiers were joined by two others, who had been guarding the thirteen men.

'Can I see now? Please?'

They raised their weapons and aimed at the bound, kneeling man, under orders from an unarmed officer.

'Just a sec, my boy.' Ben swallowed hard and tried to breathe evenly through his nose.

First Ben saw the smoke from the soldier's weapons, and the crumpling of the prisoner – who fell straight backwards on his bound wrists; then he heard the *tak-tak-tak* of the guns.

'What was that noise?'

'Firecrackers, I think, Sean. I'm just trying to see what those funny lepers are up to.'

'I want to see! I want to see!'

The officer walked up and down the line of the prisoners.

'I want to see! *Please!*'

In the centre of the rank the officer slapped a man across the face and seemed to spit in the dust at his feet. Two soldiers approached and pulled the man from the rank by the lapels of his uniform. The man went down on his knees, clasped his hands together in front of his face. He bowed down, then raised his head again, pleading.

'I want to see!' Sean tugged at his father's sleeve.

'I know you do. Just a minute, Sean. I'm just trying to see what the . . .'

The officer took a weapon from one of his men, thrust it into the kneeling man's face. The man seemed to be wailing, and the officer jabbed impatiently at him with the gun. The man raised his clasped hands into the air, begging. The officer turned around as if to spray the rank of prisoners with fire. They cringed, but the officer didn't shoot. The prisoners stood back to attention, or tried to. The pleading, kneeling man had calmed down.

'I want to see!'

'Just a minute.'

The officer circled all the way around the kneeling prisoner with the weapon trained on the man's head. The prisoner, slumped now on his folded legs, put his hands to his chest as if he were trying to pull a knife from his breast. The burst of fire from the officer's gun knocked the prisoner sideways but instantly the man was a curled-up bundle of white uniform on the parade ground.

'I want to see!'

'OK, Sean. I've counted fourteen lepers, though. Two of them are lying down now. Do you want to take a quick look before we go?'

Sean took the binoculars and adjusted them to his face. '*Sensational*,' he said. 'Look, look, can you see? The lepers are going inside. The two really *bad* lepers are having to be dragged. This is *just* the way Daniel said it would be.'

Ben didn't hear most of Sean's narration of events; he was catching his breath at the side of the road, leaning on the hood of the Euphoria.

'Come along, Sean,' Ben said. 'There's nothing left to see now.'

'They've all gone inside,' said Sean. 'Can we come back and look again on the way home? Can we?'

'We'll see about that. Come along. We're early enough to have the caves to ourselves if I step on it. Only about half an hour to go, maybe an hour.'

They drove on up the gorge and soon reached a plateau. The Berevan Mountains themselves were now visible, dusted with snow, fifty miles away, black-looking mountains that did not inspire a climbing urge. The imperative of keeping Sean ignorant of what had gone on at the long, white building had numbed Ben to events. He answered Sean's stream of six-year-old's questions as fast as they came: 'Do lepers have children?' 'Are their children lepers too?' 'Why weren't there any women or children lepers at the leper asylum?' 'How many lepers *are* there in the whole world?' 'Why do they have to live in the mountains behind a fence?' 'Do they want to escape?'

'Why are they guarded by soldiers?' 'What kind of guns did the soldiers have?'

The plateau gave way to another gorge, at the bottom of which were the Baram Caves. There had already been two road signs pointing the way. The road here was modern and smooth. Ben had expected tourist buses, hostels, themed Baram restaurants; instead he simply drove into a dirt parking lot where the map said the caves were supposed to be, or some of them. There was no one about. He stopped the car and climbed out, only to discover that his legs were shaking so badly he could hardly stand.

'Come along, Sean. Let's bring the picnic.'

They put on matching blue windbreakers. Ben helped Sean with his zip, and the boy commented on his father's quaking fingers.

'It's just all the excitement, my boy. What do you think we'll *find* in those caves?'

'I don't see any caves.'

'I think that was the whole point, Sean. To be invisible when times got tough.'

'Who were they hiding from?'

'The . . . government of the day, I suppose.'

'What did they eat?'

'They had crops and animals outside, I'm sure. Or they just stored a hell of a lot of food to last for years and years.'

'A *hell* of a lot?'

'Excuse my language, Sean. It's all the excitement. Let's get going. You won't need those binoculars. I've got the flash-light.'

There was no obvious way to find the caves, but well-worn paths leading uphill towards the sheer face of a cliff seemed the right way to go. Ben did his best to narrate as they climbed, basing what he said on the little he had heard about this place. 'Keep in mind these are *man-made* caves, Sean. Not like bat caves or pirate caves by the sea or the Carlamancio Caves of Venezuela.'

'The what?'

'OK, I made that up. Anyway people just like you and me had to dig their way in here and cut out the caves. Impressive, don't you think?'

'Did they use picks and shovels?'

'Yes they did.'

It was a steep climb, and Ben had to stop every few minutes to gain control over his nausea. He wondered if he should do something about what he had seen – though already he had begun to question whether or not it really had been a pair of cold-blooded executions. It could have been a film set – had he not seen cameras, a crew, a man in a white cap directing?

'I hope this isn't going to be a huge disappointment,' he found himself saying. 'Where are the tour guides? Where are the other people who want to marvel at these so-called caves? Caves my foot, Sean, that's what we'll say to Mama when we get back. Caves my *foot*. Show me caves!'

'What about that little hole there? And that one up there?' asked Sean.

There was a hole three feet in diameter in the side of the cliff, just at the top of the path, and another smaller hole thirty feet higher.

'You call those caves?' Ben asked, and he thought, I'm not crawling in there, not for anything.

'Let's go in,' said Sean. 'This is *sensational*.'

'You first then,' said Ben.

'*What?*'

'Only joking. Let's go. We'll leave the picnic basket here.'

On his hands and knees, Ben crawled inch by inch into the hole. The hole turned out to be a tunnel. He turned on the flashlight and pointed it ahead of him: more tunnel.

'Are you behind me?' Ben asked, hoping Sean wasn't, that

he would have to crawl back out into the sunlight. No one had told Ben there would be tunnels.

'I'm right behind you,' said Sean. 'It's really dusty.'

'You'd think,' said Ben, struggling along, 'that they would have widened the entrance for the modern visitor. *We're* not hiding from anybody.' He held the flashlight on the ground in his right hand. His knuckles were already sore. 'Hey, I see an opening, a cavern,' he said. 'We may be able to stand up in a minute. I sure as hell hope so.'

'Hell?'

'Sorry.'

'I'm right behind you. I'm not frightened.'

Ben stopped crawling and squeezed his eyes shut. Sean had said those exact words so many times during his illness – 'I'm not frightened' – that Ben and Ellen had been required to take turns to go upstairs and recover while the other comforted the boy and made a show of breezy calm.

'All right,' said Ben, opening his eyes and moving forward into cooler air. 'I'm just going to stand up.'

Ben stood, and reached behind him for Sean's hand. The boy got to his feet and dusted himself off. Ben shone the flashlight overhead into the vaulted cavern, then down to the dirt floor, then up to the far wall.

'Wow,' said father and son.

Before them was a ten-foot-high wall-painting of Jesus Christ nailed bloodily to the cross, an orange sky behind his head. The painting was unprotected, faded, smoke-damaged, but high enough on the cave wall to have been safe from vandals for a millennium or more.

'This is it?' asked Sean? '*This* is the Baram Caves?'

'I don't think so,' said Ben. 'I think there's a bit more.'

There was so much more that two hours later Ben and Sean were caked in chalky dirt, dazzled by room after room and chapel after chapel – and they were lost.

'We left the food outside,' said Sean. 'We're going to die of starvation before anyone ever finds us.' He laughed bravely when he said this.

Occasionally they came upon a porthole in the wall, and they could squint out into the sunshine. They were quite high up in the cliffside. Through one of these portholes, Ben caught sight of a paved car park full of tourist buses, as well as a gate, a coffee shop, a souvenir shop. There were people everywhere.

'You know what, Sean? I think we came in through the service entrance to these caves. Take a look.' He lifted Sean up to the hole in the wall, and could feel his son's body relax with relief. He'd been scared, all right, but he hadn't shown it.

'If we go roughly *down*, and to the *right*, we should join up with the mob at some point.'

Some of the rooms were bare, or had simple slabs carved into the walls for beds. Some of the chapels were so small only two people could have worshipped there at a time. Eventually they came to a balcony carved right into the edge of the cliff, a sort of widow's walk where they could breathe fresh air and get their bearings. There was a stunning view of the mountains and another reassuring glimpse of tourist buses hundreds of feet below. Soon they could hear voices, American voices, and they moved in that direction through a narrow passage. They blinked into a lighted room, looking like a pair of filthy spelunkers, to find a group of tourists talking excitedly about what they beheld, which was a beautiful domed chapel whose vibrant wall-paintings had clearly been restored.

'We're safe now,' said Ben, as the tourists turned around in alarm to see these bedraggled figures, as if they were real residents of the Baram Caves. 'Let's go have that picnic.'

After a sandwich and a cup of coffee, Ben started to feel better. He had succeeded in keeping Sean oblivious of the shocking scene early in the morning; he had shown him the 'lepers', he had shown him the Baram Caves. The day had been a success. There had been a point in the caves when he thought he was having a stroke: the horror of those executions; the claustrophobia of a chamber built for people in fear for their lives; the morbid depiction of Christ in every other room with blood pouring from his hands and feet and ribs, his face a vision of torture; his own hangover; his concern for Sean, who seemed to be hyperventilating. But Ben had come through it, had brought Sean through it, with no damage done. They sat side by side on a rock just up the hill from where the Euphoria was parked. They had washed their hands and faces in the restroom of the coffee shop near the main gate to the caves, but their clothes were still grimy. An attendant had given them a strange look as they'd staggered into the sunlight, but accepted retroactive payment for their visit.

'You were very brave in there, Sean.'

'I wasn't frightened.'

'Well, *I* was. I wasn't cut out to be a cave-dweller.'

Ben looked at his son and was so in love with him – with his life-long bravery, his innocence, his optimism, his serenity – that he wanted to preserve him for ever the way he was now. He had suffered so much already that it would be wicked of life to put him through more – but life was wicked: Sean would suffer more. Ben's own struggles had been dutiful, conventional ones that he endured with a pessimist's fatalism. He didn't want Sean to grow up only to believe that life amounted to a dogged pursuit of achievement. Do well in school – be the *best* in school. Never falter. Set up a trajectory in life that would lead to comfort for your family. Take responsibility, above all. Be a man, ignore the *horror* of your journey from accident to accident. Have children so you can worry yourself to death about them rather than about yourself. Ben saw Sean's life spinning away, already out of reach, into a future so certainly dire that all of mankind seemed to toil on blindfolded. Why were there not more people running, screaming, into the streets? It was no wonder that so many tranquillized themselves with alcohol, with drugs, with television. Lately Ben had experienced a recurring dream in which he paddled a canoe up a river in Africa, stopping in villages to shoot the inhabitants in the head with Mancini's handgun – telling himself he was putting them out of their misery. He fantasized also about the girl at the top of the stairs, about this simple vice that, when Ben felt under pressure or particularly upset about the turn his life had taken, he sincerely longed for – a longing he fully intended to suppress. Beautiful Ellen, he said to himself. So brave and pure and understanding. How to explain women? How did *they* hang on?

Ben reached out and gave Sean's narrow shoulders a squeeze. Sean stared out contemplatively at the Berevan Mountains, his white-blond hair ruffled by a light breeze.

'What are you thinking, my boy?'

'I'm thinking,' said Sean, 'that I really feel sorry for those poor old lepers.'

33

Ellen was worried about cholera: there was rumoured to have been an outbreak in the city. People at the club said it was true – someone's houseboy had said hundreds of people had died. Their bodies turned black and they spat up green slime and they died – on buses, in the street, in hospitals. It was highly contagious – it was in the water, in the food. Ellen washed her children's vegetables in laundry detergent before peeling them. She scalded the cutting boards with boiling water. She demonstrated these procedures to Ama and Haz, who looked baffled but willing. On the morning of Ben and Sean's trip to the Baram Caves, she had to go downtown with Nicole on the bus – Sammy took weekends off – to buy curtain rods and mattress covers and to look into buying or renting a piano for Sean. She didn't see anyone dying of cholera, but when they got home she put herself and Nicole into the hottest shower they could tolerate. Candy Mancini said Ellen would get used to it, that no one had ever been seriously ill in their neighbourhood. It was just the foreignness that made Ellen nervous, she said. It wasn't dirty, it was different, that's all. You'll get a couple of bugs, then you will be immune. You should have seen Zaire.

The house was coming along well. It was so starkly new that it felt like living in a showroom – and their furniture looked out of place in the whitewashed rooms – but it was an airy, liveable place with a wonderful view. The pool had been filled, but was soon to be covered up in preparation for winter. A temporary wire fence had been built around the property's southern perimeter to keep the children away from the steep hillside. The beginnings of a small garden were under way in front of the terrace above the carport.

Nicole was still in a peculiar mood. She missed a friend of hers named Anastasia. 'Can we go home now?' she'd ask. 'Not yet,' Ellen said, at first. Then, 'This *is* home, OK?' 'No it isn't.' Efficient as she was – even expert, by now – Ellen didn't consider herself a naturally good mother. She spent hours every day inwardly furious with one or both of her children, while having to adopt a compassionate expression and to speak in the most reasonable tone. When she didn't feel useless she felt like a slave. She could say to herself, I have produced two beautiful children. That is my role. But she didn't *want* that to be her role. She wished there were two of her – one doing what she did now, the other teaching medicine or breeding dogs or . . . or traipsing around the world with Evan Court. She told herself that in a few years things would be different. She could start again. She and Ben would have more time, more peace to be in love for real again rather than simply promising each other, between work and chores, that they were.

In the meantime it was lunch for Nicole, putting up the curtain rods, laundering the mattress covers – and nursing a prickly bolt of worry about something that had happened at Nadia and Denis's apartment last night. It was near the end of the evening, when both men were drunk and the women not completely sober, when Denis had pried a bit obviously into the workings of Planning and Resources. Ben had been firm in not wanting to discuss his job, had parried Denis's forays with questions of his own. He had even winked at Ellen at one stage as if to say, 'You see, I am impervious to this Russian's interrogation.' But then Denis mentioned something about one of Ben's colleagues, someone named Dominic

Thrune. It was an innocuous question, 'He is an Englishman, I think?' And Ben's non-committal reply came out with a sort of bashful laugh and an unmistakable gesture with his hand and wrist that caused Denis to remark, 'He is really that way?' Ben quickly changed the subject, but by doing so only affirmed his almost unconscious implication that it was true, that Dominic Thrune was 'that way'. In the car on the way home Ellen, who was driving, asked Ben if he thought that had been a mistake. Ben claimed drunkenly not to know or to remember what she was talking about. Ellen wondered if she ought to mention it again, if it really were important. In any case, she thought Ben would have forgotten by now – he had rarely been that drunk in all the time she had known him. It amazed her that he had hopped out of bed so early in the morning to fulfil his promise to Sean.

Ellen pondered this and other things as she stood in the sunshine on the terrace, looking back through the glass sliding doors at Nicole being fed her lunch by Ama. She wished Nicole would smile a little bit more often. Ellen couldn't remember the last time Nicole had laughed. It really wasn't normal for a three-year-old to be so severe. Ama made all the right noises as she goaded Nicole into eating – the little girl rarely deigned to lift her own fork and spoon – but Nicole ate impassively, without so much as a normal child's protests. Ellen sighed, and was about to go inside to cheer up her daughter when she heard the sound of footsteps crunching on the track behind the house. She went around the corner past the swimming pool and saw that it was Candy Mancini, with Caroline. Candy had never dropped by unannounced before. She wore dark glasses, and a red sweater over her tennis dress. Caroline waved cheerfully.

'Well, hello there,' Candy said, smiling brightly.

'Hi, Candy. What's up?'

'Well I just couldn't bear not to come by for a gossip, honey. I hear you went to the *most* interesting dinner party last night. You've got to tell me *everything*.'

34

On the way back to the city, with the sun low in the sky in front of them, Ben and Sean were quiet for the first hour. Sean dozed off for a while. They had agreed before leaving the caves that it wasn't worth the detour to the leper asylum, they could save that for another day. After that first hour, Ben suggested they stop for a snack and call Ellen to tell her everything was fine. Ben turned left on to a dirt road, where a sign pointed to the name of a village two kilometres away. Just for fun he shifted the Euphoria into four-wheel drive. When they arrived at the village, it turned out to be an inhospitable clutch of dwellings – no food, no phone. There were children playing in the road – boys using sticks to roll bicycle wheels, girls chasing each other about, all of them barefoot and joyful. Ben slowed down, and the children rushed to his car, slapped at the windows, shouted, climbed on to the rear bumper. Ben smiled and waved, but didn't stop. He felt strangely threatened by these children, and he was worried about the two boys still standing on the bumper of the Euphoria and holding on to the roof rack. He found a place where he could turn around without throwing the boys into the road, and drove back through the village. There were no adults to be seen, no supervision. It occurred to Ben that in the six years of Sean's life, whenever Ben had been in charge of him, he had probably not been more than fifty feet away from his son and never out of sight. Some of the boys and girls charging after his car could only have been three years old. The boys on the bumper sensibly jumped off at the outskirts of the village. Ben looked back at them in the mirror – their dusty legs, their dark hair, their palms raised, waving farewell.

'Why didn't you stop?' Sean asked.

'What do you mean?'

'I could have played with them. Let's go back.'

'I don't think so.'

'Please?'

'No, Sean.'

'They're not lepers, are they?'

'Of course not. Stop talking about lepers, Sean.'

'Then why can't we go back? I want to try that thing they do with the wheels.'

'We can try that at home.'

'I don't have a bicycle.'

'I'll buy you one tomorrow.'

'Tomorrow's Sunday.'

'The shops are open on Sunday here.'

'They are?'

'Yes.'

'And I can have a bike?'

'Definitely.'

They were back on the main road. Ben was hungry and thirsty and impatient. He wanted to call Ellen, but still didn't know if he would tell her about the executions. He didn't want her to think he had exposed Sean to something horrible, which he hadn't. He drove faster, overtaking a small truck loaded with gravel. Sean fidgeted in his seat, and he began to whine. He was tired.

'*Why* couldn't you have stopped?'

'I said you could have a bike.'

'A red one?'

'Certainly.'

'With a light?'

'Sean, it's been a long day. Come on, my boy. Pick up that map and guide us to a town. *Are* there any towns?'

Sean deliberately held the map upside down, but was quiet. Ben took the next turning, and was rewarded two miles later with a village that had a café with a telephone inside. Two white-bearded old men in baggy clothes and wool hats sat at one of only two indoor tables, talking and playing back-gammon. They looked up and nodded hello to Ben and Sean, then returned to their conversation. A younger man came through a back door and welcomed them. In sign language and in English, Ben ordered a beer for himself and a glass of water for Sean. They went outside and sat down. The drinks arrived, and just as Sean was about to take a sip of water Ben remembered the cholera scare. He took the glass away from Sean, which caused a brief scene.

'Have a cola. Have a . . . beer,' Ben said.

'No *thanks*,' said Sean.

Ben felt isolated, out here. He took Sean with him to try the phone, which didn't work. They sat down again and Ben finished the beer, which came in an unlabelled bottle. Sean looked on reproachfully. There were children playing in the road here, too, but Sean showed no interest in joining them. He was tired. So much excitement in one day – if he only *knew*, Ben thought. He put his elbows on the table and his chin on his fists, and frowned. Ben asked for another beer, because the first one had made him feel better: the hangover, the executions, the caves, the boys clambering all over his Euphoria – the beer seemed to make a dent. Sean sulked rather adorably. Ben drank his second beer, wondering vaguely what the playing children's parents did for a living. They certainly weren't lawyers. Ben clumsily paid for his drinks – he still wasn't used to the currency. He had to carry Sean to the car. Sean wasn't happy.

'Sean,' Ben said, as they bumped along towards the main

road, 'we're going to have a lot of adventures like this. I promise you. I have to work a lot but it isn't like before, when I was so tired all the time. Trust me. On weekends and holidays – I get lots and lots of holidays – when you're not in school, I swear, we'll drive around and find things to do and you can bring your friends along if you want. And you can do things with your friend Paul Mancini. You're happy, aren't you?'

Sean shrugged.

'We're going to have parties by the pool. I'll teach you tennis at the club. Isn't the food great? Don't you think Ama and Haz are friendly people? Isn't Mama just *thriving* in this *sensational* place?' Ben's questions had become rhetorical. 'Don't you think it's fantastic that your old father has found such an interesting thing to do? Isn't your school fine? Weren't those caves *incredible*?'

The sun was now so low that Ben had to lower the visor. He had forgotten his sunglasses again. He turned on to the main road, straight into the sun, and accelerated towards the city. Two beers had made a difference, but not necessarily a good one. He tried to squint away the memory of those two shaven-headed prisoners – only a few hours ago – on their knees, pleading. What was the meaning of that? Should he ask someone? Had he seen something significant, apart from the extinction of two lives before his eyes? And there was something else bothering him; it had bothered him early in the morning but had been temporarily erased by the horror at the prison and the claustrophobia in the Baram Caves: something to do with last night, with the Russians. He simply couldn't remember. He disliked not being able to remember, and he *hated* vodka.

'Look out!' Sean shouted.

Ben had strayed to the side of the road, too close to a broken-down bus. It was very hard to see with the sun coming straight through the windscreen, and Ben couldn't concentrate anyway.

'Sorry Sean, thanks,' said Ben. 'I have to be careful.'

They safely passed the bus and on they went. They were in the outskirts of the city now; the sun would set soon. They could take showers at home and wash off the Baram dust. Sean would probably fall into bed without dinner, he was so tired. Houses now cropped up on both sides of the road, with dusty tracks leading into villages larger than the ones they had visited before. Children played everywhere.

Ben reached over and patted Sean's knee, hoping the boy was in a better mood. At first Sean bit his lip and put his chin to his chest, but a moment later he looked up and smiled. If there were one thing Ben was sure of at that moment it was that Sean adored him, depended on him, trusted him. As if acknowledging this mutual love, and as if they were embarrassed by it in a manly way, both Ben and Sean, still smiling, turned their faces away from each other, back to the road.

It was an instinctive turn of the wheel: an object in the road. A ball? A tortoise? A watermelon? It was a turn to the right, not too drastic, just avoiding whatever was in the road. And then came the loud bang on the front right side of the Euphoria – Sean's side of the car, all in a haze of slanting sunlight. Ben straightened the car on the road. He looked up quickly into the mirror. Sean tried to sit up and turn around, but was held in by his safety belt. The boy unlatched the belt and tried to turn around again. Ben pushed him down with his right hand, his left white on the steering wheel.

'Don't.' Ben was surprised he hadn't shouted. 'Don't.'

Sean struggled some more. 'I want to see! I want to see!' he shouted, just as he had done at the prison.

'I don't want you to see,' said Ben. Only seconds had passed. He felt as if his heart had stopped. He spoke automatically. 'It's awful, Sean. I'm sorry. It was a dog. I know I should stop but I can't,' he said, then echoed Candy Mancini: 'The dogs are wild. If we stopped someone would claim it. There would be trouble.'

Ben looked in the rear-view mirror again and saw that the scene had quickly disappeared behind a rise. He let Sean turn around. Sean stood on the seat and looked back at the road, then sat down again.

'We can't go back?'

'No,' said Ben, who had a foul taste in his mouth, whose hair was suddenly damp with sweat. 'Buckle up.'

Sean did so. They drove on for some minutes in silence. The sun set impressively before them. Ben knew Sean was going to say something, and he focused on what it might be. He *prayed* that he was wrong about what Sean was going to say. When Sean looked up it was with the first truly furrowed brow of his short life.

'Papa,' he said, 'that wasn't a dog.'

35

Ellen stood alone on the terrace, wrapped in a shawl, sipping a glass of wine. The sun had set, and the lights had been turned on in the Soviet Embassy compound. The city was a bed of flickering lights with the old town glowing like a light bulb in its middle. Ellen wished Ben had called – he'd said he would. Perhaps he couldn't find a telephone in the mountains. She wanted to tell him about her morning – and much of her afternoon – with Candy Mancini. That woman could certainly talk, and she had a lot to talk about. What had been immediately disconcerting was that she not only knew about the Peltons' dinner last night, she knew some of the substance of their conversation. She knew they had seen the film of Nadia dancing, and when Ellen finally said, 'Come on, Candy, how do you know that?', Candy merely replied, 'They show that film to everyone.' When Ellen volunteered that she and Nadia got on well, Candy said, 'That's good, honey. That's *very* good,' and did everything with her eyes except actually wink.

Caroline adopted her customary pose in one of the deck chairs, knees crossed, hands behind her head, as if she were relaxing over a drink with friends after a game of tennis. She was becoming more like her older brother every day. Ellen couldn't believe she was not much more than a year older than Nicole. Every now and then she injected a wry remark or impatient correction into the women's conversation. The only time she showed childish embarrassment was when her mother told Ellen she was almost certainly going to win the *Prix d'Excellence* at the French School next year. After she recovered, she said, 'Yes, Mom – but if I do, my life will be all downhill from there.'

Caroline was blonde, like her mother, big-boned, like both of her parents. She always wore gaily coloured bands in her hair. When Nicole and Caroline played together, Caroline was the cheerful, charismatic leader, Nicole the glum, reluctant follower. Ellen was torn between resentment that her children would have to live in the shadow of Candy's older and rather extraordinary ones, and the idea that Sean and Nicole might profit from these friendships. She felt the same way about her own relationship with Candy, who was more than ten years older and completely in command of her life and family in a way Ellen had not been even at home. Ellen had always felt that she was biding her time, doing her duty, and that someday soon it would all lift away and she would see clearly what it was she was meant to do with her life. Candy was the sort of woman who had actually *lived*, with no expectation or desire for change.

She was also, after a Bloody Mary or two, the most outrageous gossip Ellen had ever met. The gossip poured out of her without prologue, as if Ellen knew all the characters she mentioned; over the course of three or four hours, Ellen felt she *did* know them: 'The Billionaire Beast is very *in* with Monsieur and Madame de Granges, to the extent – close your ears, Caro – that he's *in* Madame de Granges, if you follow me. At the Club only yesterday he told me she's leaving her husband. This terrifies him. The Beast has a lot of girlfriends, or so everyone says. I think he's *slightly* effeminate. He pretends what he wants is to help his country's economy. What he really wants is that billion *out of here* and a particular villa on the Cap Louise he's had his eye on – if he hasn't already bought it. He wants to recreate the fifties there, girls lounging by the pool at the beck and call of rich men. Poor Madame de Granges. I'm afraid she's almost as old as *I* am. She's in for a disappointment there, and her husband is *so* sweet. The Beast's number-one real mistress is just a hooker, if you ask me, a girl who works out of a hotel. Monsieur and Madame de Granges will be devastated, of course, and the children! Do you want to know how the Beast propositions women? I know this from experience. He goes through a whole cultivated seduction scenario, the compliments, the sudden generosity, then – I don't know *where* he learned this, probably a badly translated American movie – he says, "Baby, you are fantastic. You and me, we'll make beautiful fornication together." Of course under the circumstances no one has dared correct him. His life is such a *ménage*, I can't tell you.' Candy hardly paused for breath. 'Paul says the DiMarkos are splitting up, surprise surprise. Megan is a drunk and I've always felt sorry for Joe – he'll probably have to go home for the divorce. How people can mess up their lives like that – I mean with kids and everything – I just don't know. I wouldn't care if Paul were a *murderer*, I'd stick with him until the kids were at Yale. Aren't you the same way?'

Ellen shrugged.

'Anyway, why would you have to, honey, Ben is such a *dreamboat*.'

'I haven't heard that word in a long time.'

'But he *is*. I love the way he's so . . . *cool*. He doesn't say much, does he?'

'You don't know him very well yet. He opens up.' Ellen didn't want to talk about Ben. She knew where this would lead.

'He's so *young*.'

'He says he's middle-aged.'

'Oh, sure. What does that make me? *God*, I'm so full of lust. Shall we have another one of these?'

'Not for me. You go ahead.'

'Haz!' Candy shouted, then returned quickly to the conversation. 'My Paul is so *old*, suddenly. You're lucky to have a young man.'

'Your husband's not old,' said Ellen. 'He's –'

'Please don't say "distinguished", honey. I hate it when people say "distinguished". Oh, I love the man to pieces. I'll see him into his grave, trust me. It's just . . . Anyway we're having a little impromptu party tomorrow afternoon, after lunch. For swimming if it's warm enough. All of you come. You can meet your Ben's secretary, make sure she's no threat. I happen to know Diane, and she's nothing of the kind.' Candy told Ellen the history of Diane's adult life.

'Jesus,' Ellen said, 'stop.'

'Anyway there'll be lots of fun people – and the Beast, with any luck. You can make beautiful fornication together if you have the energy.'

'Is he really that wealthy?'

'Yes, he really is. And eventually he will be a billionaire if people continue to despise each other and blow each other up. As if they won't. I came right out and asked him how he could live with himself being, you know, literally a merchant of death, and he looked at me like I was out of my mind. He'll have his villa on the Cap Louise, he'll have his ship, he'll have his floozies drooling all over him until he can't get it up any more. The man is only thirty-nine years old, you know. Apparently the whore at the hotel does something – close your ears, Caro – *special* for him. I never know what that means, do you? I stretch my imagination and I never really *know*. I can't visualize the Beast in a hotel room having something "special" done to him by some twenty-year-old French girl.'

'She's French?'

'So I hear. She ran away from home. She's a figure of mystery. No one ever sees her. She stays at the Chevalier.'

'That was *our* hotel.'

'Did you hear anything "special" from the penthouse suite?'

'Nothing.'

'Well I think what gets the Beast going is that she's a prostitute. People can be so peculiar. She's supposed to be incredibly beautiful. So maybe the idea that she *sells* her beauty . . . ? I just have no idea what makes some people tick. At least we can be pretty sure she's making a good living. She's her own woman. For all we know she'll end up married to the Beast and living on the Cap Louise. A fairy tale.'

Caroline listened to all of this as if she were accustomed to discussions of prostitution and exotic sexual tastes. Ellen almost expected the little girl to pipe up and ask for a Bloody Mary. She would never have spoken the way Candy did in front of a child. On the other hand there was something so distracted about Caroline – just like her brother – she seemed elsewhere. She contemplated her fingernails, she closed her eyes and raised her face to the cool sun, she politely covered a yawn with the back of her hand. Her mother carried on through the list of her social set until it was time for lunch. They ate indoors. Haz served, wearing a starched white jacket that was missing a button. Now Caroline came to life. She gossiped just like her mother. Little Paul had told her Sean had a crush on a girl named Anne. Like her mother, Caroline gossiped with little regard for her interlocutors' knowledge of the characters involved. She said the American Ambassador's son had made another escape attempt – this time he'd cleared the barbed wire and made it one hundred yards down the road before he was caught by a janitor. The school's principal had been summoned specially to beat the little boy – an unprecedented punishment, in her brother's experience, all the more so because the beating was carried out in the playground in front of the whole school. Rumour had it that the principal had drawn blood on the boy's buttocks, but Little Paul could not confirm this. He did know that the implement used was a leather strap handed down through generations of French teachers dating back hundreds of years. Little Paul said the pupils had discussed the event among themselves and decided an international incident was not out of the question. The American Ambassador would be furious – and embarrassed. The principal, who had acted in a molten rage, might lose his job.

Candy and Caroline didn't leave until it was time for Candy's tennis match against the Beast. Ellen was left tired and frustrated, without any chores to perform. It was empty hours later that she found herself wrapped in her shawl, sipping her wine, watching the city flickering below. She shivered in the chill and was about to go back inside the house when she heard the Euphoria's engine at the bottom of the hill and saw its lights sweeping across the wall of the Soviet Embassy compound. She went to the top of the steps that led down to the carport, and waited. She heard the car enter. Its engine was extinguished. She heard the slam of both doors, but no chatting. She guessed Sean would be asleep after such a long day, and this was confirmed when she heard only Ben's footfall on the stairs. He came up with a finger to his lips and Sean hanging limply over his shoulder. Ellen followed Ben down the corridor as he untied Sean's boots and stripped him of trousers, sweater, shirt and socks. He took Sean into the bathroom and washed his face, arms and feet with a wet cloth. He took him into the bedroom and slipped on his pyjama bottoms and top, then slid the boy into bed. He came out again and guided Ellen into the living room.

'Good day?' Ellen asked.

'The best,' said Ben. His clothes were dirty. His cheek seemed to be twitching. 'God, I love him.'

36

Ben's manner was now so abstracted he could hardly hear his own words as he narrated a false and sometimes contradictory version of his day with Sean. He saw himself extend a hand to accept a glass of wine. He felt himself sit down in an armchair. He felt himself trying to smile through the twitch in his cheek. 'It was a prison, actually, but I let Sean believe it was a leper asylum. He was so excited. The caves were *sensational*, Ellen. You really have to come see this place. Spooky. It's a longer drive than I thought. We couldn't find a telephone. Sorry. Also . . . I didn't really know if I should tell you this . . . You might find Sean's a little bit upset tomorrow. We hit a dog on the way home. Killed, I'm sure. Sean really was upset and couldn't believe I wouldn't go back. I thought I might. I had the gun. I could have . . . But you know these dogs are wild, they don't belong to anyone. If I'd gone back someone would have tried to claim it and there would have been trouble. So just be warned, he was upset, OK?' Ben took a sip of wine, heard Ellen say something. 'What?'

'Your hand is shaking. You're spilling wine on your shirt.'

'Well, yes. It was awful.'

'Is the car damaged?'

'No. I checked. The Euphoria is sturdy as hell. Anyway it's not just that. I was so hungover this morning. I'm exhausted. The caves gave me the creeps. I wouldn't have gone in there if I hadn't wanted to set an example for Sean. He was so brave. He pretended he wasn't frightened. We had to crawl through *tunnels* . . .'

'Are you all right, Ben? What can I get you? Do you want to take a shower?'

'That's a very good idea. A hot shower. Maybe just one more glass of wine – I can get it.'

'Let me. Jesus, Ben, you're a wreck.'

'I'm not a wreck.'

Ben used both hands to drink the next glass of wine. Ellen was saying something. She was talking about Nicole. 'I'm worried,' she said. 'She's really not snapping out of it. She's depressed.'

'Three-year-olds don't get depressed.'

'That's the only word I've got. She doesn't smile. I don't know what to do.'

'She'll be fine. So will Sean.'

'I'm not worried about Sean.'

'I'm going to take that shower.'

Ben walked down the corridor on weak, trembling legs. He turned on the shower and took off his clothes. He got in under the hot, mineral-tasting spray and drew the curtain. He was alone now, so he could claw at his head and open his mouth in a mute scream and bend at the waist and knees. He pressed his fingertips into his temples, then banged a fist against the tiled wall. He lifted his face into the stream of water and took in then spat out mouthful after mouthful, until he was dizzy from not breathing. This catharsis lasted only minutes, but in its intensity left Ben wrung out and oddly calm. He turned off the shower, opened the curtain, stepped out, wrapped a towel around his waist. He used another towel to dry his hair. He wiped steam from the mirror with his hand, and looked at himself. Reflected over his shoulder, standing in the doorway, was Ellen. Ben smiled a twisted smile at his wife, and smoothed his hair with his palm.

'You look completely deranged,' she said.

'Well I . . . It's that dog. It was awful. I hoped Sean hadn't seen anything. He was falling asleep at the time. The sun was in our eyes. I don't think he saw a thing, actually. He *said* he did. But he didn't. He didn't see a thing.'

'Then why do you say he's upset?'

'Because I was so rattled. He kept asking me if I was all right.'

'Are you?'

'Of course.' Ben was still looking into the mirror, so he could see the reflection of his twitching face as he spoke.

'Good. Come on out and have something to eat. I have lots to tell you. Candy's having another party tomorrow. We have to go, I guess.'

'Terrific,' said Ben, smiling so hard his lips clicked as they separated from his gums.

Ellen went away. Ben finished drying himself, brushed his hair, put on a bathrobe. He walked barefoot down the corridor to the kitchen. Ellen was making him a chicken sandwich, and already speaking to him over her shoulder. He understood only snatches of what she said. He had to squint to focus his eyes. He leaned against the door frame. '. . . seemed to know everything about the dinner party last night . . . creepy . . . hours of gossip . . . Little Paul . . .' Trying to think was like trying to reel in a too-big fish. Planning was an impossibility. '. . . Caroline and Nicole . . . why won't she smile . . . a glass of wine?' Ben reached out and took the glass with both hands. The urge to confess had already surfaced, but had to be suppressed. Ben was sure of it, this time. He could not break down, not until they came to get him, which was likely to be soon – probably tonight. He had to say something to Ellen, something normal, cheerful. The natural thing to do would be to respond to what *she* was saying, but he couldn't follow her. He ought to say something about the Baram Caves. He ought to comment on this terrible wine. 'Your secretary will be there. Candy told me all about her awful, awful time. After talking to Candy I

191

feel as if I know all these people. Candy's too much. She also said I'm supposed to accompany you to the road opening on Wednesday. Is that so? What will I wear? Ben?'

'Sorry. Sorry?'

'The road opening. Aren't you listening to me? I'm supposed to be the doting wife. What will I wear?'

'You'll be beautiful. It's getting cooler. It sometimes snows this time of year. Bring a coat.' Ben couldn't imagine he would be at the road opening.

'Here's your sandwich. Why don't you sit down.'

Ben sat down at the breakfast table and tried to eat.

'The satellite dish arrived this afternoon but they didn't know how to install it. Someone is supposed to come on Monday or Tuesday. It's terribly ugly, much too big. The Mancinis have one so I thought it wouldn't be in bad taste. I can't live without the news.'

'The news is always the same,' said Ben, after swallowing with difficulty. 'It's Evan Court you want to watch.'

'True enough,' Ellen said, sighing.

'The news is *always* the same. You could avoid the news for the whole time we're here and it would be the same damned thing when we got home. Some of the names would have changed but you wouldn't notice.' Ben spoke automatically. He thought he sounded normal.

'Are you sure you're OK?'

'Just tired,' said Ben, slumped over and unable to sit up straight. 'I want to go to bed if that's all right. It's another long day with the children tomorrow.'

'And Candy's party.'

'That too.'

'She says the Billionaire Beast might be there – the arms dealer? Also – this is how Candy makes conversation – that he's having an affair with Madame de Granges, who wants to leave her sweet husband for him, but that the Beast's true number-one mistress is a twenty-year-old French hooker who works out of the Chevalier and does something "special" for him.'

Ben's ears pricked up. He swallowed the last of his sandwich. Ever since Sean had fallen asleep in the car – after a period of more than an hour driving in circles trying to *hypnotize* the boy into believing he'd seen nothing, or at the very most a wild dog – Ben had found himself not just quaking and sweating and dizzy with fear, but . . . pathologically aroused. The Wiesman crisis had triggered Ben's dispassionate climb to the top of the stairs; the accident – not the accident, Ben's *failure to stop*; he had rationalized that much – had soon made him wild with unfocused physical desire.

'At the Chevalier? Something "special"?'

'Hilarious,' said Ellen. 'What could that mean?'

'I don't know. What *could* that mean?'

'If you ever want something *special*, Ben, just say the word.'

'Well, you too, of course. Say the word.'

'Except,' said Ellen, 'I don't think it's supposed to be discussed.'

'Not in my family it isn't,' said Ben.

'No, I mean, men are just supposed to lash out at a woman and she likes it. That sort of thing. If you ask first you take away the element of . . . taboo.'

'If you're asking me to hit you, Ellen . . .'

'If you do I'm leaving. No, it's just an example. Tell me. Think hard. What do you think the Beast gets from that woman that's so special? And do you think he asked for it, or she just knew?'

'I'm too tired to think,' said Ben. He was listening for cars on the track outside, or sirens.

'Come on.'

'OK. I suppose if you're starting from the premise of a twenty-year-old French girl –'

'Who's gorgeous –'

'– who's gorgeous. I mean, how "special" does it have to be?'

'You're not trying hard enough.'

Ben thought he could see now that Ellen wanted to make love. He'd come home so virile and fatherly and covered in grime. He'd showered but not dressed again. She thought he'd killed a wild animal with his Euphoria. Ellen wasn't tired. She hadn't spent the day driving into the mountains, watching executions, crawling through chalky tunnels, killing on the road, hypnotizing Sean. She was sitting close enough at the table that he could smell her hair.

'I'll try to think tomorrow,' said Ben. 'Right now my mind's a blank. Really.'

'I think it's something extremely complicated. A ritual. Don't you?'

Look, Ben wanted to say: he pays a beautiful young girl for her body. He has absolutely no qualms about this because he's not married and hasn't any morals anyway – he's an *arms dealer*, for Heaven's sake. He's so rich it would be like me buying a book of matches. She tells him he's fantastic and when he's finished he simply ... *leaves*. This ought to be obvious. It's known to happen quite a lot. I want it to happen to *me*. 'Let's drop it for now, sweet,' he said instead. 'I don't think you realize how tired I really am.'

Ellen pulled her chair closer and placed her hand on Ben's exposed thigh. 'My poor darling,' she said. 'One day in the countryside and you're a wreck.'

'True enough.'

'Don't worry about that dog. It was probably rabid anyway, at the very least. Here, relax.'

'Please,' said Ben. 'Don't do that.'

'I love doing that.'

'No, really, please.'

'You don't seem to mind. Not *really*.'

'Ellen, please.'

'No, let me. Just this. I like it.'

'I'm very . . . *uncomfortable*. I said *stop* it.'

'Oh, baby.'

'How much wine have you had?'

'Not enough, Benjamin. You know, if I spend another day exactly like this one I'm going to do nothing *but* drink wine. I have to get a job.'

'You've been busy enough. We just got here, it seems like.' Ben's fists were balled on his knees. He kept his head cocked towards the track outside.

'Please, *don't*.'

'But I like it.'

Ben pulled away and drew breath to shout, then controlled himself.

'God, Ben.'

'Don't "God, Ben" *me*. Christ, Ellen, you don't have a *clue*. I'm under a lot of . . . *strain*. OK?' Ben stood up. 'You're just . . . *teasing* me.'

'Well,' said Ellen, raising her chin, 'I was *trying* to.'

When Wiesman had sacked him, Ben had gone through several weeks of detachment, but had been aware of the cliché in his mind each morning when he awoke and thought, 'This can't be happening to me.' Now he was detached again, but it no longer seemed like a cliché: this *couldn't* be happening to him. He saw himself having an irrational argument with his unsuspecting wife. He saw himself in his ill-fitting bathrobe in his house on a hill in a foreign country with his children asleep, about to shout at his blameless wife. He knew what lay in the road behind him – and ahead. Words came out of his mouth in series, correctly, angrily; and he couldn't stop himself.

'You're so . . . *selfish*,' said Ben, as if choosing a word at random. 'Give a thought to what I have been through. It's just the way it was when you were pregnant. When the kids were tiny. When they were sick. You were like some queen bee at the centre of your hive, expecting all the workers to buzz around doing your bidding. You never gave a *thought* to me, to Karin, to Monique, to Else, to anyone slaving around you. All you ever said was do this, do that. I'd come home soaked in sweat off the train with eleven hours behind me and I'd be greeted with "Read to your son." Could you have said hello first? Who the *hell* gives you the right, sitting home all day, doing *your* job – which doesn't exactly require a *degree* – to treat me like a nameless *assistant*, someone you snap your fingers at over your shoulder without even *looking* at?' This had happened to Ben before. He heard himself hurting his wife, who was not exactly soft, but could not stop himself. It was exactly, exactly like the most meretricious summing-up to which he had ever contributed. 'Look at you now. Smug. Safe and snug. Your husband has to hang his butt out there for you, for . . . for *your* children, so that *you* can be comfortable, *you* can be happy, while I'm so close to the edge all the time with the work and the stress and picking up the slack at home and *paying* for everything.'

'Ben, you're insane.'

'Oh, I'm *insane*. Is that the best you can do? "Insane"? Terrific, Ellen. Do you know what "insane" means?'

'Yes. I'm looking at it.'

'Insane is *not* what you're looking at. You're looking at someone who's got to *bottle up* every damned thing all the time, who's not allowed to complain, who is powerless to change anything, who comes about eighteenth on the list of what is important, after *everything*.'

'You're incoherent.'

'That's the last thing I am.' Ben wiped his mouth and prepared to say more, to do more damage. Then through the kitchen window over the sink, he saw lights on the track outside. 'They've come,' he said.

'What did you say?'

Ben looked down at himself. He wasn't dressed for escape. He closed his robe and tied it tightly at his waist. He felt his body pulling in two directions: towards the Euphoria downstairs; towards the French windows leading to the pool and the scrubby hill beyond. His mind raced so quickly he even had time to imagine scaling the wall of the Soviet Embassy compound, handing himself over, asking for Denis by name, demanding immunity in exchange for his defection.

'*What* did you say?' Ellen asked again.

'Nothing.' Ben wrapped his arms around himself and closed his eyes. He heard a heavy car door slam outside.

'Let me just see what she wants,' said Ellen.

Ben opened his eyes. He heard the back door open. He heard Ellen greeting Candy Mancini, who barrelled into the kitchen apologizing for having left Caroline's sweater behind earlier in the day.

'Well *hello* there,' she said to Ben. 'Nice legs.'

37

Dominic Thrune's casual clothes were a sight: a candy-cane blazer over a sky-blue chamois shirt; too-tight blue jeans belted with twine; plastic sandals like the ones the locals wore. Far from being uncomfortable surrounded by married couples and their numerous children, Dominic threw himself into the occasion beside the Mancini pool, and even threatened to swim.

'You've caught the sun, I see,' he said to Ben, who wore dark glasses to conceal what he knew were bloodshot, fearful eyes. The morning had been a tense one: Sean slept late and awoke mute and confused; last night's regrettable argument went unmentioned; Ellen, though cold, pretended normality for the sake of the children.

'I took my son to the Baram Caves yesterday.'

'I know,' said Dominic.

'What?'

'That is to say, Candy told me. Nothing escapes that woman, nor does it go unreported.'

'I see.'

'I met your wife when I arrived. What an absolute *dear*. And that's your little girl?' He pointed across the pool at Nicole, who stood all alone near the path that led to the garden, examining a purple flower.

'Nicole, yes. We're a bit concerned. She's awfully introverted.'

'You should have seen me,' said Dominic. 'I'm told I didn't speak to anyone for more than a year when I was a child. After that I spoke only to animals for a further year. I look back on that period as a sign of my latent and still unrealized genius. Don't worry.'

'Parents always worry.'

'Ah, look. Your trusty assistant has arrived.'

Diane came up the steps, followed by her son and her surviving twin daughter.

'Just think,' said Dominic, 'there used to be *two* of those.'

'Please,' said Ben, but he had been thinking exactly the same thing. Diane's daughter tossed back her long, straight brown hair and alighted on the deck. Ben lowered his dark glasses and looked over their rims at the girl, who wore a man's blue button-down shirt untucked over white shorts.

'Now, don't stare,' said Dominic.

'But she's . . .'

'Her name is April.'

'She's . . .'

'I know. She gets her looks from her late father. You're staring again.'

'How old is she?'

'She must be all of fifteen by now.'

'Oh, God.'

'So stop thinking your filthy thoughts and let's have a drink.'

Ben followed Dominic to a buffet table where beer and wine were being served by Yelam and Tamina. A stocky, hirsute man stood there chatting with Paul Mancini.

'Let me introduce you,' said Mancini. 'Ben Pelton, this is Chava Hannan.'

'Everyone calls me Chava,' said the man, shaking Ben's hand. 'Hello to you too, Mr Thrune. Fantastical jacket.'

For once, Dominic looked ill at ease. Ben knew they had just been introduced to the Billionaire Beast.

'Chava was just telling me that he feels like one of those tennis robots when he plays my wife,' said Mancini.

'She is too good. The most fantastical player at the club. If I win one game, I am a happy man. She could be professional. I get all of my exercise from her,' he said, patting his bulging stomach. 'I love her and I want to marry her but her husband insists this is not happening.'

'When I'm dead you will be first in line I'm sure,' said Mancini.

Hannan raised his glass and said something in the local language. Dominic repeated the phrase and drank.

'What does that mean?' asked Ben.

Dominic finished swallowing and said, 'It's along the lines of "Let Heaven be patient."'

'Where is your wife?' asked Hannan.

'Right over there, with my son,' said Ben.

'Ah, yes. I met her at the club. *Such* a lovely young woman. I want to marry her too.'

Ben wanted to say, 'You'll have your chance.' Instead he did his best to smile jovially at the merchant of death. Hannan was only two or three years older than Ben, but he had an air of power and accomplishment about him that made him seem older. He wore a grey pin-striped suit over a white, tieless silk shirt buttoned at the throat, which would have made Ben look like a recently released convict; on Hannan it looked like money. He wore a heavy gold watch and a large diamond ring. His black hair had been lightened to honey at the temples. His short beard had been shaved in a straight line across his Adam's apple, and was flecked with grey below his cheeks.

'As you can tell, I am unmarried,' said Hannan, his English roughly accented. 'Not for long, I tell you. The women adore me, isn't that true, Paul? They fall on their feet for me!'

'They fall on their feet for you,' Mancini replied.

'One of these women, she will be my wife and the mother of ten children, if God wills it.'

'I'll drink to that,' said Dominic.

'Ben Pelton,' said Hannan, smiling brilliantly and looking up at the taller man. 'I am very attracted to you.'

'Well I . . .'

'I am very attracted to you and your wife and . . . you say that is your son?'

'Yes, there's Sean, there. And that's Nicole, over there by the diving board.'

'They are so beautiful. And therefore I am hopeful that when you can, you will come with me on my boat. Yes?'

'That's very kind of you. We would be delighted,' said Ben.

Mancini, behind Hannan's shoulder, nodded like a woodpecker.

'Excellent,' said Hannan. 'Your children will swim. We will play backgammon for the highest dollar. I will try to make beautiful fornication with your wife but she will probably threaten to cut off my pipi. OK?'

'OK,' said Ben.

'We will drink *karat* until we shoot ourselves.'

'Fine with me.'

'Do you scuba?'

'I have scuba dived.'

'Good. Before we shoot ourselves, we scuba.'

Ben, trying to smile, caught a glimpse of April taking off her shirt on the other side of the pool. This caused him to gulp and sigh in a way that was unmistakable to Hannan, who turned and looked over his shoulder.

'Oh, no, my sweet God,' he said. 'Please, no, it is painful. Paul, cover up your guests, you are upsetting me and Mr Pelton.' He did not mention Dominic.

It was curious to see Mancini, normally himself the centre of attention and the focus of power, deferring to Chava Hannan. He had even managed to shrink in size by bending his knees and slumping his shoulders, so as not to tower over the shorter arms dealer.

'Chava has been kind enough to invite me and my family to his boat on three occasions over the years,' said Mancini.

'Yes, but it's a different boat now,' said Hannan. 'I was given this new boat by a dear old friend who now has a ship so enormous he can land his aeroplane on her. I exaggerate of course. But we must all keep going up, up, up, must we not?' The other men nodded dumbly. 'Sailing, I do not like. I like to scuba, I like to entertain. I have many friends. Come soon, before the weather gets too cool. Even at the coast, it can get cool. That is terrible because the girls keep their clothes on,' he said, glancing back at April, who was now peeling off her white shorts to the light-blue bikini underneath. 'Oh,' said Hannan, 'it is too painful. I must go make a reservation with her for her next birthday.'

Ben had been in a daze of exhaustion and incredulity all day. He had managed to go to sleep at dawn, only to jerk awake an hour later with his heart pounding and a shout almost escaping his mouth. All day his stomach had ached and his mouth had been dry and he had been short of breath. Just before noon he had retched in the kitchen sink when no one was looking. He had suggested that his family walk down to the Mancinis' house, on the pretext that it would be too crowded to park – he didn't even want to *look* at his Euphoria. Ellen walked ahead with the children. She had been so frosty since his irrational tirade the night before – which had continued for an unbelievable three-quarters of an hour after Candy Mancini went away; Ben had railed at Ellen, pointed his finger in her face, lectured, made her cry, thrown up his hands as if he were the one who was misunderstood and exploited – he knew he had to pick a moment for apology and excuses. He wanted to apologize before they came to take him away. It wouldn't be long, he knew. This knowledge made him giddy. He was surprised at how easy it was to converse with Dominic, with Mancini, with Chava Hannan. In an odd way it was as if he had been liberated from an invisible dungeon of responsibility. What would a *faux pas* mean now? They were coming to take him away. He could do as he liked on his hallucinatory cloud of slender freedom – or this brief purgatory before judgement. He imagined he looked suave now, burning on the inside with a miserable guilt and fear, pursed-lipped and debonair on the outside. No wonder Hannan had taken such a shine to him, if what he felt in his guts was for some reason broadcast as existential calm. He was out of his mind.

Sean had to be watched. Ellen hadn't brought up the accident, consummate mother that she was. Sean had said nothing, nothing at all. Ben had tried to distract him with a special kind of paper aeroplane that his own father had taught him to make when Ben was Sean's age. The trick was using heavy but malleable paper. Scissors had been necessary to cut ailerons. A paper-clip in the nose stabilized the result. He used a ladder to climb to the flat roof of the house and he flew the plane all the way down the hill, right over the Mancinis' house. It landed in the street just short of the high wall surrounding the Soviet Embassy compound. A car came round the corner and crushed the plane. Nicole looked on as well, utterly impassive in her red party dress.

'Ben Pelton,' said Hannan, licking a mouth so pink he could have been wearing lipstick, 'I love America.' In Hannan's accent, Ben saw his country's name spelled 'Amerika'. 'My favourite is New York. New York! To tell you the truth I am lying. I don't like America except for business. I love Paris. I go to Paris for the love of the place, just to be there without myself, do you understand?'

'Yes.'

'And the south of France. The Cap Louise. That is where I have my house. You will come visit someday.' Hannan had Ben by the elbow now, as if they were drunk and laughing at their own jokes. 'Up, up, up!' Hannan said. 'What more can we do?'

Ben thought Hannan must have meant 'Onward, onward, onward!', but couldn't be certain. Ben also found that he was clutching his glass to his chest with one hand folded over the other: his right hand still trembled so badly he couldn't use it to raise his glass. The wine seemed to help, though, when he could use his left to get it to his mouth.

Now Hannan moved on, shaking hands; Mancini followed him like a courtier, making introductions. Ben was tempted to follow as well, but his legs felt uncertain and his cheek had begun to twitch again. He found himself staring at Diane's daughter – she had walked to the edge of the pool and now took far too long standing there preparing to dive. Ben couldn't remember the last time he had seen that shape on a girl, that sleekness and near-grace that was still *just* too awkward. It drove him crazy. He kept staring. After the girl dived into the pool Ben shook his head, as if to clear it, and looked away. His gaze fell suddenly on Ellen's, ten feet away. She squinted at him with a kind of angry puzzlement, as if to say 'What has got *into* you?'

Ben looked away defensively. There, near the ping-pong table, were Sean and Little Paul, speaking to each other in what struck Ben as a fairly intense way for small boys. What was Sean doing with his hands? He was weaving his hands this way and that, as if they were describing . . . the Baram Caves? That had to be it. He was relating the story of his visit to the Baram Caves – those tunnels and chapels and the balcony – that's what he was doing, left, right, through the caves. Dear Little Paul, who'd seen the caves a dozen times, listened patiently. Ben was sure Sean was describing the caves.

A police car came down the road from the far end of the Soviet Embassy compound. Ben saw it right away. It was a white, van-like vehicle with an orange light on its roof and a broad red stripe along its doors. It slowly passed the parked cars of Mancini's guests and approached the road that led up to Mancini's house.

'It's the coppers,' said Dominic Thrune, who had been standing silently at Ben's side. 'You don't want to fall foul of *them*, I can tell you. The stories one hears. I had occasion to visit the Shika Prison – a guided tour, you understand. Even the *sanitized* version was ghastly. It's the parts *below ground* that are supposed to be utterly appalling.'

Ben felt he was losing his balance – he actually had to extend one arm to steady himself. The van neared the turning and slowed. A civilian car passed in the other direction. The police van turned into the hillside road and began to climb towards the Mancinis' house and, by extension, Ben's house. The police van came to a stop and its engine cut out. The passenger door opened and a trim police officer emerged, putting on his red-brimmed cap as he did so. Another policeman got out of the driver's side, then another two from the back of the van. Everyone by the swimming pool now looked at the police, as if each had a deadly criminal secret that might now be about to be exposed. Paul Mancini excused himself from Chava Hannan and walked at his full height towards the men.

Ben caught movement out of the corner of his right eye: Little Paul wanted to follow his father; Sean wanted to follow little Paul.

'Sean!'

Heads turned towards Ben, who had shouted so loudly a woman nearby had jerked her hand to her mouth in alarm – that was Ellen.

'Sean, sorry, stay here please,' said Ben, in a controlled voice, putting a hand on his son's shoulder. 'Let Mr Mancini see what the trouble is.'

'Not another robbery, I hope,' said Dominic, insouciant as ever. 'Makes me glad I live in my little hovel in the valley. You chaps in your villas . . .'

Mancini had reached the policemen, who took off their caps and shook hands with him. The guests pretended not to be interested and resumed their conversations. April pulled herself out of the pool in one long movement and dripped towards her towel. Ben squeezed Sean's shoulder too tightly, so that the boy had to pull away. He couldn't look at Ellen. He watched Mancini talking to the policemen and shaking his head. Mancini looked first once, then again, over his shoulder towards the pool. He frowned and shook his head again. Then he nodded decisively and turned to walk back to his guests. As he approached he raised a hand and gestured at Ben: 'Come here.'

38

Ellen looked on as her husband walked stiffly over to Paul Mancini; the taller man leaned down to say something into Ben's ear. Right away she wondered if this could have anything to do with the dead dog, and if Ben would be in any trouble. What could it mean but an apology and paying off the owners? Ben could use the excuse that he had Sean with him in the car and didn't want to upset him; that he had assumed the dog to be wild. Ellen looked down to see Nicole raising her hands, wanting to be picked up. Ellen hoisted the girl on to her hip.

Now Mancini beckoned Chava Hannan, who raised his eyebrows at the invitation but glided over to the other men after kissing the hand of the woman to whom he had been speaking. The men's huddle lasted half a minute, then Ben and Hannan walked quickly away towards the policemen. Paul Mancini returned to his guests.

'Some awful news, I'm afraid,' he said. 'I hate to have to say.' His guests had turned towards him in a semicircle. 'Mr Hannan's car was ambushed on its way here. This is awful. One of his men was injured. I don't know why I say that – one of his men was killed.' Mancini looked uncharacteristically ill at ease. He drew a hand backwards across his short white hair then wiped it on the side of his blue blazer. Some of the guests grumbled in disbelief or outrage, but on the whole the news was taken as an annoying interruption of a fruitful party. 'Ellen, I sent Ben along to help out if he can. I didn't think I ought to go myself. Mr Hannan is going to have to make a lot of arrangements and most of his people are at the coast. This is so . . . unprecedented. We never expected anything like this. It's going to be news. There was another bomb downtown last night. Only a small one. If this is related . . .'

Ellen watched Ben climb into the back of the van with two policemen and Hannan. She saw that as the officer on the passenger side got in, he lifted a weapon of some kind off the seat and placed it in his lap so that its muzzle pointed out of the window. The revolving orange light came on atop the van. The driver turned the van around and did not switch on the siren until he'd reached the asphalt road.

'I would have *thought*,' said Candy, in a voice loud enough to be heard over the siren down below, 'that after all that excitement some of you would want a *drink*. Yelam!'

'Hear, hear,' said Dominic. 'No need to evacuate just *yet*.'

Ellen couldn't believe Ben had sped away with the police without so much as a look over his shoulder. She hoped he wouldn't be gone too long, because she really wanted to tear into him for his inexcusable behaviour of the previous night. Their arguments – when they had time to argue, when the children were asleep – had been increasingly that way: Ben ranting and lecturing; Ellen biding her time and waiting for him to return the next day with a grovelling apology. It was childish. Last night, though, had been vicious, extraordinary. Ellen thought she had enough on her hands without an unhinged husband. She had sometimes worried that his commuter's routine had turned him into an emotional robot, but this was worse. At least it was a good sign that Mancini had trusted him to accompany Chava Hannan downtown.

'Ellen,' said Mancini, coming up behind her, 'sorry about this.'

'Well, it's just too awful.'

'I can't believe it. Sorry to send Ben off, but . . .'

'But?'

'Well, I wanted to say I'm really impressed with the way he's handled people. He's got a real . . . *power* to him. Chava latched on to him like *that*.' Mancini snapped his fingers. 'So I thought I'd let them get to know each other better, even under these circumstances.'

Ellen was shocked. 'At a time like this? His – what, when his *bodyguard* has been *assassinated*?'

'Did I forget to tell you how cynical I am?'

'You must have.'

'It's not that, really. It's just that this is our party and there are still guests to come who ought to be told. I thought sending Ben was a solution. He's a lawyer, after all – lawyers can do anything. I couldn't let Dominic go along, he would have . . . magnified the drama.'

Dominic was on the other side of the pool playing ping-pong with Little Paul, as Sean looked on. Nicole played with her mother's hair and remained mute as always.

'Hello, Nicole,' said Mancini, leaning down. 'Hello there.'

'She's in a bad mood,' said Ellen. 'Aren't you, my darling?' Nicole let her mouth and cheeks relax unattractively, like a drooping baby. Ellen sighed and spoke to Mancini again. 'How bad is this . . . incident? I had no idea he was such an important man.'

'It's not so much importance for now as celebrity. New York took a shine to him not so long ago – to his money, I mean – so he's well known in the States now. This will be news, believe me.'

'What is his name, again?'

'Chava Hannan.'

'Oh, my . . . Oh, well, of *course* I've heard of him. Sorry, I had no idea. I'd never seen his picture really unless it was in a group with other . . . Well, you know what I mean.'

'Yes.'

'When I met him at the club, Candy just called him the Billionaire Beast.'

'I wish she wouldn't do that. I suppose she disapproves.'

'And you don't? He's a complete –'

'No need to get into that. Things are more complicated sometimes than people understand. Here, have you met Diane? And this is her daughter.'

'Hello, Diane,' said Ellen, trying not to let her forced smile betray what she knew about the woman's ordeals.

'My daughter, April.'

Ellen had seen Ben staring at this girl, and didn't blame him. And she thought: there used to be two of her.

'Someone got killed?' April asked.

'You mustn't think this sort of thing happens all the time,' said Diane, cordially. 'There hasn't been anything like it for . . . well, *months*, really. Isn't that right, Mr Mancini?'

'Yes. A man named Karani. A young man. An artist – a painter, wasn't he?'

'Poet,' said Diane.

'A poet. Murdered. He was politically active. On the *right*, believe it or not. Funny country.'

'Hilarious,' said Ellen.

Most of the guests circulated excitedly: they were involved in an international incident. New guests arrived to be greeted by Candy and told the news. Yelam applied flame to the charcoal barbecue. The party would carry on. Ellen overheard snatches of conversation among the Westerners. The locals smoked cigarettes and tried to smile:

'Isolated . . .'

'Rare . . .'

'Religious left . . .'

'Religious right . . .'

'Political left . . .'

'Student radicals . . .'

'The General will have to crack down . . .'

Nicole raised her head from Ellen's shoulder and spoke for the first time in hours. '*Who* got killed?'

Ellen was saved from having to reply by the glowing return of Dominic Thrune. 'I simply *thrashed* your son,' he said to Mancini, who appeared to wince at the remark. 'I thought I ought to distract him from this business with a spot of table tennis.'

'Thank you.'

'Will this affect the ceremony at all, at the road, do you think?'

'No need to talk shop now, Dominic. Let's let the dust settle.'

'Sorry. Of course. Look,' he said, lowering his voice, 'I ought to mingle with our local friends. They look a bit down in the mouth over this.'

'Good idea. Don't be *too* jovial, Dominic. Sombre, OK?'

'Right you are.'

'He speaks the lingo perfectly,' said Mancini, when Dominic had eased himself into a group of sour-looking men and their wives. 'He'll smooth things over.'

'I love his clothes.'

Mancini sighed. 'He's a . . . character.'

April asked Ellen, 'What's your daughter's name?'

'What's your name, sweetie?' Ellen asked Nicole, lifting the girl's chin. Nicole stared into the distance. 'Come on, honey. Tell April your name.' Nicole seemed to be looking at the tall trees in the centre of the Soviet Embassy compound. 'Her name is Nicole,' said Ellen, who was exasperated by her daughter. 'She must be tired.'

'Would she like to come play with me?' April asked.

'That's a terrific idea, April, thank you,' said Ellen, who was taken aback: the men, including her husband, had been slavering over April's beauty, her sexuality, when she was still just a girl. She put Nicole down, and Nicole reluctantly took April's hand. They walked slowly together towards the pretty garden path.

'She's available for baby-sitting,' said Diane. 'She's awfully good at it. She loves children.'

'That's very kind.' Ellen couldn't bear to think of what this woman had been through. She thought it might be appropriate if she explained what she herself had endured over the years with Sean and Nicole – but thought again. Nothing could compare. Besides, Ellen had noticed that everybody seemed to know everything about everyone else already.

Tamina came out of the house, looking worried. She was a small, round young woman with one gold front tooth and a pretty peach scarf covering her hair. She got Mancini's attention from across the swimming pool and gestured with her fingers to her ear and mouth that he had an urgent telephone call. Mancini excused himself, circled the pool and went inside the house.

'This is sort of uncomfortable,' said Ellen, alone now with Diane. 'I'm not used to this. The most excitement we ever had at home . . . Well, now that I think of it, only six months ago someone walked into the local post office and shot three people dead.'

'You see?' said Diane, smiling. 'Put it in perspective.'

'I *knew* those people at the post office. I spoke to them twice a week.'

'There you are.'

'What a world,' Ellen said. Then she remembered she was speaking to Diane, a woman well acquainted with random misfortune.

'Looks like your husband has been thrown in at the deep end,' said Diane. 'Believe me, it's not normally like this at all. This is the most stable country in the region.'

'Let's hope it stays that way,' Ellen said. She wondered at Diane's willingness to stay here after all she had endured. She seemed like such an ordinary woman – dowdy, over-coifed, boringly dressed – to have experienced such a drama in her life. Ben had reported that Diane was so organized at the office he rarely had to think for himself; this trait didn't jibe with Ellen's idea of how a woman would react to the loss of a child.

Mancini came back through the French doors looking thoroughly annoyed. He bit his lip indecisively. Since first meeting him, Ellen had found Mancini too tense to be likeable – though just now he had been charming to her and Nicole. To Ellen's surprise, she saw that he was smoking a cigarette. Everyone was waiting to hear what he had to say, and pretending not to be. Mancini went first to an Englishman named Jasper LeRoy, to whom Ellen had briefly been introduced. Mancini drew LeRoy aside to have a word with him. Ellen watched this while continuing to converse with Diane about children and schools. LeRoy was something in the British Embassy, Ellen gathered. He was a neat, intelligent-looking man whose distinguishing feature was a full head of light blond hair. The few words he had spoken to Ellen had been blasé to the point of indifference: presumably he had matters of state on his mind. He looked to be in his late thirties, and had an impatience about him that spoke of ambition.

'Paul's talking to Mr LeRoy,' said Ellen, interrupting Diane's appraisal of the American School's unhealthy emphasis on organized sport.

'It could be serious then. Or more serious, I mean. Mr Mancini does things by the book. Mr LeRoy is the most senior diplomat here. I've had a crush on him for three years.'

It startled Ellen to hear these words from the apparently prim and prematurely ageing Diane. She reminded herself that Diane had married and then abandoned an Italian.

'Have you?'

'Well, look at him.'

'Is he married?'

'His wife is in England with their three children. She refuses to come out here, not even to visit.'

'How inconvenient.'

'It's . . . complicated,' said Diane. She was more discreet than Candy, who would already have told Ellen about the wife's affair with a cabinet minister and LeRoy's unseemly predilections. 'Mrs LeRoy says it's because she wants her children educated at home. They're still small.'

'I don't know how you've done it,' said Ellen, hoping she wouldn't blurt out a question or remark that was too close to the bone. 'Raising children here alone, I mean.'

Diane sighed deeply. 'April is a dream. So is Troy. It hasn't been easy. I don't know if you –'

'I know,' Ellen said quickly, placing two fingers on Diane's arm. 'I'm so sorry. I didn't want to go on talking to you without you knowing . . . that I know. There's no stopping the gossip around here, it seems.'

'I don't mind.' Diane left it at that. 'You're very good to fess up, Mrs Pelton –'

'Ellen.'

'Ellen. Most people just blush and talk about –'

'Children and schools?'

'Children and schools.'

'What was your daughter's name?' Ellen asked, emboldened and just slightly tipsy.

'Her name was Marie. Thanks for asking. No one ever does.'

'April's so beautiful, I . . .' Ellen stopped before stupidly remarking that there used to be another one of her, named Marie.

'There used to be another one of her,' said Diane. 'And yes, she's beautiful. She's sweet, too, but you know there are cracks there. Something's got to give eventually. I'm terrified she'll starve herself or worse. She doesn't do well at school. The parties she goes to . . . The boys are as predatory here as anywhere – the American boys. You'll see,' Diane said. 'In ten years, you'll be finding vodka bottles under Nicole's bed. Sorry.'

Mancini and LeRoy had finished their conversation. They shook hands. LeRoy descended the stairs to the carport without saying his goodbyes to the other guests.

'It *is* serious,' said Diane.

'Will he tell us?'

'A version, maybe. We'll see.'

Mancini next approached the clutch of locals that included Dominic Thrune. He spoke; they listened. Two or three of them glanced at their wristwatches. Dominic shook his head, then left the group and came over to Ellen and Diane.

'What a mess,' he said. 'A second bomb, it seems. You're getting *absolutely* the wrong impression, my dear,' he said to Ellen.

'How bad?' asked Diane.

'The Great Mancini says probably the worst ever. I believe "carnage" is the operative term. *Quite* worrying. Right there in Meheti Boulevard – three hundred yards from the Chevalier. Is nothing sacred? The General's going to have kittens over this, I assure you. If there's a curfew, I'll scream.'

'Who is doing this?' Ellen asked.

'If I could tell you that the General would make me Chief of Staff. You see, not everyone has such terrifically effective bombs, so when one goes off, everyone tries to claim responsibility. *Much* cheaper and more efficient to take credit for someone else's outrage, don't you think? The usual guess is that it's the political left – they're supplied by our friends over there.' Dominic gestured across the street. 'But terrorism isn't their style, unless it's a diversion. It's so frustratingly complicated. I wouldn't put it past the Communists to let off a bomb like this one and be the only ones *not* to take the credit.'

'Mr LeRoy certainly left in a hurry.'

'He is *so* divine,' said Dominic, letting down his guard in sympathetic female company. 'I imagine he's off to inspect the scene. I'm afraid this will be world news, unless there's a plane crash in America. You've no *idea* how useful plane crashes can be in keeping real news at bay.' Dominic cleared his throat. 'My dear Ellen,' he said, formally, 'on behalf of my adopted country I *must* apologize. I'm sure this is just a flare-up of some kind and order will be restored.'

'But *two* bombs? An assassination attempt? What the hell is going on? Are we safe?'

'We're safe as long as the General is safe. There has been only one attempt on his life that I know of in all my years in the country. That's about par for the course even in America, Ellen, if it isn't rude of me to point that out.'

'Was he hurt?'

'Er . . . no. No, he wasn't. His double, on the other hand . . .'

'He has a double?'

'*Had* a double.'

'This is unbelievable.'

Mancini had finished with the locals, who departed as one. Presumably they were worried about their children, their relatives, their friends – that was the reason they had looked at their watches, to place everyone they knew at the time of the blast. Mancini came over to Ellen, Diane and Dominic.

'He's filled you in?' he asked, tall and authoritative again. 'I'm afraid the party's over.'

'This is terrible,' said Ellen.

Mancini smiled. 'It's just ugly nonsense. We'll have it sorted out in no time. I mean, the General will. He's eager to meet you, by the way.'

'Me? The General?'

'He is aware of Ben's appointment and he always expresses an interest in families. He has eleven children.' Mancini was being too suave, by far. 'Don't worry. Everything will be back to normal by the time we see him on Wednesday. You'll see.'

April led Nicole back up the garden path. They were giggling together about something, and still holding hands.

'Mama, look,' said Nicole, approaching. She was animated at last – she had a friend. 'April and I found a pine cone.'

'Wonderful, darling. Come and show me.'

April, shivering in her blue bikini, smiled and led Nicole to her mother. As Nicole handed over the pine cone for inspection, April leaned close to Ellen's ear and whispered. 'We're just pretending. It's not a pine cone. It's a toy hand grenade.'

39

Ben sat on a padded bench in the back of the police van, knees almost touching those of Chava Hannan's opposite. The two policemen sitting beside them held automatic rifles in their laps: the police and the military were not necessarily distinct entities here. Grilles covered the van's windows, but Ben could see enough over Hannan's shoulder to gauge progress. His heart had stopped hammering in his chest soon after Mancini had explained about the ambush. He felt almost calm, now, sitting on his trembling hands.

Hannan had spoken a few words to one of the policemen, who relayed his message through the partition to the senior officer, who was driving. Hannan's voice was now subdued, his expression part severity, part annoyance.

'I don't know what to say,' said Ben. 'This is a terrible shock. Did you know the man well?'

Hannan shrugged. 'I don't know which it is. We are going to the scene. I change my men every year. I can't afford to let them get lazy, you know?'

It was strange hearing Hannan say he couldn't afford something. 'What will you do now?'

'We go to the scene, as I say. They just told me there's been another bomb downtown. I want to look at that as well.'

'Isn't that dangerous?'

'Think about it, my friend. It's the safest place to be. After that, I need your help.'

'Anything you want.' In an irrational way, Ben thought Hannan had saved his life.

'I need you to help me drink champagne at the Chevalier.'

'I think I can manage that.'

Ben turned around on the bench and looked through the grilled window on his own side. The van carved its way through lighter-than-usual traffic. Whitewashed apartment blocks slid past. Dozens of Fardis pulled over, giving way to the howling van.

'It's not far,' said Hannan. 'They were on their way to fetch me at Mr Mancini's house.' All of Hannan's bluster was gone, his comical bragging and innuendo.

'Someone tried to kill you,' Ben said, as if just realizing this.

'It's the first time. Everything will change, now. I am disappointed.'

'Who do you think did it? Sorry to be so naïve.'

'In my country, Ben, it is difficult to say. Much better to be naïve.'

'Is it a group? A gang? Or an individual? A competitor?'

'I don't have competitors,' said Hannan. 'It's the same ones who planted the bomb. It's the political left. The students.'

'How do they make bombs? Where do they get weapons?'

Hannan smiled for the first time during the journey. 'I sell them,' he said.

The van slowed, then stopped. Ben swivelled around again and looked through the grille. There were soldiers and policemen and photographers milling about. The focus of their attention was an American limousine facing the wrong way in the boulevard, its windows blown out all along one side. The front passenger door was open, and inside lay the reclined body of a dead man wearing a black suit and tie and a scarlet shirt. Hannan leaned forward and looked out of Ben's window.

'It's Giovanni,' he said. 'He was good with boats.'

'He was Italian?'

'Yes. No children, fortunately.'

Hannan said something to the policemen. They opened the

rear door of the van and let him out. Ben followed, uninvited but curious. The police were keeping back a large but quiet crowd. An ambulance awaited the body. The other guard, Hannan's driver, had already been taken away for treatment.

'This is an armoured car,' said Hannan, sarcastically. 'Look there.' The holes in the body of the limousine – five of them – were as big as Ben's wrists. Ben didn't ask, but he imagined Hannan knew exactly what sort of weapon could cause such extraordinary damage.

Ben held back some distance while Hannan went to look at his dead bodyguard. Even from where he stood, with police in the way and the passenger door concealing part of the corpse, Ben could see that Giovanni had been hit in the throat, from the side. Ben wasn't squeamish, and he had seen dead bodies before. He had survived a car crash in which an acquaintance – a girl – had been killed. He had skied down a mountain with the body of a middle-aged heart-attack victim on a stretcher behind him. Ellen had taken him into her medical school autopsy room in the middle of the night, to see if he could stomach it. Besides, Ben's emotions had taken such a ride in the past twenty-four hours that he had nothing left to feel. It was almost comforting to be surrounded by so many soldiers and police, to be shoulder to shoulder with them, when these were the people he had thought were going to come and take him away for ever. Ben put his hands in his pockets and watched the scene before him as if he weren't there: the damaged limousine, dead Giovanni and his scarlet shirt, the crowd of people – mostly men and boys, looking on in near silence, kissing their fingertips, trying to understand – and Ben's new friend Hannan in his shiny suit, exuding authority. Hannan looked inside the car, asked an officer some questions, looked around at the scene of the failed attempt on his life. He nodded to the officer, who gestured at the ambulance men. Hannan came over and stood next to Ben as three men lifted Giovanni's body out of the car – one of them devoting himself entirely to the head, lest it fall off. They placed the body on a gurney and, without covering it, wheeled it over and into the ambulance.

'Any word on your other man?' Ben asked.

Hannan sniffed and pulled at one of his cuffs. 'He's all right. Cut by all the glass. His face.'

'Couldn't they see you weren't in the car?'

'Smoky windows,' said Hannan. 'Let's go, now. They tell me there has been another bomb. We'll see, my friend. It's right on the way to the Chevalier.'

They clambered back into the van and drove off, this time without the siren. Fifteen minutes later, without having spoken a word, they were let out at the edge of a much noisier, more agitated crowd. The military was in charge of this one. There were dozens of soldiers pushing and shoving at a mob near riot. There were women, too, shrieking and tearing at their eyes. A lot of people had been killed or hurt. The bomb had gone off just outside a jewellery store. Hannan asked around and learned that the bomb had been packed in the saddle bags of a motorcycle parked on the broad, Parisian-style pavement. A bus had stopped only feet away, one of the smaller buses, but packed with people. Most of the victims had been on the bus. The jewellery store's windows had been blown out, and it had been suggested that some looting had occurred. There were still injured people being treated in the boulevard, some others wandering around in shock, bodies covered by blankets lying in the gutter.

'Twenty dead,' said Hannan, having spoken to a business-man whose face had been grazed by flying glass, but who was brave and calm. 'This is stupidity. It never happens here.'

Ben watched and listened to all of this in a state of such remove that he might have been reading about it in a newspaper. It felt like a reprieve, and certainly it was a distraction: a distraction from the image in his mind that had not clearly formed until he had stood trembling by the Mancinis' swimming pool: shorts, a naked chest, plastic sandals, black hair cut close to the head, bony knees, a long skinny brown arm extended – a boy. In that slanting light, in the suddenness of it, the image was just that: an exposure, a photograph.

'We can walk to the hotel,' said Hannan.

'Are you sure? Are you safe?'

'As I say. Where is safer? Look around.' Hannan sounded impatient now. He'd had a lousy afternoon. 'You can help me with your English for phone calls.'

'Your English is fine.'

'Not for talking to press. You will be my spokesman. How many other languages do you have?'

'None.'

'Come, then. Let's drink champagne and forget all this. Also talk to press.'

'Suits me,' said Ben, driving the image out of his mind by clenching his jaw.

Hannan thanked his police escort, shaking each man's hand, then crunched back over to Ben on a carpet of broken glass. For a fairly stout man, he was light on his feet. 'That's life,' he said to Ben, smiling brightly against the unreal background of chaos and death. He led Ben through the crowd, past the line of covered bodies, uphill towards the undamaged Hotel Chevalier. 'I drink too much champagne,' he said, as Ben drew alongside him on the pavement. 'I cannot resist. I am damaging myself. I drink champagne with breakfast. Also, I eat.' He patted his round stomach. 'I am not thin, like you. I have always had big appetites.'

'You have a room at the hotel?'

'I have a room,' said Hannan. 'It's natural. I own the Chevalier.'

'I didn't know that.'

Hannan's arrival at the Chevalier caused some commotion.

The receptionist, who knew Ben well from his three-week stay, looked on the American with new respect, seeing him in the proprietor's company. He handed Hannan a sheaf of messages and spoke some words to him, no doubt of condolence. Such was Ben's state of mind, he didn't object to taking the lift: he didn't even notice he was *in* a lift until he felt himself unconsciously balling his fists, and by then it was too late. As they rose through the hotel, Hannan sorted through his messages and gruffly commented on them in his own language. Ben saw himself reflected in the lift mirror, standing next to this powerful man – this merchant of death – and he felt important.

The lift opened directly into Hannan's penthouse suite – the doors opened only when he turned a gold key on an electronic panel. The suite was empty, and smelled of perfumed air-freshener straining to cover cigar smoke. The main room was lightly decorated in pastels, as if it were a beach house. Even the carpets were light. Hannan went straight to the French windows, opened them, and went outside on to a narrow balcony. Ben followed. From there they had an excellent view of the aftermath of the explosion in the boulevard down the hill. Ben could see where leaves and branches had been stripped from the two eucalyptus trees closest to the blast. It said something about the age Ben lived in that the scene of a terrorist explosion – a line of dead bodies, shouting women, television crews, a burned-out bus, limping, bleeding children – seemed utterly familiar to him. He stayed on the balcony while Hannan went inside for champagne. There were no servants in the penthouse. The arms dealer returned with a bottle, two glasses and a ringing telephone.

'I'll answer in a minute,' he said, putting the phone down on the railing. Ben held the glasses while Hannan opened the champagne, sending the cork flying into the stopped traffic in the boulevard: it bounced off the roof of a Fardi. 'To Giovanni,' he said, having poured two full glasses and placed the bottle on a low iron table.

'To Giovanni.'

The telephone stopped ringing, then started again. A filthy haze clung the length of the boulevard from the city centre to the edge of suburbia in the north. Contributing to this locally was residual black smoke from the burnt-out bus. Traffic had begun to move again. Ben sipped his champagne as the sun refracted attractively through the smog, and he felt the strength returning to his limbs. Hannan propped himself on the balcony railing, musing in silence until he needed to refill his glass.

'I can't bring a wife into this,' he said. 'I will live in France.'

The enormity of what had happened to Hannan only now dawned on Ben; he had been preoccupied with his own catastrophe.

'Do you have someone in mind? I mean, other than Mrs Mancini and my wife? And April?'

'Oh, God. It is too painful. Did you see that girl?'

'I saw her.'

'I knew her when there were *two* of them. Just children, of course. Perhaps I will marry April. In three years. We will make ten babies.'

'If God wills it,' said Ben, speaking the local language for the first time, and feeling momentarily cosmopolitan.

'I have a friend here in the hotel,' said Hannan. 'She'll be here soon. She will have been worried about me.' He looked at the still-ringing telephone. 'I don't think I will marry her. I have many girlfriends, you know.'

'Lucky man.'

'Oh, no. You are the lucky one. Your beautiful wife. Your beautiful children. *That* is life.'

'I hope so,' said Ben, 'because that's what I've got.'

224

The crowd down the boulevard was being made to disperse. The dead had been carried away.

'Giovanni got killed this afternoon,' said Hannan, shaking his head. 'Was that his job? I should visit Stephan in the hospital, but I will be too drunk soon. Have more. Get drunk with me.'

'Pleasure.'

Ben was glad to see that his glass trembled only slightly as he extended it for a refill. He didn't like champagne, but he liked its effect. For a few minutes now he'd had the strongest urge to confide everything to Hannan, someone he hardly knew. Hannan could fix anything. He would snap his fingers and make the problem go away. It was a privilege to be in the same room with him, to drink his champagne. They were like old friends, Ben and the Billionaire Beast.

After drinking another glass of champagne, Hannan answered the telephone. He spoke in his own language; his tone was that of an impatient man issuing instructions. He made a call of his own, in French. Then he handed the telephone to Ben and said, 'Please, do me this favour.'

'All right,' said Ben, as the phone rang again. He answered.

'Mr Hannan?'

'Who's calling, please?'

'Evan Court,' said the voice, a voice that assumed it needed no further introduction.

'I'm afraid Mr Hannan is –'

'Never mind that,' said Evan Court. 'He knows me. Tell him I'm on a plane right now. We'll be at his hotel by midnight. Will you tell him?'

'Yes I will.'

Ben relayed the message.

'Evan Court is . . . useful,' said Hannan. 'I will see him tomorrow evening. He's not a friend.' Ben could tell Hannan meant this in the general way, that Evan Court had seen too many wounded children to be an enormous fan of arms dealers.

Ben handled a series of calls from several countries around the world. He took the line that though Hannan was unhurt he was understandably shocked by the incident, which he deplored. Hannan drank champagne on the balcony, made calls on another telephone indoors, admitted a maid bearing a vase of flowers and an ice-chilled bowl of caviar, took off his shiny jacket, disappeared to the bathroom, returned, took off his shoes, glanced at his pile of messages.

'Maybe I should just turn the phone off?' Ben asked.

'Not yet. A few more, please.'

Ben answered three more calls before Hannan agreed that there was no purpose in answering more.

'It's just important that people know I'm not dead,' said Hannan. 'Don't you think?'

'Sure.'

'Rumours are dangerous. Thank you for your help. When I speak to journalists I always say the wrong thing. Their questions can be aggressive and they make me angry. Have more champagne and talk to me, Ben.'

Hannan had relaxed, and was in a chatty mood. He stretched out on a pale-blue sofa and put one hand behind his head; with the other hand he continued to drink champagne.

'My parents are no longer alive. They would have hated this. Not for my safety, you understand, but for our country. My father was a great man. A proud man. He did much for his country and would be disappointed it has come to this. There will probably be a little war, now.'

'Good for business?'

Hannan frowned. 'Don't say that, Ben,' he said, scolding gently, like a good parent.

'Sorry.'

Hannan perked up again. 'Call your wife,' he said. 'You

must! Tell her you will be very late. That I am upset. That you must take care of me.'

'I suppose I can do that.'

'And then we will have a party.'

40

Ellen sat in front of the television with Candy in the Mancinis'
cool and summery living room. Evan Court had filed already
from London, and was *on his way*. It was unreal to Ellen to
see a picture come up of Chava Hannan, a man she had spoken
to only hours ago, and with whom Ben was now trying to
handle the crisis. A moment later it was doubly unreal when
she caught a glimpse of Ben standing in the background as
Hannan inspected the site of his attempted assassination. Scenes
of the bombing downtown were horrific: Ellen knew that
stretch of Meheti Boulevard better than any other part of the
city. She had walked there dozens of times with the children
when they had been living at the Chevalier.

Candy was relaxed to the point of near-drunkenness after a
long afternoon. The four children were being fed in the kitchen.
Mancini was in his study, answering the telephone.

'Oh, this is *very* good,' said Candy, when she saw Ben and
Hannan on television. She used the same tone as she had when
remarking on Ellen's budding friendship with the Russians.

'I can't believe Evan Court's coming,' Ellen said. 'I've been
in love with him for years.'

'Haven't we all? I met him in Zaire. He was just starting
out. Hasn't the boy done good? He earns half a million dollars
a year.'

'I didn't know that.'

'It's the way of the world, honey. He practically makes policy
now. You just know the President's watching this just like
we are. And the General. Whatever he points his camera at,

whatever he says with those baby-blue eyes, that's *what's happening*. He creates the agenda.'

'What is he like? Did you know him well?'

Candy quite blatantly looked over her shoulder down the corridor before replying in a low voice. 'He's the *yummiest* man I've ever met. I threw myself at him in the billiard room of the club.'

'You didn't.'

'I most certainly did.'

'*And?*'

'Let's just say he didn't seem to mind. However . . . we were interrupted.'

'Not by . . .' Ellen nodded her head in the direction of the study.

'No. Or I would have had to claim intoxication or malarial fever. No. It was Evan's then girlfriend. Another reporter.'

'That must have been quite a scene.'

'To tell you the truth, I think she was used to it. The man travels constantly. He's gorgeous. He's often in danger. He's irresistible. I mean, that sort of behaviour is so *unlike* me.' Candy chuckled, so that Ellen couldn't really tell if that sort of behaviour were unlike her or not.

The children were being oddly quiet. Tamina had a good touch. When they had finished eating they came trooping in to see what was on television. The girls sat on their mothers' laps. The boys sat on the floor. Sean was clearly enthralled by Little Paul.

'Paul says there's going to be a war,' said Sean, in his thin voice.

Little Paul nodded his wise head.

'Now, Paul,' said Candy, 'that's not necessarily true.'

'There *is* going to be a war,' said Little Paul, matter-of-factly. 'And we're going to win.'

'Who's we?'

'The General, of course.'

'We're going to win!' Sean shouted, punching the air.

Mancini's footsteps could be heard in the marble corridor. He entered the room, instinctively stooping under the doorway.

'That was Ben on the phone,' he said. 'This is *very* good. He's been handling some of the press for Hannan. His message is that he'll be late tonight. He apologizes, but Mr Hannan is upset and needs the company.'

'I understand,' said Ellen. 'How did he sound?'

'Very solid,' said Mancini. 'He's a good man.'

'We saw Ben and the Beast on television,' said Candy. 'Surveying the wreckage.'

'Please don't call him that. Especially not in front of . . .' He gestured at the children.

'Who's the Beast?' asked Sean.

'No one, darling. Mrs Mancini was only joking.' Ellen was glad to see that Sean had completely shed his morning mood. He seemed to have forgotten all about the dog, or whatever it was that had been bothering him. And the more he aped Little Paul's mannerisms the better, as far as Ellen was concerned. There was something special about that child.

'There's nothing more I can do for now,' said Mancini. 'Tomorrow it's business as usual, except that I'm out of town. Tell Ben to take his time coming in to the office if he has a late night. Hannan can talk and talk, and he'll be pretty shaken up. Ben's done good work today.'

'Thanks, I'll tell him.'

Ellen took this as her cue to leave; leaving took a quarter of an hour because Sean wanted to stay with Little Paul. Candy promised he could spend the night soon. Little Paul pretended to be aloof – Sean was just six, after all – but Ellen could tell he liked being idolized by a younger boy.

In the car on the way up the hill, Sean was quiet again. Nicole fell asleep in thirty seconds. At home, Ellen put her to bed, then went back into the kitchen to find Sean sitting on the floor. She wanted him in bed as soon as possible, because she had just remembered that her parents would have heard the news. They would be worried, and Ellen ought to call them.

'What's the matter, my darling?'

'Nothing.'

'Come now. Maybe you're a little tired? It's getting late. It was a long day and you had a big dinner.'

Sean shrugged. Ellen hated to see him this way, even if it were only exhaustion.

'Is there something you want? Do you want to read a book? Remember, we have some new ones Granny sent.'

'No.'

Ellen saw now that he was near tears. This was so unlike him she worried immediately about his health.

'Do you feel all right? A belly ache?'

'I feel . . . fine.'

'Oh, good.'

Sean had rarely cried out of emotion in his life – only out of pain. Now a fat tear wept from one of his eyes, down his cheek and across to the side of his mouth. He wiped it away, but it was followed by another from the other eye. Ellen got down on the floor and put her arms around him. He shuddered in her arms and she felt her panicked heart beating against his shoulder.

'My darling, my darling, what is it?' She knew he would have to sniffle away for a few minutes before he spoke. She kissed his hair and stroked his back. She reached down and unlaced his shoes. He was limp in her arms, still crying. He had never cried exactly this way before. 'Do you miss your friend? You had such a good time today.'

Sean sniffed again, as if to say 'No'. It took Ellen ten minutes or more to bring him around, to make him smile crookedly, to dry his face, to feed him a piece of chocolate reserved for the most special occasions.

'Now, my little guy. You can tell me, can't you?'

'No, I can't.'

'What do you mean?'

'It's a secret.'

'Whose secret, Sean?'

'*My* secret.'

'I see.'

'And Paul's.'

'Oh. Did he tell you a secret? If it's secret, then you mustn't tell me.' Ellen beamed at her boy, who was smiling, who was going to be fine.

He swallowed the last of the chocolate, then said, 'No, Mama. It's *my* secret. I told *him*.'

41

Ben and Hannan had watched the sunset from the balcony, an almost gory red-and-purple affair splashing the sky directly above the still-smouldering bus. Street sweepers were out with brooms made of bound faggots, clearing away the glass. With more than a bottle of champagne in their systems, the men had spoken of their childhoods: Hannan's in the shadow of his powerful father and four older, beloved sisters; Ben's provincial, steady, calm – and of their dreams for the future: Hannan's titanic and nearly realized; Ben's necessarily factitious under the circumstances, but still conveying a father's hope that his children might thrive if he did his duty. Their conversation touched on culture and politics, it swirled around these and other issues, with Hannan doing most of the talking and holding by far the stronger opinions.

Quite how or when exactly Ben found himself sitting indoors next to a girl named Monika, across from Hannan and a girl named Marie-Ange, he found he couldn't quite piece together. He remembered the lift doors parting, emotional embraces on Hannan's part, the popping of at least two more champagne corks, another look at the bomb damage from the balcony, another toast to the memory of Giovanni, a visit to the gold-plated bathroom to relieve himself and splash cold water on his face – and here he sat, with someone named Monika. She was a smiling, chesty girl with a dark, wide, pretty face and long brown hair. Ben hadn't absorbed her nationality. Her English was poor, but what there was of it she wasn't afraid to use.

Hannan's friend was a real beauty. She cheered up the arms dealer in no time – if his mourning for Giovanni hadn't been an act all along. She laughingly held a flame to his first barrel-like cigar of the evening. She smoked cigarettes elegantly and had a surprisingly low laugh for so slender a girl. She flirted with Ben from fifteen feet away without even looking at him – or rather, *by* not looking at him. Ben had no doubt this was the girl Ellen had mentioned last night. She spoke French with Hannan. When she smiled her eyes twinkled and dimples appeared beneath her cheekbones. She had straight, shining brown hair as girlish as April's. Her black cocktail dress was nothing more than a tight shift covering a third or less of her long, brown body.

Ben tried to concentrate on Monika. He wasn't drunk, not yet – he didn't think so. It was the fatigue, and the great wave of guilt that had only begun to crash over him, that made him feel giddy and disorientated. For a few minutes now he had wanted to ask Hannan's permission to use the telephone: it occurred to him that his parents and his sisters might be worried. He was inhibited by Hannan's unrepayable generosity, and by the suspicion that he wouldn't, at just this moment, sound to his relatives as if everything were satisfactorily under control.

Monika proved to be Yugoslavian. She drank little, but was alone in eating the otherwise untouched caviar. Ben thought he recognized in her mannerisms a girl who had her heart set on being provided with cocaine, but who had small reserves of the substance in her handbag if none were forthcoming. She had long eyelashes and pretty blue eyes and, although Ben had never put a priority on voluptuousness, a sort of *earthy* figure that he imagined gave off an aphrodisiac fragrance.

Hannan called out from across the room: 'I'm feeling much better – beautiful girls are saving us, Ben. Cigar?'

'No, thank you.'

'Whatever you desire, my good friend. If you are *very* lucky, we will dance.'

Ben fought with himself now. There was a struggle going on within him. He argued to himself, in a small corner of his conscience, that he had done nothing wrong in twenty-four hours. There was nothing wrong with sitting here, helping Hannan through his trauma. Nothing wrong even when Monika touched his hand, then intertwined her fingers with his. Her girl-smooth skin, though it registered in Ben's body, was a gesture of support at a difficult time. She must have looked at Ben as if he were an important businessman – *wasn't* he an important businessman? – in need of distraction on a difficult day.

The dancing wasn't really dancing, as Ben had ever known it – more like a cocktail-party conversation between two newly-wed couples standing in the middle of a room, accompanied by soft popular music ten years old, hugging each other when the urge arose. Ben wanted to hug Marie-Ange. When he did so, his head swam. Even hugging Monika had its effect. He was taller than everyone in the room, so they seemed almost to be worshipping him. He found to his surprise that he had made all three laugh, several times, having made strictly serious observations that they seemed to take as satire. Hannan, his extinguished cigar still clenched in his teeth, swayed almost imperceptibly and extended his arms like a Greek dancer to envelop not just the girls but Ben as well.

Marie-Ange seemed to Ben, after a while, to be the physical composite of Nadia and April: Nadia's grace, April's freshness. He horrified himself by whispering in her fragrant ear, when Hannan had turned his back to relight his cigar, 'I love you.' I *love* you? he asked himself, directly afterwards. I *love* you? What was he saying? And why was he saying it to an arms dealer's girlfriend? Marie-Ange responded by gently stroking Ben's lower back, looking him directly in the eye and *smoulder-*

ing in a way Ben could not remember having experienced since he had been seduced by an older girl at Harvard – a girl then Marie-Ange's age. She brushed Ben's forelock with her fingertips, then retreated into Hannan's casual embrace.

'Remember, we are in mourning,' said Hannan, solemnly, refilling everyone's glass. 'To Giovanni.'

'To Giovanni,' chorused the others.

'Now we go to bed?' Hannan enquired of the girls.

Ben, still under the impression that he was not misbehaving, was suddenly reminded of a remark a classmate had once made that had lodged permanently in his memory. The classmate had just returned, shaken, from his brother's stag night and wedding in California. 'Don't do orgies,' he had said, wincing. 'You'll just end up with some hairy guy's dick in your mouth.'

Ben cleared his throat. This was the moment to make his excuses. He could take a taxi home and be there before Ellen went to bed. He could expend some of the build-up in his libido on his deserving wife.

'Good idea,' he heard himself say, mainly because Marie-Ange had her hand on the small of his back again. She looked so . . . delicious to Ben, so unmissable. He was already a drunken, whoring monster and had been, technically, for months. For a day he had been a murderer. What possible moral reasoning lay between him and the sweet unknown of a girl like Marie-Ange and, for that matter, Monika? He had never needed to draw an ethical line at such a matter, because the thought had never entered the realm even of his fantasy world that such a situation could ever arise in his life. And now here it was, shimmering before his eyes in a twilight of fatigue and fear and champagne.

The girls knew the way to the bedroom. Ben followed, with Hannan right behind him. The bed itself looked like a normal billionaire's purple-silk-sheeted affair, fifty feet away at the far end of an unnecessarily large room that also contained a sitting area in the foreground, a hot tub in the middle distance, and a grooming centre worthy of an opera house. The girls were naked in the hot tub before Ben could loosen his tie. He undressed in the dim, almost smoky light, and slid into the tub between the girls. Hannan, having lighted candles, arranged glasses and bottles around the circumference of the tub and inspected himself for a second or two in a triptych make-up mirror, did likewise.

I'm not doing anything wrong, Ben said to himself. I am taking a bath with friends. This is the way they must do things in this wonderful country. If Ellen were here I would behave no differently; nor would she.

The tub began to bubble. The oiled, scented water rose to the bathers' necks. The others were smiling, and Ben imagined he was too. His feet touched other feet, his thighs other thighs. He stretched out his arms and lay them on the rim of the tub, so that his thumbs made contact with both girls' still-dry hair. There was no need to speak, only to relax.

'Now,' announced Hannan, 'we will play the game. We will play the Strait of Hormuz!' The girls laughed; they knew the game. 'Ben, my friend, you are an oil-rich state. So am I. These girls – come along, girls – are the oil tankers.' The girls lay on their backs in the roiling water. 'Now, we pass these tankers safely through the strait. You must manoeuvre them only this way.' Hannan demonstrated, cupping one of Marie-Ange's breasts and pushing her slowly along, until Monika came by and was guided in her turn. 'Isn't this fun?'

'It certainly is,' said Ben, as Marie-Ange floated over to him, on her back, her breasts islands in the water. He did as Hannan had done, and pushed her safely around the circumference of the tub.

The game lasted ten lazy minutes. The girls sat up again, looking relaxed. When Hannan eventually leaned over to kiss Marie-Ange, Ben spent an uncomfortable minute not wanting to watch, but not wanting to look at Monika either, until she took matters into her own hands and floated over practically into his lap.

Being kissed by Monika, and having her wet, smooth body pressed against him, was so wonderful that Ben stopped rationalizing the moment to himself and gave in to the full sensuousness of the experience. He was not thinking ahead; he was not paying attention to his immediate future. A few minutes passed in something like ecstasy, until Hannan drew his short, brown, hairy body out of the tub to fetch towels. During his absence, Marie-Ange glided to Ben's side, stroked his chest, kissed his ear. Ben almost laughed; he wanted a photograph of this to send to Alan Yates. This was the sweetest pleasure he had ever known. His eyes were closed. A glass of champagne was held to his lips. He drank. Marie-Ange's hand came delicately up between his legs. Hannan helped the girls out one by one and they wrapped themselves in oversized towels bearing the scarlet crest of the Hotel Chevalier. Ben climbed out, his body unapologetic for a moment until he covered and dried himself.

The bed had plenty of room. Boys on the outside, girls on the inside. Monika closest to Ben, believably happy. Parts of Marie-Ange were within reach. Ben lost himself in all of this until he was between the girls and had even more of Marie-Ange to himself. He thought he heard her whisper into his ear, inches from her real lover, 'I love you.' This had a powerful effect, though Ben still recoiled from the idea. He heard himself say, 'This is what I want,' and a second later he was alone with his thoughts and his confusion, his face between Marie-Ange's thighs. After luxuriating there for some time, he looked up – he wanted to see her body arched in the eerie light of Hannan's bedroom – and he saw Hannan, propped casually on one elbow, not involved, smiling at him.

42

'Hello, Daddy, it's me.'

'Ellen?'

'Yes. I thought you might be worried.'

'Ellen! It's Ellen! She's all right! Are you all right?'

'Yes, fine. This is a very good connection. How are you?'

'How am *I*? How are *we*? Ellen, we've been watching this thing all morning, worried to death. Are you coming home?'

'Of course not, Daddy. Of course not. Everything is just fine.'

'Why are you whispering?'

'Because the children are asleep. It's been a long day. The house echoes.'

'Where's Ben? Is Ben there? I want to talk to him.'

'Ben's not here.'

'Not there? Where's your husband when that whole town's been blown to smithereens? Not there?'

'It's a long story. Listen, Daddy. Did you see on television the famous businessman they tried to assassinate?'

'Of *course* I did. They thought he was dead. Barbarians!'

'He's not dead. We were at a party with him when it all happened. He's fine. In fact Ben went with him downtown to help sort things out. Ben's with him now.'

'With the man they tried to assassinate? At a *party*? Why isn't Ben with *you*?'

'It isn't dangerous. It's part of Ben's job. It's very important. Ben's boss asked him. You should be impressed. Ben's boss is very pleased with him.'

'What kind of country is that you're living in?'

'It's a fine country.'

'And what kind of a husband leaves his family – his wife and his children – in a time of crisis, with bombs going off all around you?'

'Daddy, you sound . . . you sound *Jewish*, Daddy.'

'How dare you, I –'

'I'm only teasing. May I speak to Mom? I'm sure she's worried too.'

'Oh, sure. Here's your Jewish mother. Come on!'

'Mom?'

'Hello, sweetheart.'

'Tell Daddy everything's okay.'

'I will.'

'He sounds . . . apoplectic.'

'He *is* apoplectic.'

'It's bad timing, because I wanted to invite you two for your first visit. Actually, it *isn't* bad timing, if you could just persuade Daddy of this, because it's going to be safer than ever now. The government's going to crack down. There won't be any more trouble for a while. How *are* you?'

'Never mind me. How are the children?'

'They miss you. Otherwise, perfection. Sean has a terrific best friend, Ben's boss's son. Nicole's still quiet, as I wrote to you, but adjusting I think. We're going to take trips outside the city. It's the most interesting country. You must come.'

'Ben's not there? Is that what I heard?'

'That's right. He's right in the thick of things, Mom. You ought to be very proud. We're here just months, and as we speak Ben's dealing with the world's press on behalf of Chava Hannan.'

'They mentioned him. The man they tried to kill. He works for the CIA.'

'I hadn't heard that. He's just a businessman. A very wealthy one, too.'

'The pictures are awful. They show them every hour. Children . . .'

'I know. I've been watching too. Did you see Ben?'

'What?'

'Ben was on television, in the background. Look for him next time the headlines are on. I know I shouldn't be excited about something so . . . so ghastly, but to think that we're somehow *part* of this drama.'

'You're very good to call, darling. I think your father wants another word. Please be careful.'

'Don't worry. I love you both. Goodbye.'

'Ellen?'

'Yes, Daddy.'

'I want to talk to Ben. You tell him to call me. Have him call me from the office tomorrow. It'll save money.'

'He's awfully busy.'

'Sure he is. Too busy to look after his family during a crisis. Do you know they said there might be a war?'

'Only a little war.'

'Oh, well, that's all right then. I'm so glad you're *enjoying* this, Ellen. We're worried to death here, and you're making jokes.'

'It isn't dangerous. You'd have to be here to see how safe it really is. We're in a suburb, almost. No one wants to hurt us.'

'In your letter you said Ben had a gun.'

'For dogs, Daddy. I shouldn't have told you about that.'

'I want you to know that I do appreciate your writing every week.'

'Thanks.'

'No, I mean it. You're a good girl. I just can't believe I've lost all power over you. If I could I'd have you out of there and home on the next plane. Maybe not a plane – those terrorists! On a boat or something.'

'You haven't told me anything about you. I read it's very cold.'

'Oh, we're fine. Fine, fine. Except our *only daughter* is living in a *war zone*.'

'You make me laugh, Daddy. You're adorable.'

'I am *not* adorable. I'm a bitter old man who's lost his family.'

'Thank you for trying to make me feel better.'

'I don't want to make you feel better, I want you to come home. Leave Ben there if he likes it so much.'

'We all like it. Sean speaks French. Once we're more settled I'm going to find all sorts of interesting things to do. We're going to make excursions.'

'Take the gun.'

'Daddy . . .'

'The world is a dangerous place, Ellen. The idea that Ben would quit a perfectly good –'

'Oh, Daddy, Ben didn't . . .'

'Didn't what?'

'Nothing. Nothing. He's done the right thing. Right now, he's doing something so important you wouldn't believe it. He's with a very powerful man. It's exhilarating. Evan Court is coming here to cover the story. Nothing like this has ever happened to us before.'

'I should think not.'

'You have to trust Ben. He's a good man, Daddy. He's been under a lot of strain. He feels the pressure. But you can trust that he's doing the right thing.'

43

'*Now, do,*' said Ben. He was trying to say '*No, don't.*' His mind dragged through the possibilities: feigning cramp; pretending to become unconscious; biting one of his companions so hard he drew blood. But still he carried on, or was swept along, and to be kissing Marie-Ange and sweeping his hands across her body in many ways mitigated the now undeniable fact that a murky arms dealer had Ben's penis in his mouth. He didn't know exactly where Monika was but he suspected she was similarly engaged with Hannan. Ben thought he was drunk now, but not nearly drunk enough. Marie-Ange's hot breath on his face kept him where he was; it was an irresistible force that had the effect of detaching Ben's body from his mind – which now played a home movie of Ellen and the children smiling in the sunlight on the lawn back home in America, in the autumn, Ellen's bright loving eyes directed purely at her husband, Sean reaching up to him (wearing a knitted hat over his bald head), Nicole toddling across the lawn (her jaw wired so that when she laughed her face looked like a grimace of pain).

Hannan eventually stopped what he'd been doing, and there was a general rearrangement of limbs and attitude. What Hannan tried to do next was so utterly out of the question that Ben created a diversion by neatly inserting himself into Marie-Ange's body and rolling her on top of him. This was better. Then Ben startled himself by reaching up and grasping her by the back of her head, pulling her down so he could whisper again with his lips pressed against her ear: 'Can you make him come?' This was far and away the most direct and pornographic remark Ben had ever made. He felt her silent laugh in a short blast of air from her nostrils that seemed to say, 'Of course I can. You first.' With Monika's aid, both objectives were promptly achieved, and escape looked a possibility.

If regret or guilt can follow on the heels of a man's climax like a black curtain dropped on a lighted stage, then so can a spasm of embarrassment. The awful clarity with which Ben now viewed his situation was like a spotlight on his wickedness and humiliation. Already thinking of entering his house where Ellen lay sleeping, he imagined the perfume of three other people on his body, of lipstick and strands of hair, of Hannan's . . .

'Anyone care for another bath?' Ben asked, into the darkness.

In the hot tub, Hannan looked gloomy and unsatisfied. He poured Ben more champagne and floated over to sit next to him. The girls leaned back and closed their eyes. Ben wondered how much they were paid, and if they were paid merely to act as bait for men to whom Hannan was attracted – or if indeed Hannan was so omni-sexual that Ben's presence had simply been a coincidence; that the merchant of death had only been trying to be a good host. Ben's innocence astounded him. He also wondered at his previous belief that life would amount to muffled, commuter-line orgasms of greater and greater infrequency until making love became an intellectual curiosity, like modern art.

'I thank you, Ben,' said Hannan, not touching him. 'We are good friends.' He raised his glass.

'Thank you, too,' said Ben, doing likewise.

'We will be seeing a lot of each other?' This was said in a way that required a response.

'I'm sure,' said Ben, noncommittally. He really didn't know a thing about Hannan, or how or if he fitted into Planning and Resources.

'You will stay the night? It's very late.'

'I . . . don't think so,' said Ben, looking over at Marie-Ange. 'My wife. My children. They'll be worried.'

'Of course. You're right. I'll send for a car in a few minutes.'

'Your car?'

'Of course. I have another.'

'You know what,' said Ben, 'I think on this *particular* occasion I won't take you up on your generous offer. You've lost one car already today. I'll get the hotel to call a taxi.'

'I understand.'

Ben got out of the tub, dried and dressed himself. He reached down and shook Hannan's wet hand. For the sake of appearances he got down on his knees and kissed both girls on the cheek. He saw himself out – steeling himself as the lift doors parted and wringing his hands as he descended to the lobby. He had already made up his mind that the past thirty hours or so of his life simply hadn't happened. If he could convince himself of this, he would be cleansed. Ben could start again. They hadn't come to get him. Hannan had no stake in gossip. He could start again. No one had seen him yesterday, no one had seen him tonight.

He walked across the hotel lobby to the concierge's desk and asked for a taxi to be summoned. Standing there next to him, smoking a cigarette, was someone who looked familiar. For a moment Ben feared it was someone from the Mancinis' party. The man caught Ben's eye.

'Good morning,' said the man.

'Hello,' Ben said, then moved towards the revolving doors. His body felt loose and relaxed as he stood on the pavement with his hands in his pockets. No one was about. It was after three o'clock in the morning. A taxi arrived in minutes. A bell boy came out of the hotel to open the car door. Ben tipped him and got into the back seat. The cab smelled nauseatingly of strong local cigarettes. He told the driver his address, then slumped back in the seat to ponder his chaste, responsible future. He had almost fallen asleep when he suddenly placed the familiar man at the reception desk. Evan Court had come to town.

44

The house was quiet. Ben had asked the driver to let him out two hundred yards down the hill, so there was a better chance Ellen wouldn't be awakened. He put his key in the lock and gently opened the door. He entered the still-unfamiliar house and took off his shoes. Ellen had left some lights on, and there was a note from her on the kitchen counter saying that Mancini wouldn't expect him at the office in the morning if he'd been up late. The note also said, 'I saw you on television.' Ben washed his hands and face in the sink, and thoroughly wet his hair: he'd worried all the way home that it was still wet from Hannan's hot tub. He washed out his mouth from the tap – remembering too late the cholera scare – then went into the living room and looked out of the French windows at the view. There were lights on in the top floor of the office building inside the Soviet Embassy compound. The city lay in its smoky basin, street lights flickering along the boulevards. Ben sat down in a deep armchair and felt that he was looking through the eyes of a changed man, a reformed man: do good work; support and protect your family; be kind and patient; show the family how much you love them . . .

'I was trying not to make any noise,' Ellen said, as Ben opened his eyes. 'The children are hungry.'

Ben groggily looked at his watch. It was seven o'clock. He had been asleep for three hours.

'Go to bed if you want,' said Ellen. She wore a winter dressing-gown and slippers. It was a chilly morning – hard to believe that April had been able to swim in the Mancinis' pool only yesterday. 'I didn't even hear you come in.'

Ben rubbed his eyes. 'It was late,' he said, adopting a policy of sticking as close to the truth as he dared without actually confessing to his first bisexual, adulterous orgy. 'After three, I think.'

'I left a note.'

'I saw it. Maybe I'll take a shower and see how I feel. Sammy will be here in an hour.'

'You look awful. Did you get terribly drunk?'

'That's an ugly way of putting it. Hannan was pretty . . . distressed.'

'I'll bet he was. But Ben, you looked so *businesslike* on television.' Ellen smiled. 'Candy and I watched you together. She called you a "dreamboat" again. If we stay here much longer she's going to trick you into having an affair.'

'Impossible,' said Ben, only gradually bringing into focus what he had done just hours ago. 'I really have to take that shower and swallow an aspirin.'

Because it was natural for Ben to give his wife a hug and a kiss, he did so. She crinkled her nose. 'What did you eat?' she asked.

'Caviar,' said Ben.

45

Ben felt dreadful, but knew he had to get out of the house. Sammy was on time, so Ben kissed his wife and children goodbye and walked out into the cool, sunny air where the car awaited him. Sammy looked like someone who was ordinarily talkative, but his spoken English was still so poor he said only one word during the half-hour journey, as they passed the spot of yesterday afternoon's atrocity: 'Boom.'

Ben made it upstairs to his office without seeing anyone. He closed the door, hung up his suit jacket, sat down behind his desk and waited for something to happen to him. In his previous job there had never been any question of having to wait: work came to him in a relentless, sometimes exhilarating torrent. Things here were subtler and, in normal circumstances, rather relaxing: a meeting with Mancini, a lunch with a junior minister of agriculture or transportation, the dictation of a letter or two in the afternoon, tea in his office with Dominic to discuss what was known as the 'quiet marketing' of the organization's contribution to the development of a country that was either going to streak into modernity in one generation or tear itself to pieces in the attempt.

There were two envelopes on Ben's desk. One was a personal letter, the other an overnight fax from Mancini's house that Diane or the receptionist would have delivered at eight o'clock. Ben read the fax first. Mancini thanked Ben, in large, almost juvenile handwriting, for looking after Hannan. He also added a somewhat worrying postscript: 'Wonderful news on the Russian front. Your friendship with him is to be encouraged.

Don't worry. We'll talk about that. Keep up the good work.' A second postscript said that Mancini would be out of the office until Wednesday, and that Ben should 'hold the fort'.

Ben's telephone rang. It was Diane, asking if he wanted tea and buttered toast. She knew, somehow, that he'd had a late night. Everyone knew everything here.

Ben opened the letter, which had been posted locally on Saturday but did not bear a return address. The letter had been typed on an electric typewriter. Ben's eye travelled to the signature: 'Denis'. In formal English that read as if it had been edited by a committee in Moscow in 1950, the letter spoke of the author's great feelings of goodwill towards Ben and Ellen, and expressed the hope that their friendship might blossom despite the sometimes harsh climate engendered by a Cold War that had serious people contemplating the suicide of all mankind.

The tea boy came in. Ben looked up and smiled automatically at him, then was blinded by the image of the child in the road. He'd been this boy's age, had the same bristly haircut – Ben thought he could remember a missing tooth, it had become that clear. The tea boy put Ben's glass of tea and a plate of warm bread and butter on the desk. Ben thanked him – he had learned how to say 'Thank you'. The boy left, closing the door behind him, and Ben's face fell into his hands. This monstrous act that he could never erase – even if they didn't come to take him away, he would be haunted until he died. It was too much to take in. The urge to confess pounded away at him – he knew he would confess, some day, to someone. But in the meantime, how could he function? How could he speak to Ellen? How could he look Sean in the eye? He would never be happy again – the idea, even the value of happiness had lost all meaning.

Ben's telephone rang again. It was Dominic Thrune. Dominic

sounded peculiar, not his usual jocular self. He was on an outside line.

'There's a small matter I need to discuss.'

'Fine. I'm not busy.' Ben's knuckles were white on the receiver, but his voice sounded normal to his own ears.

'Something perhaps we could talk about outside the office. Will you meet me?'

'Of course.'

'Do you know Monsieur Romny's?'

'I've heard of it, yes.' Monsieur Romny's was a brand-new French restaurant, not the sort of place Ben imagined Dominic would feel at home.

'One o'clock, then?'

'See you there.'

Ben spent some time fighting the urge to return to the scene of the accident. It was out of the question. No one had seen him. If he didn't have Ellen and the children, of *course* he would turn himself in and take his punishment. But priority had to be with his family. Would he be able to find the exact spot? Would there be flowers there? A police roadblock?

He could seek his father's advice. He could confess to his father, who would understand, and who would calmly narrate a lawyerly version of how and why Ben had behaved in the only way he could under the circumstances. Ben's father would suggest an act of atonement. A donation to a charity. The adoption of a local orphan. He would insist that Ben stop *pitying* himself and just be glad he'd not been caught and Sean was unhurt. It was an accident. Life is one accident after another and there are winners and losers and you play the hand you're dealt.

Ben would never commit adultery again. There was a start. He would somehow *impose* a morality on himself that would go beyond his vague understanding of right and wrong: not to be embarrassed, nor to feel ill with guilt – that had been his only gauge of morals. Now that he was a child murderer, though, the simple and exquisite act of making love to Marie-Ange looked benign enough. He held his head again and squeezed his eyes shut.

Diane knocked and entered. She looked momentarily startled by Ben's appearance.

'Are you all right?'

'I'm fine. Good morning.'

'You got Mr Mancini's message?'

'I did indeed.'

'Was it awful, with Mr Hannan?'

'It wasn't great,' said Ben. 'It must be pretty scary almost to have been assassinated. To be a marked man. Any word on who did it? It's frustrating not to be able to read the newspapers.'

'Not that I've heard. It's impossible the two things weren't related.'

'Pretty big coincidence. Who would want to kill Hannan?'

'All I know is that he procures arms for the whole region. It's the normal, shady thing. The list of people or groups or even governments that would want to – what do they always say, "Send a message"? – It's a long list. It could even be . . .' Diane pointed towards the north wall of Ben's office, which was in the direction of the General's modern but palatial headquarters.

'Hannan's going to need more security.'

'That's for sure.'

'It makes me wonder. Are *we* in any danger? I mean Mr Mancini, P&R in general?'

Diane contemplated the question. She'd been through so much, Ben thought, that she probably tried not to give much thought to the next horror that would visit her and her family. 'No need to worry,' she said. 'We're the good guys.'

At noon Ben put on his jacket and left the building. He

bought an outdated London newspaper and arrived at the restaurant half an hour early. The restaurant would have been out of place anyway, but was more so now for being only a hundred yards from yesterday's bomb blast. Was this Dominic's little joke? Ben could see the marquee of the Hotel Chevalier beyond, where he had incontrovertibly committed adultery less than twelve hours ago. He shuddered, and entered the airy restaurant.

Dominic was already at the bar, reading a newspaper of his own. Ben approached him and said, 'Slow day?' Dominic looked terrible.

'You look terrible, Ben,' Dominic said.

'I was just going to say the same thing. Thanks.'

'Quick, have a drink. Catch up.'

'I . . .' Ben really wanted to refuse. 'I will, thank you.'

Dominic's hands were trembling slightly – one of them holding the remainder of a filterless cigarette between thumb and index finger, like a dart.

'I'm having a gin and tonic,' said Dominic, 'because I am *depressed*.'

'Fine with me.'

Dominic was not so strangely dressed as usual. He wore a fine herringbone jacket over a tieless white shirt and khaki trousers. He still wore his desert boots, however, and a copper bracelet.

'Catching up on last week's news?' Dominic asked, gesturing at the London paper as Ben placed it on the bar. 'Here's today's.' He closed and flattened his local newspaper – there were just two national papers.

'Is there a report on Hannan?'

'Indeed. It seems the LFP were responsible,' said Dominic, with considerable sarcasm. He referred to the ethnic group that lived near the presumed oil in the east.

'Is that true?'

'Almost certainly not. Here, your drink.'

'Thanks. And the bombing?'

Dominic showed Ben the front page, which bore a photograph of a tourist-bus crash – on the coast of a neighbouring country, of course – in which a retired English couple had been killed. 'Not a sausage.'

'I beg your pardon?'

'Sorry. Not a *word*. The blast and the carnage go unmentioned. Marvellous system, really, dictatorship.'

The men sipped their drinks. Ben could see that Dominic was in some sort of pain – whether physical or emotional, he couldn't yet tell. Then Dominic turned his face and Ben saw a livid bruise on the side of his neck, beneath his left ear.

'God, Dominic. What happened to you?'

'A *contretemps*,' said Dominic, trying to smile. 'It's in a way why I wanted to see you. I didn't go to the office this morning, knowing the Great Mancini wouldn't be there.'

'Well, what?'

'I'm afraid you won't be . . . happy about this. In fact I'm certain you'll be *shocked*, frankly.'

'I doubt it,' said Ben.

'Oh, then, all right. It's just that I don't think you're going to *like* this.' Dominic took another sip of his drink, then looked into the glass as if he'd seen a hair or an insect. 'I sort of, in a way, fell in love,' he said.

'Yes?'

'Yes. But you see . . . with a *chap*.' Dominic paused here, as if he expected Ben to push away his drink and depart. He raised his eyebrows in his usual expectant way, searching Ben's face, reaching blindly for his cigarettes and lighter.

'I do see,' said Ben. 'Don't worry, Dominic.'

'I'm terribly relieved. No no, *terribly* relieved. I knew I could trust you.' He lit a cigarette and snapped shut his lighter. His next few sentences came smoking out: 'You see the thing is,

254

Ben, here in this *marvellous* country where I have chosen to make my home, something of a taboo is involved, one not so long ago extant even in Britain. A taboo in fact reaching the stage of judicial censure, sadly enough. One is simply not *allowed*, on pain of imprisonment and all that entails, to be in love in the way that I quite suddenly and for the first time find that I am.'

'I think I knew that,' said Ben. He tried to be casual, modern, even though he had never had this sort of a conversation with a man and the thought of what followed from Dominic's admission vaguely repelled him. It helped his equanimity that he had been in bed with a man a few hours before. 'Anyone I know?'

'I find it hard to believe that you would. It's not too important who he is, except that – really I shouldn't be so *fucking* arch, sorry – except that he's the son of someone quite prominent.'

'The son?'

'Now, not to worry. He's twenty-seven.'

'Ah, well.'

'And a local.'

'Should I ask?'

'No. Do not ask. The point is we were followed, yesterday evening, walking home. After the do at the Great Mancini's house and all the brouhaha surrounding Hannan, I'd met my friend at a restaurant. We were going to my little shack in the hills – I live practically in a *caravan*, you know, you *must* see it – and we sensed this person's presence. My friend is a bit of a hothead, you know, and he decided we should round a corner and lie in wait for the sinister shadow on our tail. I begged him not to. He insisted. So we lay in wait and . . .' Dominic sucked on his cigarette and exhaled his conclusion: 'A jostling ensued. I was struck, as you can see. My friend was hit in the ribs and below the eye. Whoever it was dashed away, leaving us battered and terrified.'

'Is your friend all right?'

'He is robust. But this left us very worried.'

'Was it the police?'

'No.'

'How do you know?'

'Because,' said Dominic, 'he smelled of vodka.'

Ben absorbed the meaning of this statement over a period requiring him to finish his drink.

'One more,' said Dominic, 'then we'll go to our table.'

Ben didn't refuse. He wanted to ask the obvious question – 'Why are you telling me this?' – but first he wanted to hear all of what Dominic had to say. Even after all that had happened since Friday night he still dimly recalled Ellen's reprimanding him for having said something compromising about Dominic in front of the Russians. What could he have said? And what did it matter to the Russians if the Communications Director of P&R – technically Ben's subordinate – might be vulnerable to blackmail?

Their new drinks arrived. Dominic rubbed his bruise and frowned. Ben wanted to say, 'You think *you've* got problems.'

'It is all so *fraught*,' said Dominic. 'And sorry to drag you into our little drama. It's just that I could never go to Mancini about any of this – he's disapproving to the point of blindness on the matter. You *did* know, didn't you?'

'What, about your . . .'

'Yes.'

'If I say no I'll look like an idiot. If I say yes will you be offended?'

'Not in the slightest.'

'Well, yes, then, of course. I wasn't aware that it was supposed to be a secret. Not that I told anyone,' Ben added quickly. 'You've been living here too long. At home it isn't a problem at all.'

'Now you're being naïve, Ben.'

Ben thought for a moment. 'Of course you're right. I'm sorry. But you don't go to jail.'

'Or undergo torture.'

'Or that.'

'Now,' said Dominic, pulling at his cuffs and trying to smile, 'what do you think our Russian friends want from me?'

'I'm just learning about what's going on here,' said Ben. 'But don't they just look for weaknesses wherever they can, bide their time? I don't know how it works.'

'That's probably right. The thing is, Ben, I *do* know things. I'm telling you this because we're on the same side.'

'I'm not on anyone's "side". This is my job. This is my life. Whose "side" am I supposed to be on?'

Dominic smiled again, more naturally. 'You had dinner with Denis and his serenely graceful wife on Friday evening. You watched a ballet film. How do you think I know that?'

'Mancini?'

'Correct. He'll want you to befriend Denis further.'

Ben remembered Mancini's note, Denis's letter. 'Will he?'

'Yes. He'll want you to get drunk with him again and listen for the slightest hint of anything . . . useful.'

'I'm not a spy,' said Ben.

Dominic reached for his cigarettes. He looked over Ben's shoulder at some new arrivals. The restaurant had begun to fill. 'Well, *I* am,' he said. 'I suppose it's not so obvious as the other thing.'

Ben, as before, tried to be casual. 'Oh, it's obvious all right,' he said. 'I just couldn't tell what side. Does Mancini know, or is he blind to that as well?'

'I think one could say,' said Dominic, 'that it's why he hired me. Or was made to hire me. It certainly wasn't for my administrative skills.'

Now Ben spoke recklessly, because of the drink and the guilt and the exhaustion. 'You're fitting into a mould, Dominic,' he said. 'You're English. You drink. You're gay. Where do they find you people?'

'Cambridge, old boy,' Dominic said.

'Even now?'

'Especially now. They send us hither and yon to be preyed upon and turned – a neat trick, when you think about it, since these days we are men of absolute *steel*.'

'If you're such a man of steel,' Ben asked, 'why have you told me this? You don't know anything about me.'

'Oh no? You don't think so? I'll get to that over lunch. Oh my,' he said, looking over Ben's shoulder again and raising his hysterical eyebrows. 'Who do we have here?'

Ben turned around and looked towards the door. There, being greeted by a bowing *maitre d'*, were Marie-Ange and Monika.

'My goodness,' said Dominic. 'You'll never guess who *she* is.'

Ben turned back to Dominic so the girls wouldn't see his face. 'I've never seen them before,' he said, automatically. The words sounded guilty even as he spoke them, but there was no way Dominic could know *everything*.

'The tall one, the absolute beauty, is Chava Hannan's lady-friend,' said Dominic.

Ben sneaked another look.

'I don't know if I approve of your wandering eye,' said Dominic.

'Don't be ridiculous. She is something, though. Whoever she is.'

'Shall we go to our table?'

'I'll just . . . go to the men's first.' There was a route that could take Ben to the toilet and back round to Dominic's table without having to make eye contact with the girls. He made his way around the periphery of the now-crowded restaurant, which, though nominally French, actually served local food with a French accent. Ben pushed on a freshly painted door labelled *'Hommes'*, washed and dried his face and hands, looked at himself in the mirror. He smiled mockingly at himself, as if he were someone else – a client, perhaps, caught in the net of his own lies. Ben's mundane law duties had never given him the opportunity to represent really bad men – just overreaching, greedy, unscrupulous men compounding their errors until they were out of all proportion to any original goals. They came from a world where everyone stretched at the limits of the law until, having transgressed here, then there, further transgressions were necessary to cover the initial breach; and so on, in a cycle, until the machinery of justice plucked them out of a grey area and pronounced them criminally black. If representing these people had taught Ben anything over the years, it was that to succeed in life, a bad man had to be the *worst*. The honest, meanwhile, would have to pray for their reward in Heaven.

Ben prepared himself for going back out into the restaurant and rejoining Dominic Thrune. He didn't know if Dominic were really a spy or not, and it didn't matter to him. There were spies, and spies. Dominic was probably a fantasist. He'd fallen into difficulty, and he did like a drama. Ben had half-expected Dominic to say, 'It's *you*, Ben, it's *you*.' This had happened to Ben before. It was precisely his obliviousness to homosexual attraction that seemed to serve as a magnet to a certain kind of man.

With one last glimpse of himself – looking exactly the opposite of what he was, or the way he felt – Ben turned and went back through the doors. Head down, he circled over to where Dominic was seated at a corner table. He was reading the newspaper again. Ben sat down with his back to the room, but there was no doubt in his mind that the girls would recognize him eventually. He had to trust in their professional discretion. He also had to hope that Hannan wouldn't join them – though it was unlikely he would; he would be avoiding public places until he had tightened his security.

'Now, this,' said Dominic, slapping an inside page of the newspaper with the backs of his fingers, '*this* is interesting.'

'Tell me,' said Ben, who felt lazy and had no appetite.

'The Vodis are on the rampage.'

'Vodis?'

'Colonel Vodi and his younger brother. I have no adjectives for Colonel Vodi. One looks to Nazi Germany for comparisons. He's not in the government, but everyone knows who he is. He trains a large number of men – they always say "elite", don't they, when they mean "sociopathic"? – just north of the city in the middle of nowhere. They're supposed to be ultra-secret but everyone knows where they are and what they do. They're collectively known as "the Vodi". They're a sort of presidential-guard-in-waiting. Hundreds of men. The most *gloriously* severe uniforms. Vodi himself looks like a vampire with a moustache. There are all the usual horror stories about him, his sadism and all that, and pressure has been put to bear on the General to be . . . more subtle. The idea is that the General's image ought to be as benign as possible – he speaks English, you know. If he's to be our friend he has to put a leash on men like the Vodis.'

'Why do you say they're on the rampage?'

Dominic lit another cigarette and looked down at the newspaper. 'I have to read between the lines, here. It's a straight, rather sad news story, but I can tell trouble is brewing. It has to do with Vodi's younger brother. I wouldn't want to be *this* person,' Dominic said, tapping the page with his index finger.

'Who?'

'Whoever ran over and killed Colonel Vodi's little nephew.'

46

Ellen had nothing to do. Sean was at school. Nicole was playing with Ama. Haz had washed the car, stripped the beds, made lunch, covered the swimming pool, mopped the kitchen floor, repaired a loose table leg, hauled the garbage down to the road, helped install the satellite-television dish, carved and painted a wooden soldier for Sean, oiled a door hinge, gone shopping for food, baked a chocolate cake and ironed two loads of laundry. Ellen worried that she would turn into a younger version of Candy Mancini – that she would descend into genteel alcoholism, that she would learn to play tennis only to be thrashed at the game by Candy every afternoon, that she would spend all her time at the club gossiping ruthlessly about friends and acquaintances. She needed a job, but what was the point? What she'd always wanted was a career, not a stop-gap to keep her occupied only to leave it all behind in two or three years and start again from scratch. Should she get pregnant again?

She knew Ben had done the right thing in coming here – it would broaden their outlook, and the children's – but Ellen's subordinate position in the family had never been more glaring. She thought she might start a diary, for publication. A title had even occurred to her: *A Woman, Abroad*.

At two o'clock in the afternoon, the telephone rang. Ellen considered not answering it, in case it was Candy. She wasn't comfortable with close friendship being imposed on her so quickly. She certainly didn't want to go to the club. She could make the excuse that she had to pick Sean up from school, even though Ama or Haz could easily do it for her. She didn't even need an excuse: she could say 'No' to Candy Mancini.

'Hello? Oh, hello, Candy.'

'Come on over to the club. Have you had lunch?'

'I don't think I can do that, Candy, thanks anyway. I have to pick Sean up from school soon.'

'Oh, *what* a shame,' said Candy. 'That's really too bad. I've got Evan Court here at my side. He *longs* to meet you.'

'I'll be there in fifteen minutes,' Ellen said.

Girlishly and almost blushing, Ellen changed her clothes, brushed her teeth and hair, put on an informal but attractive Norwegian sweater. It was getting cold. She asked Ama to pick Sean up from school, and to take Nicole along. She drove the Euphoria down the hill, past Candy's house, out on to the road, around the Soviet Embassy compound and up another hill to the club. She left the car in a nearly empty parking lot near the tennis courts, and walked to the side entrance closest to the club's bar.

Candy sat alone at a corner table, drinking a beer. She wore her tennis outfit, dark glasses, a cardigan and a checked handkerchief tied around her head.

'Now you think I was only kidding, don't you, honey?'

'You weren't, were you?'

'Me? Of course not. Evan's on the phone. He's always on the phone. Have a drink. He'll be back in a minute.'

There was another glass of beer on the table.

'All right,' said Ellen. 'I guess I'll join you with one of those.'

Candy gestured towards the bartender to this effect. 'I've told Evan all about you,' she said. 'And about Ben, and about all the excitement of yesterday. When I described Ben to him he said he thought he'd seen him in the lobby of the Chevalier last night. Or rather, this morning at about three o'clock. Is Ben simply exhausted?'

'Yes. But it was important for him to be there, I suppose.'

'Absolutely. Ah, here comes our golden boy.'

Ellen turned around to see Evan Court entering the bar from the club's lobby. She found that she wasn't immune to the effects of meeting a famous person: she felt she knew him, her heart beat faster, she wanted to make a good impression. She even knew his clothes, having seen him wearing them on television a dozen times: a beige linen jacket over a dark-blue chamois shirt, khaki chinos, yachting shoes. He was taller than Ellen had imagined, he had a soft tan, his thinning blond hair trailed above his head like a nimbus.

Evan greeted Ellen with a two-fisted handshake and a kiss on each cheek. He had beautiful teeth and a smile that the humanitarian, on-camera Evan Court had rare occasion to deploy. He had a lot of energy. He sat down and lit an American cigarette. His blue eyes danced with excitement.

'I've got Hannan,' he said. 'Six o'clock. He said he hates me but will talk to no one else.'

'Well done,' said Candy.

Evan turned to Ellen. 'What does your husband – Ben, is it? What does your husband make of Chava Hannan?'

'I haven't had a chance to . . . debrief him,' Ellen said.

'Well he looked a right mess when I saw him – your husband, that is. In the hotel? Around three in the morning? A tallish man wearing a grey tweed jacket? Chiselled features? Dark hair parted neatly on the right as you look at him? Polite but curt? American? Looks like a lawyer?'

'He is a lawyer.'

'He ought to steer clear of Hannan – that's my advice, for what it's worth.' Evan couldn't sit still. He smoked in a fidgety way, he took a sheaf of papers from his leather briefcase and arranged pages on the table, he spoke in disjointed sentences. 'Hannan's a dangerous little bugger. You've met him?'

'Yes. Yesterday, at Candy's house.'

'So you've seen him ooze the charm?'

'In a way.'

'I know who tried to kill him.'

'You do?'

'It was the General. Had to be. Process of elimination.'

'Will you say that on television?'

Evan laughed, still shuffling documents on the table top. 'I'll tell you what I'll say – and no one's interested anyway. I'll say that it has been "reported" that the LFP were responsible for both the assassination attempt and the bombing downtown. I don't know the first *thing* about this country. What the hell should I say? I'm a reporter. I report.'

Ellen cleared her throat. 'I watch you all the time,' she said. 'I see you in the evenings when the children are asleep. You're everywhere.'

'Thank God someone's watching,' Evan said, smiling.

'Is this a big story?'

'It all depends,' said Evan, implying that it would be a big story if he deemed it to be: he could shine his torch elsewhere if necessary. 'Maybe I'll stick around for a few days and see if there isn't a little war.'

'Why does everyone say there's going to be a war?' Ellen asked. 'When was the last one? I feel so stupid, living here and not knowing these basic things.'

'I don't really know myself,' said Evan. 'Candy? Can you enlighten us?'

'About four years ago there was a *sort* of little war,' Candy said. 'Little Paul loved it. We had a blackout for two nights. We drove around with blue plastic covering the lights of our car. The General took the island of Corbair, without much of a fight. I think the point is, though, Evan my dear – and you must tell your millions of viewers this – the *point* is that everyone's looking for a spark to light the tinder-box. And I mean the big one. It's as if they *want* it to happen. Put us all out of our misery.'

'What am I missing?' asked Ellen. 'What "big one"?'

'I believe she means a rather larger, more general war with the Soviet Union,' said Evan, still smiling.

'This country?'

'No, the whole world.'

'That's the silliest thing I've ever heard. The world war's going to start over something important, like . . . well, Berlin, or Jerusalem. Anyway I always assumed we'd be blown up by accident, not because we disagreed about – what did you say? An island?'

'My whole life,' said Candy, 'since I was old enough to listen to my parents – for about thirty-five years now – I've thought it was going to happen every day. My husband disagrees with me, but *he's* been to war and been shot up for his pains. I'm still waiting. I can't believe I brought children into this world.'

Ellen wondered if Candy were tipsier than she appeared. True, Ellen had grown up in a house with a stocked bomb shelter, and history had taught her that there were no apparent limits to human cruelty, but the arms race and the Cold War seemed to her a deliberate, permanent stand-off. It would last for ever – of course it had to – but it would be in the back of people's minds, like their own mortality.

A waiter brought a plate of black olives, a bowl of almonds and three more glasses of beer. Evan put away his papers. He lit another cigarette and blew the smoke towards the ceiling. 'The question is,' he said, 'how do you cover nuclear war? This has come up, I'm not joking. Should correspondents and their crews be provided with radiation suits so we can get right *in* there if we survive? Will people be in the mood to watch television?'

'I can't believe you two talk this way,' said Ellen. 'A bomb goes off in the street here – I mean *here* – and you're getting your radiation suits ready.'

'It's the Ferdinand Principle,' said Evan.

'Meaning?'

'Archduke Franz –'

'Oh, I see. I get your point. Jesus, what a world. How do you cope with the awful things you see? I'm sorry, you must have to answer that question every day.'

'Do you want the idealistic version – the one about the ceaseless search for objective answers, just doing my job – or the truth?'

'The truth, please.'

'The truth is that I have just a couple of priorities: making sure I'm safe, physically safe, as far as that is possible. Then, making sure my crew are safe. After that, it's a matter of getting to the next job so I don't have time to think about what's gone before. I mean, how do you imagine doctors deal every day with cancer, or . . .' Evan's voice trailed off, betraying the fact that Candy had thoughtfully briefed him about Ellen's life. 'I'm used to it,' he continued, 'and it's not every day, you know. I've only had a couple of real scares in ten years. This morning I interviewed the parents of two children killed on the bus yesterday afternoon. They're in pain. I'm not.'

Ellen loved Evan's familiar voice, his soft accent, the humorous wrinkles around his otherwise professional eyes.

'Evan tells me he's afraid of flying,' Candy said. 'Isn't that hilarious? Our intrepid reporter, afraid of flying?'

'Now, Candy, that was our little secret. Think of my image, please.'

'Is it true? I don't like flying either,' said Ellen.

'The funny thing is I don't mind small planes, helicopters. I mean I've landed on frozen lakes, in jungle clearings, all that – and really enjoyed it. It's anonymous airlines I can't stand. Completely irrational, of course. I have to drug myself and drink. Luckily I slept fairly late today. I sent my boys out to film the road, the dam. I'm *so* annoyed that Candy's husband is out of town. He's the one I want to talk to. He's got the General's ear – isn't that right, Candy?'

'They're bosom buddies.'

'Why don't you just speak to the General yourself?' Ellen asked.

'He's not in the mood. And he's never liked television. He's uncomfortable with his appearance.'

'He looks all right to me,' said Ellen, gesturing at a portrait of the General on the wall. The General's image was everywhere – almost as ubiquitous as that of the founder, Meheti. Whether in uniform or mufti, he always looked fatherly in a stern, military way. There was no popular idolatry surrounding the General, and his image was kept in proportion: stability, gradual modernization, a firm hand where national security was concerned.

'I'm not sure what it is. There are rumours. He may be blind in one eye. A scar? He just won't do it, never has.'

'It's none of those things,' said Candy. 'I've met him. He looks fine. He's just a handsome soldier. He even speaks pretty good English. I think it's *you* he's afraid of, Evan. He thinks you'll ask him about torture of political prisoners, or something. Just to get him riled.'

'Not that I would.'

'Evan is secretly *very* right wing,' said Candy.

'Oh, nonsense,' said Evan.

'He is, he is. He writes for a London magazine and says the *most* controversial things. You'd be fired if your employers could read, Evan.'

'Nonsense.'

'Evan likes dictators, if they're on our side. Come on, Evan. Admit it. Ellen won't tell anyone.'

'Let's talk about *Ellen*, shall we?' Evan said, not really put out by Candy's teasing.

'No, please,' said Ellen. 'I'm just a miserable housewife.'

'But at least a very attractive one,' said Evan.

'Oh, here comes the big bad wolf,' said Candy. 'Do you two young people want to be left alone?'

'Please, Candy,' said Evan.

'Well I just think I ought to do my bit for this girl, Evan, she has *so* much pent-up —'

'Candy,' said Ellen, blushing.

'Yes, really,' said Evan. 'That's enough of that.'

'Is he as dishy as I said?' Candy asked Ellen. She really was tipsy. It was so hard to tell. When she spoke she waved her hands too emphatically. She wasn't drunk, it occurred to Ellen, she *was* a drunk.

'I apologize,' said Evan. 'I shouldn't have said what I did — even though I meant it. It's a reflex. I move around so much. There's never any time.'

Ellen wanted to say, 'Let's go to your hotel.' Instead she said, 'It's quite all right. Don't worry. Everyone's tense.'

'Tense!' Candy shouted. If there had been anyone else in the bar their heads would have turned. 'Hah! I'm about to *explode*! Here I am with the *dishy* Evan Court and my husband is out of town and my children are being looked after and *you're* "very attractive". I'm going to *gas* myself. *Damn* you, Evan.'

'I see,' said Evan.

'You invited me,' Ellen said.

47

Ben could hardly hear what Dominic was saying – blood had rushed to his ears on hearing about the Vodi nephew. His mouth had gone dry, and he almost choked on the foul-tasting wine Dominic had ordered. Dominic seemed to think there was something Ben could do to help him and his boyfriend. He couldn't go to Mancini. Ben had 'such charm', which might be deployed in the direction of Denis the Russian, to have the Russians call off their dogs. Ben felt himself nodding his head, as if he really thought any of this were in his power – or that he would even live long enough to help Dominic in any way.

'There might be something you could trade,' said Dominic, looking defenceless in the corner of the restaurant. His eyes pleaded with Ben to find a solution.

'But if your friend is so powerful,' Ben managed to say, then he ran out of breath.

'His father,' said Dominic. 'And yes, powerful. But powerful in, shall we say, the wrong direction. He is the wrong kind of powerful.'

'I can't begin to guess what you mean.'

Dominic took a sip of wine and adopted a resigned, desperate tone. 'Religious,' he said.

'Oh, *terrific*,' said Ben. 'This isn't wise at all. Get out of it, Dominic.' Ben could casually suggest this solution because he did not believe in homosexual love.

'I would *die* for him,' said Dominic.

'I understand. I *think* I understand. But consider the danger you're putting your friend in. If I have a word with Denis it might backfire. They'll get the police on to you next.'

'I was only asking for a favour,' Dominic said, trying to look pathetic, and succeeding. 'I'd tell them anything, really I would. But they're just clumsy thugs and they wouldn't believe that I can't help. I really can't. What do I know? They think I know Mancini's master plan. I don't. They think I know why we're building the road. I don't. Why must they pick on me?'

'You've exposed yourself.'

'You could put it that way.'

'Dominic, try to relax,' said Ben, who was so far from relaxed himself he was already trying to grind his brain through the logistics of getting his family out of the country by nightfall.

The restaurant was full now, and noisy. Ben didn't dare turn and look over his shoulder. He had ordered soup and bread, and didn't think he had the appetite even for that. Dominic hadn't touched his food either. Ben had to get away before the afternoon dissolved into a *karat*-soaked binge.

'You probably think,' said Dominic, slurring his words a bit now, 'that here I am, someone who knows his way around, knows the people and the language, ought to be able to look after himself. But I'll tell you something. I toil away in the engine room – I have no idea what goes on upstairs.'

'You said you were a spy.'

Dominic's eyes bulged. 'Do I *look* like a spy? For Heaven's sake. I was only teasing you.'

'It makes sense,' said Ben. 'If you really were a spy you'd keep your voice down.'

'There are things going on upstairs, Ben. Find out for me. Throw me a sop. It's no different *my* asking than it is for Mancini to try to get you to cosy up with the Russians. We all *hate* the Russians, by the way.'

'I can never tell if you're being serious.'

'I shouldn't have bothered,' Dominic said. 'Now I am *com-*

pletely miserable. I don't know why I thought you would want to help. You're probably one of *them*. Of course you are. What was I thinking?'

'You ought to go home and get some rest,' said Ben. 'I'm sorry about your trouble.' As he said this, he felt what could only be a premonition: but no, he'd seen Dominic's eyebrows rise on his forehead, looking at something behind Ben that seemed to astonish him. A moment later Ben felt a hand on his shoulder. Ben started and turned. There was Marie-Ange, leaning down and smiling, her red dress falling away from her shoulders.

'I thought it was you, Ben,' she said, kissing his cheek. 'What a lot of energy you have, even to be awake. Hello,' she said to Dominic. 'We were just leaving. See you soon? Goodbye, Ben.'

Ben hadn't said a word. Marie-Ange evaporated, leaving behind a scent Ben remembered. Ben found that his eyes were closed. When he opened them, Dominic was looking down at his fingernails and clucking.

'I say, old boy,' he said. 'I may have a few chips left on the table after all.'

48

Ben summoned Sammy at half past five in the afternoon. He sat in the back of the polished black car, a folder of unexamined documents open on his lap. He had behaved as normally as he could all afternoon. He had kept two appointments: one with a local hydraulic engineer, who drank three glasses of sweet tea and treated Ben like a school principal; the other with an American advance-man for the eminent founder of P&R, who drank bottled water and confessed for no reason whatsoever that his wife and children had left him two months ago because he'd had an affair with the wife of an Indonesian diplomat. Ben had smiled and nodded at these men – he'd reassured the engineer and stroked the ego of the advance-man – all the while inwardly boiling away and wondering where to turn. He switched on the reading light in the car, so Sammy would think he was working. It was dark and cold outside and the air smelled of snow. The streets were less crowded than usual; the traffic actually moved along. The small buses that ferried hundreds of thousand of people in and out of the city every day were decorated with colourful lights, like cheap res-taurants. There was a noticeable increase in military and police presence downtown – fogged breath and cigarette smoke rose over groups of soldiers wearing woollen caps and mittens. Presumably the General's crackdown had already begun. How many more men would be taken to the long, white building in the mountains? How many more taken out into the yard and shot? The sight of those executions seemed an age ago.

What am I *doing* here? Ben thought, as the car turned off

the boulevard and headed into the hills. What was Wiesman *thinking*? Was I fired because Innis is a black man? I got this job because some trainee spook said he thought Mancini's boy looked 'queer'. Accident, accident, *accident*. Pack up and go? That's it. Just leave, and write to Mancini expressing regret. It hadn't worked out. Ellen wasn't happy. Nicole wouldn't *speak*, the country disagreed with her so much. Just get out. Leave Dominic to his Russians, Mancini to his General, the Vodi brothers to their devices, that dead boy to his rocky grave, Hannan to his whores and his billion.

In the hills there were construction sites where shifts of workers laboured round the clock. Houses and apartment buildings glowed from within like Halloween pumpkins. Pulleys squeaked as they hauled up concrete from the street below. Flood lights illuminated the ubiquitous sight of men sifting, sifting against their rectangular sieves, every shovelful another piece of a wall, a step, a foundation. None wore a hard hat.

Sammy drove darkly, silently, cautiously. Farther up the hill, grander residences appeared out of the gloom, behind their walls, their razor wire, their guardhouses. Children still played in the street, in the last light – riding bicycles, playing hide and seek, coming home late from friends' houses, roller skating, kicking soccer balls. The last thing Ben saw before his head lolled back in sleep was a pair of boys Sean's age, standing ten feet apart and speaking to each other through pretend walkie-talkies.

Ben was awakened by Sammy's gentle prod on his shoulder. Cold air poured into the heated car. Ben's squat, white house was there, just a few feet away, for him to enter and to be enveloped by the bosom of his family. He thanked Sammy in English, gathered his documents and briefcase, walked through the cold to the front door. It had started to snow.

Ben entered the house, put his briefcase down on the floor, reached instinctively to loosen his tie. There was a mirror on the wall in the entrance hall: he looked at himself and saw a youngish man who had slept too little – not a monster. He tried to wink at himself, but only managed a twitch. He could hear activity in the kitchen. He went in that direction and found Haz and Ama labouring over dinner, a process that included – on Ellen's paranoid anti-cholera instructions – washing salad and fruit and vegetables in soap and hot water. Ben smiled and said hello. Haz smiled and pointed at his own ear, then drew attention to the sound in the living room, and said, 'Television.' Ben nodded and smiled again at the hard-working couple. 'I'll go see.'

Ellen and the children were curled up together on the sofa watching the new television set, purchased from Sammy's cousin downtown and now attached to a dish on the roof that looked like a military radar installation. Ellen blew Ben a kiss. The children looked up, then back at the television. Ben took off his jacket and draped it on the back of the chair in which he had slept early in the morning. He took off his tie and placed it on the jacket. The television trumpeted commercial noises. Ellen made an apologetic face that said 'It's a special occasion.' Ben wanted a cup of coffee but was still too uncomfortable with Haz and Ama to ask for one, and too embarrassed to make one for himself in their presence. He sat down.

It was six o'clock. The news came on. Ben watched himself in the background of the bomb wreckage, Hannan importantly to the fore. Ellen smiled at him. The network switched to a view of the undamaged Hotel Chevalier, then inside to Evan Court and Chava Hannan, sitting together on the same leather couch where Ben had first met Marie-Ange and Monika. Ben cleared his throat and looked on, his features sculpted into an important-businessman's expression.

Evan Court didn't bat an eye when Hannan stated without equivocation that the LFP had been responsible for both outrages. Hannan looked suitably sorrowful as he expressed his condolences to Giovanni's family. The interview lasted no more than two minutes. Evan Court's cool rage was visible only in the corners of his eyes as he signed off and returned his viewers to home base, where the subject was quickly changed to something that might conceivably be of interest to a mostly American audience – in this case a professional basketball player who had died of a heart attack in the middle of a game. Ellen switched off the television.

'That was so odd,' she said. 'I met Evan Court today at the club. He says it's not the LFP. He says it's the General.'

'You met him?'

'Candy introduced us. They've met before. He's a real . . . dynamo.'

Haz came into the room and indicated with a bow that dinner was served. Ben was so bewildered by all that had happened that he simply stood up, automatically, and went into the dining room to begin a domestic life that even in the best case would be a permanent, unnerving sham. He held Ellen's chair for her, helped Nicole on to her raised seat, tried to grin at Sean – who looked back at him with an expression close to scorn, or suspicion.

'What's the matter, Sean?' Ben asked, terrified by the thought of what the child might say. 'Are you feeling a little tired, maybe?'

'You said you would get me a bicycle.'

'Did I?'

'A red one with a light.'

'*Did* I?'

'Yes. And you haven't.'

'Sean, I'm so sorry. It's all the excitement. We'll find you a bike one of these days. I promise.'

Haz served leek-and-potato soup. Nicole wouldn't touch this, but Ellen wanted to establish a grown-up pattern. Ben was still not accustomed to the unpleasant silence that descended on

275

the family as Haz made his tour around the table. Ellen had learned to try to keep speaking – soon it would seem natural to have a servant hovering around. Now she thanked Haz and said how *sensational* the soup smelled. When Haz had gone back through the swinging door to the kitchen, Ben sighed with relief.

It was time to have a conversation. Ellen asked him about his day. She asked Sean to repeat a story he'd told about school: a Vietnamese boy, wearing a conical straw hat, had turned green with some sort of food poisoning and, inverting the large hat like a bowl, vomited into it in the middle of the playground. Ellen asked Nicole to report on her day, but the little girl just stared unhappily at her untouched soup and whispered, 'No.' Ellen had not yet sought professional confirmation that Nicole's occasional muteness might be connected with her jaw having been taken apart, put back together again and wired shut for months.

Ben wanted this scene to disappear. He wanted the children not to exist – just for a while, just for a year or so, just long enough for him to confide in Ellen and *have it out*, to justify his actions; to explain how he really felt, how he adored her. He would even explain about the girls and Hannan last night – well, no, perhaps not that . . . At any rate, and *especially*, he would talk about Victor Wiesman, about the unfairness, the randomness: it should have been Innis, everyone knew that, Innis was *useless*. He was kept and Ben was turned out on the street because Innis was a black man and it wasn't done to sack a large firm's only black employee – it was that simple. It had to be. People like Ben weren't *fired* – Ellen understood that, didn't she? She knew he wasn't a failure. He could have started again – it might even have been an upwards move – of course it probably *would* have been, in time. But now here they were, this was their situation. If he could just get some time to think. Everything moved too quickly. He hadn't had a reasonable, humorous conversation with Ellen for years, since Sean was born – or even before that, with all the pregnancy scares. Why did other people appear so relaxed? Even his divorced friends and acquaintances seemed to take it in their stride, to move on, to make plans. Is this the way they perceived *him*? A family man? A provider? Someone who played by the rules? A husband and parent having an interesting adventure abroad?

Spoons clicked in soup bowls. Ellen was asking Sean about the Vietnamese boy again, and about Daniel and Anne and Little Paul. Ben wanted all of this to cease. He wanted to start over, do things properly this time. Failing that he wanted to stand up, ask for silence, list his crimes to his family in a firm voice and ask for forgiveness and solidarity at a difficult time. What real harm could come from that? Ellen would back him up, would agree he had done the right thing, would know he wasn't a failure or a killer or an adulterer or . . . a liar? Would she forgive him for lying to Sean? For *hypnotizing* him into believing it had been a dog? Ben's eyes were unfocused now, as he thought of his parents and his sisters and how utterly supportive they would *pretend* to be . . .

'Ben?'

'Sorry?'

'We lost you for a second there. Sean was just asking about the bicycle again.'

Ellen stared at her husband as he parried Sean's demand for an immediate, night-time visit to a bicycle shop in town. Clearly, Ben was exhausted. He was trying so hard to make things go well, to turn things around, and he'd done a wonderful job. He'd swiftly gained the confidence of his powerful boss. He'd charmed the over-charming Hannan. Mancini had put him in charge of the office while out of town. Ben had made the effort to show Sean a good time over the weekend. He'd gamely drunk more alcohol than ever before to put the Russians at their ease. He was doing all he could.

The end of the meal saw Nicole straight to bed, Sean in front of the new television, Ben in the shower, Haz and Ama throwing away perfectly good food in a poor country and Ellen at the French windows watching the snow fall outside. It had already settled an inch deep. Snow swirled over the hillside above the house, caught in the security lights on the roof. The French School had instructed Sean to purchase black rubber boots – the same as the ones the workmen wore, but in miniature – and Ellen reminded herself to take them out of the closet and put them by the front door. Outside, the snow fell hard enough to obscure the lights of the city. Even on the road at the bottom of the hill, the lights of occasional cars or trucks were unfocused and yellowed by the snow. One of these cars turned into the road that led up the hill to the Mancinis' house. Ellen squinted into the night and made out that it was larger than the Mancinis' Euphoria, and taller than either Sammy's or Chauffeur's cars. It climbed the hill and slowed at the Mancinis' carport. Someone got out and approached the open doors, went inside and emerged a few seconds later. Ellen moved to another window where she had a better view. It was a military van, similar or even identical to the one that had brought the news of Hannan's assassination attempt only yesterday. Ellen could make out the red stripe along its side. The soldier climbed back in and gestured to the driver. The van's lights beamed through the thickening snow as it nosed and bumped off the steep and uneven track – a proper road had been promised by spring. The van did a five-point turn on the narrow track, then bounced back down the hill to the road. It turned back in the direction it had come from, and disappeared around the corner of the Soviet Embassy compound.

Ellen had to conclude that this was some sort of security check that might become routine in the aftermath of the bombings. If so it seemed rather cursory. She walked down the corridor to the bathroom. The light was still on, the mirror was still steamed, but Ben wasn't there. Ellen went into the bedroom and saw Ben lying uncovered in his underwear, face down, asleep. She stepped silently to the side of the bed, covered his body with a blanket and switched off the light.

49

Ben endured Tuesday with a calm fatalism that took him by surprise. He did nothing to assist, nor to hinder, the advancement of Planning and Resources. At night he slept for stretches lasting twenty minutes or less before his conscience woke him and reminded him of his predicament and his shame. He was able to sleep again only when he managed to convince himself, like some oleaginous defence attorney, that a child had died on a dusty road solely because of Victor Wiesman's cowardice and bad judgement. At dawn he awoke thinking of Marie-Ange, and everything she represented to a man's sense of purpose and accomplishment in life: it was appalling to contemplate. It also caused him to nestle closer to Ellen in their bed, slowly to rouse her, to make love to her with the conscious thought that his relatively unfamiliar attentions might betray his . . . betrayal. When he sighed 'I love you,' he heard the same voice and the same tone and the same words he had so improbably spoken to a stranger, and convinced himself that he had meant *Ellen* at the time – it had been confusion, fear, champagne, nonsense. When Ellen said 'I love you,' drawing the sheet and blanket back over them against the cold, it sounded so profoundly sincere and obvious that Ben had to squeeze shut his eyes and make further redundant vows to himself that if he managed to escape from the crisis Victor Wiesman had set in train, he would devote himself as never before to the happiness of this pure and courageous woman. He held her in his arms now – not *too* hard, not *too* apologetically – but so closely that he could feel her precious heart against his guilty one, slowing, slowing. 'I love you,' she said again. 'I love *this*.'

At half past eight, Sammy came to the door on foot, his trouser legs soaked to the knee. His car couldn't climb the track in eight inches of snow. Ellen drove both men down to the road in the Euphoria. They watched her return safely to the house in four-wheel drive, then got into Sammy's car and slowly made their way into the city. The building sites had been temporarily abandoned. Only the main boulevards had been ploughed. Few shops had opened this early in the morning. The air was clear and the sky a rare dark blue. Schools must have been closed: there were no children about. Soldiers blew into their cupped hands and stamped their boots. Last night's car and bus crashes – against trees, in the sewer, on the pavements – were silent and snow-covered. The eucalyptus trees hung low over the avenues, gleaming in the low sun, dripping like leaking taps. The drive to his office was one of the most beautiful sights Ben had ever seen.

He endured a day made difficult because of the snow: no appointments could be kept, Diane was out of the office, Mancini was unreachable. Ben's only executive act was to confirm that the evening's road opening would go ahead. In doing so he spoke to one of the General's official spokesmen, an elderly-sounding man with excellent English and good manners: he was a civilian. Ben could not say for certain that Mancini would be able to attend the ceremony, but nominated himself as stand-in.

At noon Ben phoned Ellen. He asked her to invite the Russians to dinner next week, and to be prepared to drive to the road opening in the Euphoria. He said it would be wise if she picked him up directly from the office. Sammy's car wasn't up to deep snow, and more snow was expected. He phoned Candy Mancini, who hadn't heard anything from her husband in two days, and told her he would step in if need be. Candy said, 'You're so brave.' Ben ate no lunch, and spent much of the early afternoon looking out of the window at snow flurries and skidding car accidents. He felt better. It seemed that with enough distance between him and the weekend, a sort of life might be resumed. At two o'clock he walked to the Hotel Chevalier and drank a beer, ate a bowl of peanuts, kept an eye out for Hannan. At two-thirty he was back at the entrance of his office building, waiting like a good man for his trusting wife. The Euphoria pulled up at quarter to three, Ellen glowing with excitement behind the wheel.

'What a day! Do you want to drive? It was like a toboggan ride coming down here.'

'I'll drive if you like.'

Ellen moved over to the passenger seat. Ben took the wheel of the Euphoria for the first time since Saturday night.

'They should have postponed this,' said Ellen. 'It's starting to snow again. And it will be almost dark before it's all over, won't it?'

'The show must go on,' said Ben. 'And I'm in charge. There's no sign of Mancini. I suppose I'll have to give a speech. Dominic wasn't in the office, so I don't know. He writes the speeches. It's been a very odd day.'

'It started well,' said Ellen.

Ben was so uncomfortable behind the wheel of the Euphoria that he drove hunched over, peering into the snow, fists tight on the steering wheel. They were headed south, right through the centre of the old city. Ben had never been here before. The streets were narrow and, because of the snow, almost deserted. The shops and houses looked as if they had been carved out of the hillside, like the Baram Caves.

'I took Nicole here,' said Ellen.

'You didn't tell me. Where did you go?'

'To a sort of bazaar.'

'Oh, I've heard of that.'

'Sensational. Nicky loved it. You wind down and down a

kind of cobblestone street with tiny shops on both sides, for *miles*. That's where I bought the grey carpet.'

'I didn't notice. Sorry. I'm sorry.'

'Don't worry about it. Anyway I felt completely safe in there – these people just want to sell, sell. I actually *bargained*, Ben. Can you believe it?'

'No, I can't.'

'Sammy came with us, of course. But it's not at all threatening. People here are wonderful.'

'I'll tell the General you said so.'

'Boy, *he* must be in a bad mood. Do you think this is OK?' Ellen asked, opening her cashmere overcoat to reveal a dark-beige, woollen suit.

'Beautiful. But you won't be taking your coat off. The ceremony is outdoors. It's still snowing, even.'

The streets were so empty it was eerie. Some people shovelled or swept snow from their doorsteps, others scraped at the windscreens of rusting Fardis, others grouped around charcoal braziers for warmth. The cramped old city soon gave way to a flat stretch of recently constructed housing – the newest part of the city and home to more than one million people. The streets here had been laid out in advance – straight and soulless. Kerosene lamps flickered in the windows of row after row of drab apartment blocks. Underdressed children threw snowballs at the Euphoria as it passed.

The city ended so abruptly it was shocking: barren plateau, not a house, not a farm. The two-lane road stretched straight into the whited distance. Until the ring road was built, this arrow of highway had continued uninterrupted for three hundred miles to the coast. Ben kept his distance from a truck just ahead: a boy, a teenager, sat on its canvas covering, holding a dog with one hand and his snowy cap with the other. Without having to consult the map, Ben found the turning that led to the site of the General's ceremony. There was the new road, eight lanes wide, under half a foot of snow. Part of the road had been ploughed and designated as a car park.

'Remember, I'm a dignitary,' said Ben, as he followed the hand signals of a soldier and parked the Euphoria. 'Don't let it go to your head.'

It was not perfect weather for a road opening. Several dozen people – and one sheep – had gathered on a stretch of what would have been tarmac, but this afternoon was a field of snow indistinguishable from the surrounding plateau. They might have been standing in the middle of a desert. There was very little wind, though; the snow fell gently on the assembled crowd. This included dozens of workmen symbolically holding shovels and spades and other tools of their trade. They all wore identical coats and black watch caps.

Ben quickly found a familiar face: a sturdy politician who was the current Minister of Transportation and had designs on the presidency, should that office be reinstated in his lifetime. His name was Orla Panni, an overweight, humorous man well known to be of high intellect and capability. He wore large, thick glasses with wide, black stems. His moustache was bushy enough to catch falling snowflakes. On being introduced to Ellen he bowed as he shook her hand. He apologized for the weather. He spoke perfect English, with a British accent. He was the sort of man who was so instantly likeable that one doubted his future in politics.

Ellen wanted to ask Panni if there was going to be a war, even a little one, but chose instead to compliment him on his lovely new road.

'It is fabulous,' he said, gesturing at the snowy expanse. 'Tomorrow it will be a traffic jam. But our city will breathe again.'

Panni introduced Ben and Ellen to other members of the General's government and representatives of the business community, among them two chic women. Ben explained that Paul

Mancini had been stranded by the weather, inspecting a coal mine in the north. Ben felt drained, and unsafe. He was used to the permanent nausea now, the foul taste in his mouth, the feeling that he was about to be tapped on the shoulder.

Someone tapped him on the shoulder. He turned with a reflexive jerk to find Dominic Thrune standing there, wearing a reasonable overcoat and a cream scarf that covered his bruise.

'I didn't mean to startle you,' he said. 'I brought along some . . . words. If you would care to utter them at the appropriate moment? That would be after the sheep, before the General.'

'The sheep?' Ellen asked, having shaken Dominic's hand.

'It's the part I won't watch. They have to slaughter the sheep. This ceremony coincides with a festival. Two birds with one stone. It's worse when there's snow.'

'I don't mind a little sheep slaughtering,' Ben said. 'In fact I relish it.'

'Each to his own,' said Dominic. 'I will avert my gaze.'

Ben took a single typewritten page from Dominic and read it to himself. 'Would you be offended if I made these points in my own words?'

'By all means do. The Great Mancini likes everything written out. He is not one for extemporizing. Sorry there wasn't more notice. I should have warned you but I've been . . . preoccupied.'

'I understand.'

Ben was a good speaker. Not all lawyers were, or had to be. Even in the present circumstances he thought he could get through ten minutes of congratulating these people on their road, singling out those most responsible, stressing his organization's commitment to development, progress and cooperation, naming the damned thing 'Meheti', like everything else.

The General arrived, as Generals will, in a convoy of limousines and military vehicles. Security had to be tighter than ever now. The crowd assembled itself in a sort of receiving line leading to a podium where the speeches would be delivered.

The American, British and Canadian ambassadors arrived at the same time as the General. Ben had met none of these men before. When he was presented to them it was a simple matter of saying 'And Ellen, my wife.' No one else seemed to have brought along a wife. Ellen's cheeks glowed in the cold. She looked like the wife of someone important. She *was* the wife of someone important. When introduced to the American ambassador, she mentioned that their children were in school together. She did not say that she had heard about his son's escape attempts, his knives and rope, his beating at the hands of the French principal. The ambassador smiled in a pained way, and moved on.

The General went straight to the podium without being introduced. It was down to Panni to tell the General who Ben was. The General wore a civilian suit and no hat. He was a handsome man, darker-skinned than the majority of his compatriots. The country had celebrated his fiftieth birthday six months ago. He had light-blue eyes – also rare here – and his hair was cut so short he might have shaved his head two weeks ago. His English, though throatily accented, was confident and even cordial. He exuded strength, in the same way Mancini was able to do: he was a soldier. He knew Ellen's name.

Standing to his right was another man, who spoke no English. He was a slender, dark, beady-eyed man of about forty, wearing full dress uniform over a white turtleneck shirt and no overcoat. He had unfortunate, rat-like teeth and minuscule ears. He held his red-striped cap in the crook of his arm and stood almost to attention. The snow whitened his slicked-back hair. Panni introduced him to Ben with two words: 'Colonel Vodi.'

50

She was a clean young sheep. Even her hooves were polished. A civilian in a cheap suit over a heavy wool sweater held on to the sheep with a short leather leash. He led the sheep to a spot near the podium where the snow had been cleared and a shallow trench dug in the hard ground. Two other, similarly dressed men joined him there, to help hold down the animal. The first man took off the leash and held the sheep by the neck with both arms. Each of the other men took two of the sheep's legs.

Ben had a good view of this, just past Colonel Vodi's simian profile; he wondered which of the other officers might be Vodi's brother. A fourth man approached the sheep and produced a long, curved knife. He wore a floppy black hat like a rolled-up executioner's hood. Ben glanced at Dominic Thrune, who had bowed his head and raised the collar of his overcoat to cover his ears. What followed was expert and fascinating. The sheep hardly had a chance to squirm as the man with the knife raised her chin and deftly sliced into her throat. He pulled the head back and cut again, so that the head came neatly off. The head was placed to one side as the sheep's blood ran from her neck into the ground. The man with the knife worked quickly at each leg and then, with the help of the other men, tugged at the fleece so that it came off in one piece, like an overcoat. The perfectly skinned carcass lay steaming in the snow for a few moments, before being taken away to be gutted, roasted and – along with some of her less ceremoniously dispatched sisters – enjoyed by the dozens of deserving labourers who had looked on hungrily at the proceedings. Ben made a mental note to thank the workers in his speech.

Ben had spoken publicly innumerable times – in court, at weddings, at conferences, at meetings, at a cancer-support group and, at Harvard, to gatherings of his club. Here, in the snow, with the sheep's carcass being dragged away, with most of his audience not able to understand English, with Colonel Vodi's eyes boring into the back of his head, before statesmen and ambassadors, he felt a catch in his throat as he approached the microphone. The snow fell faster now, and he looked out at the crowd like a member of the politburo addressing Red Square. Ben's horror and guilt seemed to drain away for a moment. He felt grown up. If Alan Yates or Victor Wiesman could see *this*, he thought. He felt warm and powerful in his navy-blue overcoat, his hands on the low lectern, the microphone beneath his jaw, the hushed labourers and dignitaries awaiting his words. If his *father* could see this.

Ben saw his fogged breath float on the still, cold air as he introduced himself. He heard his low, clear voice amplified from behind, deadened by the snow. He made his points in order: the value of cooperation, determination and hard work – a nod to the dark rows of workmen here – and the desirability of progress and economic development. He used the road itself as a metaphor in this regard. He led up to a climax – which had to be a paean to the General – with a concise and, to his own ears, rather moving exegesis on geopolitics and the dangers of fanaticism. He had seen with his own eyes, he said – and only three days ago – the fruits of rabid political ideology. As he completed his address and turned to acknowledge the General, he caught Dominic's eye. Dominic looked like a swimmer who had spotted a shark's fin: mouth open, eyes wide, hand raised slightly in a gesture that said 'No . . .' Ben smiled into dampened applause, gave way to the General after shaking his hand, resumed his place between Ellen and Colonel Vodi.

Vodi, who had lost a nephew – his brother's only son, Dominic had said – just days ago, stood rigidly at Ben's side. His squinting eyes peered through a mask of ugly scorn. It had been natural enough for Ben to assume that he had nothing to do with the Vodis' tragedy: the drivers here were lunatics, world famous for it, people were killed on the roads every day. Vodi's brother wouldn't live in the outskirts of the city, would he? Vodi's boy wouldn't play alone, unsupervised, shirtless . . . The image came back to Ben once more and he was again stricken with dizzy disbelief.

The General was not a loquacious man. His brief speech ended to applause that, because so many wore gloves, was more thudding than clapping. The workers went off for their feast in a temporary barracks nearby. The dignitaries milled about for only a few minutes, Ben and Ellen among them, before the main convoy swept the highest-up away. Ben took Ellen's arm and caught up with Dominic, who was on his way alone to the car park.

'Dominic, wait up.'

Dominic stopped and turned. He said nothing. His hands were stuffed deep in his coat pockets.

'Dominic, what's the matter? What did the General say in his speech?'

Dominic glanced at Ellen, as if he were uncomfortable speaking in her presence. His curly hair was full of snow. He pursed his lips and tilted his head. 'You were an absolute *smash*,' he said, pouring sarcasm. 'What *is* it about you? The General singled you out.'

'He did?'

'That *rubbish* you spouted – I thought –'

'Hold on, Dominic. That's the line, isn't it?'

'Yes, but you don't *say* so. My *God*. I was *mortified*. I gave you the text, didn't I?'

'But the General liked it.'

'Well of *course* he did. But *we* don't like the *General*.'

'We –'

'Oh, bloody *hell*,' said Dominic, moving on. Ben and Ellen followed. Over his shoulder, Dominic muttered, 'I really thought, about halfway through your . . . your *threnody*, that Mark Antony was among us. You carried me away, Ben. Luckily he understands English. If he were to read that in translation, as others will, it will sound as if you personally want to make love to the ghastly man.' Dominic paused in the near-darkness at the edge of the car park and drew a bottle of clear liquid from one pocket of his overcoat. He took an unapologetic swig, then replaced the bottle. This gesture was oddly ungracious, as if Ben had expected to be offered a sip.

'Dominic,' Ben said, 'you're going to have to explain this to me. Calmly. In the office. Tomorrow. You will be *in* the office tomorrow?'

Dominic turned and walked away without replying. Ben didn't call after him. Instead he walked with Ellen to the Euphoria, which was covered in a quarter of an inch of light new snow.

'He's having a rough time,' said Ben.

'Maybe it was a bit naughty of you not to use his speech.'

'I only expanded it a little. You heard him. The General loved it.'

'Sounds like Dominic thinks the General is the bad guy.'

'Well, he's *our* bad guy at the moment. That's what it's all about. I have no idea what Dominic meant. He's always sounded very pro the General,' Ben said, as the Euphoria's wipers easily cleared two arcs on the windscreen.

'I think I understand him,' said Ellen, 'if you want my little-wife opinion.'

'I cherish your little-wife opinions.'

'I think he means that support for someone like the General is temporary, so you don't want to gush on the record in case he's next year's bad guy. It wouldn't reflect well on P&R. Or is that too obvious?'

'You're right as always,' said Ben. 'OK, maybe I screwed up just a little.'

'Well, *I* liked it. Oratory, Ben, it really *gets* me.'

'I could have been Lieutenant Governor by now.'

'Oh, terrific. I'm proud of you, Ben. I really am.'

Ben concentrated on driving. It would take more than an hour to get home in these conditions, and it was already dark. He hoped the children were all right. He looked forward to a light dinner and a glass of wine, early to bed with Ellen in his arms, a completely reformed man. There was nothing to worry about except his soul, and he didn't believe he possessed one. Tomorrow he would attack the day. He would learn about this country in due course, he would become an expert on the whole region. After P&R he could move to State, to the UN, to academia, back to the law – there were so many possibilities. And he would keep his trousers on.

51

Mancini had said, 'They'll come at night.'

Ben awoke in total darkness and heard the noise. He had no idea what time it was. He and Ellen had come home in time to put the children to bed. He remembered a snack and two glasses of wine and such exhaustion . . . There was the noise again. He thought of the gun. 'Shoot at the ceiling,' Mancini had said. 'Shout and shoot, shout and shoot . . . Don't shoot *at* anyone, you'll just kill one of your kids . . . It's been known to happen.' Ben had practised this in his mind – and there was the noise again. Not a child's noise. The gun was under the mattress near his head; the clip was in a locked bedside drawer; the key to the drawer was under the carpet, within easy reach. Ben thought of only two possibilities: run-of-the-mill burglars, easily scared away; and Vodi's men, which would mean the end of the world.

Ben rolled out of bed and on to the floor. He searched for and found the key. He unlocked the drawer and removed the clip. He reached under the mattress and withdrew the gun. He inserted the clip and chambered a round. He crawled along the side of the bed towards the door. Ellen hadn't moved. The bedroom door was open – it always was, so he and Ellen could hear the children. He crawled into the corridor. There was a dim, flickering light at the far end – a torch? Ben stood up and, taking Mancini's advice as seriously as if it were a military order, shouted, 'All right then!' and fired two shots at the ceiling.

The noise was much louder than he had expected. It half-deafened him in both ears. The light at the end of the corridor didn't go away, but there was a frantic noise from the living room – someone fleeing? A glass broke.

'Get out!' Ben shouted, and fired another shot upwards at forty-five degrees.

Ben heard another noise at the end of the corridor: 'Ben? Ben?'

Ben reeled at the sound of the voice. A moment later he said, 'Ellen?'

The silhouette of Ellen's head rounded the corner from the living room. She switched on the corridor lights. Just then the door of the children's room opened. Sean and Nicole came out to see what was going on, what the terrible noise was. Ben stood there in the harsh light, naked, holding the gun horizontally in both hands: it must have looked to the children as if he'd been firing at their mother.

'It's all right, my darlings,' said Ellen, rushing towards the children and glaring at her paralysed, naked, armed husband as she passed. 'It's all right.'

Ellen bundled the children back into their room, and closed the door. Ben lowered the gun and looked at the ceiling: three clean holes. The bullets had probably reached the Soviet Embassy compound, or at least the Mancinis' swimming pool. Ben walked ahead down the corridor, shivering, the gun cold against his thigh. The flickering light turned out to be the new television. He noticed just in time the broken wine glass on the floor. The clock on the wall told him it was quarter past three in the morning. Ben circled round the broken glass and sat down on the sofa. There was a blanket there, still warm from Ellen's body. Ben wrapped the blanket around his shoulders. Staring at the television screen, he raised the gun and pressed its barrel against his temple. A woman on television told him about a singer who had drowned in his swimming pool; the coroner, interviewed live, said the singer's blood contained such large quantities of barbiturates and alcohol that it was unclear how the young man had negotiated the two-hundred yards through his mansion's grounds to the pool. Another woman came on the screen to tell Ben that the basketball player who had died of a heart attack in the middle of a game had left thirty-eight million dollars to his widowed mother, ignoring eleven illegitimate children. Ben fingered the trigger. A fashion designer had outraged Milan with a model wearing a dress made entirely of his dead lover's skeleton. A clever man from Edinburgh had developed a foolproof hangover cure that involved suction cups and electricity. A liver-transplant patient complained that his donor must have had a worse drinking problem than he, the recipient, ever did, and that he now craved vodka in the morning. Ben squeezed gently at the trigger, angling the gun slightly towards the back of his skull. Evan Court came on the screen, standing in the Meheti Boulevard outside the General's headquarters, in the snow. Evan could confirm that the General had launched a midnight raid on Sereni Island. This unprovoked act was bound to mean war.

Ben remembered Haz and Ama, in the quarters at the back of the house. Surely they would have heard the gunfire? They didn't have a telephone. They hadn't come over to the main house to investigate. Ben would be terribly embarrassed to be *seen* shooting himself. Evan Court had been replaced on the screen by a man with a head of hair shaped like an armadillo's shell, who had something to say about a political scandal that had rocked Washington and the nation at large: a vice-presidential underling's second wife's son by a previous marriage was alleged to have been caught with a prostitute. Ben thought of the girl at the top of the stairs. He thought of Marie-Ange. The armadillo spoke of weather patterns in western Australia. The gun was heavy in Ben's hand. He was about to put it down when Ellen entered the room, wearing a night-gown, and stared at him in wild amazement.

'Ben? Ben? Could you please let go of the gun?'

'Of course,' Ben said. He wanted to shoot the television. Instead he put the gun down on the glass-topped table before him. 'I can't *tell* you how sorry I am,' he said. 'How are the children?' Ben was amazed by Ellen's calm. He thought she would just come at him, slap him around for a little while because he had scared the children. Instead she sat down next to him, shaking her head but saying nothing. Ben wondered what he ought to say: 'Everything will be all right'? 'Did you notice there's a war on'? 'Sorry about the ceiling'? 'It won't happen again'? He held on to Ellen and thought, *I'm all she has.* Ben looked at the television. They had returned to the story of the General's raid. A map of the region was shown. Sereni Island was highlighted – a speck among other specks, big enough only for a single enemy garrison, worthless even for tourism. The military action was sword-rattling, symbolic. The General wanted to draw attention away from domestic conflict. He wanted to suggest that the neighbouring country – an enemy of such long standing that no one could remember why they hated each other so much – might be behind the elements of dissent at home: the LFP, the religious right, the political left.

'I'm so . . . sorry,' Ben said. Those were the right words. 'I'm so *sorry*.' He kissed her hair. 'I don't want you to worry. Ellen, I'm sorry. I love you *so much*. I don't know what came over me. I was suddenly so frightened. I thought there was someone in the house, coming to get . . .' Ben swallowed as the thought dawned on him. 'Coming to get *Sean*.'

52

Ellen drove Sean to school in the Euphoria. It was a fantastically bright, sunny morning and she squinted against the glare of nearly a foot of snow. Earlier she had driven Ben down the hill to the road, where Sammy waited. They hadn't mentioned last night's calamity. Ben looked embarrassed and ashamed of himself. He couldn't meet Ellen's eye even as he kissed her cheek and got into Sammy's car.

Explaining the gunfire to Sean and Nicole had been surprisingly easy: 'Isn't Papa brave? There could have been *thieves*, and he was trying to frighten them away.'

'Were there thieves?' asked Sean, who had been interested in thieves since he was two years old.

'No, sweetie. But if there *had* been . . .' Ellen smiled her way through this conversation, changing the subject as often as she could, wishing she could say, 'I have no idea what's bothering your father. He may need to *go away*, for a while.'

Driving slowly back home, Ellen passed the front gates of the Soviet Embassy compound. She had never seen the gates open before, but this time they were. A car emerged. The car flashed its lights, so Ellen stopped, thinking she ought to let it go ahead. It was a Fardi, not well equipped for the snow. Instead of moving on, the car stopped and the driver's fogged window was wound down. It was Nadia Tumarevna, waving a gloved hand and smiling her theatrical smile. Ellen pulled over. Nadia stepped balletically out of her car – wearing high fur boots and a tall fur hat – and came over to say hello.

'What a day,' she said.

'It's beautiful. I never expected so much snow so soon.'

'I'm so happy to see you, Ellen,' said Nadia. 'I haven't been to the club since last time. I think I have some news for you.'

'News?'

'Oh, Denis wouldn't want me to say, I think.'

'Go *ahead*,' said Ellen, sounding to herself like Candy Mancini in her gossiping stride. Only after saying this did it occur to Ellen that it might be something political, something to do with the war, or Hannan. 'You don't *have* to say,' she added.

As the Soviet Embassy compound gates closed automatically, Nadia looked both ways up and down the deserted street. 'You and I should celebrate,' Nadia said, rubbing her gloves together. 'I think I'm going to have a baby.'

'Oh, Nadia!' Ellen reached out of the window and squeezed her wrist. 'This is sensational! But you must have known last week?'

'Not for sure. Now is for sure.'

'This is *sensational*. I'm so happy for you. Denis – is he thrilled?'

'He *says* so,' Nadia said, first frowning in thought, then beaming at Ellen with a white smile that stretched from cheek to glowing cheek. 'He is the happiest man in the world.'

'Come to our house for dinner,' Ellen said. 'Just the four of us,' she added, thinking that to invite the Mancinis would be a terrible idea, and remembering that Ben had asked her to make this invitation in any case. 'Before Christmas, anyway.'

Nadia shook her head. 'We are going on home leave for three months.'

'Well then, I'll arrange it when you're back. I have your number. I'm *so* thrilled, Nadia. Will you have the baby here?'

'Oh, yes,' said Nadia, looking both ways again. In a low voice, she said, 'Is better than Russia, I tell you. And you will teach me *everything*.'

'I can't wait,' said Ellen.

The women parted with blown kisses. Ellen drove home feeling much better. She parked the Euphoria and climbed the stairs – Haz had swept them clear of snow during her short absence. She could hear the telephone ringing indoors – a loud, old-fashioned bell-ring that reminded her of her parents' house. Through the French windows she saw Haz answering it, and she waved to him. Inside, she kicked off her low boots and went into the living room, expecting to have to speak to Candy. She took the receiver from Haz and thanked him.

'Hello?'

'Ellen, this is Evan Court.'

'Evan? How nice to hear from you.' Over the telephone, Evan's voice sounded exactly as it did via satellite from far-flung war-zones: 'This is Evan Court.'

'How are you, darling?'

No one other than her parents and Ben had ever called her 'darling' before; she reminded herself that Evan originally came from somewhere in England. 'I suppose I'm fine,' she said. Ellen could see through to the dining room, where Ama sat at the table with Nicole, drawing a crayon picture in silence.

'I'm ringing just to say I have to cancel this afternoon at your club – sorry.'

'I didn't even – Candy didn't –'

'I'm off with the boys to Sereni Island.'

'Oh, my.'

'Having a look to see what this little war is all about.'

'How will you . . . *get* there?'

'Oh, the air force will be kind enough to give us a lift. Look for me on the air, will you? I look forward to your critique.'

'Of course I will. Please be careful, Evan.'

'As always. It's only a short hop from here. I'm at the coast.'

'But I saw you after midnight, here in the city.'

'Staying up for me, were you?'

'Oh . . .'

298

'I got a flight out of here just after dawn. Slept on the plane. Anyway, must rush. See you anon, darling.'

Ellen blushed, put down the telephone. She took off her coat, hung it up in the hallway, then wandered into the dining room to say hello to Nicole. The child looked up from her drawing, her jaw slack, her mouth slightly twisted, as if in annoyance. Ellen felt a now familiar combination of worry and anger at the sight of her daughter continuing to behave this way. What had Ellen done wrong? Why was Sean so relatively outgoing, after all he'd been through? Ellen pretended to be interested in Nicole's craggy, grey mess on the piece of paper – then, hearing a strange noise, went towards the kitchen to investigate. In the corridor leading to the bedrooms she found Haz, standing on a ladder, repairing the three holes in the ceiling. Ellen couldn't imagine where he had found the supplies for such a job, unless the builders had left some behind. Haz smiled at her and nodded his head, as if repairing the weapons damage of a master's residence were a natural part of a houseboy's duties. Ellen smiled back, then quickly turned on her heel and grimaced in embarrassment. She went into the living room and, to take her mind off the unwelcome turn Ben seemed to have taken, switched on the television and searched the airwaves for Evan Court.

53

'Hello?'

'Ben, my good friend, it is Chava.'

Ben had dreaded this call for days. He'd wanted the whole memory to evaporate. 'How are you?'

'I am on my boat, here at the coast. I thought with the war . . . I should move her, no?'

'Good idea.'

'We could practically hear the action from here; it isn't far.'

'Is it serious, do you think?'

'We will have to see. Now listen to me, there is a small matter. I thought it was my duty to tell you.'

'Go ahead then.'

'You may just possibly find, as I have done . . . that you have a little problem.'

'A problem?'

'Yes. Just a little one. But I have good news.'

'Good news? You haven't told me the problem yet.'

'My friend, my good friend. You may find you have . . . the clap.'

Ben, who had been sitting with his feet on the clean desk, felt the chair give beneath him. At exactly that moment he thought he sensed a stabbing pain at the base of his bladder. 'You –'

'Not to worry! Not to worry! The best doctor in the city will solve the problem for you – he will deliver antibiotics to the desk of the Chevalier, if you want. No need to worry, really, Ben. If you have a problem, just get in touch with him. I'll give you the number.'

'But my . . . wife,' Ben said.

'Oh dear. You have –?'

'Yes I *have*,' said Ben, trying to keep his voice down.

'Oh dear. Oh dear, oh dear.' Ben heard a champagne cork popping in the background, and seagulls. 'I have a plan,' Hannan said, and Ben could hear him licking his lips. 'A plan of genius! Don't worry. I once embarrassed myself in this way. In Paris. I had the lovely woman's chef pour medicine into her orange juice in the morning, into her soup at lunch, into her coffee after dinner. *Voilà!* She never suspected a thing. You know, sometimes the girls can't feel the clap. This is what you shall do.'

Ben automatically took down the telephone number Hannan gave him, and the doctor's name. He had never had a venereal disease before. He knew nothing about them. By 'clap' did Hannan mean gonorrhoea specifically, or did the term cover a broader range of diseases – even exotic, local ones?

'You know,' said Ben, 'I'm just horrified. Marie-Ange didn't look the least –'

'Now, don't blame the girls,' said Hannan, chivalrously.

'OK, look, could I have some phone numbers for you as well? In case I need your help?'

'But of course.' Hannan listed three numbers. 'Now I must go. Tomorrow, New York! Then I have to do some *very* sneaky things, but I will be back in a few weeks. Let's have a party then, my friend.'

Ben had an appointment in forty-five minutes, across town. Sammy was waiting downstairs. Ben needed to urinate, but didn't dare. He dreaded doctors. He was the kind of hypochondriac who thinks he has every conceivable illness but will never confess his symptoms to a doctor for fear of hearing bad news. He had a list of persistent symptoms that he thought about all the time – that used to keep him awake at night. His feet tingled. The skin on his shins was numb to the touch. His left knee clicked. His kidneys hurt, always. For years he had felt a dull pain in the right-middle of his back that he assumed was either lung cancer or cirrhosis of the liver. The tumour in his skull, which he assumed had been set in train by a blow to the head during a baseball game in high school, hurt during warm weather.

Ben took his feet off the desk and placed them squarely on the floor. He gripped the rests of his chair. He pushed himself into a standing position and began to pace about his office. His shoes squeaked on the polished parquet. *Gonorrhoea.* He went to the tall windows and looked out at the boulevard. Only piles of sooty snow remained. The eucalyptus trees dripped sparklingly in the sunlight. Sammy's car was there, its engine running. Ben squeezed his genitals through his trousers – very gently at first, not wanting to know the news. Was that a twinge, there? He thought his bladder did feel peculiar, or was that another one of his dark, persistent symptoms? He put a hand in his pocket and pulled on the tip of his penis, as if initiating urination. How long did this disease take to manifest itself? Was there hope? He pulled a little harder until – was that pain? Was that gonorrhoea, or was that just what it felt like to have one's penis pulled halfway to the knee in cold weather? He knew he had to go to the toilet sooner or later, and that it might as well be now.

He left his office, looked both ways, then clipped across the marble landing to the gents'. He decided to go into the cubicle, to muffle any screams. He lowered his trousers and sat down, so that he could relax. He found he couldn't start the flow. Was this good, or was this bad? He leaned back against the cool tile wall, cursing Hannan, cursing Marie-Ange, cursing Victor Wiesman whose fault all of this was. Could I have a reprieve, just this *once*? he asked. With all the other things going on, and now that I am a *reformed man*, would it be too much to expect good luck this one time?

He breathed in, he breathed out. He felt disassociated from his urinary tract. He'd heard that if you turned on a tap it helped, so he reached out to the sink and did so. Still his bladder didn't speak to him. He pressed two fingers into his abdomen. There . . . there . . . Something was happening. Something was welling up. Ben closed his eyes and concentrated. It was just the fear, that was all. As soon as this was over he would be back to normal.

The urine began to flow at first in droplets, just a leak, and Ben detected no special pain. When it surged out at a more normal rate, tears sprang to his eyes: it felt *hot*, and it stung meanly at or near the tip. Ben forced himself to finish, as if he would never have to urinate again, then dropped his head into his hands.

54

That evening Ben bought a bottle of whisky on the way home.
His afternoon meeting had gone badly. Two of the three men
he had met – all of them local bankers – chewed gum after
lunch, and the third twisted a toothpick in his mouth beneath
a soiled moustache. This drove Ben mad and prevented him
from focusing on what he was supposed to say to them. Ellen
knew of Ben's horror of noisy mastication, and he would use
this as an excuse for the whisky.

At home, all was phonily cheerful. The ceiling in the corridor
had been repaired. Dinner boiled and roasted away. Sean was
doing his homework at the dining-room table. Nicole sat next
to Ellen on the sofa, waiting for the news to start on the
television. Ben went into the kitchen and poured himself a
large whisky, drank it right there, then poured himself another.
He thought this might kill his gonorrhoea. He had already
decided, during the drive into the hills, that it was impossible
for him to have passed on the disease so quickly. Everything
was going to be all right.

He sat down in the armchair next to the sofa where Ellen
and Nicole were snuggled together. Evan Court soon came on
to the screen, live from Sereni Island, standing handsomely in
a conquered machine-gun nest. The General had taken the
island in no more than two hours. There had been few injuries.
Forty-eight enemy had been captured and were already on
their way home. International protests had been lodged. The
situation was still tense.

'Your Evan is something else,' Ben said. 'How do you suppose he *got* there, so quickly?'

Ellen shrugged. She didn't want to say that she had spoken to Evan. She felt thrillingly adulterous.

Dinner, from Ben's anaesthetized point of view, was downright joyous. He regaled his family with stories from the city. He drew Sean out on the subject of school. He tickled Nicole's ribs and thought he almost made her smile. He beamed at Ellen. Afterwards he went to the bathroom, urinated, and had to bite his wrist to stop himself from crying out. He single-handedly put both children to bed – after a quick aperitif and a visit to the French windows to gaze down upon the blackout in the city and the new military guard at the bottom of the track – and read Sean a special story about the Knights Templar. He apologized to Ellen for still having to catch up on his rest, and went to bed drunk enough to be able to sleep until morning.

That evening was a breakthrough, and was to set a pattern. Ben waited only two days before contacting Hannan's doctor, visiting him in an alcoholic haze of hypochondriacal panic, who duly arranged to have Ben pick up his medicine at the reception desk at the Hotel Chevalier. The course of antibiotics lasted only six days, and it proved effective. Ben had put out of his mind the possibility that Ellen might have been infected. He kept the house stocked with whisky. He outdid himself with the children. He presided seigneurially over the dinner table.

Paul Mancini, who smoked cigarettes all the time now, opened up to Ben, confided his dreams for the expansion of P&R's involvement in the country's dramatic regeneration. Forests were to be planted, a modern harbour built; a pipeline was being negotiated, a new airport at the coast had been mooted. The war had helped. The General's position at home had been consolidated. The international community was not in the mood to intervene – even the Russians seemed half-hearted in their condemnation of the General's unprovoked attack. Evan Court had gone to Angola. Dominic Thrune was still nervous, still needed Ben's help, but the tension on all fronts gradually eased. Ben thought he might be regaining control. When he didn't have an appointment for lunch he took walks around the city, buying presents to send home for Christmas, absorbing the atmosphere, contemplating what he now thought of as a parallel life: of *course* he could have taken Victor Wiesman's advice, rested for a few months, caught up with Ellen and the children, got another job. Of *course* he could have, but the bold step he had taken had written him a new biography. The other Ben Pelton might as well still be living back home, commuting, working like a dog, sweating like a desert tank-driver when in court, suffering in-law weekends, Thanksgivings, Christmases. The other Ben Pelton, his eye on near-immediate partnership, fantasized about early retirement – perhaps a triumphant return to Law School, where he could be tweedily sardonic in front of classrooms full of shockingly young and impressionable proto-lawyers. The new Ben Pelton was far away, where no one could see him.

Christmas came and went blissfully unobserved, except that Sean got his red bicycle at last; Nicole got a plastic racket and a sponge ball because on the rare occasions when she expressed enthusiasm for anything it tended to be tennis. The new, parallel, whisky-drinking Ben Pelton had survived his rocky start. The city was quiet, violence-wise. Ben had met and befriended some impressive locals from the professions – they tended to be more thoughtful, quieter, more . . . *civilized* than their American counterparts: Ben had already begun to adopt the American expatriate's *hauteur* regarding his home and countrymen.

The Peltons employed April to baby-sit, so that they might

have a cultural life. After films, plays, lectures or exhibitions, Ben drove April home to Diane's house, biting his lip against the urge to ask her leading questions about her private, teenage life. At weekends, they packed up the Euphoria and drove off into the rugged countryside to see the sights: classical ruins, healing baths, crusader castles. Ellen noticed how slowly and carefully Ben drove, how his hands never left the sides of the steering wheel. Ben's festering guilt, meanwhile, was like one of his long-term medical symptoms – a lump or a twinge that might or might not be cancer: he tried not to think about it. At night he sedated himself with strong drink. At work he wrote unnecessarily elaborate memoranda, some of which he never sent to anyone. He had come to the conclusion that life was a simple matter of waiting for the next thing to happen, good or bad. He felt helpless where his future was concerned, and his instinct at the moment was to pass the weeks and months like someone in disguise, his figurative trilby pulled low over his brow.

If there were to be no redemption, Ben thought, there could always be amnesia. Hadn't he already recovered from ten thousand small trespasses and embarrassments that had seemed insurmountable at the time? This too would fade into the fog of the past. Each day he shaved and dressed, said 'Good morning' to Sammy, negotiated the day's work and returned in the evening to his grateful family: another day to be checked off the calendar of his life. It was normal. *He* was normal. Everything was going to be fine. The children adored him. Ellen adored him – he could tell by the way she looked at him over those grown-up dinners. Everything was going to be fine.

55

Ellen wondered how to go about helping Ben. She couldn't guess what had come over him unless it was still the Wiesman débâcle, which he had never seemed quite to shrug off. He drank every evening. He fell into bed right after the children. He spoke in a stilted way, like a sarcastic headmaster addressing an especially dim and guilty boy. His *laugh* had changed. Ben used to laugh charmingly, if rarely, without opening his mouth wide: he had laughed with his eyes. Now he laughed frequently, at anything – head tossed back, teeth exposed, forcing out an alien, asthmatic noise. His eyes were glazed. He sweated. He had lost weight. On their few excursions into the country – which Ellen had to organize herself – he refused to speak while driving and would stop the car if the children made the slightest scene. When the telephone rang at home he answered it in the kitchen, even if Haz and Ama were there.

Ellen wondered if she should tell Ben's parents, or Mancini, or her own local doctor (whom Candy had recommended). She had a routine appointment with the doctor soon anyway. She thought she might bring the appointment forward, because she had noticed a slight discharge, unlike anything she'd had before. Normally she was good at medical self-diagnosis, but this was different. It wasn't a urinary-tract infection. As her appointment with the doctor neared she began to wonder, in an abstracted way, if she might have a venereal disease. She studied Ben's strained features over the dinner table to see if this were remotely possible, and decided it was. Because of this foreknowledge, she had time to prepare her retaliation if the doctor were to confirm her suspicions: she would say nothing about it to Ben, not right away. She would watch him. She would guard this secret like a concealed weapon, see how long Ben carried on not telling her the truth: find out how disturbed he really was.

As always in her adult life, Ellen had to go through the motions of her routine for the sake of the children. Her moments away from them were rare. Three times a week she attended language lessons in the basement of an apartment building halfway to the centre of town. Her five fellow pupils were all women, of four different nationalities, all facing the same relatively empty days as Ellen did. Their teacher was a fiercely handsome young man named Hugo who smoked cigarettes throughout the lessons and encouraged his pupils to join him. He had made it clear on the first day that he was a political dissident and fully expected to be carted away to prison one day. Ellen suspected that in reality he lived with his parents and exercised his political conscience only in the voting booth.

Hugo was a flirt, and an enthusiastic teacher. Ellen was relieved to find that she had shed her high-school embarrassment about speaking a foreign language, and could repeat what Hugo said in a loud and confident voice. The language's total unfamiliarity was somehow reassuring, unlike dimly remembered and intimidating French. Ellen's intellect – once so important a component of her character but now long unemployed – gratefully lapped up this new knowledge as if slaking a seven-year-old thirst. It made Ellen happy when Hugo praised her. She learned the alphabet, and after only a few weeks was reading and copying out simple sentences. She was reminded during this process that children are taught nothing but propaganda.

None of the other women proved to be friend material: they were diplomatic wives, older than Ellen, with mean, frustrated faces and expensive tastes. Ellen had no intention of going native here, but she found it offensive that these leathery, thin-lipped, well-fed women should flaunt Italian shoes and French scarves and Swiss watches in so poor a country. Nor did any of them show the slightest interest in the new language; it was as if they had been ordered to attend classes by their husbands. They mumbled, they patronized Hugo, they didn't do their homework.

Gonorrhoea? Ellen wondered. Some potent local strain, perhaps? Boiling with a fury that she was not yet allowed to release, she smiled at Ama and Haz, smiled at Hugo, smiled at Madame Soubrier – she even smiled at Ben when he came home from the office. She could just add *this* to the list of ways she didn't want to turn out: with a whoring, drunken husband who'd gone to seed – a marriage in ruins, left alone to raise two children on alimony prised from the soiled clutches of a *failed attorney* ... Ellen wished she hadn't been raised so strictly, so coldly, to be so phlegmatic, so diagnostic. Otherwise she could just go at Ben with a kitchen knife and ask questions once he got out of the hospital. Instead she calmly arranged for Sean's classmates' younger sisters to come over to try to befriend poor Nicole. She helped her quiet, expert servants keep the house in order. She wrote faithfully not only to her own parents but to Ben's, and to his sisters, saying everything was fine and not to worry about occasional disturbing news reports from the likes of Evan Court. The war, which hadn't really been a war, was long over. There would probably be an election soon. Foreigners lived safely segregated from the rabble. The locals were super. There was so much to see and do. In the summer the children would swim and swim, at home and with the neighbours. The family might take their first holiday in Paris or Rome – or both. Everything was ideal. Ben had made the right decision. As a husband, Ben was an absolute *triumph*.

Sean was eager to learn to ski. Little Paul had already done so at an all-weather *piste* of white plastic bristles on the roof of the Pleasure Dome at the north end of Meheti Boulevard. This building contained an Olympic-sized swimming pool, a ten-pin bowling alley, four cinemas, a running track, a boxing gym, a natural-history museum and a children's electronic-games arcade. Little Paul offered to come along and coach Sean on the boy's first outing to the *piste*. Candy drove everyone there in the Mancinis' Euphoria. The girls came along to watch. Paul and Sean casually spoke French to each other, as they did at school, as if it were a secret language. It made Ellen nervous to have Candy behind the wheel at any time after midday, but she seemed in a naturally good and sober mood and said she might do some skiing herself. Ellen had gone through the motions of inviting Ben along – it was a Saturday – but he had complained of back trouble and an almost crippling need for sleep.

It was a brilliantly sunny day, not too cool. The roof of the Pleasure Dome had a terrific view of the old city, especially from the top of the miniature J-bar ski lift. An adult would turn perhaps four times in descending the gentle, watered slope of bristles, but small children could snowplough this way and that and make good progress in an afternoon. There were appropriately dressed ski instructors on hand, who pretended to take the rooftop as seriously as they would the east face of the Vandrellane.

The rooftop wasn't crowded today – there was still real skiing available in the Berevan Mountains. The boys were fitted with skis, poles and boots. The lift was slowed down and an instructor held on to Sean and walked beside him as he was dragged unsteadily to the nearby summit. Little Paul could handle the lift by himself. Ellen walked up a concrete staircase at the edge of the slope, and put on dark glasses against the bright sunshine. She glanced down at her hand on the wooden banister and found herself noticing how youthful

311

it looked. She actually paused there to study her hand more carefully. She held it up to the sunlight. It was a girl's hand, not the hand of a mother of two and the wife of someone suddenly exhibiting symptoms of imbalance.

A northerly wind had swept the capital's basin almost clear of fumes. The city sparkled as it had never done before in Ellen's experience. Looking to the north she could make out her own house and the Mancinis' – two glinting white seashells against a beach of brown hillside. The forbidding Soviet Embassy compound stretched across the near horizon like a walled forest.

Sean had completed one run of the slope, with the instructor holding on to his waist from behind. Little Paul followed, falling once. The boys came back up on the lift, rosy-cheeked and smiling.

'This is *sensational*,' said Sean, his skis clattering and crossing as he was held nearly off the ground by the breathless instructor.

Sean began his next run, but Little Paul stayed by Ellen's side. Candy had still not come out on to the roof; she may have been in the bar.

'I'm never going to be a good skier,' Paul said, 'but I do enjoy it.' The boy had a way of speaking that startled Ellen every time she heard it.

'You're already a fine skier,' Ellen said.

'Look at Sean,' said Paul, smiling fondly. 'He'll be better at this than I am in about fifteen *minutes*.'

'Now, Paul.'

'I think Sean's a remarkable boy,' Paul said.

'Why, thank you, Paul. How ... *remarkable* of you to say so.'

'I was a little worried about him at first.'

'What, settling in?'

'Yes ... And other things.'

Near the bottom of the hill the instructor let go of Sean and let him slide to a stop by himself.

'What other things?' Ellen asked. She still wasn't used to Little Paul's manner. With his big blue eyes and pale skin he could sometimes look even younger than his age – despite having inherited his parents' height – and yet Ellen found herself listening to him as if he were Sean's schoolteacher at the end of term.

'Oh, the whole mess about the accident. He was really upset, wasn't he?'

Ellen had to think for a moment before remembering the dog. 'I suppose he was. Not for long, though. He told you about that, did he?'

'He sure did. He said it was a secret.'

'Yes, well, I imagine it should really be a secret, Paul.'

'So no one finds out.'

'Right.'

'I understand,' said Paul, his expression severe.

Sean came back up on the J-bar, absolutely beaming with joy. He was on his own. His instructor was going to lead the way for Sean's first solo run. Sean set off slowly, biting his lip in concentration.

'Poor Sean,' said Ellen. 'You're right, now that you mention it. He was pretty quiet for days after the accident. The same thing happened to me, when I was Sean's age or a little older. My father was driving.'

Paul's eyes grew wide. 'Where *were* you?'

'In America.'

'Did your father stop the car?'

'Yes, of course. I mean, it's different in America. You have to stop and go back. Here it's pretty likely no one will miss them. That's what my husband says, anyway.'

Paul crinkled his nose. 'Is that true?'

'I think so.'

'So what happened?'

'We stopped. I don't really remember very much of this. We turned around. My father explained what was going on, what we'd hit. There was a woman there crying and sort of *wailing*, which was more upsetting than anything else. There was quite a mess, but it wasn't as if it were my father's *fault*, or anything. They can just run right out in front of the car, the way it happened with my husband here.'

'Did the woman call the police?'

'The police? I don't think so. It was obvious what had happened. I think my father might have offered to pay her, once she calmed down.'

'*Pay* her?'

'I know, it seems silly. He just felt . . . guilty.'

'I should think *so*,' said Little Paul, leaning on his poles, looking as indignant as was possible for an eight-year-old boy.

A pair of military helicopters took off from the General's headquarters to the north-west. Ellen had never seen this group of walled-in buildings from above. Built only twenty-five years ago, it looked more like a barracks than a residence, but the people took it as a good sign that the General didn't live in the Meheti Palace in the hills – a preposterous, French-built throwback of terraced gardens, parterres, ornamental bodies of water and boxwood *allées*. The helicopters banked and headed north towards the mountains.

'I don't think I was all that traumatized,' said Ellen, who was touched by Little Paul's concern. 'I hardly remembered it until now. Accidents happen, you know. It was just an accident. Sean understands that.'

'Oh, so do I,' said Paul, still looking serious.

A pair of middle-aged women, shouting at each other in Italian, were coming up on the lift. Ellen recognized one of them from her language class. Their outfits were so bright Ellen had to look away. The louder of the two got her skis tangled in the rising J-bar. The lift stopped, and the woman was rescued. In her embarrassment, she fell several more times before making it to the exit at the bottom of the hill. There she crossed paths with Candy, who got out of her way and made for the staircase to join Ellen and her son at the summit.

'Anyway, it was probably wild,' said Ellen.

'Wild?'

'Here comes your mom. Yes, wild. If my husband had gone back someone might have claimed it. There might have been trouble. That's what your mother says, too.'

'My *mother*?'

'Well, yes. I think my husband said that was her advice when he first came here and his taxi ran over a dog. It was probably wild, she said.'

'A *dog*?'

'Yes, of course.'

Candy stopped halfway up the stairs to watch Sean skiing by, and to applaud him.

'Mrs Pelton,' said Little Paul, fixing her with his adult blue eyes, 'I don't know what you are talking about. I probably shouldn't say this. But mine is a different secret.'

'What do you mean?' asked Ellen, kneeling down and putting a hand on the boy's shoulder.

Little Paul waited a second, saw his mother resuming her climb, and said, 'It wasn't a dog.'

56

Ben walked out of the P&R office building into warm sunshine, bent on food and drink and the solitary pleasure of reading an out-of-date newspaper. It had been a good morning, he thought: plans for the visit of the Eminent Founder were falling into place; Mancini was out of the capital for a few days again, leaving Ben in charge; the warm weather had put everyone in a good mood. An inexplicable, icier-than-usual atmosphere prevailed at home; this was a further reason why Ben felt relieved to be alone, in the sunshine, free and anonymous for at least two hours.

Dominic Thrune lurched into sight down the boulevard. Ben considered turning around and walking in the opposite direction, but it was too late: Dominic hailed him and gestured for him to hurry up. Ben nodded and cut through the milling pedestrians to greet his colleague.

'Ah, here you are,' said Dominic, too loudly, as if for someone else's benefit. He clapped Ben on the shoulder and fell into step with him, as if they had a prearranged destination. '*This* is the weather we've been waiting for. Trust me, it will stay like this for weeks now, just *glorious*. The winter can be a bit *grim*, don't you think? Yes, even I can get the blues in winter. But now all will be well with the world, the birds will sing again, the people will rejoice and we will be *choked* in smog as God intended.'

'Hello, Dominic,' Ben said. Dominic had been almost invisible at the office. The two men had spoken only once in private since Dominic's altercation with the presumed Russian: Ben had assured him that everything was being done to help. 'You're in a good mood.'

'And why not? Just look around.'

It was true: the men had removed their rough woollen hats and coats; the women wore skirts or summer dresses. The city had come alive again after a blink of winter. People sat out of doors, the bus windows were open. The shouts of children could be heard from school playgrounds. Restaurants and cafés had reclaimed the pavements up and down the boulevard and a smell of dry earth and fresh plaster carried on the air.

'Where shall we go?' Dominic asked. 'I have something of just the *slightest* importance to convey to you. If I dare.'

Ben wanted to decline, but said, 'Oh, all right. I could use a little drama in my life. And a drink.'

They went to one of the interior-courtyard restaurants, the same one where Ben had first dined with Mancini and overdone it on the *karat*. Ben sat down on an iron chair and took off his suit jacket. He loosened his tie. The air smelled sweet away from the boulevard, and it was comfortable sitting in the shade and meeting the eye of an eager young waiter who would bring sedative refreshment. Ben thought, *this* is why I do what I do, why I have done what I have done: to spend a lazy lunch-hour or two in the sweet-smelling air, almost my own master, an evening swim awaiting me unless a nap intervenes.

'It's about Colonel Vodi's brother's boy,' said Dominic, rubbing his hands together. Then, to the waiter, a sentence in the local language Ben had come to understand: 'Two large gin and tonics, please.'

Dominic took his smoking materials out of his jacket pocket and toyed with them before lighting a cigarette. 'But I'm spoiling a *very* good story,' he added, as Ben tensed and adjusted himself in his chair. 'Is something wrong?'

'Nothing,' Ben said. 'Go on.'

'I'll just wait for our drinks. This is enormous. This could be *international*.'

Ben squinted at Dominic. He felt relieved: Dominic wouldn't speak this way if his news affected Ben directly. 'Take your time,' he said.

The waiter returned bearing their drinks on a copper tray, along with a bowl of olives and a plate of sliced lemons.

'Cheers,' said Dominic. 'My *Christ*, what a lot of excitement.' He took a sip of his drink, smacked his lips. 'Do you remember that chap from the consulate, Jasper LeRoy? The simply *divine* Jasper LeRoy?'

'I do. I met him at Mancini's house.'

'That's right – on the fateful day. Dear old Jasper and I were having one of our little *conversations* together as we sometimes do, and in between reminiscences about our *ghastly* time at school together – you didn't know? – he had some fairly startling things to say that might, my dear Ben, change all of our lives. Am I being dramatic enough?' Dominic seemed to have aged five years just in the months Ben had known him. His cheerful eyebrows still arced happily on his forehead as he spoke, but overall he looked drained and dispirited.

'Plenty, Dominic.'

'Jasper is still *such* a head-boy sort of figure to me. I mean, I can certainly understand *my* ending up here, doing this, it makes perfect sense – but LeRoy? I would have had him pegged as Governor of Hong Kong, at the very least. Perhaps there is still time. His father was *utterly* Foreign Office. Perhaps he thinks about me the same way. In his mind I ought to be entertaining grand ladies and dashing young men in my Tuscan villa, writing epicene plays on the side. We're all vaguely *failures*, don't you think?'

Ben did not reply.

'I mean, I've been in love with Jasper LeRoy since I was eleven years old, and he had to come *here*, to my secret hideaway, to

318

torment me. Sorry. You probably don't like to hear about that sort of thing.'

'I don't mind, Dominic.'

'You haven't met his wife and children,' said Dominic dismally, gesturing at the waiter for the same again. 'You would not, I assure you, have found the post-adolescent Jasper LeRoy contemplating marriage.'

'People change.'

'No they bloody *don't*. Anyway. Dear old married Jasper's had his ear to the ground and discovered the most alarming thing. I am sworn to secrecy but I assume he told me because someone in P&R needs to know, and if I know, why shouldn't you?'

'Exactly.'

'Do you remember the day, a weekend, when you saw us at the dam?'

'I do, yes,' said Ben. 'You sort of shooed me away.'

'Well, yes. That,' said Dominic, 'was the day Vodi's nephew was knocked down.'

'Ah.'

'And killed.'

'Yes.'

'We had our mysterious meeting, and lunch. Mancini's boy was there – an *oddish* child, don't you think?'

'Special,' said Ben.

'Quite. So at the end of business, much of which I was asked not to listen to – they banished me to the bar, don't you think that's *awfully* strange? – off everyone drove. Mancini in his big Euphoria, with his eerily articulate boy.'

'I see,' said Ben, beginning to see.

'According to Jasper, Mr Mancini and the boy and the car were spotted on the road back home. There are witnesses. It all adds up.'

'Oh, my God,' said Ben, because that was what he thought

it appropriate to say. He no longer had spontaneous emotions.

'There was damage to the Mancini Euphoria consistent with such an accident. Vodi's brother had a man investigate. The Colonel and his brother are *not* happy.'

'This is all . . . shocking,' said Ben. 'I mean, really *shocking*. Do you think it's true?'

'I don't think so,' said Dominic, with a peculiar slyness. 'But if so it's a tragedy. The poor man! You know I can be sarcastic about the Great Mancini but I do admire him. I owe him a lot. If this has happened to him – I mean, one does pity the boy and . . . *Mrs* Vodi, whoever she may be – but Mancini – I say, did you notice anything even *remotely* different about him since that day?'

Ben thought for a quarter of a second. 'He smokes cigarettes,' he said.

'Ah! Precisely. And I mean, wouldn't *you*?' Dominic asked, lighting a cigarette of his own.

'If I'd killed someone's little boy? I sure think I would.'

The food arrived: stuffed peppers, artichokes, cucumber and tomato salad, red wine.

'The *frightening* part,' said Dominic, continuing to smoke even as he buttered his bread, 'is that Vodi's brother is after Mancini now. Plotting his revenge. LeRoy's view is that he'll do something to Mancini's son. Have I mentioned that both Vodis have the morals of Satan? And that the younger one is if anything more bloodthirsty? The stories one hears. If his sort of character is hereditary, Mancini may have been doing the world a favour by –'

'Dominic . . .'

'Sorry. Of course. You have a little boy. You wouldn't want to see him squished into the dust.'

'Please. I can't believe you are *enjoying* this.'

Dominic put out his cigarette, took a sip of wine, poked at his food without eating anything. 'What are we going to do?'

'We? Us?'

'Well, why do you think I'm unbosoming myself of this sensitive intelligence, Ben, unless it's to ask for your advice? We have to tell Mancini, is what I think. To warn him. Jasper wants nothing to do with it.'

'No,' said Ben, much too quickly, but Dominic didn't seem to notice.

'Why not?'

Ben filled his mouth with food so he had time to think. If Mancini were warned, he might pull strings, even use the General to protect himself and his family from the Vodi brothers, all the while protesting his innocence. It might even occur to *Dominic*, eventually, that Mancini wasn't the only Western Euphoria-driving man with a boy in the passenger seat to take that route on the same day.

'It had occurred to me,' said Dominic, suddenly lowering his eyebrows and staring at Ben so hard the American froze in the act of reaching out for his wine glass, 'that you and your son were on the road that day. Isn't my memory a wonderful thing? Don't say anything, don't worry,' he added, as Ben opened his mouth and started to smile innocently. 'I'm not going to mention this again. It's only that I was the one who told you about the reports of the accident, and I don't believe it is possible for a man to blanch *quite* so arctic-white as you did. I knew then.'

57

The doctor Candy had recommended held his surgery in a residential neighbourhood downtown, where a single street might complain of seven different architectural styles. Ellen's doctor's building reminded her of a Manhattan brownstone, and evidently the doctor lived upstairs from his professional quarters. She rang the brass doorbell and was admitted by a uniformed nurse. The nurse was pale, freckled, pretty. She led Ellen along a corridor to Dr Servizan's waiting room. Ellen sat, within reach of Western magazines – without wanting to touch one – for no more than five minutes. Her predecessor, a short, slender businesswoman, left in what looked like high spirits. Ellen was ushered through.

Dr Servizan's office might have belonged to an estate agent: no medical equipment except for an antique wooden box labelled 'Sterilizer'; an exquisite, well-worn carpet underfoot; a broad, banker's desk; seascape water-colours.

'Mrs Pelton,' said Dr Servizan, coming around from behind his desk. He was a short, friendly looking man with a greying brush moustache and a cheerful squint behind his heavy spectacles. 'Sit down, please.' He gestured at a green leather-clad armchair at one side of his desk.

There followed a brief interview, during which Ellen grew nervous. Though she was a doctor's daughter, and had once thought of herself as a thoroughly medical person (she had dissected a cadaver named 'Patrick'), new doctors always made her uncomfortable. In this case, in a foreign country suffering from an intimate discharge that Dr Servizan would presently wish to look at, Ellen wanted to disappear. Until she had used it to have children, Ellen had never been happy about having a body, rather than existing simply as a mind floating immortally in the ether. Doctors reminded her of her body. Doctors were the ones who were going to say, 'You're dying.' Ellen wondered what kind of doctor she would have made, how she would have broken the news. She would have been a paediatrician, had Ben or his equivalent not come along to rob her of a career. She would have fixed children instead of *having* them fixed. She would have said to parents, as Doctor Friend had said to her, 'I'm afraid the news isn't great.' That was it for Ellen, really. That was the end. 'I'm afraid the news isn't great.' Trying to keep her composure each time she saw Sean from then on had drained every volt of her energy, and still did. Perhaps, she thought charitably, that was the real reason Ben had begun to behave so strangely.

Ellen answered questions about her medical history; Dr Servizan took notes. His excellent English was accented in the manner of the global diplomat, like one of Evan Court's far-flung interviewees reassuring him that peace was finally in sight.

'I do have one complaint,' Ellen said, at last. So far she had simply listed past ailments in a clinical way. 'A discharge,' she said, flatly.

To her surprise, Dr Servizan raised his hand to silence her. He sighed and put down his pen. 'I don't think,' he said, 'there will be any need for a physical examination.'

'And why not?' Ellen asked.

'Because,' said Dr Servizan, 'your husband came to see me.'

58

Ben stood alone on the observation deck at the airport, waiting for the Eminent Founder's plane to land. Mancini had sent him on this errand because Ben and the Eminent Founder, whose name was Peter Knox, shared an alma mater. 'You can reminisce,' Mancini had said – though Knox had graduated in 1940, shortly before joining the Navy and going off to save the Far East from the Japanese. Knox was also a lawyer. Perhaps they could reminisce about *that*, Ben thought, except that Knox was one of those fellows who without any apparent effort had founded his own partnership, moved to Washington, rubbed elbows and become an indispensable adviser to presidents and all-round policy sage before he'd unpacked his bags. Knox was considered a visionary. Raised on a diet of Franklin Roosevelt, he applied New Deal principles to the international stage. A benighted foreign country was not, to Peter Knox, very much unlike Tennessee. He understood the dynamics of the Cold War, and his instinct told him that private development for friendly nations was unlikely to be undermined at home – quite the opposite. He had never known failure. By the age of fifty he had already been well on his way to becoming one of those quiet legends who grew into their patrician features and actually felt *sorry* for each president in succession and said so in self-deprecating memoirs.

A plane glinted in the sunlight, miles away. Ben thought about what it would be like to be a quiet legend, to be a Great Man. He imagined a life of oak desks and musty libraries and low male voices planning the world's future through whorls of cigar smoke. He imagined financial security, to the point where bills were paid by trusted others, elsewhere. Property was divided seasonally. 'Summer' and 'winter' were verbs. Whole kleptocracies were on first-name terms with Peter Knox; dictators had his private telephone number and secretly feared him; the General would want to see him right away.

The plane landed smoothly, if dustily. Ben waited on the observation deck to watch the disembarkation. Two ramps were driven out, one for steerage at the back, one for first class at the front. Knox, Mancini had said, travelled alone. Sammy had the car running kerb-side at the airport's main entrance. Ben hoped Knox hadn't been expecting a military band, a red carpet, a convoy of cars with flags on their fenders.

Knox appeared at the top of the ramp. Even from a distance he looked painfully thin and stooped. He put down his briefcase and put on his suit jacket. He straightened his tie, picked up his briefcase again, and limpingly descended the stairs. Ben rushed down to be in time to greet him when he emerged from VIP customs.

The arrivals hall, which was also the departures hall, was not too crowded. Half a dozen chauffeurs or bus drivers waited, smoking, leaning against a newly whitewashed wall under revolving tourist posters – the Baram Caves, the coast, the antiquity. Predictably, Knox was first to come out from customs, through a side door. A porter followed him, pushing a trolley that bore one large case.

Knox recognized Ben by default, extended a hand and pronounced his own name in a raspy voice that emanated from a skeletal, jaundiced, weary face. His thin white hair was plastered to his skull but curled once at the collar. He had a long, pointy nose that he had to direct upwards at a steep angle because he was quite small. Standing next to Mancini he would look like a child.

'It's good to be back,' said Knox, as Ben ushered him the

short distance to the exit. Knox looked around, sniffed the air, and added, 'Shit hole.'

Shocked though he was by Knox's unlikely remark, Ben managed a nervous laugh. In a moment they were outside, in the cool air, Sammy waiting with the back door of his brilliantly polished car open. Ben tipped the porter, then went around to the other side and let himself in. He was beginning to feel important again – it was like being with Hannan.

'What time is it?' asked Knox, looking at a watch that drooped from his spindly left wrist.

'Three forty-five.'

'That explains it. I was expecting it to be dark. *Look* at this God-damned place, would you?'

They were not, so far, fondly sharing first impressions of Harvard Yard. Knox had a few more gruff remarks to make before he deigned to turn his wet blue eyes on Ben. For a man of only sixty-nine, Knox looked old.

'Did you bring children here too?' he asked.

'You mean like Paul Mancini? Yes.'

'Crazy business. Crazy.'

'They seem happy. The children are fine.'

'Each to his own,' said Knox, adjusting his teeth. For a man who had supposedly scaled the heights on brilliance and charm, Knox had so far made a sour impression.

Ben made the remarks that were required of him: how bold P&R's projects were, how successful, how important. On a personal note, Ben said, he was delighted to be making a contribution. Ben finished his monologue and braced himself for a dismissive expletive, but Knox merely nodded in acknowledgement. He looked tired, perhaps ill.

After a long pause, shielding his eyes against the sun with his hand, Knox said, 'I've heard good things about you, Ben.'

'Thank you, sir.'

'It's hard to keep up with everything at the moment. I rely

on my people.' P&R operated in three other countries, and Knox had a law firm to run as well.

'You must be awfully busy.'

Knox made a gesture with his head that Ben took to mean, 'Not in front of the driver.' Then he said, 'Interesting times.'

Knox reached down, picked up his briefcase, put it on his knees, clicked it open, took out a manila folder. His mouth made a clicking sound again as he looked inside the folder and withdrew a printed page.

'I'll go to the Chevalier first,' he said. 'There's time for a shower and a change of clothes and a bite to eat. You'll come with me. I have questions and they need answers. I'm borrowing Hannan's suite. Have you come across Chava Hannan?'

Ben thought about the phrasing of Knox's question. 'I certainly have,' he said.

'Oh, wait a minute, that's right. I was briefed on this. You were the one – good work. You were the one who helped out when there was all that trouble.'

'Well, really, Paul Mancini just asked me –'

'I've heard good things, as I say. Hannan's very important to us.'

'So I've gathered.' Ben still didn't know why.

'I hope to see him while I'm here. At the coast. You'll come with me, if he's so sweet on you.'

'Whatever you want,' said Ben. 'Oh, look,' he added, as Sammy accelerated, 'it's your road.' They had turned on to a section of brand-new motorway, Knox's ring road.

Knox sat up in his seat and peered out at the smooth, black, eight-lane marvel and said, 'Traffic already.' It was true. Already the ring road looked overused, insufficient. 'I suppose the city centre's cleared out?' Knox asked.

Ben hesitated. 'Not so's you'd notice,' he confessed.

'I'm not the least surprised. It was a sarcastic question. And the traffic's not *our* fault.'

Soon Ben found himself back in Hannan's penthouse, having suffered the private elevator at Knox's side. Everything was revoltingly familiar: the summery sofas, the sharp surfaces, a terrible glimpse of the hot tub as Knox opened the door to Hannan's bedroom. Ben went out on to the balcony while Knox showered. Knox emerged just a few minutes later, with one of Chava Hannan's monogrammed towels wrapped around his waist, drying his hair with another. His emaciated torso was as shapeless and hairless as a lump of white clay on a potter's wheel.

'Do me a favour,' he said, so relaxed in his near-nudity that Ben might have been his son. 'Get Mancini over here, all right? I don't feel like going to the office. We'll discuss things here, maybe have a bite to eat.'

While Knox went into the bedroom to put on some clothes, Ben phoned the office and the message was relayed to Mancini. Then he asked the hotel receptionist to go outside and tell Sammy he could take the rest of the day off: Chauffeur could take up the slack. During the twenty minutes it took Mancini to be driven to the hotel, Knox finished getting dressed and, through the bedroom door, asked Ben a series of questions so precise he might have been reading from a list. Ben had seen written communications from Knox, and knew him to be a details man. His letters looked like questionnaires, and required numbered, bulleted replies. This mystified Ben, who, in Knox's shoes, would have left everything to minions and held only the big picture in his legendary mind.

When Knox had run out of questions, he enthused about the Meheti Dam. 'I can't wait to clap my eyes on it,' he said.

'It really is impressive,' Ben said, with somewhat forced excitement. 'I am amazed by how fast it is possible to build something so . . . *big*.'

Knox frowned, started to say something, stopped himself, looked quizzically at Ben.

'Yes?' Ben asked, prompting him.

'Oh, it's . . . I have to be careful here, I think.'

'What do you mean?'

Knox was saved from having to reply by Paul Mancini's arrival. As the two men shook hands, Ben was surprised to see that Mancini appeared nervous. If he weren't so tall, he could almost have been said to be fawning. He asked the usual questions about Knox's journey, the state of his health, the level of his comfort here in Hannan's penthouse.

'This place makes me laugh,' said Knox. 'What these walls have seen, right? In case you didn't know, Ben, Mr Hannan is just the *littlest* bit of a playboy.'

Ben wanted to say, 'Well he sucked *my* cock, Mr Knox.' Instead he shrugged and said, 'I only saw him on the day his car was shot to pieces.'

'That sure pissed him off,' said Knox. 'He said he had half a mind to fight back, if he could be absolutely sure who really did it. Say, would you fellows be against a drink? I don't know what time zone I'm in any more.'

Room service was called and delivered a chariot stocked with drinks, ice and snacks so quickly they might have been waiting in the lift.

'That's better,' said Knox, who had swiftly poured himself a bourbon and water. Mancini plucked a small bottle of mineral water from a silver tray, then reconsidered. He decided not to drink anything. Ben casually opened a bottle of beer and poured it into a glass. He toasted Knox's arrival, which seemed to annoy Mancini because he wasn't holding a glass. Mancini was making Ben nervous. He didn't sit down. He looked out of sorts. Perhaps he wanted to smoke but didn't want to ask permission. Ben wondered if he ought to excuse himself, or at least ask if they wanted him to stay. There was a clandestine air about this meeting, holed up as they were in Hannan's tacky boudoir. Ben's instincts proved correct, as Mancini finally said, 'Peter, if you'd prefer, Ben could wait downstairs.'

'Oh, no, absolutely not,' said Knox, waving his rather full glass. 'We just won't discuss our most *sinister* plans in front of the young man.'

Mancini tried to laugh, but it was obvious that there really were things Ben was not to know. He didn't mind. He no longer minded about very much of anything except to continue to be in good odour at home. He'd watched Ellen for any hint of disease or suspicion and decided he'd dodged that particular bullet as well as the first, biggest one. In her eyes, he was a *noble* husband.

'I think I'll have another of these,' said Knox, standing up with his suddenly empty glass. They were due at the Institute for Political and Religious Understanding at six o'clock, where there would be no alcohol. Knox was to meet Roffe Furan – known universally as Roffe – a sort of religious prodigy at only twenty-five and the leader of a legitimate political party with revolutionary intentions, short term. His raw charisma made intelligent people worry, but at least he wasn't on the Left. Far from it. Ben had never met Roffe, but Diane had seen him speak and reported that he was mesmeric. It didn't hurt, she also said, that he looked like a particularly favoured god. Ben had seen Roffe's picture on posters here and there around the city, and agreed that there was something messianic about the young man – a starry look to his black eyes, a delicate and humane-seeming nose and lips, shoulders slender under a black cloak.

When Knox had his second drink in his hand, Ben couldn't resist drinking another beer. Mancini changed his mind and mixed himself a vodka and tonic. Weeks ago he had expressed to Ben his horror of Roffe's religion, and clearly dreaded meetings with the man.

'Look at us,' said Knox, with a big, successful-man's grin, 'pounding it down before it's too late. Are we dressed all right? We don't have to wear *hats*, do we?'

Roffe's poster photographs showed him wearing a delicate, white, crocheted skull cap with a small coloured bobble hanging over his wise brow.

'No, nothing like that,' said Mancini, who had met with Roffe on several occasions at the Institute.

Ben hadn't been aware that he would be accompanying Knox and Mancini to this sensitive meeting, and he boldly said so.

'Nonsense,' said Knox. 'Come along, why don't you? It's all just hand-shaking and touching base. We'll be out of there in minutes. Right, Paul?'

'I don't . . . *think* so,' said Mancini. 'He's windy. He will want to tell you a lot of things you don't necessarily want to know. Beautiful room, though, where he greets people. Beautiful carpets.'

'I'd better call my wife, then,' said Ben. 'I'll tell her not to expect me for dinner.'

'Will she mind?' asked Knox.

'Oh, Christ no. It's routine. She'll welcome the peace once the children are asleep.'

Ben went over to one of the telephones and dialled an outside line. Ellen would be thrilled by this news. How *well* Ben was doing. The Eminent Founder had taken such a shine to her husband that he bared his torso to him after a shower within an hour of first saying hello. He kept him in the room during his exchanges with Mancini. He invited him along to meet the mesmeric Roffe. And this – Peter Knox – a man who *made a difference*, whose every day and every act were precious to the future of his country and to the future of the world. Ellen would get the picture now – she would see what Ben was doing, and how well. Ben exhaled with self-satisfaction and dialled his home number.

59

When the telephone rang, in its old-fashioned, clanging way, Ellen happened to be standing at the French windows at home, watching Haz remove the swimming pool's blue cover. The winter seemed to have lasted only weeks. Soon the children would be swimming every day. Candy had said, 'You and Ben can throw *young* people's parties late at night, under the stars.' Haz was a serious, hard-working young man; Ellen felt self-conscious watching him pull at the heavy cover, slipping now and then in the overflow, risking disaster. She would have to have a chat with him and Ama about the children, now that the pool was uncovered: no running, no swimming without a grown-up actually *in* the pool with them.

And there was the phone. It could only be Ben; Candy was playing tennis. Ellen sniffed with sarcasm and disdain and turned to look at that beige, ringing apparatus, that telephone, with her *shit* of a husband almost certainly on the other end. Her horror after hearing Little Paul's secret had only been allowed a few days to settle into her awareness before Dr Servizan's news had its own try at pushing Ellen beyond mere worry. She had lived with the information long enough to have thought it through. Ben hadn't visited some brothel during the day, in that filthy city: it could only have been the night Ben had stayed out with that creep Hannan. The same way she knew where and when both of her children had been conceived, she knew where and when she had contracted this . . . this *dose*. This *clap*. A delicious mixture of anger and humiliation had kept her steely for a while, but now, as she approached the telephone, she thought she might have to lash out, lest she show *any* sign of weakness before the rotten man who had done this to her.

'Hello?'

'Babe. It's me.'

When Ellen first knew Ben, he had sounded just like this: confident to the point of arrogance. It had taken time for life – not Ellen – to grind him down; at least two years under Victor Wiesman's wing before the air was let out of him, a couple of years with Sean to reorganize his priorities and soften, soften into the routine he would use to protect himself from life and to dig a moat of money around his family. When that was taken away, no wonder he overreacted. When Sean was ill, it was Ellen who had said, optimistically, 'We won't let this destroy us.' Ben had nodded, not looking at his wife, and gone out for a walk in the rain.

'Hello.'

'Look, I'm with Paul and Mr Knox. They want me to come along to see Roffe this evening. At the Institute? I won't be late, but I'll miss dinner. I'm truly sorry about that, babe.'

This last was meant to sound as if Ben were the President of the United States' General Counsel and was needed at an evening powwow in the Oval Office – but he hadn't forgotten about the little woman at home, no sir, and he was *truly sorry*.

'All right.'

'Everything going well at home?'

Ellen had turned around to watch Haz take a last pull at the blue tarpaulin, which he was trying to fold rather than roll into its original cylinder.

'Splendidly,' she said.

'You sound . . . muted. I didn't wake you, did I?'

'No.'

'Well, good. Kiss the kids, all right? I won't be late.'

'Yes.'

333

Ellen banged down the receiver with such force that she cracked both sides of the plastic cradle. She wanted to shout, but the children were in the kitchen with Ama, eating a snack of fruit and cheese. She had already harangued Ben at such length and volume in her imagination that she couldn't wait for the real performance. And then, when he was like a beached jellyfish under her shoe, she would take the children with her and *leave*. She would wait a little longer and watch this man, though – who had, Ellen now believed, hit and probably killed a person in the car, then told Sean to *lie* about it; slept with someone who gave him the clap, and transmitted the disease to his wife – and observe him like a gerbil in a cage. She would write a diary, to be used in court for the divorce proceedings – if they ever let him out of jail in *this* country once she turned him in to the authorities. She would go and visit him in the Shika Prison to watch him beg, and to check on the state of his torture wounds.

Ellen wished she could tell someone right now. Her friends at home seemed too far away at the moment, and Ellen's humiliation too great. Her divorced friends would say, 'It's the tip of the iceberg. You've found out just one or two things. He's probably abusing Nicole. Get out.'

Was it the tip of an iceberg? Ellen thought it must be. Ben had always been so smooth – and he loved girls. But if he could automatically lie about probably killing someone – and somehow force his own pure boy to join a cover-up conspiracy – how could this *not* be part of a larger pattern?

Ellen was going to leave Ben – suddenly and permanently. She would not even warn the children, so that they would know Papa was an untouchable black memory of the distant past, that the door was slammed on him for ever. An irredeemable man, never to be seen again.

Ellen put a cardigan over her shoulders and went outside for some fresh air: she didn't want the children to come out from the kitchen and disturb her perfect fury. Haz was just beginning to drag away the tarpaulin to the shed behind the pool house, and Ellen had to fight an urge to help him. She took a deep breath and went around the corner of the house to the small garden that overlooked the Mancinis' house and the Soviet Embassy compound. This reminded her to try to contact the Russians, Nadia and Denis, who must by now be back from home leave. Perhaps she would tell Nadia about Ben's crimes, set the Soviets on him for blackmail.

Haz came back from the shed, and Ellen signalled to him. She thanked him for removing the tarpaulin, and explained that Mr Pelton would not be coming home for dinner. As she did so, she noticed over Haz's shoulder a car coming up the track from the road. Another identical car – they were both anonymous white Fardis – waited at the bottom of the track. When she had finished instructing Haz, he nodded, turned around, and noticed the cars.

'What can they want?' Ellen asked. 'Are we expecting anyone? Anything?'

Haz shook his head.

The car stopped next to the Mancinis' carport, almost out of sight. Ellen knew there was no one at home – Paul with Knox; Candy at the club with Tamina and the children; Yalem at the market; the gardeners on their day off – and wondered if she ought to call the police.

A darkly dressed man got out of the Fardi. He reached behind the seat and slid out something long and thin and heavy, like a shotgun. He jogged out of view towards the steps and reappeared seconds later next to the swimming pool. The object in his hand was an iron bar or pipe.

Haz turned to Ellen and gave her a look that asked, 'Do you want me to go down there?'

Ellen shook her head.

The man walked around the pool house to the back bedrooms, again out of view. There came the sound of a glass pane being smashed. Ellen reflexively put a hand to her mouth. She looked at Haz. Without saying a word, Haz went straight into the house to the telephone. Ellen thought of evacuating her children, locking them in the Euphoria, making a run for it, but was frozen at the railing. The figure down below came back around the house, breaking every window he came upon. He broke the French windows in the pool house. He broke the broad, high window of the Mancinis' living room. When he had broken every window he could reach, he threw the pipe or bar into the swimming pool and ran back down the steps. He turned his Fardi around and drove back down the track to where the second car waited. They set off in opposite directions: two carbon-stained white Fardis among thousands upon thousands in the city.

Ellen made for the telephone to track down Ben and Paul Mancini. As she turned, she looked up at the hillside and there, a hundred yards away and crouched down next to a boulder, were Ama and Sean and Nicole: Haz had sent them off to safety before calling the police.

60

'It's for you, Paul,' Knox said, looking both worried and annoyed. The telephone call had come just as he and Ben and Mancini were about to leave Hannan's suite for the Institute. 'It's Ben's wife.'

This news interested Ben. His wife, on the phone to Mancini, when she knew where her husband was? Almost impossible to guess what the matter could be, not in the seconds it would take to find out – but Ben had, after all, a fine brain: the Vodis had made their move. One of the children was kidnapped or dead. Mancini's reaction to the phone call seemed to confirm this, as he registered shock and incomprehension – then more so as he said, without even looking at Knox for approval, 'Tell Candy I'll be right home.'

When Mancini put down the receiver Ben went up to him and said, 'Paul, I'm so sorry.'

'What?'

'I mean . . .'

'Look, I'm sorry, Peter,' Mancini said, mercifully ignoring Ben. 'Someone's smashed up my house. I have to go back and make sure my family's all right. See what's going on. Talk to the police. Ben here can go along with you. This is the strangest thing. Never heard of anything like it.'

'Anyone hurt?' asked Knox.

'No, everyone's fine. No one was in the house.'

'Thank God for that.'

The three men left the hotel together. Mancini shook hands with Knox without another word, and got into a taxi. Ben signalled to Chauffeur, idling across the boulevard, to bring up the big, tail-finned car. Knox looked displeased as he crossed his thin legs in the back seat, as if this meeting with Roffe warranted more attention than the partial destruction of Mancini's house.

'Who would do a thing like that?'

'I just can't imagine,' Ben said. 'I have never heard of anything like it. Let's hope they catch whoever it was. I mean, it shouldn't be too difficult – it was broad daylight. Maybe my wife or one of the servants saw something.' Ben certainly hoped not. A confession by the vandal might elicit a blanket denial from Mancini, and draw attention to the other Euphoria, just up the hill. Ben felt giddy. The shock had worn off gradually, and for some time now he had been able to go minutes at a stretch without remembering the impact, without his stomach tensing and his eyes squinting as if to shut out the memory. Events at Mancini's house had brought it all back full-force.

The Institute for Political and Religious Understanding wasn't far from the General's headquarters. A sort of failed cement Parthenon, the building dated back thirty years, when it had been the old government's Department of Public Information. Its front colonnade was pitted and discoloured, its steps crunchy with unswept crumbs of the building's dilapidation. Chauffeur stopped at the front entrance, put on the parking brake, leapt out and opened the door on Knox's side. Ben got out of the car on his own, and noticed that Chauffeur not only wore the expression of a trained bodyguard, but held his right hand close to his bulging left lapel. It had never before occurred to Ben that Chauffeur – and Sammy – might be armed.

Ben almost took Knox by the elbow as they climbed the steps: the man was frail, and probably tight. At the summit, an aggressive-looking young man explained that he would accompany them to Roffe's presence. The atmosphere at the Institute was unlike anything Ben had so far experienced in

338

this country. All he had known was an almost ritualized cordiality, but here the ambience felt threatening. Still it was thrilling to be playing a role, as Ben saw it, on the international stage with the likes of Peter Knox.

Roffe held court in an upstairs sanctum decorated with exquisite carpets and embroidered cushions and an enormous framed mosaic on the wall that had once floored a Roman palace.

'I hope I don't smell of booze,' Knox said, out of the side of his mouth.

Roffe stood at the far end of the long room, in conference with a group of people that included several women. The group dispersed and Roffe approached, flanked by two men who wore identical red shifts and baggy white trousers cinched at the ankles. The religious prodigy himself wore the little cotton skull cap with bobble, a light beard, a heavy white ankle-length robe and white plastic sandals. His arms were folded deep inside his robe, making hand-shaking impossible and causing the two Americans involuntarily to bow in greeting.

Roffe was as striking to look at as had been advertised. His perfectly sculpted face was of an even, dark-brown colour that contrasted startlingly with his light-blue eyes. He spoke English slowly, even pedantically. He interrupted himself every now and then to mutter a religious incantation in his native language. When Knox explained what had befallen the Mancini household, Roffe's serene features turned to alarm and concern and he said, 'This is a shame and a travesty. There will be arrests,' he added, as if he already ran the country.

Roffe had learned his English and his French in Paris, where his father had worked in a lowly position at the Embassy. Overwhelmed by spiritual epiphany at the age of fifteen, he had returned home to study his religion in earnest, and to rise to the top of the Institute by the age of twenty-two. Rural adoration was quick to follow. In a hierarchical culture this was unheard of, and it accounted for some people's suspicion that he possessed mystical powers. Mystical or not, his power was now considerable. He openly supported revolution – the complete dismantlement of the existing government and a leap to theocracy – a stance referred to in his literature as 'change'. This would normally have meant his disappearance into the bowels of the Shika Prison or to the long, white building in the mountains to the north. His standing as a quasi-prophet prevented the General from taking such action.

An obligatory tea ceremony preceded any real business. Ben always wished these things could be hurried along, but no: the great urn, the red-hot knife, the special little silk pouches of sugar, the three-thousand-year-old tongs to grasp the actual tea leaves themselves, the ivory fan, the silver lime juicer, the pouring thrice from a considerable height – all of these had to be employed or performed while the men looked on in contemplative silence.

No one had said so, but the formal purpose of this encounter between Roffe and Knox was to ensure that, in the unlikely event of the religious leader assuming power, P & R's business would continue unimpeded. Theocracies needed roads and dams and mines and airports just as much as democracies or dictatorships did. Also unmentioned was the fact that Peter Knox was a conduit to the President's ear – and that what Roffe said that evening, any assurance he could give, would be relayed to the State Department before Knox went to bed that night. It was necessary for Roffe to be *wildly* anti-American in public; this did not mean that he privately ignored the value of people like Knox and the power they represented.

Ben didn't say a word as pleasantries were exchanged. Roffe sat on a cushioned bench beneath a scarlet canopy, while the Americans sat on simple wooden chairs. He spoke, Christ-like, in parables. Knox impressed Ben – this gruff and sickly man had perked up, and spoke with charm and intelligence about the smallest things. He flattered Roffe just to the brink of plain sycophancy, and was flattered in turn through Roffe's glinting eyes. Ben would have found the whole process stressful even if he hadn't been preoccupied by events at Mancini's house – so preoccupied that he didn't notice when Knox asked him to leave the two men alone for a few minutes.

'Ben?'

'Sorry?'

'If you don't mind?'

'Excuse me?'

Knox made a circulating motion with his index finger and said, 'Take a stroll.'

Ben walked off thinking he'd probably lost *this* job, as well. *God*, he needed to concentrate. He walked almost the full length of the room, pretending to be interested in the mosaic, which depicted a scene of mythological drowning. With hands in pockets, practically *whistling* with nerves, Ben crossed to one of six broad windows on the other side of the room. This looked out on to a courtyard, where a dozen or more men were engaged in athletic prayer. Ben hadn't prayed, ever, much less prostrated himself and crawled about in obeisance. Even when Sean was ill, Ben hadn't prayed – cursed, yes.

Knox's tête-à-tête with Roffe went on for an uncomfortable length of time, nearly an hour. Ben walked up and down the room, smiling at Roffe's two bodyguards, accepting more tea, feeling guiltier and guiltier each time he did so. The worshippers in the courtyard dispersed as the sun set. Ben only returned to Knox's side when the two men stood up and began to say their goodbyes. Roffe had his hands outside his robe now, and could shake hands. It was now he who seemed to be bowing. What could Knox possibly have said? Roffe's silvery eyes were as bright as ever, but he clearly deferred to Knox as he hadn't done when they first met, and accompanied him – and Ben – all the way outside to the top of the steps. He said something about God in his own language, and returned to his quarters. Chauffeur stood on the pavement at the bottom of the steps, holding the car door open, squinting first to the right, then to the left, then right and left again. He *was* armed.

Knox settled into his seat with a smile on his face.

'Should I ask?' Ben asked. He had no idea what was going on.

'I'll sleep like a baby tonight,' said Knox, rubbing his hands together and yawning. His gracious, old-school summing-up went, 'That's one more s.o.b.'s pecker in my pocket.'

Ben wanted to know how, in one brief meeting, Knox had got Roffe's pecker in his pocket, but didn't ask.

'He liked you,' Knox said.

'Liked me? I didn't say a word.'

'Didn't you? I thought you charmed the socks off him.'

'He wasn't wearing socks.'

'Well, then, you see? You'll be hearing from him. He said so.'

They drove along in silence for a few minutes. The boulevards were alive with people enjoying the warm evening – businessmen in shirtsleeves, teenagers on motorbikes. Ben had come to the conclusion, while pacing up and down Roffe's long room, that the attack on Mancini's house had nothing to do with him – it was a coincidence, it was political, it was anti-American or anti-rich-people vandalism. It wasn't Colonel Vodi or his brother.

Knox fell asleep in the car on the way back to the Chevalier, then jerked awake with a click of false teeth. Rather than inviting Ben inside for a drink, or dinner, he shook hands and said, 'I'm turning in. Thanks for your help. Good work.' Chauffeur let Knox out of the car, got back behind the wheel, pointed the car towards the hills, and drove to Mancini's house.

Even from a distance, the house looked different – dark and mysterious. When Ben climbed up from the carport he saw

Haz helping Mancini and Yelam tape plastic sheets over the shattered windows. Haz was indefatigable.

'What a mess,' Ben said. 'What can I do to help?'

'Nothing. We're just finishing.' Mancini looked wild; Ben had never seen the great warrior frightened before. 'Candy and the kids are at your house.'

'Of course.'

'I'm going to stay here, in case he comes back.' Mancini made a trigger-pulling gesture with his right hand.

'Did anyone see anything?'

'Ellen did. A man in a white Fardi.'

'Strange.'

'I'll say,' said Mancini. 'Listen, Ben, I didn't want to tell Candy – and don't you go telling Ellen either . . .'

'Sure.'

'I got a telephone call after the police left. Like they knew I was alone in the house. And a man's voice says, "Do you love your son?"'

'Jesus.'

'Now just what in the hell do you think *that's* about?'

61

Coast-bound in Hannan's narrow jet, Ben sat by himself in a calfskin armchair, across a table from Mancini and Knox. He had never been in so small a plane, and found it noisy but exhilarating on take-off. He also felt like a personal assistant rather than an Associate Director, left in the dark on subjects and frequently asked to leave them in private. This didn't bother Ben too much; they were obviously involved in some sort of eyes-only deal with Hannan – something ugly, perhaps, but necessary for good business and the general welfare of the West. It was a tense time, despite some openings in Eastern Europe – some said the most dangerous ever. An ally like the General, with Hannan's assistance, was indispensable. It didn't bother Ben that he hadn't been invited along to meet the General last night – even Mancini hadn't accompanied Knox. Ben wondered if Knox thought he had come away with another powerful, world-stage pecker in his pocket.

What had been nagging Ben was Ellen's continued coldness at home. He had been so cheerful, so *successful*, that he wondered what could be wrong with her. After dinner she went out of her way to occupy herself with the children, when Ama could equally well have bathed them or played with them or put them in their pyjamas for bed. When the children were asleep, Ellen prepared herself for bed, put on a dressing-gown, came out into the sitting room with a cup of tea or a glass of wine depending on her mood, and installed herself with a magazine on her lap and Evan Court on television in the corner. This left Ben, if he had come home in time, puzzled as to how he should occupy himself. Did she not like it in this wonderful country? Did she not love it that her husband was now soaring over a far-off land in a private jet that seated a maximum of ten, in the company of at least one quiet legend? Did she not see that their future together – with the children – was like a stroll down a springtime lane bordered by cherry blossoms? Was she unhappy for some other, unforeseen reason? Ben hated to think along these lines. Any concern he might have that Ellen might in some remote way be 'unfulfilled' was really laughable, given how well the children were doing and what he had contributed to their lives until now, which was *everything*. He had even thought about how he could eventually explain to Ellen what had happened, show her how impeccably he had behaved in not exposing Sean to the horror on the road. What strength that had taken, what *nerve*.

He rested an arm on the deep-set porthole to his left and looked down behind the wing at the barren plateau. From above, this part of the country looked like a rusty, corrugated sheet deeply grooved by long-dry riverbeds. He and the other two men had been drinking champagne and orange juice, as it was breakfast time. The taste made Ben feel ill, but as usual he was glad of the alcohol. It was even more nauseating to be looking down thousands of vertical feet from this fragile tube piloted by a man who had sat next to Ben at the airport for five minutes, complaining in broken English about his wife who wanted to live in Singapore. And down there, the most inhospitable landscape, where for thousands of years glorious armies and screaming hordes had crisscrossed one another – Ben had a history book on the subject at home on his bedside table; he had been meaning to read it since his family's arrival. It all seemed so long ago now, and look at him: everything was going beautifully, if he just didn't worry. That's how people like Hannan got ahead, and people like Knox. They ploughed on, regardless.

Mancini had said nothing more about the attack on his house, as if the episode embarrassed him. Ben had noticed that the whole mess had been cleared and new glazing completed within fifteen hours, such was the magic of Mancini's power and anger. Ben hadn't asked, but he was certain Mancini had hired a guard to stay with his family – perhaps Chauffeur had gone straight back there from the airport. This made Ben feel much better. Everything was going to be all right.

After an hour, the plateau gave way to dark, rocky hills, then to irrigated fields, then to pine forests. Knox slept. Mancini read something inside a folder, perhaps one of poor Dominic's recent offerings. Dominic lived on the edge these days, and Ben found himself spending more and more time covering for the Englishman at the office. Ben still intended to have a manly word with Denis on Dominic's behalf, but the opportunity hadn't arisen. He thought he remembered Ellen having said something about dinner with the Russians, but he drank so much in the evenings these days that he didn't dare ask her in case he had already been told.

The coast was visible on the horizon before the jet began its descent: a curved strip of light blue after such an expanse of nothing, it might have been an oasis. The plane slowed and nosed downwards quite steeply. The port of Turga was visible out of Ben's window as the pilot circled out to sea and banked back towards the airport.

'Ben,' said Mancini, leaning forward and pointing. 'Look, just there. You can see Hannan's tub.'

Ben shaded his eyes against the sun and looked down. There was no mistaking what Mancini had pointed at. She looked like the Sydney Opera House compared with the minnows docked nearby. Even from fifteen hundred feet in the air, Ben could make out the three decks, tiered and pointed like a knight's visor. The little stone buildings of the old town bordering the harbour seemed to tremble on their ancient foundations at the apparition of this white leviathan in their midst.

Minutes later the plane touched down and taxied straight to a waiting limousine on the runway apron. During the walk from ramp to limousine door, Ben felt the first real heat on his back since that day at the Baram Caves. It was the sort of limousine where four people could sit comfortably facing each other; Ben sat facing backwards. The windows were so darkly tinted he couldn't see out. It was impossible not to feel criminal, on the run from justice, inside such a car.

Knox yawned and said he looked forward to a cup of coffee.

'Have you been on the yacht before?' Ben asked.

'Not this one. The last one. He's come up in the world, our Chava Hannan.'

'This one has a helipad,' said Mancini. 'For the quick escape. I was on the last one three times,' he added, boastfully. Mancini had become prickly since learning that Ben was to come along on the trip to Hannan's new ship. That hadn't been the plan. Ben's presence diluted the power-quotient of the gathering. Mancini had confessed to Ben that he still had his sights set on an ambassadorship at the next election. His foreign tours might have come to an end, but the idea of retirement made him ill. His children were young, and he still had plenty to offer. And, damn it, he *looked* like an ambassador.

The limousine drove as close to the harbour as possible, but it was too long to reach the quay itself. The three Americans had to walk down a cobble-stone alley to the harbour – the driver having indicated that he would bring their luggage along later – then a hundred yards or more to the pier at the end of which, dominating the horizon, Hannan's yacht was moored. When they reached the pier and began to approach the vessel, Ben noticed a group of local boys, slippery-brown and naked, jumping from the edge of the rotting wooden pier into the murky, oily water. They were diving for coins thrown by lunching yacht-dwellers, most of whom were European. Ben was reminded of Diane's tragedy, then of April. He bit his lip. He seemed to remember that he had touched April's leg the other night, while saying goodbye after driving her home from baby-sitting. He couldn't remember for *certain*, and it was more likely that he had dreamt it, but he . . . he feared perhaps he might have *groped* April in some way, and he had to try never to do that again or it might get back to Diane. Anyway he could always laugh it off, couldn't he? Touched her leg? Oh, maybe.

Ben craned his neck to look up at the yacht's name: *Hector*. Weren't yachts supposed to have only female names? Ben was no sailor, but the name *Hector* offended him. Perhaps it had something to do with war, and that was the reason Hannan had chosen it.

The Americans rattled up the gangplank to the first deck, led by Knox. They were saluted aboard by a young man who wore the full ship-master's warm-weather outfit, or so Ben imagined, of brilliant white shoes, knee-socks, shorts, button-down epauletted shirt and billed cap. They were ushered directly inside to an area that looked like the lobby of a Miami hotel, then up to the second deck where Hannan awaited them at the distant bow. To reach him, they had to walk through a greenhouse, two bright and open lounges each with its own bar, an informal dining room and an outdoor sunning area. The furnishings and decor seemed to Ben to be simultaneously brand new and out of date, but the sheer *excessiveness* of such a construction was all the owner needed to project himself. Ben recalled that Hannan had said there was an indoor swimming pool aboard, a gym, two cinemas (in case adults and children wanted to watch different films) and as a matter of course all the amenities of a modern businessman's hotel in America. Ben also seemed to recall that during one of their heart-to-hearts on that awful night, Hannan had said something about having been 'given' this ship.

In Ben's mind all moved in slow motion as the three Americans emerged into glaring sunlight and the presence of Hannan – Knox to the fore, slight in his dark-blue suit, his white right hand extended to meet Hannan's brown one; Mancini so tall his head blocked the sun from Ben's eyes for a moment, walking deferentially in the wake of his boss; and Ben, behind, in his khaki suit, plucking sunglasses from his shirt pocket, putting them on – he felt like a particularly important spy, Hannan's favourite. At the same time he was nervous. After what had happened in Hannan's hotel he had never wanted to see the man again, to have to pretend that he hadn't been revolted at the time and furious afterwards. But here he came, Hannan, hand out, enormous smile, owner of this cathedral yacht.

Hannan *hugged* Ben. He hadn't hugged Knox. He hadn't hugged Mancini.

'My friend,' he said, pulling away but holding Ben by the shoulders. 'My *good* friend.' He hugged Ben again. Ben hugged him in return – it was required – but as Hannan was the shorter man Ben could only do so bent at the waist with hips well withdrawn. Over Hannan's shoulder he could see Knox and Mancini looking suitably solemn: Ben had been the man at Hannan's side on that very emotional evening, after all.

Hannan wore a loose white muslin jacket with the same Nehru-ish collar as his business suits, over a black crew-neck T-shirt and black jeans. The coastal sun had smoothed and darkened his skin, which offset his gleaming, acquisitive smile. Ben had the conscious thought that Hannan looked too small, too compact, too *alone* to be responsible for the tons of ship beneath his feet.

'You need coffee,' Hannan said, reading at least Knox's mind. Coffee was immediately produced, and an eleven-hour meeting began. This was conducted fore and aft, above decks and below, over food, over drinks, over snooker, over tea, while swimming, while enjoying a sauna, over more drinks, over caviar, in the library, over dinner, with cigars and brandy. The meeting covered political trends, geological surveys, demographics, Swiss banking, South Africa, the General, Roffe, Vodi, Knox's children, Mancini's children, Ben's children, Hannan's late father, the weather, the *Hector*, exchange rates, the British Prime Minister, the long-oppressed ethnic minority in the east, women, self-worth, God, death, sex, time and money.

This was Ben's longest exposure to Mancini, who seemed suddenly unimpressive, toadying, unimaginative by comparison with Knox and Hannan. When the *karat* inevitably flowed, he looked vacant, waxy. Every now and then he perked up and said something just *slightly* irrelevant. Knox, on the other hand, was sharp as can be and quite masterly when it came to combining threats and flattery. Every so often he asked Ben to leave them alone – Ben strolled about the ship's decks, just as he had strolled about Roffe's long room – so that ghastly secrets could be exchanged. Ben didn't mind.

It was during one of these circuits of the yacht that Ben spotted Marie-Ange coming down the pier and climbing the gangplank, having evidently been in town for a day of shopping: a minion trailed behind her carrying several bags and one hat box. She glanced up, saw Ben, and waved. She looked so fresh and happy, so unlike the one person in history who had contaminated Ben with a venereal disease. She disappeared into the yacht and did not return to the men's company until late at night, and then only to make her excuses and go to bed. By that time Knox was exhausted, Mancini was quite drunk, Hannan looked itchy and Ben wanted nothing more than a few hours' sleep before tomorrow's journey home to his loving family. Instead, he found himself alone with Hannan outside on the second deck, having a thimble of *karat* poured and diluted for him. He wanted to say, 'This is fine if you keep your hands off my penis.'

'It's too cool. I have an idea. There's a place we can go.'

'I don't think –'

'I am feeling a little . . . mischievous, Ben.'

Hannan's teeth gleamed in the electric light shining on the deck from lamps above the main cabin door. The harbour was quiet. It was past two o'clock in the morning.

'I *really* don't think –'

'Come,' said Hannan, taking Ben's elbow. 'This is special.' He led Ben upstairs to the top deck, the one part of the yacht the Americans had so far not visited. Hannan had planned this in advance: flickering candelabras lighted the way. Ghostly crew opened doors, took instructions from Hannan for snacks and more icy *karat*.

The room Hannan wanted to show Ben was a library crowded with *objets* from this part of the world, and Hannan began a slightly slurred museum-curator's lecture on what Ben beheld: knives in jewelled scabbards, colourful manuscripts inked on bleached leather, gilt-edged books, miniature marble sculptures of the human head. The room was elaborately enclosed against the elements, but its contents were so out of place in this gaudy gin palace that Ben almost remarked on the incongruity – then it occurred to him that Hannan might prefer his treasures mobile. One day they might end up on the Cap Louise.

Hannan had begun now and then to slip accidentally into his native tongue, but Ben got the gist of what he was saying: how proud he was of his country, of his ancestry, of his cultural inheritance. He said what high hopes he had for P&R's future projects, especially if the Soviet menace and the more local menaces of Roffe and Colonel Vodi could be kept at bay. The only hope against the Russians was the General – Hannan was sure of this. To that end, he said, he and Knox and Mancini had decided on a perfectly *wonderful* scheme, which he was tight enough to assume Ben knew about in a general sense. Ben did not, but listened with suddenly sharp ears. It had to do with the Meheti Dam, as Ben had vaguely sensed. Hannan would supply the material. Mancini would supply the manpower. Knox would supply the money.

'And?' Ben finally had to ask.

'I am making mischief by telling you details,' said Hannan. 'But I throw it to the fates. Perhaps I want you to know so that there is . . . insurance.'

'Go on.'

Moonlight seeped into the library through smoked glass overhead. Hannan toyed with an eight-inch-long china lizard. His face was suddenly sober and serious, as if until now he had treated Ben as a friend and a co-libertine, and it was time for business.

'The Meheti Dam will be destroyed. Boom, you see? On the day of its opening, or soon after.'

'I knew that,' said Ben, though he hadn't known.

'And did you also know that our Russian friends will be the culprits?'

'I had surmised that they would be,' Ben lied.

Hannan led the way back outside, on to the top deck of the towering vessel. A red helicopter occupied the helipad down below in the stern. The dry hills were dark against the starry sky. Ben used the natural silence to take in the ramifications of what Hannan had just divulged. It was an enormous concept. Here Ben stood, shoulder to shoulder on the top deck of an ocean-liner-sized yacht with a murky arms dealer who had committed an unnatural act with him and now planned to pin the blame of a terrorist outrage on the Soviet Union. It felt good, especially as the *karat* circulated to Ben's brain. He couldn't wait to tell Ellen, to tell his *father*. He would think about it in the morning.

'There's another funny story,' said Hannan. 'I have to tell you.' Hannan really was shoulder to shoulder now, making physical contact. 'Your Mister Paul Mancini. I have a surprise for him. Well, many surprises. But he doesn't know this – I tell you specially. He is going to make the most *enormous* political contribution in America. You mustn't say a word, Ben! He will be ambassador to this country, or to somewhere else. Also he will be one of the, you know, *glamorous* ones, the non-civil-servant I think?'

'That's very good of you,' Ben said. 'Very generous.'

Hannan placed a palm on his chest and shrugged in modesty. 'Generous, I don't know. I have my little mischief. And this is why I tell you specially about the dam. When Mancini is gone, you take his place. Peter Knox agrees. He likes you very much.'

'But I haven't done a damned thing,' said Ben. 'I just sort of hang around. I picked him up at the airport. Every now and then I agree to leave the room.'

'He told me, he told me. He likes you. And this way, you see, as Knox would say, I have your pecker in my pocket.'

Ben wanted to say, 'As long as it's just your *pocket*.'

62

'Now, no splashing,' said Ellen, sitting with Candy Mancini by the side of the Peltons' pool. It was a crowded scene in the water: Sean, Nicole (buoyed up with armbands and a rubber ring), Little Paul, Caroline (who swam strongly), April and four friends of the boys from the French School, including the Vietnamese boy who never took off his conical straw hat, even when swimming.

'I keep having to engineer things,' said Candy, 'so that my husband doesn't see that boy's *hat*. He'd have a heart attack.'

'I've never dared ask,' said Ellen. 'Did Paul have an awful time?'

'I think the truth is,' Candy said, 'Paul had the time of his life. Not that it wasn't ghastly, you know, but I think that he was so *good* at it – if you spend four or five years with everybody telling you you're a hero, and you carry out your responsibilities, well . . . We don't talk much about it because we disagree, we've always disagreed, about the war. Not that he would listen to me for one *second* on the subject. Who am I to say? I was too young. But Paul was in there early and did a very good job, is all I can say, and made a lot of life-long friends. He looked at it as his first job, and he wanted it to be a success. He had faith in his superiors. And you can imagine, after that disaster, once we got married and he began diplomatic work and then P&R, it was really one fiasco after another – he has sort of left a wake of destruction since he was twenty-two, wherever in the world he's gone. Let's hope it doesn't happen here. Today wasn't promising.'

Candy was referring to one of the first organized demonstrations to have taken place there for more than ten years. It had caught the expatriates by surprise, because they didn't read the local newspapers or listen to the radio. No violence had been reported, but according to Diane (who had dropped off April at Ellen's house), the security forces had been unprepared for the turnout. The actual nature of the demonstration had not been made clear yet, but it was suspected to be a show of general protest by an otherwise incompatible collection of Roffe's supporters, the middle-class intelligentsia, various persecuted ethnic minorities and a much-feared nationalist group that everyone thought supported Colonel Vodi.

Nicole came over to Ellen to be dried off. She was the only one of the children not to wear a bathing suit in the pool – she flatly refused, and Ellen didn't want to push the issue. Ellen dried Nicole's hair, her shoulders, her body and her feet, then took the little girl, wrapped up in the towel, into her lap.

'What else can I do for you, my angel?' Ellen asked.

Nicole didn't speak, but pointed at a hairbrush sticking out of Ellen's handbag.

'Do you want me to brush your hair?'

Nicole nodded, still not saying anything, then looked up and *nearly* smiled. 'Papa.'

Ben slowly climbed the steps from the carport. Ellen hadn't heard the car drive up, what with the noise from the children in the swimming pool.

'Well, *hello*,' said Candy, who was closer to Ben than his wife. 'You look *awful*. How was the trip?'

Ellen hadn't really looked up from brushing Nicole's hair.

'Super,' said Ben. 'A little quiet on the return flight, if you know what I mean. I don't think I have to spell it out. I'm surprised Paul wanted to go straight to the office.'

'Chava will have that effect on people,' said Candy. 'Have a swim, why don't you?'

355

'Perhaps I will,' said Ben, glancing over at April on the diving board.

Ellen had to be careful not to hurt Nicole's head as she brushed the girl's hair; her anger hadn't dissipated in the least.

'Hello, girls,' Ben said, leaning down to kiss Nicole on the back of her neck. He waved at Sean, who was playing with Little Paul and April over at the diving board. 'It feels like I've been away for a week, but the kids haven't really noticed. Have you, Nicole? In fact they'll just think I'm home early for a change.'

Ellen watched Ben walk over to say hello to Sean and Little Paul, and to wave at April, who was now in the water. April waved without smiling and dived under the water with a kick of her legs. Ben went inside the house, having announced that he needed a drink and a shower and a change of clothes.

A disturbing thought had occurred to Ellen during the past hour: April, though barely post-adolescent, was only a few years younger than Ellen had been when she met Ben and gave her life over to one man, supposedly for all time. It made Ellen close her eyes and shake her head. It also annoyed her, on top of everything else that had been making her seethe inwardly for so long now, that when Ben drove April home in the Euphoria after a stint of baby-sitting, having had something to drink, he guided her out of the door with a hand around her waist or on her shoulder or even on the back of her head. This was wrong, this was inappropriate. 'Oh, she's a nice girl,' Ben would say, on his return. 'I really like her, you know? She's so wonderful with Nicole.' And in a lame feint, 'What a *looker*. Makes me feel like a dirty old man.' What sort of sad fantasy was he indulging?

Ben came back outside, drink in hand, wearing knee-length white swimming trunks and a baby-blue towel around his neck. Ellen eyed him up and down and tried to make her expression say, 'You've gone to seed.' But he hadn't gone to seed. The exhausted man in a suit who had returned ten minutes ago from a stressful business trip at the coast had been transformed into the slender, cocky, irresistible boy she had fallen in love with and married. Still, she thought she hated him.

'Ooh, sit here,' said Candy, patting the chair next to her. Ben sat, crossed his legs, took a sip of his drink, smacked his lips. 'Did you hear about our little *riot* today?'

'We were informed on the plane,' said Ben. 'That's one of the reasons I came straight here. The traffic must be awful.'

Candy reached over and patted Ben's thigh. 'You've got to tell us *everything*. Was there an orgy?'

Ellen looked up, tossed the hair from her eyes. 'Yes, Benjamin. Was there an *orgy*?'

'Sadly, no,' said Ben, smiling suavely. 'Very much a business trip. We did take the chopper off the boat this morning to get to the airport, though, got a little tour of the area from above. A bit sick-making, to tell you the truth, after a certain amount of *karat* in the wee hours.'

'What,' said Candy, '*karat* and no orgy?'

'Well, if *you'd* been there,' said Ben.

Ellen, holding Nicole in her arms, wanted to scream. Instead she ran her hand up and down the towel on the little girl's back, warming her and trying to calm herself.

'Oh, look,' said Ben, waving. 'Sean can jump off the diving board now. He couldn't do that before, could he?'

'Yes,' said Ellen.

'I don't remember that. Good boy.'

Sean climbed out of the pool, got back on the diving board, made sure everyone was looking before he jumped in again.

'Everything at the coast was *very* hush-hush,' said Ben. 'I can't say a thing.'

'Oh, go on,' said Candy.

'Absolutely tip-top secret.'

357

'According to Paul,' said Candy, 'we're not even supposed to know you were at the coast, with the Beast.'

'Oh, well, keep it under your hats then, girls. Was everything all right around here? We were worried.'

'Sure you were,' said Candy. 'But yes, everything was fine. It was the oddest thing, though, don't you think? No one has ever heard of anything like it.'

'No news from the police?'

'Are you kidding? They always grill the servants, the gardeners. It's almost as if they don't believe it really happened, not here. Robbery, sure, but just breaking someone's windows? There's no point, that I can think of.'

'Unless it was political,' said Ben.

Ellen listened to this exchange, and thought: Ben knows something.

'Probably just run-of-the-mill anti-Yankee stuff, don't you think?' Ben asked.

'If so, it's a first,' said Candy.

'Are you going to do anything extra about security?'

'I'll have to speak to Paul. I assume so. Maybe a gate and a guard at the bottom of the hill – you know, for all of us. We never thought we'd need that sort of thing here. In Kinshasa we had two men with machine guns, around the clock. Paul does seem worried, though. Did he seem worried to you, Ben?'

'I wouldn't say that. A little tense, maybe. Who wouldn't worry about his family?'

With that Ben finished his drink, put down his glass, stood up, stretched and dived lazily into the deep end of the pool. He swam over to April and the children and splashed them in just the way Ellen had asked them to stop doing.

'Are you two all right?' Candy asked, her powers of social observation as finely tuned as ever.

Ellen made a gesture to mean, 'Not in front of Nicole, please.'

In the pool, Ben horsed around with Sean in a too-obvious

way, putting on his ideal-father act when he still must have been burning up inside – Ellen had to believe this.

'All I meant was, you're not worried about this nonsense downtown, are you? You don't have to be. As long as there is a Cold War, the world is safe, this country is safe for us. That's what I think. We won't let the General down. We'll let him act as he needs to act. We do this all over the world, don't we?'

'I suppose so. And I wasn't worried. I'm not worried about that at all. I think I'm still getting over . . . you know – Sean, and this little one.' Ellen kissed Nicole's temple.

'Oh, honey,' said Candy. 'I know and I'm *so* sorry. I almost *forget*, you see, because everything always seems so fine with you and Ben and the children. If you would just do me a favour and keep reminding me, I'll hold your hand when you're blue. All right, honey?'

'Thanks,' Ellen said.

Candy leaned over in an intimate way and put a rough, tennis player's hand on Ellen's forearm. 'I just want to say how happy I am you're here, honey,' she said, in her tipsy but thoroughly sincere way. 'You've made a big difference and I want you to know that. We can be partners, Ellen. In your case it's not that easy . . .'

'What do you mean?'

'Your Ben is new to this. He may not tell you much. Paul is a bit more . . . forthcoming. We're veterans. We've been through this before. Do you know we were married *ten years* before Little Paul came along?'

'You told me, yes,' Ellen said. Candy did sometimes repeat herself. She had told Ellen that one miscarriage had put her off the idea of children for a while; that a tropical illness had rendered her husband completely impotent for more than a year – a condition never *entirely* resolved to this day, Candy had divulged more than once; Little Paul and Caroline had been conceived under stressful conditions, the Rhythm Method in reverse. Candy tried to joke about this.

'Anyway we're in good hands,' said Candy. 'Our men are in charge.'

Candy was so direct and friendly, Ellen had the strongest temptation just to tell her everything: the accident, the lying, the venereal disease, the groping of April. But she couldn't – not yet. It was the greatest test of her character so far, keeping a lid on what she knew, biding her time.

63

Technically, Ellen was in charge of both children. It was a Saturday afternoon. Ama and Haz had gone home to their village for the weekend – according to Ellen, 'To get her pregnant. She's got that look.' Ben stood alone on the flat roof of his house, overlooking the swimming pool and the Soviet Embassy compound, collecting his thoughts. The children played down below, next to the pool, waiting for permission to swim: it had been only half an hour since lunch. Ellen was somewhere out of sight.

It was quite a view, from the roof: the brown-red mountains to the north still capped with snow, the layers of foothills two-dimensional at such a distance, the northern suburbs, the golden gates of the Meheti Palace, the great boulevard leading straight to the heart of the city, the cheap housing white on its southern edge, the whole basin choked in a fat blanket of sulphurous smog. It relaxed Ben to let his eyes focus on the distant horizon. He'd had a psychological scare that morning, when a starkly obvious thought had finally dawned on him – something he should have recognized on the day of the accident: if the same thing had happened in America, he would have stopped, turned around, driven back, administered first aid, called the police – no matter *what* horrors Sean had to witness. This was the truth, Ben was sure of it. He would have cradled the boy in his arms and comforted him as he died, if necessary – or perhaps saved his life.

Ben sat on the low wall that surrounded the roof like a parapet. The white satellite dish loomed over his shoulder like a giant carnivorous jungle flower. He looked down at his children, who had not noticed their father spying on them from above. Sean's thin hair had gone nearly white in the sun. He squatted on his haunches, trying to put a broken plastic soldier back together – a toy Ben had looked at and knew to be beyond repair. Sean wore only a pair of black shorts. His vertebrae stuck out from his skinny back like a vestigial dorsal fin. Nicole looked on impassively, sitting naked and cross-legged on the deck with her hands in her lap. The sheer amount of *worry* Ben had invested in these children, it made him sick to think that they were the only real reason he had been put on Earth. Where was the consolation?

Ellen came out on to the deck. 'Oh, that's *never* going to work,' she said to Sean. 'We might as well throw that little guy in the garbage.'

'I can fix it,' said Sean, biting his lip.

'Are you warm enough, Nicky? Do you want a shirt, or something?'

Nicole shook her head. She had a new haircut: boyish and so adorable that on first seeing it Ben had hugged her too tightly, until she cried out.

'You can swim whenever you want, my angels,' Ellen said. 'Little Paul and Caroline might be coming over later. I just spoke to Candy. Little Paul's been sent on *errands*, isn't that great? He can shop for groceries all by himself now. You'll be able to do that soon, Sean.' The Mancinis had tried to guard Little Paul for a few days after their house had been attacked – and after the threatening telephone call – but abandoned the idea as being an overreaction to a vandalistic prank.

There was a small market just beyond the French School, along with an electrician, a hairdresser, a tiny cinema that showed only local films, a tea room, a restaurant and a religious bookshop. A child could walk there in twenty minutes. Ben had gone there with Sean and Nicole, many times. He let Sean do the talking. Asking for a dozen eggs, a pint of milk and a loaf of fresh bread, Sean sounded like a local. Ben really had to learn the language.

After two more minutes of spying on his family, Ben felt so troubled and lonely that he had to move over to the other side of the roof. From here he could look down into the grounds of the Soviet Embassy compound, and imagine all of the sorry Communists labouring away on world domination, oblivious of the devilish plans being hatched by Hannan, Peter Knox and Paul Mancini. Ben felt like folding one of his ace paper aeroplanes, writing word of the conspiracy on its wings and sailing it over Mancini's house into the compound for someone like Denis to stumble upon. He thought seriously about this. He had seen the dam – and he had studied maps of the surrounding area. There were two villages within five miles down river. No more than thirty crowded dwellings in each – but here that meant hundreds of people. Would they not be swept away in the flood? It had entered Ben's vulnerable mind that he had it in his power to save those people, and that such an act might in some way absolve him of past crimes. There would be children in those villages.

'Treason,' Ben muttered to himself, aloud. Treason? He didn't really know. He didn't work for the government – did he? He hadn't signed a contract that said he had to keep a lid on international plots. It was rather fun to think along these lines. What would Victor Wiesman say – what would Alan Yates say? – when Ben popped up on their television screens being interviewed by the likes of Evan Court, having caused an international incident – a scandal that might cause fingers to twitch on keys inside missile silos deep beneath Ben's fertile homeland and the icy steppes of the north?

A motorbike buzzed along a paved path in the compound, ridden by an elderly woman. Ben could imagine a conversation on this roof with Ellen's bigoted old father, who was absolutely

363

obsessed with the Soviets' treatment of an obscure Christian cult in Georgia – perhaps they would build an equivalent of the Baram Caves for themselves and disappear for a few centuries? Ben heard himself chuckling, also saying 'Sean, Sean, Sean,' under his breath. Had he drunk too much wine at lunch, on top of the wine he had drunk before lunch, and the Bloody Mary (two, actually; it was the weekend, after all)? The elderly woman stopped her motorbike at the entrance of the main office block, the one topped with a jungle of antennae, and removed a stack of envelopes from one of the saddlebags. These, presumably, related to world domination. She took them inside the building. 'Sean, Sean, Sean,' Ben whispered to himself. Ever since Sean's illness Ben had lived with a helpless terror for the boy's welfare. He sometimes wished Sean had never existed, even that Sean had died, so that he wouldn't have to worry this way. 'Sean, Sean, Sean.'

There came a yelp from the swimming pool. One or both children must have jumped in. There was a pool in the Soviet Embassy compound as well, where dark-haired Communist children swam wearing their dark woollen bathing suits. Ben had watched them through binoculars. 'Sean, Sean, Sean.' His little shrieks came up from the pool. How old would Sean have to be before Ben could sit him down for a chat about the accident? Eighteen? Thirty?

'Help!' It was Nicole's voice. She *never* shouted.

Ben raised his head like a wild animal catching a scent. The low cement wall overlooking the pool was only thirty feet away, but he didn't move. Where was Ellen? *She* was in charge.

'Help!' Nicole would only shout this way if she or Sean were in danger. Sean, Sean, Sean. Was that *gurgling* Ben heard, now?

Ben had the conscious thought, as he dashed across the roof, that by saving Sean's life he would for ever redeem himself for all that had gone before, and at the same time *show* Ellen that she, too, could behave irresponsibly. Where *was* she, when her children were drowning? Fizzing with adrenaline, Ben jumped up on the low wall and, without pausing to look over the edge, as if he were bouncing one last time on a high diving board, launched himself head-first towards the swimming pool.

Had Ben's trajectory fallen one foot short, he would have killed or paralysed himself. As it was he cleared the edge of the pool by such a narrow margin that he scraped his chest and knees as he crashed into the water. As he thrashed to the surface he felt to see if his genitals were still attached to his body, then looked for his drowning children. There was Nicole, standing naked at the edge of the pool. And here, under the water, feet away, was Sean. Ben dived down and caught the boy first by the hair, then under the arms, and hauled him to the surface. He would administer first aid, just as he had been taught only twenty-five years ago during a fifteen-minute course given by Mrs Fornter. He would save Sean's life. Nicole would be his witness. Then they would all go looking for Ellen to tell her she had let the family down, that she was a terrible mother, that anything Ben had ever done could never compare with her turning her back as Sean drowned.

'Ben!' It was Ellen, standing behind Nicole with the sun over her shoulder. 'Just what the *hell* do you think you're doing?'

She looked angry and frightened, which struck Ben as strange given that he was completely in the right. She pulled Sean away from Ben and made sure the boy was unhurt.

'Where were you?' Ben asked, choking on pool water. 'Sean could have drowned.'

Ellen looked at him in disbelief. 'I was sitting *right here*,' she said. 'And you came flying off the roof. You scared us all to death. You hit Sean. You could have killed him.' Then, to her son, 'Are you all right, my darling?' She tried to make light of Ben's folly. 'Wasn't that . . . a *sensational* dive, my guy? Wasn't that . . . *unexpected*?' She glared at Ben.

'The kids were in trouble,' Ben said, reaching the edge of

the pool. Nicole gave him an odd look and backed away. 'I *saved* them.'

'I have an idea,' said Ellen, with a mischievous look that almost made her look unattractive. 'Maybe Papa would like to try that dive *again*. What do you think, Sean? Nicky?'

'Yes!' shouted the children.

Ben pulled himself out of the pool and looked down at his wet clothes, his wet shoes, then up at the roof. He had dived fifteen feet vertically, ten feet horizontally. 'Is that what you want?' he asked the children, knowing he could never repeat the dive without that kick of terror.

'Yes!'

The telephone rang inside the house.

'I'll get it,' Ben said, kicking off his soaking shoes, not looking at his enraged wife and bemused children.

Ben dripped his way inside and picked up the phone.

'Oh, it's you, Ben,' came Candy's after-lunch drawl. 'Did I just see you dive off your roof? I happened to be looking out of the window.'

'Sean dared me,' Ben said, looking over his shoulder at his family. 'Stupidest thing I've ever done. I nearly didn't make it to the water.'

'Well, honey, thank goodness you did. Now listen, the reason I'm calling is to ask if my Little Paul is there with you. That's why I was looking out of the window, to see if I could get a glimpse of him. He is there, isn't he?'

'He's not, no,' Ben said.

'Well he went shopping more than an hour ago and isn't back yet. He was just supposed to buy orange juice and lemons and a chicken.'

'Maybe he ran into some friends?'

'Maybe,' Candy said.

'Do you want me to walk down there and take a look? I could take Sean and he could ask around.'

'No, no. Thanks anyway. I'll stroll down there and find the little guy. It just isn't *like* him, as the saying goes. Never mind.'

'Do give us a call when he turns up, all right?'

'Of course I will.'

Ben shivered in his wet clothes. He went outside to tell Ellen what Candy had said.

'Was she worried?' Ellen asked, unsmilingly.

'She didn't really sound worried, not yet.'

'I should go down and help her look.'

'I already offered. She said she didn't need help. And that she'll call when he turns up.'

Ben walked to the railing above the carport and looked down at the Mancinis' house. Their Euphoria emerged, Candy at the wheel, and drove more quickly than usual down to the road and turned right towards the French School and the market beyond.

'Candy's on her way,' Ben said. 'She said she was going to walk but I suppose she is the *slightest* bit concerned. She said he had only been an hour, though. Round trip can take an hour. I told her he had probably run into friends.' Ben heard himself trying to sound blasé. 'She'll find him in no time.'

'Did she say where Big Paul is?'

'No, but I know where he is. He's down south for the weekend looking at irrigation. I may go out with him there next month. It's an interesting project. All local engineers, very proud of themselves.'

Ben received another arctic look from Ellen. He really had no idea what was bothering her. If she had any idea what *hell* he had gone through for the sake of his family, Ben thought, she would wipe that hostile look off her face. And now this, Little Paul missing. The likeliest thing was still that Candy would drive back with the boy in the passenger seat of the Euphoria, minutes from now. That was the likeliest thing.

64

The greatest crisis in Candy Mancini's privileged life had arrived in the form of a grimy white Fardi whose passenger plucked Little Paul from the pavement outside the religious bookshop, in front of two witnesses who tried their best to describe him to the police but came up with only the most generic, moustachioed, cropped-haired, twenty-to-thirty-year-old, dark-haired civilian man wearing black leather jacket, blue jeans and white trainers. Candy had come straight to Ben and Ellen's house so that Ben could track down Big Paul. This Ben managed to do, through Diane, though Mancini would be unreachable until evening; the awful news awaited him where he was staying, at the house of P&R's local 'man in the field'. Mancini wouldn't be able to fly home until tomorrow morning at the earliest: Ben had to fill his shoes. Candy was so wide-eyed and breathless with shock it took half an hour to get her to focus on what had to be done. During this period Ben did everything he could think of: called the American Embassy and, after speaking to someone entitled Chief of Security, left a message for the ambassador himself; left messages at P&R in Washington; gave his telephone number to the local police; called Dominic Thrune and asked him to come over in case translations were necessary later on in the evening; left messages on all three of Hannan's phone numbers. Ellen kept the children occupied in the kitchen, but they knew what had happened. She came out into the living room every few minutes to commiserate with Candy and to say irrationally optimistic things.

Candy wasn't *quite* hysterical, but she did burp with laughter every now and then, when she wasn't dabbing at her eyes with the tissues Ellen had provided.

'I have to pull myself together,' she said. 'I have to pull myself together. Oh, why did Paul have to be *away*?'

'Don't worry,' Ben said. 'I'll stay with you tonight, or Ellen will, if you want. Unless Little Paul comes home before then, as I'm sure he will, Candy. Everything will be just fine. It's some sort of mistake. Little Paul will be fine, don't worry.'

'It's *unprecedented*,' said Candy. 'Why now? Why us? This has happened to *no one* else. This *can't* be happening.'

How familiar that sounded to Ben, who hadn't yet begun to debate with himself on the topic of how he was going to solve this problem, as was probably within his power. Could he be sure? The only thing he could really imagine doing was to confide everything in Dominic Thrune.

'Could it be political?' Candy asked. 'So much has been happening – bombs, these demonstrations, out of control – I should have taken everything more seriously instead of just *sitting* here on my . . . Is this political, Ben?'

'I just can't imagine that, Candy, no. Not a child. No one does that, do they?'

'You're right. So, what? Money? We're not rich.'

Ben, who had been discreetly drinking every time he had an excuse to go to the kitchen – Candy refused to touch a drop – could have answered her worries in three words: 'Vodi's little brother.' In fact he almost did so, clearing his throat and squatting on the floor next to Candy's chair, putting a hand on her knee. Dominic drove into the carport just as Ben had decided he ought to speak and put Candy out of her torment. Now Ben closed his eyes in horror at what he had almost done. 'It's Dominic,' he said, standing. 'I'll let him in. He'll be very helpful, I know he will.'

As Ben watched Dominic climb the steps from the carport,

he remembered the first time they'd met – Ben in limbo on his first day in the office, Dominic wearing his Victorian Egyptologist outfit and full of haughty praise and optimism for this country. Was it possible that Dominic had gone grey, in just a few months? His face was pinched, worried – also handsome and commanding, despite the man's clownish clothes and mannerisms. Perhaps good old Dominic needed a crisis to come into his own.

'Right,' he said, smiling and loosely shaking Ben's hand. 'Show me to the mother.'

Ben gestured towards the open French windows.

Arms wide, Dominic swept into the living room, fell to his knees, hugged Candy and burst into tears. 'My *darling*,' he said, sharing the tissues and holding both of her hands, 'this is perfectly awful. *Devastating*.'

Ben glanced at Ellen. Why had they spent the past two hours insisting 'Everything is going to be fine'?

'Oh, Candy, Candy. What will we do? Have you heard anything from the kidnappers?'

'No, nothing,' Candy said, her arms around Dominic's sympathetic shoulders.

Dominic was a marvel. 'Will they *kill* him?'

'I don't know.'

'If they say "We'll kill him if you call the police," will you call the police?'

'I don't know.'

'Oh, Jesus *Christ*, this is terrible. Ben, *alcohol*!'

Ben decided to pour everyone a glass of local red wine – except Candy, who still refused – which people got used to eventually even though it tasted of resin. Dominic knelt at Candy's side, not weeping any longer but stoking her agony with his own outrage. 'It has to be the Russians,' he said. 'Bastards!'

Candy began to relax, as if to compensate for Dominic's

hysteria. 'When Paul comes home tomorrow,' she said, 'we'll find Little Paul, won't we? We'll get the General's help. Hannan's help. He'll solve this. Do you know where he is? He *could* help, couldn't he?'

'I've left messages at all his numbers,' said Ben. 'I'll call him again if you want. Do you think he could be helpful, Dominic?'

Dominic frowned. 'Look,' he said, 'this is complicated. Ben and I have to have a little conversation. Ellen, sit with Candy while the men sort through their options. All right? Candy, I am *so* sorry.'

Outdoors, on the far side of the swimming pool, Dominic lectured Ben.

'I think,' he began, 'you may have gone too far. I've not enjoyed being the only one to know about your . . . *mishap*, but honestly this is far, far too grave a matter now. You'll have to have a word with the Great Mancini, don't you think? You are responsible for the welfare of his son. Put yourself in his place. What would you have *him* do?'

'You aren't telling me anything I don't know,' said Ben. 'I just have to think. I want to do the right thing. I always want to do the right thing.'

'Don't . . . over-*analyse*,' said Dominic. 'Or I'll have to do this for you.'

'Dominic, listen. If it's about the Russians – I've got everything planned. My contact has been out of the country. His wife is pregnant. They're coming over to dinner. I'm just going to instruct him along the lines we discussed. Are they still bothering you?'

'Well it's wonderful how you have *leapt* to our aid, Ben, but perhaps the Russians aren't the biggest problem looming on your horizon just at the moment?' Dominic smiled. 'Honestly, Ben, this country was going along just fine until you arrived. What have you *done*?'

'It isn't funny, Dominic.'

371

'No, it certainly is not. I imagine you are trying to put yourself in Candy's position. She's going to need to be sedated when this sinks in. I've brought something for her. I dare say it's yet to sink in for you. Ben, listen. Listen to me. Someone's snatched her boy, and we think we know who it is. Am I right?'

'Yes.'

'Action is required, Ben. Can you hear me?' Dominic asked this because Ben had the distant look of a stubborn child, or a corpse. 'Ben?' Dominic looked over his shoulder to see if the women were watching; they weren't. He put a hand on Ben's shoulder. 'It'll be all right, you'll see. Everyone likes you, Ben. Everyone believes in you. You just have to tell poor Candy what's going on, not let her suffer this way.'

'I will, I will,' Ben said, thinking he wouldn't, he wouldn't.

'Good. I'll hold your hand, if you like. Figuratively. Shall we go? And have a drink afterwards, for heaven's sake?'

'Not . . . yet,' said Ben. 'I'll tell Mancini when he gets back tomorrow. I don't want to tell Candy. And I don't want Ellen to know. Dominic, listen, you've got to help. You're the only one who knows. You're my friend, right? You've got to see this from my point of view. If I can tell Mancini, man to man, solve it that way – get the General involved, right? That's the ticket. Then we can spring Mancini's boy and not get . . . *me* involved. I have to think of my family. What if this Vodi comes after Sean? Sean had *cancer*, Dominic. Ellen doesn't know anything. Dominic, I got *fired* from my job, that's why I'm here. I'm just trying to limit damage. I'll speak to Mancini tomorrow, as soon as he gets here. It's the best way for Little Paul as well, I'm sure of it. These things have to be handled quietly. And Ellen would never forgive me if I put Sean at risk for *anything*. The little guy had cancer, Dominic, do you see? I've been trying to protect him. That's why I didn't stop and turn around. Dominic, listen, I know things about P&R I can trade with the Russians, if you'll just stick with me on this. All right? I know things you just wouldn't *believe*. All right? I'm going to blow the whole thing out of the water when the time is right. I'm going to save the lives of a lot of people, I really am, I really am. I don't need to tell you what this means. I may even bring in Evan Court. Tell him everything. That *is* what I'm going to do. I was *fired*, Dominic. They *fired* me.'

'Stay here,' said Dominic. 'I'm going to get you a tissue. Mustn't let the women see you this way, old boy.'

Dominic left Ben alone. When Dominic returned, Ben had composed himself sufficiently to apologize, but not enough to change his mind about what tactic to adopt in the face of a crisis that was obviously of his own making.

'I *think* I understand you,' said Dominic, impatiently. 'But might I suggest that by putting Candy through a night of this horror you are not exactly endearing yourself to her husband, our boss? You don't want to be fired *again*, do you?'

'Mancini has children,' Ben said. 'He'll understand why I've had to do this. You have to look after your own children first. You wouldn't understand that.'

'Oh, dear oh *dear*,' said Dominic. 'You ghastly man. How *dare* you take that line with me, you self-pitying *shit*. You're the child-*killer*, Ben, remember?'

This assault was so fierce and unexpected that Ben didn't know quite how to react. Dominic filled the silence, his lips close to Ben's ear. 'I'll take your word for it that it is in your family's interest to *torture* Candy Mancini for the next few hours. Please be kind enough to *anaesthetize* her – I can help on that front. If you don't tell Mancini what we suspect the *moment* he lands, I will. Do you understand?'

'Sure.'

'You're an odd chap, Ben, you really are,' Dominic said, reflectively, leaning away again as if to appraise his colleague like a painting. 'You aren't facing facts.'

'Don't be ridiculous. It was all an accident. These things happen. I've just been trying to do the right thing.'

'I never said it wasn't an accident. Quite obviously it was. But people have responsibilities to each other, Ben. You take responsibility for your actions, if you're a grown-up.'

'Oh, really?' Ben looked Dominic in the eye. 'And why should that be?'

Dominic thought carefully, then replied, 'Funnily enough I have never had to ask myself *why* human charity should exist, only to remark on its beauty and its necessity and its surprising *abundance*, all in all.'

65

It had been a busy night, which had included visits from police, the military and the US Embassy. Dominic played at Master of Ceremonies and charmed the visiting locals. Ben ached inside and thought of blue-eyed Little Paul, physically *held* somewhere, at best. Even the children stayed up late, Sean and Nicole, in their matching blue-and-white-striped pyjamas, playing the Kidnapping Game and comforting Caroline, who would be spending the night. Candy, who did not lose consciousness until shortly before dawn, looked as if she might expire. She seemed to have aged one year per hour after midnight.

Ben slept for three hours on the sofa in the living room. Mancini, who had been told what had happened the moment he returned to the house of the P&R man-in-the-field, would fly into the capital's secondary airport at ten-thirty in the morning. Ben had grandly volunteered to meet him, alone. Ben left the house at eight o'clock, before the exhausted children were awake and only just after Ellen had come out to stare at him with undisguised anger.

Ben drove off in the Euphoria in concentrated mood: he was about to confess to Mancini, to liberate Little Paul, to organize an anti-Vodi coalition with the General (desirable in any case), solve this whole problem. The secondary airport was due west of the city, a V-shaped pair of old concrete runways and a control tower the size of a shack. Ben looked down at his clothes and saw that he was wearing exactly what he had worn on the day of the accident, right down to his boots. It was a

Sunday, an informal day, and it was an informal airport.

Ben parked his Euphoria on the sandy verge of the north–south runway. Mancini's little plane wafted down, buffeted from side to side and bouncing rather dramatically on landing as if a passenger had taken the controls from a pilot in cardiac arrest. Ben had spoken to Mancini the night before, briefly, in a rush of courageous, manly euphemism:

'See you in the morning then, Ben?'

'Right you are, Paul.'

'Take care of yourself.'

'Same to you.'

'Make sure Candy's OK.'

'Will do.'

'Give Caro a kiss for me.'

'Of course.'

Mancini's plane taxied towards the control tower, then stopped. Its two propeller engines were shut down one at a time. A door opened and unfolded into a ramp and staircase. Unconventionally, the harried-looking pilot was first to emerge. He rushed away to a private car and drove off with the same recklessness he had indulged in landing his aircraft. Mancini was next out of the cabin, putting on dark glasses against the strong sunlight. Ben swallowed self-righteously and walked over to greet him.

'Ben, thank you,' said Mancini, shaking hands. 'Thanks so much. How's Candy holding up?'

'She's probably still asleep. I don't have to tell you how upset she is. Come on to the car, there's something I have to tell you.' Ben felt grown up as he said this; proud and certain of himself. He was going to solve the problem.

They walked back to Ben's Euphoria, Mancini stooped and rumpled, Ben feeling utterly in control because he was about to purge himself, open a vein. Mancini tossed his briefcase and overnight bag into the back seat, opened the passenger door,

pulled in his long legs. He looked old and defeated. Ben had
been so intimidated by this Vietnam warrior, since the first
time they met along with unlucky Ross Howard under the
Maliki painting in Mancini's ballroom office, that it was shat-
tering now to see the tall man slumped in the passenger seat,
his short white hair mussed, his confidence replaced by a
narrow-eyed despair and white knuckles on his high-raised
knees.

'Any news?' Mancini asked. 'Anything at all since last night?
The police?'

'No, no, I'm sorry. But I can explain all that,' said Ben,
beginning to smile to himself. This was his most courageous
act. After this, everything would be fine. 'Its a conspiracy. They
wouldn't tell you even if they knew something.'

'What does *that* mean?'

'I have a theory about this. I think I can solve your problem.'

'What? My "problem"? You call this a "problem"?'

'I can get Little Paul back.'

'You? Spit it out, Ben.'

'This isn't political, is my view. Don't you agree? I mean
. . . not *children*.'

'I never thought it was,' said Mancini, sitting up straighter
in his seat.

'And it isn't plain kidnapping, for money. No one could get
away with that here, and with a target like your family the
General *himself* would come down on them. There would be
no place to hide. Not worth it.'

'I'd thought that, too.'

'So,' said Ben, driving slowly downhill towards the city on
P&R's own brand-new airport spur of the ring road, 'it has
got to be personal.'

Mancini turned his head and looked at Ben for the first time
since they had left the airport. 'I beg your pardon?'

'Someone with a grudge. Someone who wants revenge. A

personal grudge and, obviously, a strong one. Any enemies on that scale, Paul?'

'Of course not. We already –'

'Exactly. This,' said Ben, as if crossing towards the jury in front of Judge Ladatt's bench, 'is a case of mistaken identity.'

Mancini reddened. 'You'd better hurry up and tell me what the hell you're talking about. And *step* on it, will you? Why isn't Chauffeur here?'

'It's Sunday,' said Ben, accelerating.

'Now go on, tell what you're talking about. By the way, you smell like a still.'

'It was a late night,' said Ben, who had also drunk just the tiniest *inch* of whisky from the bottle before leaving the house this morning. 'Right. You remember when your windows were smashed? I suspected it then. I thought –'

'Ben, we already –'

'Just wait a sec. I thought to myself, "This is a case of mistaken identity." There were no other explanations. And the phone call you got, about whether you loved your boy?'

'Come on, of course I've thought of that. You agree this is related?'

'I do indeed. Because I know who wants revenge.' Ben began to talk rapidly now, nodding his head as if all of what he had to say and ask had already been agreed: 'I'm telling you this because I just know, father to father, that you are going to understand why I never said anything before. Why I haven't said anything until now. I *know* you are going to understand. But at the same time, I also need your word that you will solve this without causing any problems for me or my family.'

Mancini cocked an eyebrow. 'I have no idea what you're talking about. You're not making any sense at all.'

'Sorry. But I need your word. When I tell you what I know, you will act on it in a way that does no harm to me or to my family.'

Mancini's jaw stiffened, and he squinted at Ben. After a long pause, he said, 'I promise.'

'Last year, not long after we came here, there was an accident in the mountains. A boy was killed.'

'I know all about that. Colonel Vodi's younger brother's boy.'

'Yes,' said Ben.

'There were no witnesses.'

'There were,' said Ben. 'But their information was suppressed. That's what I believe, anyway.'

'Why would that be?'

'Because Vodi and his brother wanted their own revenge.'

Mancini waited for Ben to continue. Ben drove more slowly than ever now, and eventually pulled over into the breakdown lane.

'You were on the road that day, with Little Paul,' Ben said. 'It was a weekend. You'd gone out to inspect the dam and you'd brought Little Paul along. Someone must have seen a dark Euphoria near the scene – there had been a tail-back of traffic, a broken-down bus with lots of people by the side of the road.'

'How do you . . . ?' Even in his agitated and sleepless state of mind it took Mancini only a moment to understand what Ben was trying to say.

'Now, listen,' said Ben, whose mouth was dry but whose eyes were moist. 'We have a deal. You would have done the same thing. I couldn't let my boy know. I couldn't let Ellen know. I have to be responsible for my family. I couldn't have gone back. There would have been trouble anyway. I didn't know if he . . . I couldn't let Sean see. Sean had *cancer*, Paul, do you understand? We've got our deal, anyway, you and I. You'll have all the help you need from the General and the Embassy without dragging me, dragging me and my family into this, now that you know. That's why I didn't even tell

Candy last night, even though it hurt like hell to put her through that pain. I know you understand. I know you would have done the same thing. I can see that you would. And the General wants rid of the Vodi brothers – this is his perfect pretext. I've thought it all through. Believe me, this has been *agony* for me, to face all of this alone. You've probably seen how . . . *tense* I've been. Anyway I'll help, I really will, anything you need. This can be solved today. You tell the General it's Vodi, without explaining how you know – American intelligence, maybe? He goes after Vodi, calls it political – the *shame* – and the Vodis are finished as a political force. Hannan and I discussed this in another context. It's what the General wants. The General is basically *good*. He doesn't want Roffe *or* the Vodis. Right? Are you following this?'

'Get moving,' said Mancini, pointing a long index finger straight ahead through the windscreen. 'Right now.'

Ben drove on. 'But you do understand? You see what decisions I've had to make? And we have a deal? Father to father?'

'That's right,' Mancini said, coldly. 'Father to father.'

'We'll get Little Paul back,' said Ben, steering the Euphoria over into the fast lane.

'You're damned right we will,' said Mancini.

'Of *course* we will, Paul. This is absolutely the right thing to do. I can talk to Hannan, if you want – and Knox. They *like* me. The General doesn't need an international incident right now. He's got the left wing whipping up demonstrations and Roffe looking stronger every day and the Vodi boys in the wings thinking the military will do whatever they –'

'Just drive,' said Mancini.

'The important thing, part of our deal, is that you don't even tell your wife. You don't even tell Candy. Right? I mean I love her but she gossips with the best of them and one weak moment might mean –'

'Ben?'

'Yes?'

'Just drive.'

'Right.' Ben drove for a few seconds without speaking, opened his mouth to do so, but was interrupted.

'I've got a question for you, Ben,' said Mancini.

'Go ahead.'

'Was it this car?'

Ben analysed the question, then replied, 'Yes. This car. It's my only car. The one we're in now.'

'Where?'

'The north road. You know where.'

'No, Ben. Where on the car.'

The air came out of Ben's lungs as the flashing image came back to him, so it took a moment to reply. Before doing so he rubbed his nose noisily with his sleeve. He didn't want to come apart in front of his boss, when everything was going so well. 'Right front, way over to the right, there, I guess. Just at the corner of the bumper. No damage. Well, just a *tiny* dent, like you'd make in a parking lot and not even leave a note about. Right front, there.' Ben pointed. He felt himself falling, now. 'Paul,' he said. 'He ran out. He ran out for a ball, or something, the sun was in my eyes. I wasn't going too fast. I didn't want Sean to see. It was an accident. He must have been running out for a ball. I'd just missed some people at the broken-down bus. Sean had said "Look out!" I was very tense – I'd had a long night with the Russians and the caves scared the hell out of me. Ah. Ah. Sorry, look. Paul, I got *fired*. That's why I came to work for you. Do you understand? I got fired. *Me*. Benjamin Pelton. *Fired*. I lost my job, Paul. A fucker named Wiesman *fired* me, completely out of the blue, instead of a useless black guy named Innis who was totally, totally a useless black guy. Is that fair? My in-laws don't even know, Paul, that's how bad it is. Do you see? Do you see?'

'Pull over. Now,' said Mancini. 'I'll drive.'

66

Little Paul had been missing three days. Ellen had spent much of that time with Candy Mancini, who felt so impotent she just sat by the swimming pool with her legs tucked up under her chin, smiling like an idiot and saying, 'Paul's taking care of it. Paul's taking care of it.' Her long legs, Ellen noticed, were mottled with pre-cancerous blemishes from ankle to knee. Three days was probably the longest she had gone without playing tennis since the age of six. Much as Ellen tried to empathize with her friend and neighbour's tragedy, she could not begin to imagine Paul's being *held* somewhere, and she had to wonder if it weren't more likely that he had been murdered.

Ellen's language classes had been cancelled indefinitely. Her flirtatious teacher, Hugo, had disappeared. There were rumours that he hadn't been kidding, that he was a dissident, and that because of recent disturbances dissidents were being taken away. This seemed unreal to Ellen. Nothing *felt* different in the city, except that it was getting hot and the smog rose even to suburban altitudes.

Candy's gardener toiled in the heat, wearing dark-green overalls and a cap that bore the logo of an American tractor company. Ellen had never spoken to the gardener: there was a caste system to servants here, and gardeners knew to keep to themselves and leave discreetly when their work was done. He was paid in cash by Yelam, from a carefully controlled store of money in a kitchen drawer.

Ellen had run out of encouraging things to say to Candy.

She wished she could be more like Dominic Thrune and simply collapse into tears and keep on crying until this whole affair was resolved one way or another. Candy couldn't decide whether or not it had been a good idea to keep the crisis under wraps, as her husband had decreed. Mancini might not have been ambassador, but he was important enough for his son's disappearance to make the Western press on a slow news day. Evan Court was back in the city, covering the demonstrations, and Candy had told him everything over the telephone, to seek his advice in the matter. He had spoken to Paul Mancini as well. They knew they could trust Evan to sit on the story if they asked him to. He was due at Candy's house any minute. Ellen looked forward to Evan's perspective and to having someone with whom she could share the responsibility of minding Candy – a chore that had become increasingly like a suicide watch.

Ellen had been watching Ben carefully. The crisis had energized him, in a strange way. He was inappropriately boastful as he reported his secret meetings with the US Ambassador, his telephone conversations with Knox and Hannan, and rumours of an imminent meeting with the General himself. He hadn't reacted like a parent – more like a detached, professional trouble-shooter. He seemed overconfident. He said the 'problem' would be resolved in another day or two. Mancini, in his shock and fear, seemed over-reliant on Ben, leaving strategy to the younger man and praying for good news. Ellen had the strongest sense that Ben and Mancini knew more than they let on.

'We should have heard something by now,' Candy said, for perhaps the fiftieth time in five hours. 'What sort of game is this? My little boy! Ellen, I want him back. What are they doing to get him back? What are they really doing? Oh, my little boy, my little angel. Little Paul! Where can he be, out there? Oh, Jesus! Paul's taking care of it. Paul's taking care of it.' Candy hugged her knees and rocked forwards and back, forwards and back.

Ellen had tried every tack in attempting to reassure and console Candy, who was so distraught the damage would certainly be permanent no matter the outcome of this drama in her life. Now Ellen merely changed the subject: 'Roffe's marching today, in person,' she said. 'It's the first time. That's why Evan Court came back, isn't it? Do you think there will be another little war? It seemed to work the last time.'

Candy didn't reply. She kept rocking and looked wide-eyed in the direction of her gardener, who had brought along some lettuce to feed the two tortoises whom Little Paul had named Romeo and Juliet. The gardener looked to be in his seventies. He cut the grass with hand shears, crouching down and resting his free hand on one knee. Ellen wondered if Candy thought the gardener had something to do with Little Paul's disappearance. The people here were honest, but sometimes desperate. Servants were always the first suspects. Yelam and Tamina had been interviewed for hours when they returned from their village, even thought their alibi was as strong as it could possibly be. Tamina had wept, and Yelam had vowed personally to kill whoever was responsible.

It wasn't the servants. It wasn't the stooped old gardener. It looked increasingly political – but a child? And where, anyway, were their demands? No one had heard anything. Not Mancini, not the police, not the government. Ellen imagined the inevitable conversation with her father in which she would have to admit that her next-door neighbour's son had been kidnapped in broad daylight at the local market and probably killed.

A few awful minutes later Evan Court arrived, by taxi, looking beautifully solemn, the way he did in places like the Sudan, or Afghanistan, or Los Angeles. He wore khaki shorts and a sun-faded blue polo shirt. His legs were the colour of toasted bread. His eyes were so full of concern when he said hello to Candy that Ellen wanted to grab him by the back of his head and kiss him.

After all the right things had been said, Ellen asked Evan what was going on downtown.

'It's sort of eerie,' he said. 'It's as if all these different sides have decided to get along for the moment and just protest in general. There isn't any one issue. You've got the students, the religious nuts, the anti-corruption democrats, the human-rights campaigners, the old-school communist intellectuals, everybody with no business getting along together marching.'

'Is this a good thing or a bad thing?'

'Good, I think,' said Evan, as the breeze played with his thin blond hair. 'In my experience the religious freaks are the ones you've got to watch, and to see them joining in with all the others is highly unusual and interesting. There may be hope for a peaceful revolution, and the General has a history of being willing to step aside.'

Candy seemed to be in a trance. Evan did his best with her, but after three long days she was inconsolable.

'When your husband says the word,' Evan said, with dashing authority, 'I'll go on the air world-wide with this. Do you understand, Candy?'

Candy nodded.

'My opinion is I ought to break the story right away. What's holding Paul back? He told me he's heard nothing at all, not a thing. So why wait any longer?'

Candy shrugged and shuddered at the same time.

'I just don't get it. He must know something,' said Evan.

'That's what I've thought all along,' said Ellen, happy to have her suspicions confirmed by an expert journalist who earned half a million dollars a year. 'And I think my husband does too. They're together all day long, scheming.'

'Well, my offer stands. I'll stick around as long as I can. You tell me the moment Paul changes his mind, OK?'

Candy nodded and started to cry again. Evan put his arms around her neck and hugged her, then did something Ellen wouldn't have dreamed of doing, but something that suddenly seemed appropriate: he started talking about the first time he met Little Paul, when Little Paul was a baby in Zaire. Candy sobbed so hard it became catharsis, and in ten minutes she was actually in control of herself and trying to be optimistic. Ellen walked Evan to his car and thanked him for his help.

'Get your husband to tell you what's going on,' said Evan, sincere again, kissing Ellen on both cheeks. 'This whole thing stinks out loud.'

67

Ben lay on his back, in bed, heart beating too hard – Ellen asleep a foot away with her back to him – thinking everything was going to be fine. It had been a narrow escape, but they were almost there. The General was said to be going to try to put the squeeze on Vodi's incensed younger brother. Little Paul was probably being kept in the elder Vodi's headquarters north of the city, where he trained his élite troops. The General would agree that Vodi's brother had acted in a justifiable fit of rage, and need not be punished. These were the rumours, anyway. The General was said to be grateful for Paul Mancini's restraint in not letting out this damaging story, and he trusted the American intelligence that proved Mancini could not have been responsible for the boy's death.

Ben wished he could sleep. It was going to be another long, long day. Despite all that had happened, Ben and Ellen thought it was a good idea to go ahead with their dinner with the Russians. Ben was glad of this because he had a whole new plan: he was going to tell Denis about the plot to blow up the dam. This had been mere fantasy a few days ago, the day of Little Paul's disappearance, when Ben had launched himself from the roof. Now it made perfect sense to him. Just tell Denis, get those sad old Communists moving, get rid of the bomb or the mines or whatever they were, save all of those villages – more, *much* more than make up for accidentally running over the crueller Vodi's son.

Part of Ben couldn't believe Mancini hadn't immediately told the authorities that Ben was responsible. What an honourable man: his son, *held* somewhere, and yet he kept his promise to protect Ben and Ben's family. Remarkable, really. When this was all over Ben would ask Mancini what in the world he could do to repay the favour.

Ellen stirred at Ben's side, but did not awake. How peculiar *her* reaction had been, Ben thought. Her frostiness had lasted weeks now, when ordinarily she held a grudge for two days at the most. And the children too, now that Ben thought of it. It was as if Ben, alone, lived in a world where commerce existed, where tragedies occurred, where men had to take action to ease their path through life; and Ellen and the children stayed cocooned at home, relying on him, needing him to do everything for them. Perhaps some day he would sit them all down and tell them what it was he had done: how he had brought Little Paul home at considerable risk to himself; how he had saved dozens of people's lives by divulging a secret casually learned to a citizen of the despised Soviet Union. It was dramatic. Ben was making a difference. Victor Wiesman could be dead, for all Ben knew of events back home, and Alan Yates divorced.

Ben got out of bed at dawn. He shaved. He dressed. He ate a piece of toast. When Sammy arrived he got into the car, flapped open yesterday's London paper (Sammy always brought a paper along; he was a superb chauffeur; Ben was going to give him two-hundred dollars for Christmas) and read about the far-away real world.

Mancini wasn't in the office, and rarely had been since the crisis began. He would still be at home now, taking Candy's pulse to see if the sleeping pills had killed her yet. Ben was in charge of the office, where the focus was on the opening of the dam, now just two weeks away. Ben mentally rubbed his hands together in anticipation as he imagined Mancini and his spook cronies from the Embassy waiting for the structure to blow up and then . . . *nothing*. Ben's intention was to be supremely casual with Denis tonight: take the Russian outside after dinner, comment on the view, remark as an aside that someone was going to blow up the dam and blame it on the Russians. Denis would nod knowingly and never mention it again.

Ben had another thought, as he took off his jacket, hung it on the stand next to the door, opened the window to the full blare of Meheti Boulevard, installed himself behind his desk: why not, while he was at it, tell Evan Court? Ellen had said the reporter was in town, covering or even fomenting the revolution. Why not tell Evan Court? A little insurance, that's what it was, in case the Russians failed to defuse the bomb, or the mine, or whatever it was. If the dam blew up, killed lots of children down-river, Ben had his insurance in Evan Court, who could tell the world that one brave man with a conscience had tried to put a stop to the lunacy. Look, Ben could say, I'm a private citizen. I'm not on anyone's *side*. I just think blowing up that dam is a shameful waste of money; it might kill people; if we annoyed the Russians by lying about such a thing it might mean World War Three; so we're actually, Evan, saving *all the children in the world*. Journalists were said to go to prison rather than divulge their sources. Ben would not come under suspicion, because he wasn't even supposed to know about the plot.

Ben thought about his parents. They would be *so* proud, if only he could tell them what he'd done. Right now they would be asleep, the bedroom window open a crack, the perfume of flowering rhododendrons and lilacs floating up to their snoring nostrils. They would awake at six and dutifully turn on the television to see Evan Court reporting from the main drag of their son's temporary city. But they wouldn't really *know*. They wouldn't know that their son had played a key role in the unfolding drama.

Ben looked at his telephone and thought of calling Victor Wiesman. Wiesman stayed up late drinking brandy and smoking cigars and pretending to care about his wife. What if Ben just dialled the number and asked for Wiesman and listened to him saying 'Hello? Hello?' It amazed Ben that his feeling of hurt and betrayal had not abated, not by one degree, in all the months since Wiesman had fired him. Ben lived in pure rage. He could call Alan Yates, wake him up. 'Hello? Hello?'

Diane knocked and entered. Even she didn't know what was really going on behind the scenes, but someone who had lived her life could guess it wasn't good. She did everything for Ben and didn't ask questions. She had been less friendly with Ben for some time, and Ben wondered if April had said anything about those vaguely remembered pats on the knee that could so easily be misconstrued – or even about that . . . Had Ben tried to *kiss* April? Well, certainly, if he had, it was 'Goodnight, and thanks,' just good manners. Had he *kissed* April? Ben wondered if there were something wrong with his diet, if he were missing out on an important vitamin that would straighten out his thoughts. No time to visit a doctor, though, not now, not in a period of crisis. Ben looked up and realized Diane had been standing in front of his desk for some time.

'Sorry. Yes? I was . . . preoccupied.'

'Is this not a good time?' asked Diane. 'I have no idea what's going on around here. I have something important I wanted to say. More to Paul, but in his absence . . .'

'What is it then, Diane?'

'I'm leaving. I'm leaving P&R.'

'Diane. No. Please.'

'Yes. I have to. I'm thinking of the children. I don't like what's going on. It's never been like this before. I'm going home.'

'But everything's going to be fine. Why now?' Ben had focused on Diane's face and saw how tired she looked, how defeated.

'I've been thinking about this for months. I didn't want to say anything. I don't feel well. I wanted to carry on. I can't do that any more. I want April to have two years of high school back home. I want her to go to college. I have to leave.'

'But where will you go?'

'I have a brother in Texas. I'll go there. I'm worried about my health. My brother is a doctor.'

'What's wrong?'

'I don't want to talk about it. I'm not well. I have to leave.'

'But what will I do without you?'

Diane frowned and turned to go. Over her shoulder she said, 'That's a selfish way of looking at things, don't you think?'

After she went out, Ben chewed on Diane's insolent remark for a few minutes, staring at the treetops through the open window. The poor woman didn't have the first idea of the intrigues surrounding her. She was probably spooked by the newly secretive atmosphere around P&R and that, combined with a restless populace even now assembling downstairs in Meheti Boulevard, had put her over the edge. Let her go back to Texas, thought Ben – the woman has been through enough.

At noon, having accomplished almost nothing at his desk, Ben went out to look at the protesters. There was said to be an anti-American element to some of the marchers – most notably Roffe's followers – but Ben didn't feel threatened in the slightest as he walked downhill in the sunshine towards the Hotel Chevalier. All of the demonstrations so far had been peaceful, even on the part of supporters of the LFP. There was no one masterminding this slow increase in public dissent. It reminded Ben of college, when protests and candlelight vigils normally didn't begin until the weather turned fine. The men, who outnumbered women twenty to one, were in their shirt-sleeves and went bareheaded. It was a youthful crowd. Some carried banners, many written in English for the sake of Evan Court's camera and commentary. From what Ben could see the march was made up predominantly of people interested in gaining some measure of 'human rights', which in this country meant a guarantee that someone like Vodi wouldn't burst in to one's house in the middle of the night and carry one away to an unspeakable fate, simply because one had written or published a snide essay in a national paper. It was a problem this country shared with most other countries in the world, but no less annoying for that.

The marchers, crowded together, shuffled along at a slow pace. The military looked on in small numbers, as if the General had uncharacteristically decided that a limited presence would stem international interest, and that the protesters would gradually lose their initiative, get bored and go home. It didn't feel like a revolution. It felt like a strike, a transitory protest.

Ben went into the Hotel Chevalier. He nodded to the familiar faces at reception, and walked through to the outdoor bar where he had first met Candy Mancini and, later, Ross Howard. As he sat down Ben couldn't tell if that day felt like a long or a short time ago. He did remember how elated he'd felt on arrival, how eager to do a good job and to watch his family thrive. He'd had to claw his way back from disaster, and he was by no means in the clear yet. Mancini had to hold his nerve – but what more likely man to do so than a Lieutenant Colonel in the Green Berets, a great warrior, a man with nerves like piano wire and a past full of sensational conspiracy?

Ben nibbled at peanuts and olives and drank a glass of beer. He could hear mild chanting from the boulevard, which he didn't understand. He really would have to learn the language one of these days. He ordered a second beer and looked at his watch. He knew he ought to check in with Ellen to see if there had been any news. He went back out to reception and asked to use the telephone. The line was busy. He rang Mancini's house; also busy. They were likely to be on the phone to each other. Ben went back to the bar, finished his drink, went back out again to the telephone. Ellen answered on the first ring.

'He's out! He's back!'

'Fabulous,' said Ben, quietly, trying to sound as if he'd known all along that Little Paul would survive and be released. 'Is he home now?'

'Yes, yes. He arrived about twenty minutes ago, in a taxi, for some reason. Can you believe this craziness? Anyway, I can't talk, I'm going straight down to see him. Candy *fainted* when she heard.'

Ben had covered the mouthpiece of the telephone while he bit his lip with relief. The concierge noticed and looked away, perhaps suspecting that Ben had just learned of a parent's death. Ben struggled to control his emotions. He'd done it. He had *clawed* his way out of his difficulties. He had risked his own hide to help save that little boy – was he not now redeemed?

'Big Paul sounded stern as always, but I have a feeling he's going to need a holiday after this,' said Ellen, bubbling over with happiness and relief. 'He says Little Paul is completely unharmed and even *unfazed*, in the weird way he has. Apparently the first thing he said was "I beat them all at backgammon," and produced the cash to prove it. He's the most amazing boy, I adore him.'

Ben could breathe regularly again. 'You'd better go see him,' he said. 'Give him a squeeze for me.'

'I will.'

'Tell Paul and Candy I'm . . . glad it worked out.'

'This has been the worst thing ever.'

'Not quite,' said Ben, 'but I know what you mean.'

'All right, I'm off,' said Ellen. Ben could hear Nicole in the background, wanting to know what was going on. This was a good sign. 'I assume we're still on for dinner with the Russians now that this is all over?'

'I think so,' said Ben. 'We don't want to arouse suspicions. By the way,' he said, 'any idea who took Little Paul?'

'Well, it's quite scary. I probably shouldn't say over the phone.'

'Go ahead, Ellen.'

'I'm not sure we're at all safe here any more,' Ellen said.

'Why is that?'

'Paul said something about how it actually *was* political, in the end. Unprecedented. He hopes it won't leak out. We hope Evan Court doesn't find out, either. We trust him not to report the story but if he found out about that . . .'

'Found out what? Who do they say did it?'

Ellen sighed, worried again. 'Big Paul says it's the LFP.'

68

Ben went back to the bar thinking what a genius Mancini was. What an absolutely brilliant idea it had been to incriminate the wretched old LFP. They deserved it, didn't they, after all of those bombs, those dead children, Hannan's slaughtered driver? Ben ordered a cheese omelette, a tomato salad, a bottle of French white wine. Little Paul was safely home. No need to think about this unpleasantness ever again. He had heard Nicole's voice in the background as if she'd regained it out of relief for Little Paul's return. You had good luck and bad luck in life – everything was an accident – and the time had come for Ben to have good luck. He drank two glasses of wine before his omelette arrived. He ate with relish.

Ellen had overreacted. There was nothing to fear, now. There was no reason to leave the country. Little Paul had come home. The demonstration, still audible from the boulevard, was a standard, periodical catharsis. Ben found he could *stare* at his mental image of the boy in the road without having to gag. There were casualties everywhere, every day. It had been an accident. The boy in his black shorts with his crew-cut hair, his face looking up for a last instant, he was a casualty. And he was a Vodi boy.

Ben felt his shoulders heaving. He breathed hard through his nose as he swallowed more wine. He thought about paying the bill and getting out of there. The outdoor restaurant had begun to fill with hotel guests and local businessmen. He had to be on his best behaviour tonight, with the Russians. He ought to ring Mancini to thank him and to say how happy he was that Little Paul had come home at last without complications.

Three Western men, casually dressed, came out of the hotel into the sunny courtyard. Ben glanced up at them from where he sat in the shade of the courtyard's lone eucalyptus tree. The first man, who looked about twenty-five years old, had long, curly red hair and was unshaven. The second man, twice the first man's age, had an ashen complexion beneath feathery grey eyebrows and above a biblical grey beard. The third man was Evan Court.

They went straight to the bar and were served tall green bottles of local beer without having to ask. They were in high spirits. Evan Court wore a rumpled white Oxford shirt beneath a light-blue linen jacket, white chinos and scuffed, camel-coloured desert boots. The bearded man spoke in a loud American voice — so loud that other patrons stopped their conversations and looked at him. He crescendoed through his sentences so that only their tail ends could be understood: '. . . as far as I could throw him . . .', '. . . a long-tailed cat in a room full of rocking chairs . . .', '. . . lower than a snake's belly in a wagon rut . . .'

Ben caught Evan Court's eyes. The reporter looked away, then looked back again. He excused himself to his colleagues, and made his way over to Ben's table.

'Evan Court,' he said, extending a hand. He wore a leather bracelet.

Ben shook hands without standing up.

'You're Ellen's husband, right?'

'That's right. Ben Pelton. Have a seat.'

Evan sat down. 'I saw you that night,' he said. 'Or that morning, I suppose it was, last time I was here.'

'You have a good memory.'

'I saw your wife yesterday. Awful business, with Candy's kid.' Evan frowned and paused, as if in mourning.

'Haven't you heard?' asked Ben. 'Little Paul's free. He's home.' Ben wished he could add that he had been personally responsible for the boy's safe release.

Evan made a whistling sound to indicate that he was relieved. 'Any idea who was behind it?'

'LFP,' said Ben, firmly, as if this were a fact. Mancini really *was* a genius.

Evan frowned again. 'That doesn't sound right,' he said. He had powdery smooth skin that might have been lightly made-up for the camera. Ellen had told Ben that this reporter earned half a million dollars a year.

'I have it on good authority,' Ben said. 'Anyway, the boy's in good shape, no harm done.'

'It still doesn't sound right.'

Ben filled his glass, emptying the wine bottle, and asked Evan if he had time for lunch and a chat. 'I have a story for you,' he added, so suave in his narrow escape that he might have been Chava Hannan after a mighty arms deal with Indonesia.

'Sure,' said Evan. 'We're done for the day.' He gestured at his colleagues, who were eating bar snacks and laughing over their second beer. 'I interviewed Roffe this morning. Know him at all?'

'Yes,' said Ben, who had done nothing more than loiter in the religious leader's presence, out of earshot.

'I think,' said Evan, 'he may be the most frightening man I've ever met. And I've met the lot.'

'Oh, I don't know about that,' said Ben, as if he were privy to young Roffe's most ambitious schemes, and had found them tame.

A waiter who knew Ben well came over to take Evan's order. Having already eaten, Ben asked for another bottle of wine to accompany Evan's meal. He had redemption to celebrate, after all, and across the table sat the conduit for his greatest humanitarian act of all.

Ben inspected Evan and decided they must be exactly the same age. Evan's thin blond hair had been disorganized by his morning's work with Roffe and the demonstrators. He smoked continuously and looked annoyed when his food arrived, as if having to eat meant an unwelcome break from cigarettes. This was a man who had to look out of his hotel window every morning to find out where he was. He was unmarried and he had no children and was therefore, in Ben's eyes, irresponsible.

'Your friends,' said Ben, nodding towards the bar. 'They work with you?'

'Camera and sound,' said Evan. 'They'll find their own entertainment. What's your story, then?'

'Ah,' said Ben, pouring wine and feeling like an arms-reduction negotiator on the shores of Lake Geneva. 'That.'

Ben had rehearsed this moment for days, while never expecting actually to have the opportunity to divulge his secret to Evan Court in person. He had imagined an anonymous telephone call, or using Dominic as an intermediary, or meeting Evan at a remote site along P&R's ring road. They were perfectly safe here, in the Chevalier courtyard, their voices dampened by the waterfall in the carp pool, by the eucalyptus tree, by the conversations of businessmen nearby, by the loud voice of Evan's bearded American colleague at the bar.

'I am going to tell you something so important it may be the scoop of your career,' said Ben, in a low, conspiratorial voice. Part of him couldn't believe he was doing this. Vast political and historical forces clashed overhead, and here was Ben – who had been *fired* – lighting another fuse. He *had* to, though: this was part of his redemption. 'Everything I am going to tell you is true. But I need certain assurances from you. It would destroy my life – and Ellen's, and the kids' – if anyone found out I was the source. Are you the sort of guy who goes to jail before revealing a source?'

Evan laughed. 'I've never been in that position. I usually just film people killing each other. No sources involved. But if it makes you feel any better, I swear to God and on my father's grave that I will never tell a soul we had this conversation. Unless they torture me – I draw the line there. Can't abide torture.'

'That's good enough for me,' said Ben, whose head swam with relief and far too much wine on a hot afternoon. 'Now, first of all, I'm not a spy or anything like that. I'm a – I *was* a lawyer. I haven't been here very long. P&R – Planning and Resources, that's my company, Mancini's the boss – was a . . . detour. I just sort of administer the place – Mancini travels a great deal. Our biggest project is the Meheti Dam –' Ben gestured towards the mountains to the north. 'Have you heard about that?'

'Yes.'

Ben described the dam anyway – its location, its size, the 'leisure activity' involved. 'It's *sensational*,' Ben said, reminding himself of Ellen and Sean. 'But some very disturbing information has come my way. From Chava Hannan, who must have thought I knew all about it. I didn't. I didn't know anything. Mancini must be a spook,' Ben added, rambling now, reaching out for his glass. 'It's the craziest idea. I can't let it happen. I have my reasons. Children . . .'

'Just slow down,' said Evan, who had stopped eating and resumed smoking. 'Take it easy and tell me what Hannan said.'

Ben felt the way he had when he almost told Ellen about the girl at the top of the stairs. He should stop now. He'd already mentioned the dam, but Denis was going to take care of that, thanks to Ben. He could stop right now, or make something up. He loosened his tie and leaned forward over the table and whispered: 'We're going to blow up the dam. Blame it on the Russians. Is that clear enough for you? *Blow it up*. "Boom," Hannan said to me. He's probably providing the explosives, the mines, or whatever. I've seen Mancini at secret meetings at the dam, with locals. There are villages downstream. People will be swept away. I'm trying to stop it. I have a way. The Americans are going to do this to prop up the General. It's wrong. Do you understand me?'

'I believe I do,' said Evan, who had gestured towards the bar for another bottle of beer. 'I'm interested.'

'Interested? Jesus, this is *huge*. Think about it.'

'Keep your voice down, please.'

'Sorry, but you've got to think of the consequences. This is a Bay of Pigs. Have you ever had a bigger story? I mean, it's *disgusting*. The *President* must know about it, wouldn't you think? Come on, I expected you to be *angry*.'

Evan's beer arrived and the table was cleared of plates and cutlery. He looked over his shoulder at the other people in the courtyard, and at his colleagues at the bar. 'This isn't something I'm used to doing,' he said. 'You want me to confront Hannan? Mancini?'

'No, no,' said Ben, urgently, drunkenly. 'No, no. It's insurance, don't you see? I'm going to *solve* this, *save* those people. You just wait. Remember what I've told you. If I fail, and the dam blows, you'll know I was right. And you *bust* these people, these criminals.'

'I see,' said Evan.

'But *do* you see?'

'Quietly, Ben.'

'*Do* you see? It's a *disgrace*. I mean, you hear about this sort of thing, it always sounds like a conspiracy theory, all crazy – but it's *happening*. I can stop it, though. I think I can stop it.'

'How are you going to do that?'

'I can't tell you,' said Ben, blinking in sunlight that had rounded the eucalyptus tree. 'But I have a way. I have a channel. If that dam doesn't blow a week from Wednesday, you'll know I was right.'

'Or completely wrong,' said Evan.

'What? You don't believe me?'

'Of course I believe you. It's a big story, Ben. Try to relax. We'll fix this, don't you worry.'

'They're insane. They could kill a lot of people. I've looked at maps.' Ben hated the idea that Evan might think he was talking to a drunk. This was so important. It was so *noble* of Ben. 'And for what? Are they afraid there will be a revolution? Here? Forget about it. The General's in charge as long as he wants to be.'

Evan Court cocked an ear towards the boulevard. 'I don't know what you've seen, mate,' he said, 'but there are a million people outside. The General's coming down.'

'Oh, come off it.'

'Count on it,' said Evan.

69

It had been a hectic two hours for Ellen getting the dinner party organized, after an emotional afternoon at the Mancinis' house welcoming back Little Paul. The boy really was miraculous. He seemed to have grown taller while in captivity, or this was the impression he gave when he boasted of beating his kidnappers at backgammon and teaching them how to make a proper omelette: 'Plenty of butter in the mixture, isn't that right, Mom? And a *dusting* of paprika?' Candy, who had not had a drink during her son's absence, drank vodka and orange juice and sat on the sofa looking as rosy and satisfied as a Tudor barmaid. Paul Mancini, after half an hour of hugging his boy, went to bed and slept all afternoon. The police were summoned to debrief Little Paul, but they seemed oddly uninterested in his description of his captors and the place north of the city where he had been held. Coming home in a taxi turned out to have been Little Paul's idea, after he was left alone in a suburban street. Ellen could see how proud the boy was of having endured this unforgettable adventure. The only way in which he seemed immature was in his inability to see how near collapse with anxiety his parents had been. 'Did you miss me at *all*?' he asked, and Candy had to cover her face with a cushion.

The Russians were expected at eight o'clock. At six, Ben returned from the office and promptly fell asleep. Ellen had to rouse him at seven so that he could shower and pull himself together. The smell of wine seemed to come straight out of his pores – that and someone's cigarette smoke.

'My darling,' he said, taking off his clothes as the shower water warmed up, 'everything is going to be fine now.' He said this as if it had been their own child who had been kidnapped, and as if the whole country surrounding them didn't seem to be on the brink of revolution.

Ellen didn't pursue any sort of conversation with Ben. She wanted to get through the evening and talk about the future in the morning. Despite everything that had happened, Candy Mancini said she expected to stay here. 'It doesn't matter who the *government* is,' she said. 'All governments need money.' She believed in this country and its serious, civilized people. She believed in her husband. She didn't believe Evan Court – whom she had called 'an absolute *dish*' to his face – when he said the General would be toppled and sent into exile. Evan thought someone like Vodi would assume power and a period of even worse oppression would follow. Candy tended to think the General was invincible and that in the grand scheme this was not entirely a bad thing. It could be *so* much worse, she said: just look at Roffe. And the Left: a rabble of too-clever Trotskyites with too much time on their hands, tossing the occasional Molotov cocktail into a bank or a post office or a train station. The General looked downright reasonable by comparison and, after all, most countries tortured people now and again and there was nothing anyone could do about that. Now that she had her little boy back Candy really didn't care *what* happened.

Ama and Haz, who had overheard policemen and knew exactly what was going on with the neighbours, had been infected by everyone's relief and happiness. Haz had announced that he would bake his 'world-famous' apple tart to serve to the Russians. Ama played outside with Sean and Nicole. Sean had tried to react to Little Paul's return with almost adolescent detachment, but his lower lip betrayed his emotion. He looked dazed, and went to bed of his own accord at seven-thirty.

Fifteen minutes later Nicole fell asleep in Ama's arms. Although the peace and quiet was welcome, Ellen half wished the children had stayed awake so that she could show them off to Nadia. They were her only accomplishment, after all: she couldn't show ballet films of herself.

The Russians arrived at a quarter past eight. Nadia was splendidly pregnant. She wore a short black cocktail dress that clung to her body so tightly that in profile she looked like the photographs of naked pregnant women Ellen had studied in books about childbirth. Denis looked tiny standing next to her. Nadia's graceful long legs looked too slim to support her egg-shaped belly.

Ben had bought a bottle of vodka for the occasion, which he produced on the guests' arrival. In solidarity with Nadia, Ellen declined the drink even for toasting purposes; the men sank two shots before anyone had sat down. Denis was obviously somewhat overawed by the Peltons' house, modest though it seemed to the Americans. He asked leading questions about how much such a place might cost, and was only denied a tour on the grounds that Sean and Nicole were asleep. Nadia cooed over recent pictures of the children that Ellen had framed and put on a glass side-table next to the sofa.

Wearing a new white jacket, Haz served canapés from a brass tray, one hand behind his back, asking softly 'Madame?' when he came to Nadia. Ellen was so proud of him she wanted to say so even in front of guests. She thought that if they stayed in the country much longer Haz would become her best friend. He was her ally. He was so serious and adorable in his white jacket, with its Nehru collar. Who had taught him to say 'Madame'? He must have consulted Yelam, at Candy's house, and practised. Ellen suddenly found this unbearably poignant, and wanted to rush into the kitchen to kiss the man and his wife and shower them with thanks.

Denis smoked cigarettes and drank champagne when it was

offered. Ellen watched her husband conversing with Denis, and thought Ben looked oddly cocky, even arrogant. They talked about the demonstrations downtown, some of which Denis had probably organized. They were careful to comment only as citizens of the world, rather than as enemies locked in abstract battle with the potential of erasing all of mankind in a day. Ellen and Nadia, together on the sofa, talked about babies. This made Ellen so happy that she couldn't stop smiling at Nadia's perfectly lovely, creamy face, or reaching out to put a palm on her hard belly. Babies were her only area of expertise. After a few minutes she couldn't help asking Nadia to come down the hall to look at her sleeping children. Silently, in dim light, they looked down at the face, first, of Nicole, then of Sean. Nadia reached down and lightly touched Sean's hair. Ellen could sense the pleasure and anticipation resonating in Nadia's body. After they had crept out of the children's bedroom and closed the door, both women put a hand to their bosoms, shook their heads and quietly laughed with sighs of emotion. Ellen desperately wanted to tell Nadia about Little Paul's ordeal, but stopped herself. She found that she was physically drained from the afternoon with Candy. She would never forget the feeling of Little Paul's arms around her neck when he hugged her, a little squeeze with his fingertips that meant, despite his bravado, that the child had been really, *really* frightened.

The women rejoined the men, who were talking in low voices about Roffe. Ellen wondered if this were wise of Ben, under the circumstances. Ben wore a severe charcoal suit and a thin navy-blue tie. He sat leaning back with his legs crossed and his hands clasped behind his head, like a White House aide posing for informal photographs in the Oval Office, or a newspaper editor. Ellen wondered if Ben fantasized that he was contributing, in the presence of a Russian, to the Cold War battle for this outpost of spurious freedom. Ellen just wanted to run away with Nadia, help her have her baby. From the moment she had met Nadia, Ellen had been so attracted to her that it reminded her of elementary-school crushes.

The men had another vodka before dinner, toasting the baby's health. This made Ellen so uneasy she almost had to leave the room. She wanted to sit Nadia down and explain to her at length and in detail what it had been like to have a broken child, how she would never get over it, how it had quite clearly ruined her marriage, how crazy Ben was, how every second with Sean was an excuse for tears. Instead they sat down at the table and talked about the quality of local vegetables and the unbelievable fact that this country was a net exporter of fruit.

Haz served course after course with a solemn, sleepy look on his face, when he must have been fizzing with anxiety on the inside. The men grew noisier and noisier as they drank their wine, and began to find manly common interest in things they knew nothing about. Denis admitted that he dreamed of visiting New York City, while Ben decided to praise Soviet courage at Stalingrad. Wearing the same silk suit as he had on their first meeting, Denis confessed to an admiration of Abraham Lincoln. Ben remarked that he had read bits of Tolstoy. Ellen told Nadia about both of her deliveries: the first scary, premature and painful; the second scary, prolonged and by emergency caesarean section. She wanted to ask Nadia about old boyfriends, about living in the world of theatre, about Russia, about sleeping with the same man night after night for ever.

The world-famous apple tart was a triumph. When Haz came out of the kitchen to clear away the plates, Nadia touched his sleeve and said, in the local language, that it was the most delicious desert she had ever eaten in her life, and that Haz was a genius. As Haz backed away, when no one else was looking, he winked at Ellen. This touched her, and made her hope Ama was as pregnant as she appeared. Ellen wanted to lose herself in babies, it was all she had ever really done or been good at. She wanted to *kill* Ben, who for no reason had begun to describe his parents' house back home, and to suggest that in America everyone lived that way. What had got into him? During the whole Little Paul episode he had peacocked around as if he had all the answers, as if he alone could withstand the stresses of a kidnapping. He had started to tell Denis about Harvard – always a bad sign. Most alarmingly, he told Denis he was going to ask Mancini for a pay rise. Ellen found herself thinking, quite clearly: I have to get my children away from this man.

70

Ben thought things could not be going more splendidly. His manly conversation with Denis had set exactly the proper tone, it was leading in the right direction. Ellen and Nadia were getting along so well they might have known each other all their lives. Ben had been troubled by second thoughts in the shower, after his nap: did he really know enough about Knox and Mancini to betray their plot, especially as it had been wicked old Hannan who let the information slip? Now, chatting reasonably with Denis about world affairs, he thought he did. Denis seemed to him perfectly placed to act on Ben's revelation: not too senior, not sinister at all – in fact humane and sensible. Anyone who had succeeded in marrying Nadia had to be honourable. Ben was going to do this thing, this one good act to wipe away all sin. Some day soon he would tell Ellen what he had done, what courage he had shown. He would never tell her about the boy in the road – that was impossible – but this one good act of unpatriotic deceit was something he could hold up and be proud of for the rest of his life.

During dinner Ben dropped hints that he had something important to tell Denis, something private and in the grey realm of espionage. Denis reacted as if he heard this sort of thing all the time. He had no *idea*. To Ben it was monumental, a scandal that could bring down the US administration. There could be *money* in this, Ben thought, well down the road when memoirs were called for. The Cold War was going to go on for ever, though, or end in the obliteration of the human species. Ben had always believed this, but he had never lived accordingly. Now he had an opportunity to make a difference to blameless innocents in those villages downriver from the dam. Finally things were going well. Sean's health seemed to be holding. Nicole had smiled at Ben only this evening. Little Paul had been returned safely. Mancini had *kept his word.*

'Shall we take a glass of wine outside?' Ben asked Denis. 'I'll show you the view.'

Leaving their wives at the table, the men stepped through the French windows and circled round the swimming pool. All evening Denis had been unable to contain his envy of Ben's house. Looking down now on Mancini's much more opulent spread, he actually sighed in a dismal Russian way.

'It is beautiful,' he said. 'In winter I can see it from my office.'

'Do you work right there, in the big building?'

'Yes. You can see, there, where the light is still on. I have a colleague who works late every day. He's not married, no children.'

'Everything is going to change for you now, my friend,' said Ben, raising his glass. He assumed Denis was as drunk as he was, and hoped the Russian held his vodka and wine well enough to remember this conversation so he could go back to his office and act upon it. 'Here's to a baby as beautiful as your wife. We're so happy for you. Ellen will love to help out. She's an expert. Do you know if it's a boy or a girl?'

'Girl,' said Denis. 'Keep secret, all right? Nadia wants me not to tell.'

'Got you,' said Ben. 'Now here's a secret of my own.'

Ben imparted his information as if he were reading from a written document. He didn't even look at Denis as he spoke. He looked instead at the glowing beehive of the old city, miles away, and felt the warm breeze sweeping up the hills to his exclusive patch of foreign land. He spoke as clearly and succinctly as he would have in chambers with Judge Ladatt. Denis didn't interrupt.

When Ben had finished Denis simply said, 'I understand. You are doing a good thing.'

'I want two things in return,' said Ben, who had finished his glass of wine and found that he had to hold on to the railing to steady himself. 'The first is, obviously, that you won't tell anyone where you learned all of this. Not that I give a *shit*,' Ben added, rather spoiling the high moral tone he had adopted while betraying his country. 'I'd just lose my job and be disgraced, but that's happened to me before and I'm all right.' Ben had to wrestle with himself not to lose his grip on what he really meant to say. 'And the second thing is,' he continued, 'a personal matter. Your boys over there –' Ben gestured at the Soviet Embassy compound '– are hounding a friend of mine, Dominic Thrune, who works at P&R. Call them off, Denis. Do you understand?'

'We would never –'

'Just *do* it,' said Ben, imperiously. 'I don't want to hear another word about it. It's the least you can do and if I hear he's been hassled one more time I'll bust you all the way back to Red Square.' Ben heard himself say this, and couldn't quite believe it. He had been carried away by the thrill of his intervention and, as planned, by the drink.

'I understand you, Ben,' said Denis, swaying slightly in the breeze. 'I will take care of it. You are a brave man.'

Yes, I really *am*, thought Ben. In his opinion the matter was closed. He'd had a brush with doom, and survived thanks to keeping his nerve, careful planning, Mancini's honour and Denis's self-interest. All that remained was to go to bed and get some sleep.

The men returned indoors. Significant goodbyes were quickly exchanged. Ben drank a quick shot of vodka to congratulate himself, and joined Ellen in the bedroom.

'Have you checked the children?' he asked, trying to take off his trousers without falling down.

Ellen rolled her eyes and did not reply. She had already put on plaid cotton pyjamas. She got into bed, turned on the reading light and opened a book. Ben climbed in on his side, wearing nothing but boxer shorts. He got out again and went into the bathroom to brush his teeth. He smiled at himself in the mirror as he did so, and winked. He went back to bed and lay on his back, smiling. Ellen would understand soon enough.

71

'They'll come at night,' Mancini had warned. Ben was so tranquillized by alcohol that Ellen had to physically shake him out of sleep.

'There's someone trying to get in the house,' she said. 'Quick, quick. Someone's working on the lock.'

Ellen's reading light was still on – she hadn't yet gone to sleep. Ben snapped awake and thought about his gun. After the embarrassment of having shot up the house for no reason, he had locked the gun and ammunition in separate cupboards in the laundry room and hidden the key behind the drier.

There came a terrible crashing sound from down the corridor. Whoever it was had grown impatient with the lock and smashed the French windows.

'Sean,' said Ben.

'What? What? *Do* something.'

Ben thought they had come for Sean, that it was Vodi's brother out there.

'Get across to the children. Get them out through the window.'

Ben tried to get out of bed and fell on the floor. He was horribly drunk. He pulled himself to his feet as Ellen fled through the open door and across the corridor to the children's room. He looked around for a weapon but there was nothing he could use except his voice: he stumbled into the dark corridor and began to shout: 'Out! Get out! I have a gun! I'll shoot! Get out!' He was thinking 'Sean, Sean, Sean . . .'

Without turning on the light he staggered forward. He could hear two men speaking urgently in the local language.

'Get out!'

He bounced first off one wall of the narrow corridor, then the other. He almost fell down again as he entered the living room. He didn't want to turn on the light because he didn't want to see the intruders. He wanted them to get out. He could hear the crunch of glass under their feet. Only seconds had passed, but he could imagine that the children were already outside. Ellen would have told them to wake Ama and Haz in their little dwelling out the back, that there were robbers in the house. They would take the children up the hill to safety. Ellen probably couldn't squeeze through the window herself, so she would be cowering in the children's bedroom.

Ben heard the men's voices again. He could see them now, their dark silhouettes. They weren't leaving. They came straight at Ben, both of them, and he felt himself being pushed to the floor, a knee in the small of his back.

'Get out! Take anything!'

Ben was struck on the back of the head by one of the men's palms. His chin hit the floor and he bit his tongue. His wrists were being tied together with a leather strap. He was picked up and marched across the room towards the smashed French windows. Broken glass cut into the soles of his feet. He cried out in pain and was struck again. He was pushed and dragged past the starlit swimming pool, down the stairs to the carport. They bundled him into the back seat of a white Fardi. One of the men got in beside him and rolled him over so that his chin rested on the back of the seat. The other man climbed into the driver's seat and started the engine. As they drove off, Ben looked up at his house and watched it recede. 'They're safe,' he thought, tasting blood from his bitten tongue. 'They're safe.'

The car bumped down the road, skirted Mancini's house. Ben looked up through the rear window to see that there were lights on inside. Squinting through the pain of his tongue and his feet and his wrists, Ben saw a tall figure standing on the terrace of the house. He could even see the glowing tip of a cigarette. There stood Paul Mancini, calmly watching.

72

Ben found himself in what looked like a disused classroom, but its two windows were barred. There was a narrow cot in the corner. He had been given a pair of trousers, a denim work shirt and plastic sandals. His feet had been cleaned, disinfected and bandaged. He sat on a metal chair at a low wooden desk antique enough to have a steel inkwell embedded in its upper right-hand corner. There was a blackboard on the wall in front of him, blank except for the smudged chalk-dust of past erasures.

Ben had fallen asleep in the car in a narcoleptic fit of drunken relief. At last, they had come for him. His family had escaped. It was all entirely appropriate. This is what he deserved, and then some. When he had awakened in the classroom, dressed and bandaged, head throbbing, tongue bitten, he had experienced the most unusual and intense emotion: he was relieved; his troubles were at an end. After torturing him they would take him to the long, white building in the mountains and they would shoot him. He would cease to exist except as a pile of bloody clothing and a mess that had to be cleared away and burned.

Ben was sure of this because his captors had made no effort to disguise themselves. He could tell by their haircuts and bearing that they were soldiers in mufti, calm and efficient and acting under a superior's orders. Every so often one of them came in with a bucket to see if Ben needed to relieve himself, which he had not yet done. It was light outside, and when Ben went to the barred window he saw an empty soccer pitch, barracks, low fog and a grazing mule. It occurred to him that this was where Little Paul must have been held, and again the sensation of relief washed over him. Little Paul was safe. How could he have thought for a *moment* that Mancini wouldn't immediately tell the authorities who was really responsible for killing the boy in the road? If Ben had just tried to imagine himself in Mancini's shoes, his son *held* somewhere, he would have seen this coming.

Ben looked forward to his torture, and imagined what it might entail. He planned to laugh, and to urge on his torturers. They could not possibly cause him pain, because he was going to die, he was already a corpse. Whatever they did to him would amount to the rest of Ben's life, and wasn't life there to be appreciated? His family was safe. Ben had done his duty. He had sacrificed everything.

On the second afternoon of Ben's captivity, a man entered the classroom and sat down in a chair behind the teacher's desk. This was Colonel Vodi's little brother. He shared the colonel's simian features and his alert black eyes. He wore a black leather jacket over a cleaned and pressed white button-down shirt, tight blue jeans and black loafers. A heavy gold bracelet clanked as he put his fists side by side on the desk. He stared hard at Ben, who tried to stare back but found it difficult to hold such a threatening gaze.

After a few minutes, Ben cleared his throat and asked, 'Do you speak English?'

The man waited a further minute before nodding his head.

'I know who you are,' said Ben. 'I know why you've brought me here. I understand.'

Ben wished to convey to this man that he was not afraid, that he deserved his punishment. He was one of life's casualties. He had not been a success. He remembered the day Victor Wiesman had sacked him, how he had gone to sit on a grave eating a tongue sandwich: this can't be happening to me. What an idiot. Ben had let everyone down. He had condemned his children to lives of resentment – if they remembered him at all.

'Do you want to ask me any questions?' If this man had killed Sean, Ben would have been at his throat the moment he walked through the door. 'I'll tell you anything you want to know.'

Vodi continued to stare at Ben without speaking. His fists were tense on the desk in front of him, but his expression was one of curiosity rather than rage. He even cocked his head to one side and squinted, like an entomologist confronted with a new species of spider.

'Is there anything you want to ask me? I can talk all day about my . . .' Ben had almost said 'children'. 'About my wife. I'm afraid she's not too pleased with me at the moment. Women, you know.'

Ben found that he was elated. You don't kill someone's child and get away with it, no matter what kind of monster the father is. And there are losers, even in America. Ben was an American loser. All flowed from Wiesman, right down to the pile of bloody clothes being dragged off the parade ground. There was a sort of glory in a fate like Ben's. He would lose nothing but continuous anxiety interrupted by moments of unbearable tragedy. People like Ben were never happy. They strove for things they didn't need or want. This was much better, being stared at by murderous foreign eyes, about to be tortured into a confession he would make in the first instant, shot in a parade ground or out on the soccer pitch or right here against the blackboard. Ben welcomed it all. He was a failure, and he wanted to be a *complete* failure. He wanted to *excel* at failure, be the best failure there ever was. To *hell* with Wiesman, to *hell* with Alan Yates.

Vodi stood up and went over to the window. He clasped his hands behind his back and looked outside, as if there were anything to see but a grazing mule. Ben remained seated, pupil-like, at his antique children's desk. He tapped his right sandalled foot on the cement floor.

'You can ask me anything, you know,' he said.

Vodi turned around and stared at Ben again. Ben tried to recall what little he had learned about the man he had come to think of as the Lesser Vodi. He had no other children. He did his older brother's dirty work. The Vodis were nationalists, warmongers. They wanted a proper and efficient totalitarian dictatorship, not the General's on-again, off-again variety that too frequently gave way to the vote. They frightened even Hannan. They were pro-American. They were anti-Roffe to the point where the religious leader greeted each day as if it were likely to be his last.

Ben could feel that he was smiling, and he tried to stop. The Lesser Vodi might not like it if the cowardly murderer of his son sat there and smiled behind the classroom desk. Vodi couldn't know that Ben was a failure, a casualty. He couldn't know that Ben had reacted badly to broken children, been fired, misbehaved, let *everyone* down.

'Don't worry,' Ben said. 'I know why I'm here.'

Vodi went back to the teacher's desk, but did not sit down. He resumed staring at Ben.

'I'm relieved,' Ben said. 'This is exactly right. Don't worry.'

Vodi squinted at Ben, still curious and full of distaste. After half a minute of this he walked to the door. With his hand on the latch, he turned around and took a last look at Ben. He almost said something – his Adam's apple bobbed – but didn't. Instead Vodi spat on the floor, rubbed the slime in with his shoe and left the room.

If he had been in any doubt before, this gesture of Vodi's seemed to confirm Ben's fate. He could wait, as he had done for months now, for the sound of the boots in the corridor. He hoped and assumed it would be Vodi himself who pulled the trigger. He felt he had no attachment to the world. He never wanted to see his family again. He wanted to disappear. All of this was going to be seen to by Vodi and his men. Ben no longer had responsibility for anything, and this made him happy. When they came to kill him he wouldn't even look up at the sky, wouldn't try to experience a lifetime in one moment – it all made him sick. He didn't belong here, he had never belonged anywhere. His life had been artificial. Until now he had never had the courage to admit to himself that he hated every minute of being alive, every second. The sooner it was over, the better.

Ben got out of the chair and went over to the cot. He lay down on his stomach and closed his eyes. He wanted to put himself to sleep by counting random memories; nothing surfaced but a grey wall, as if he had been imprisoned all his life.

73

'I hope he's good at backgammon,' said Little Paul, cheerfully.

'Now, you run along and play with Sean,' said Candy, who was helping Ellen pack. They sat on the end of the bed in the master bedroom of the Peltons' house. 'I have to have a serious and confidential conversation with his mother.'

Little Paul danced away to the dining room, where Sean was putting the finishing touches to a painting of Madame Soubrier. Nicole and Caroline were having a snack in the kitchen with Ama. Ellen's children had been told that they were flying out of the country this evening, with no plans to return. They would fly first to London, then onward to Ellen's worried parents in America. The Mancinis were going to stick it out as long as they could, which meant not very long: Roffe was in charge now.

Ellen had spoken to the police, to the embassy, to Evan Court. She had done what she could, in a surprisingly lethargic fog of anger and mixed feelings. When Candy heard that Ben had been taken, she said, 'I know everything, honey. What do *you* know?' It had been six days now. Ben wasn't coming back. Ellen had explained everything, truthfully, to his parents. Ben's father had been typically chivalrous and said, immediately, 'Let's get you and the children home, dear. That's the priority.' This was hours before the streets filled again and Roffe glided into the Meheti Palace, seizing power in a suitably mystical way. The General ceded to him in a solemn radio broadcast, taking Roffe's word for it that elections would be held the following year, that parliament would be untouched, that the Vodi brothers would be neutralized. He accepted Roffe's decision that he ought to remain in charge of the armed forces, and expressed his regret that the country was now at war again. He asserted his confidence that the nation's brave soldiers would prevail, as they had done without fail against this particular enemy for more than eight-hundred years.

'Are you OK, honey?' Candy asked. Packing had been easy, as if Ellen had never really unpacked in the first place. 'I'm so worried about you. You know we'll do everything we can at this end. We'll get him home, I'm sure. Everything has changed now. Just remember, even Roffe needs the Americans.'

Ellen couldn't explain the way she felt now, it was too awful: she felt exactly as she had when Ben commuted to the city and worked all the hours there were. She never saw him then, or only when he was ragged with fatigue and worry. For all the fear and other emotions she felt, Ben might as well have been on a business trip, or just working late yet again without even calling her, it felt so normal.

'He gave me the clap,' Ellen said, out of nowhere.

'Oh, *honey*,' Candy said.

'Can you believe that?'

Candy paused for only a moment. 'I sure can,' she said. 'I've been trying to shake something Paul gave me, ever since Kinshasa.'

'Oh, God.'

'We love our men, though, don't we?'

'No,' said Ellen. 'I don't. I really don't. He lied to Sean. You don't lie to your children. I will never forgive him. He killed some little boy.' The women had been speaking as if they believed Ben was still alive.

'Maybe he meant well,' said Candy, immediately laughing at her hopeful remark. 'Sorry. I should have said what a *shit*.'

'Exactly.'

'Oh, honey,' Candy said again, and moved closer to Ellen on the bed. She put an arm around Ellen's shoulders. 'You've had an awful lot of bad luck, haven't you?'

'Bad luck has nothing to do with it. Bad luck is Ben's excuse for everything. I'm not going to go around feeling sorry for myself. That's all Ben ever did. He thinks he's the centre of the world. When things went wrong with Sean you would have thought it was Ben who had the disease. He moped around and pretended he had to work a hundred hours a week just so he wouldn't have to be at home to help out. Same with poor Nicky. Ben took it as a personal insult, an affront. Ben *Pelton* wasn't supposed to have these things happen to *him*, no sir. And when he lost his job . . .'

'He lost his job? I can't believe you never told me.'

'That's why we're here. I'm not even supposed to mention it, as if it never happened. I think in Ben's mind it *didn't* happen.' Ellen paused for a moment, trying to gather in what was really going on. She looked at Candy and asked, 'What do you think they're going to do to him?'

'Oh, honey, I don't know. I'm so sorry.'

'What does Paul think?'

'He just feels guilty. I don't think he even wants to see you, to tell you the truth.'

'Well he shouldn't feel guilty. Tell him that for me. He did the right thing. Unlike *some* people I could mention.' Tears finally came to Ellen's eyes as she said, 'He killed a little *boy* . . .' Ellen leaned away from Candy and pulled her hair behind her ears. 'I don't want the children to see this. They have no idea yet. I said, "We're going to see Granny and Grandpa," as if they lived around the corner. They have no idea. They think Ben's in Wassa, finding oil.'

'He might as well be,' said Candy. 'God, is this strange.'

Ellen composed herself. 'I'm not just going to *retreat*, you know,' she said, with a hiccuping laugh. 'Of course I hope

Ben's going to get out of this, but he's really . . .' Ellen had to laugh at her understatement: 'He's gone *too far*.'

'That's the spirit.'

'I did all I could.'

'Of course you did.'

'He was a coward.'

'Of course he was.'

'He couldn't *cope*, and that's what it's all about. You have to *cope*. Are all men like that?'

Candy thought for a moment, tilting her sun-tanned face to the ceiling. 'Not all,' she declared. 'Most, though.'

'Evan was incredible,' said Ellen. 'When I told him what had happened to Ben, and asked him not to report it for now, do you know what he said?'

'Tell me.'

'He said "How about a date?"'

'Amazing.'

'He was very funny about it.'

'I hope you accepted,' said Candy, narrowing her eyes.

Ellen didn't reply. She stood up and went to the window. Outside, on the hill behind the swimming pool, Sean and Little Paul played marbles – the Gravedigger's Game. Caroline and Nicole looked on. Ama and Haz were there too, sitting on a cement pillar, holding hands. Ellen had given the couple the equivalent of two thousand dollars, which could buy them a house if they ever wanted one. She was going to miss them most. Despite the necessary, formal distance that usually had to be observed, she had enjoyed their days together with the chores, with the children, *coping*. She had told them the absolute truth about Ben, that he had killed a local child in an accident and was in prison somewhere. Ama had wept and left the room. Haz had stiffened his jaw, contemplated a possible servant–master breach of etiquette, and given Ellen a hug. He hardly ever spoke anyway, and his English was still poor, but he made the effort to collect what he wanted to say: 'Madame, I am so sorry for you. He will come back. Now I will bake a chocolate cake for the children.' He guided Ellen to the armchair in the living room and said, 'You cry here. I cook.'

Candy joined Ellen at the window. 'I don't want to sound too hard about this,' she said, 'but you're doing the right thing. You've got to get out. It would be awful for the children if you stayed. We'll do everything here, don't worry. With Ben, with the house. No matter what happens . . .'

'I could come back alone,' Ellen said. 'I could leave the kids with their grandparents. I can't just . . . *leave* him, not like this. Not now.'

'You're doing the right thing, trust me. I hate to say this but I don't think Ben's coming back. I didn't think Paul would, but this is different. Vodi's got his man this time.'

'I just can't believe this is happening. Listen to me, I sound like Ben.'

Ellen had never felt so confused and torn. She surprised herself with her relative calm. She hated and pitied Ben at the same time. She wanted him safe, but she wanted him away from her and the children.

The telephone rang on the bedside table.

'I'll get that,' said Candy. 'It might be Paul.' She confirmed that it was after answering by nodding significantly at Ellen. She said only a couple of words to her husband before putting down the receiver. 'He says to turn on the television. He can't talk now. Something terrible has happened.'

The women went into the living room and turned on the set. Ellen expected the story to concern Ben's fate. When the picture appeared it was of Evan Court standing, microphone held beneath his chin, on a barren ridge overlooking what had been the new Meheti Reservoir.

'They've blown up the dam,' said Candy. 'Look, it's all been swept away. My God.'

Evan spoke of casualties down-river, using the familiar tone Ellen had known so well for years before meeting him. He sounded weary and displeased with the way people treated each other. He mentioned Peter Knox by name, and Planning and Resources. He managed to imply, without actually saying so, that the political Left, now in league with the LFP, was behind this atrocity. The turbulent last days, which had seen Roffe catapulted to power, had been too much for the Soviet-backed factions, who needed to galvanize their support now or it would be too late. This attack was symbolic of their anti-imperialism as well as of their fierce opposition to Roffe and his new government.

Evan Court signed off and was thanked by the presenter at headquarters with the customary wish that Evan would take care of himself 'out there'. The viewers were assured that they would be hearing more details from Evan once the situation clarified itself; for the moment it was back to the day's main story: a professional golfer had been struck by lightning and was said to be paralysed from the neck down.

'Well,' said Candy, after Ellen had turned down the volume, 'everything Paul's ever done has been blown up in one way or another. I suppose we really have to move on, now. Too bad. Any chance of a cocktail? I'm parched.'

'Of course, I'm sorry,' said Ellen. 'The packing is done. The kids' travelling clothes are all laid out. I think maybe I'll join you.'

Ellen went alone into the kitchen and got a bottle of wine out of the refrigerator. She opened it and poured two glasses. She had only hours left in this place. Sammy would drive them to the airport early: for the past week there had been quite a lot of people trying to get out of the country.

She carried the wine and glasses out to the living room, where Candy had turned up the volume on the television. The film footage had come in of the damage to the villages down-river from the exploded dam. Candy sat on the sofa with her head in her hands. She might have been weeping, but if so it wasn't for the victims of this outrage. She had collapsed periodically this way ever since she got her son back.

'I'm the one who's supposed to be comforting you,' Candy said. 'I'm not doing a very good job.'

Ellen didn't reply. She had so thoroughly made up her mind now that she didn't need further support. She drank her glass of wine and watched images of the exploded dam and the ensuing flood, listened to Evan Court's disappointed voice. Then she put down her glass, stood up and went outside to fetch the children. It was time to get them ready, time to leave.

74

Ben had been roughly transferred to a smaller, darker room. There was a hole-in-the-floor toilet that functioned. He was brought food – bread or a candy bar or a piece of fried chicken – once a day. Vodi had never returned after his first, staring visit. Ben slept almost all of the time, on a mattress on the floor. There was a barred window, but he rarely looked out of it for very long. He had seen the occasional soldier walking across the soccer pitch, but no training, no parading. The barracks across the way seemed mostly unoccupied. The mule continued to graze.

Ben had counted six days, but had not recorded them in any way and hoped he would soon lose track. He was blankly comfortable with his grey thoughts, and didn't even look up if one of the men came in to throw him the bread or the candy bar or the chicken. He had no appetite and no resolve and no expectations except for a swift, unheard bullet.

It only vaguely occurred to Ben that he might be a hostage rather than a criminal awaiting summary revenge on Vodi's part. He didn't mind. He was so relieved. It seemed impossible that there was a world outside going about its business. He didn't, or couldn't, think about his family when he was awake. He lived in anticipation of the shuffling boots outside the door. They came, once, and Ben sat up; they passed by. He went back to sleep. Sometimes he did have a dream that awoke him, back to the blank grey – of Sean or Nicole raising their arms to him to be picked up; of Ellen during the spring when they'd first met, holding the back of his head as she kissed him.

On the seventh day Ben was not fed. There was no one outside. Even the mule was gone. There was a tenseness in the quiet of the barracks. At midday, though, the soccer pitch came suddenly alive with activity. Fifty or more soldiers assembled and stood to attention in the heat. An officer put them through an ambitious drill, his orders echoing off the barracks walls. There was something urgent about the way this drill was carried out. Something was going on – another demonstration to be quelled? Another symbolic little war? Ben wondered if some of these men would make up his firing squad.

The shuffle of boots returned to the corridor, and this time it stopped outside the door. Ben, who had been standing at the window, turned around. He heard voices pitched at the level of argument. He heard two bolts being unlocked and pulled back. Then, strangely, the footsteps carried on down the corridor. There was silence for a few moments, so Ben sat down on his mattress. He couldn't imagine that they had really unlocked the door. He had no intention of getting up and walking over to find out. He would stay right here, waiting for his bullet.

There came the sound of a single pair of feet and Ben thought, this is it, this is Vodi. He remained seated with his legs crossed underneath him and his hands folded on his lap. The footsteps paused some way down the corridor. Another door was opened, then closed again. The footsteps came closer, closer, until they stopped outside. The door opened.

A familiar, egg-shaped head popped in, as it had so often at the office.

'I say, old boy,' said Dominic. 'Fancy a lift home?'

Ben was so startled he swallowed the wrong way and began to cough.

'Dear, oh *dear*,' said Dominic, entering the dark room. 'Have they treated you *abominably*? Let me have a look at you.'

Ben felt himself being pulled to his feet.

'Such *cheekbones*,' said Dominic. 'They *starved* you, poor thing. Oh, *very* fetching,' he added, plucking at the shoulder of Ben's filthy shirt. Then, much more seriously, 'I say we get you to my car.'

Ben began to feel a weight pressing on his shoulders, as he realized he really was leaving this place, that he was going back out into the world. He groaned, and Dominic mistook this for a sign that Ben was in physical pain.

'Can you walk?'

Ben nodded, but didn't move. The open door in front of him led to an unknown he thought he would never have to confront again, like the doors of lifts he had always feared to enter.

'Come along, then,' said Dominic. 'Come along now. I can't honestly say we have all the time in the world. I will *thoroughly* entertain you in the car. You go off to fester in a cell for a few days and you can't *imagine* how the world has changed. We missed you Ben – you're so *good* in a crisis.' Dominic's sarcasm had returned. He had dressed for the occasion in a faded safari jacket, below-the-knee khaki shorts, red knee-socks and desert boots. He put an arm around Ben's slumped shoulders, took one of his hands and guided him to the door as if Ben were a blind man.

They walked as quickly as they could to an open door that led outside to a gravel drive. Dominic helped Ben into the passenger seat of his unkempt orange Fardi. Unarmed soldiers marched along the nearby road, clenched fists swinging high.

Ben stared straight ahead as they drove out of the military base, then closed his eyes when he saw that they were going to go past exactly the spot where he'd hit the boy. Dominic, who seemed angry now, continued to speak without expecting replies.

'We could go to my house,' he said. 'Humble though it be. Shall we go there?'

Ben shook his head and opened his eyes.

'Your house might seem somewhat . . . *empty*,' Dominic said. 'Your family quite sensibly bolted. Do you understand?'

Ben nodded and closed his eyes again.

'Your *close* personal friend Mister Roffe has "assumed power", as the phrase has it. This goes some way towards explaining why you are no longer languishing in a urine-drenched cell. The Vodis are probably in Switzerland by now. Did I mention there's a war on? Just the *tiniest* little war, you know, for the purposes of *consolidation*.'

Ben sat with his hands on his knees. He opened his eyes and took in the sight of children walking home from school, of old-fashioned-looking tanks thudding towards the city on the verge of the road, of teenagers on scooters heading out for a routine night on the town.

'Now there's the little matter of our *dam*,' said Dominic, scratching one of his hairless knees, steering the orange Fardi with one hand. 'Do you want to know about the dam?'

Ben nodded.

Dominic reached under his seat and retrieved a half-pint bottle of Russian vodka. He offered this to Ben, who refused it, then poured a small amount down his own throat.

'Someone,' Dominic said, swallowing, 'has done away with the dam. Any idea who might have wanted to do that?'

Ben shook his head. He coughed some more to clear his throat and spoke for the first time: 'Was it blown up?'

'Yes,' said Dominic, delightedly. 'How clever of you. It was *terribly* dramatic, Ben. I'm surprised you didn't hear the explosion all the way from your rat-infested prison. I was at the office at the time, of course, simply *toiling* away. The word came through from the Great Mancini himself. All of our efforts for nought, you know. It was devastating. We congregated in Mancini's ballroom and thought to ourselves, "Oh, *bother*." Mancini was *most* sincere. He specifically blamed the Russians

– in league with the beastly Left and the even beastlier LFP. Are you sure you don't want to come to my house?'

Ben nodded and said, 'We're going to *my* house.'

'Perhaps they've left you some clothes,' said Dominic. 'You look like a peasant in those.'

Ben tried to concentrate. 'How did you find me?'

'The divine Jasper LeRoy knew where you were. The Great Mancini did his best to intervene. All of these gods, Ben. They have such power. And they all thought you were going to be killed, which would have been terribly embarrassing, and rather a shock to you, I would have thought. Oh, the *strings* we pulled.'

'No, you didn't.'

'Well, no,' said Dominic, 'we didn't *really*.'

'Was anyone hurt?' asked Ben. 'When the dam went?'

'My dear, it was *cataclysmic*. It's all been hushed up but I've seen the pictures. Dozens swept away. Candy's good friend Evan Court has been keeping us informed.'

'What did he say?' asked Ben. 'Who did he say was behind it?'

'He was so *firm* about it. A Soviet atrocity. Typical. Trying to destabilize the region. Clumsy timing, what with Roffe, but they must have thought it was their last chance. *Bastards*,' said Dominic, chortling.

'You know, don't you?' said Ben.

'You could not *torture* out of me what I know.'

75

Ben knew where he wanted to go, what he wanted to do. He hardly listened to Dominic as they drove through the outskirts of the city. The gun was waiting for him in the cupboard – Ellen didn't know where the key was. He felt so depleted, so let down by his freedom. Where was his punishment? In the cupboard at home.

'I'm not just going to leave you,' said Dominic, as they rounded the corner of the Soviet Embassy compound. 'Let me come in. We'll take *stock*, Ben.'

The Mancinis' house looked deserted.

'Have they left too?' Ben asked, just finding the breath to do so.

'My information is that they're with Hannan, on his ship, *plotting*.' Dominic drove confidently up the hill and stopped not in the carport, but by the back door of Ben's house. 'We'll have to feed you,' he said. 'Let's see if they left any food behind. They only departed last night.'

Without thanking Dominic, Ben got out of the car and walked ahead into the unlocked house – presumably left that way for Ben's benefit. Dominic followed behind. Ben walked through the kitchen and turned right down the corridor towards the bedrooms and, beyond them, the laundry room. He could hear Dominic's falsely cheerful voice behind him: 'I say, marvellous good fortune! They've left not one but *two* bottles of chilled white wine!'

Ben had to lie down on the tiled floor to get at the keys behind the drier.

'And salami!' called out Dominic. 'I say we have a picnic by the pool!'

Ben retrieved the keys and stood up again in his prison-issue clothes and plastic sandals. He reached up, unlocked both cupboards and took out the weapon and ammunition. He inserted the clip as he heard the pop of one of the wine-bottle corks in the kitchen.

'Please say you'll be joining me!' shouted Dominic.

Ben came back down the corridor, gun at his side. The house seemed to echo more than usual, even though all the furniture remained. His family had left in a hurry. This puzzled Ben.

'Oh, *dear*, oh dear,' said Dominic, in the kitchen, when he saw what Ben was holding. 'For goodness' sake not in *here*,' he added, gesturing at the carpet Ellen had bought. 'At least come outside.' Dominic led the way out to the pool. Ben dragged himself along behind him, lazily taking off the safety catch of the gun with his thumb.

Dominic sat down in a deck-chair and arranged wine, salami and cheese on the glass-topped table. Ben sat down in another chair next to Dominic, with a view of the smog-bound city below. Dominic poured two glasses of wine without looking at Ben, or at the gun. He took his glass and drank; Ben left his alone.

'I'm sure you're going to want to know *everything*,' said Dominic. 'But where to begin?'

Ben toyed with the gun and breathed rapidly through his nose.

'First of all there is your acquaintance Mr Roffe, who is now in charge of the country, as I told you in the car. This is grim news for everyone except me, because it means, if you recall, that I have at least one close friend in high places.'

Ben could hear what Dominic was saying. He knew what Dominic was trying to do. He sighed and blinked his eyes and tried to remember the strange sensation of happiness he had experienced alone in that classroom, at the end of it all.

'Now Ben, I fear you'll have been *rather* distressed – or *more* so, if that's possible – to have learned the other great news of the day. That is to say – and did you actually *hear* me, in the car? – the fact that someone blew up our adorable dam?'

Ben looked up at Dominic for the first time.

'Isn't that the most *shameful* thing?' Dominic had lit a cigarette. 'As I told you – and were you actually *listening*? – fingers have already been convincingly pointed at your chums across the way.' Using his cigarette, he indicated the Soviet Embassy compound. 'Your country is *most* displeased.'

Ben wanted to speak, but found he couldn't.

'Listen to me, Ben. I'll be frank. I know what you did.'

Ben looked over at Dominic again and managed to say, 'Who . . . ?'

'I hope you won't be *too* surprised that I had a little conversation with Denis, don't tell a *soul*. He and I have the most splendidly agreeable relationship, though we've never met in person. He was most unnerved to hear what you had to say, and he needed my advice. The point is, Ben – and I do hate to disillusion you this way – Denis is on our side.'

'But I . . . I told Evan Court.'

'Oh? And exactly whose side do you think young Mr *Court* is on? Goodness, Ben, we must school you in some of these basics.'

Ben hadn't noticed that as Dominic spoke he had been leaning closer and closer, until he could reach out and gently remove the gun from Ben's limp hands. Dominic stood up and there was a splash as he dropped the weapon into the swimming pool.

'I let everyone down,' said Ben.

'If you ask me,' said Dominic, in a loud, confident voice now that he had disarmed Ben, 'you have been *bloody* lucky.

434

Can you try to *grasp* that, Ben? Don't be so completely *pitiful*.'

'I let everyone down.'

'I think what you are feeling,' said Dominic, still standing and sounding rather angry, 'is what in English we call *remorse*. Can't you just leave it at that?'

'My family . . .'

'Tricky, that,' said Dominic, 'but as you once so rudely implied, family is not my area of expertise.'

Ben stood up, which took some effort. He was weak and hungry. He noticed that his clothes smelled. He took off his shirt, his sandals, then his trousers. Before Dominic could reach out to stop him – even if he had wanted to make the gesture – Ben dived into the deep end of the swimming pool. He opened his eyes and he could see the black gun lying on the bottom near the drain. He swam straight down towards it, feeling the pressure in his ears. He hovered over the weapon until he could hold his breath no longer, then rose to the surface.

'Ah, all refreshed,' said Dominic.

With his arms on the edge of the pool, Ben collected himself.

'I'll find you a towel,' said Dominic, 'to cover your modesty.'

Dominic went inside the house, leaving Ben to confront the idea, once again, of starting over.

When Dominic came back Ben struggled out of the pool, dried himself, wrapped the towel around his waist.

'All better?' Dominic asked.

'Oh, sure,' said Ben.

The two men stood side by side at the railing, looking out over the city. All looked normal down there, and at this time of day they could even hear the bleating horns of Fardis.

'A lot of good all this meddling has done,' said Dominic. 'Roffe's the worst of all possible worlds, if you ask me. Never mind. "Up, up, up," as Hannan would say.'

'Where will you go?' asked Ben.

'Oh, I shall jolly well stay right here. I'm suddenly well

connected, as I explained to you. Anyway it's *you* lot Roffe can't abide, for some reason.'

'I can't stay? My family can't come back?'

'I don't *honestly* think,' said Dominic, scoldingly, 'that was ever an option.'

'I'm going to pack up here then,' said Ben, furrowing his brow. 'I'll pack everything and send it all home to Ellen.'

Dominic shrugged. 'You're the *expert*, Ben.'

The swim had cleared Ben's head. The sun was hot on his back as he remembered Dominic's local saying about the leper's bell. Next time, he thought, I will be ready. I will be listening. An optimism began to surface in Ben that was both irrational and necessary.

'I haven't thanked you,' Ben said.

'Not at all,' said Dominic, bowing.

'I'll start over again.'

'That's the spirit.'

Ben felt that he was breathing regularly. He and Dominic took in the view for a few more minutes. The sight put further perspective on Ben's past and future struggles. He thought of home, wherever that would prove to be. He thought of the children.

Ben and Dominic had turned around and were walking towards the bottle of wine and the salami and cheese on the outdoor table when they spotted a car on the road at the bottom of the steep track beyond Mancini's empty house. The car crawled uncertainly beside the high brick wall of the Soviet Embassy compound. Dominic went ahead to pour wine, while Ben watched the car. It wasn't a Fardi, it wasn't a military vehicle, it wasn't a limousine he would have associated with Hannan. It was an American car, chunky and dark blue. It turned in at the track that led up to Ben's house. It slowed at Mancini's house, then continued up the hill. It stopped outside Ben's house. A man wearing a light khaki suit got out of the driver's side; his twin from the passenger side. They both wore dark glasses and moved lazily, as if bored.

Ben looked at Dominic, who had taken a sip of wine. Dominic raised his eyebrows and smiled.

'Shall I see what's the matter?' Dominic asked.

Ben looked back at the men, who were making their way to the steps beside the carport. He felt lifted up, ecstatic.

'I'll go,' Ben said, catching Dominic's eye for the last time. 'It can only be good news.'